1

The Master of the Shell

by Talbot Baines Reed

Copyright © 9/18/2015
Jefferson Publication

ISBN-13: 978-1517414733

Printed in the United States of America

Table of Contents

Chapter One.

Twice Accepted.

The reader is requested kindly to glance through the following batch of letters, which, oddly enough, are all dated September 9th, 18—:

Number 1.—William Grover, M.A., Grandcourt School, to Mark Railsford, M.A., Lucerne.

"Grandcourt, *September* 9th.

"Dear Railsford,—I suppose this will catch you at Lucerne, on your way back to England. I was sorry to hear you had been seedy before you left London. Your trip is sure to have done you good, and if you only fell in with pleasant people I expect you will have enjoyed yourself considerably. What are you going to do when you get home—still follow the profession of a gentleman at large, or what? Term opened here again last week, and the Sixth came back to-day. I'm getting more reconciled to the place by this time; indeed, there is no work I like better than teaching, and if I was as certain it was as good for the boys as it is congenial to me I should be perfectly contented. My fellow-masters, with an exception or two, are good fellows, and let me alone. The exceptions are harder to get on with.

"As for the boys, I have a really nice lot in my house. One or two rowdies, who give me some bother, and one or two cads, with whom I am at war; but the rest are a festive, jovial crew, who tolerate their master when he lets them have their own way, and growl when he doesn't; who work when they are so disposed, and drop idle with the least provocation; who lead me many a weary dance through the lobbies after the gas is out, and now and then come and make themselves agreeable in my rooms when I invite them.

"I fancied when I came here I should get lots of time to myself—enough perhaps to write my book on Comparative Political Economy. Vain hope! I haven't time to turn round. If my days were twenty-six hours I should scarcely then do all I ought to do here. Ponsford is getting old, and leaves the executive to his lieutenants. He sits aloft like Zeus, hurls a thunderbolt now and then, and for the rest acts as a supreme court of appeal. Bickers, my opposite neighbour, is still a thorn in my side. I don't know how it is, I try all I know, but I can't get on with him, and have given him up. Moss, I believe, who is Master of the Shell and head of a house, has come to the end of his endurance, and there is some talk of his throwing up his place here. It would be a pity in many ways, and it might be hard to get a good man in his place.

"By the way, if there is a vacancy, why should not you enter the lists? I see you smile at the idea of anyone exchanging the profession of gentleman at large for that of Master of the Shell. But it's worth a thought, any how. Let us know where and how you are; and if you can run down this way for a Sunday, do, and make glad the heart of your friend,—

"W. Grover."

No. 2.—Arthur Herapath, Esquire, Lucerne, to Sir Digby Oakshott, Baronet, Grandcourt.

"Dear Dig,—Here's a game! The gov's been and lost a lot of the luggage, and ma won't go home without it, so we're booked here for a week more. He's written to Ponsford to say I can't turn up till next week, and says I'm doing some of the mug, so as not to be all behind. Jolly good joke of the gov.'s, isn't it? Catch me mugging here!

"Stunning place, this! We went a picnic to—I say, by the way, while I remember it, do you know it's all a howling cram about William Tell? There never was such a chap! This is the place he used to hang out in, and everyone says it's all my eye what the history says about him. You'd better let Moss know. Tell him, from inquiries made by me on the spot, I find it's all humbug, and he'd better get some chap to write a new history who knows something about it. I was asking Railsford—by the way, he's a stunning chap. We ran up against him on the Saint Gothard, and he's been with us ever since. No end of a cheese! Rowed in the Cambridge boat three years ago, Number 4, when Oxford won by two feet. He says when you're rowing in a race you see nothing but the fellow's back in front of you. He's 6 feet 2, and scales 12 stone 14 pounds. That's why they put him Number 4; but he rowed stroke in his college boat. He's having a lot of fag about our luggage, but I'm in no hurry for it to turn up.

"How are all the fellows? I guess I'm missing a lot of fun this week. Get some of them to keep something; till I come back. How's Tilbury? By the way, who am I stuck with this term? I don't want to get chummed again with that young ass Simson. Tell Moss that. Any more rows with Bickers's lot? There will be when I come back! I've got half a dozen of them in my eye. Gov. says I'll have to wake up this term. What a go! If I don't scrape into the Shell at Christmas, he says he'll know the reason why! So look out for no-larks.

"This fellow Railsford's put me up to a thing or two about mugging. He was a hot man at Cambridge, and says he knew Grover. He's gone with Daisy up a mountain to-day. Wanted to take me, too, but I told them I didn't see it. I tried it once, that was enough for me! Ta-ta, old man; keep your pecker up till I come, and then mind your eye!

"Yours truly,—

"A. Herapath, Ll.D."

Number 3.—From Miss Daisy Herapath to Miss Emily Sherriff.

"Lucerne, *Tuesday*.

"My Dearest Milly,—We are in *such* trouble! Two of our boxes have been lost between Como and here. One of them contained my new black grenadine with the Spanish lace. I have positively nothing to wear; and had to appear at *table d'hôte* in my blue serge and one of mamma's shawls. Just imagine! It is such a sad end to our holiday. I am longing to get home. Travelling abroad is all very nice, but one gets tired of it. I feel I shall like to settle down in town once more.

"Poor papa has had so much trouble with the boxes, and must, have spent pounds in telegrams. It was really Arthur's fault. He sent the porter who was booking the luggage for us to get him some chocolate from the buffet, and the consequence was the train went off before all the boxes were put in the van. Dear Milly, *never* travel abroad with your young brother!

"I have been quite lazy about sketching the last few days. I can't tell you how lovely some of the sunsets have been. It is the regular thing to sit out in the hotel grounds and watch them. I wish so often you could be here to share my pleasure, for papa and mamma are afraid to sit out, and Arthur is so unpoetical! There are a great many Americans here. The fashion of short steeves seems quite to be coming in again! I shall have to get mine altered as soon as I come home. Some of our party went up the Rigi to-day. The view from the top was beautiful; but the place is spoiled by the crowds of people who go up. I so much prefer the quieter excursions.

"I must go to bed now, dearest Milly. It will be lovely to see you soon. When one is away from home, one feels more than ever how nice it would be to have one's friends always about one. (What a lot of 'ones'!)

"Ever your very loving friend,—

"Daisy.

"P.S.—We met the Thompsons at Como. Did you know Edith was to be married this autumn, quite quietly, in the country? The Walkleys are here, and one or two other people we know. Arthur has struck up with a Cambridge fellow, named Railsford, whom we met on the Saint Gothard, and who took *so* much trouble about the luggage. It is so nice for Arthur to have a companion. Dearest Milly, he (M.R.) was one of the party who went up the Rigi to-day; he speaks German so well, and is so attentive to mamma. Don't be too horribly curious, darling; I'll tell you *everything* when I get home. (He is *so* good and handsome!)"

Number 4.—Francis Herapath, Esquire, Merchant, to James Blake, Esquire, Solicitor.

"*Private and Confidential*.

"Dear Blake,—Being detained here owing to a miscarriage of some of our luggage, I write this instead of waiting till I see you, as it may be another week before we are home.

"During our travels my daughter has become engaged to a Mr Mark Railsford, apparently a very desirable and respectable young man. You will wonder why I trouble you about such a very domestic detail. The young gentleman was very frank and straightforward in making his proposal, and volunteered that if I desired to make any inquiries, he was quite sure that you, his late father's solicitor, would answer any questions. I have no doubt, from the readiness with which he invited the inquiry and his satisfaction in hearing that you and I were old friends, that you will have nothing to say which will alter my favourable impression. Still, as my child's happiness is at stake, I have no right to omit any opportunity of satisfying myself. Anything you may have to say I shall value and treat as confidential.

"I understand Mr R., under his father's will, has a small property; but of course it will be necessary for him now to find some occupation, which with his abilities I have no doubt he will easily do. As usual, the young people are in a hurry to know their fate, so it will be a charity to them to reply as soon as convenient. Excuse the trouble I am giving you, and, with kind regards to Mrs B. and your sister,—

"Believe me, yours faithfully,—

"Fras. Herapath."

Number 5.—Mark Railsford to William Grover, Grandcourt.

"Lucerne, *September* 9th, 18—.

"Dear Grover,—You have often in your lighter moods laughed at the humble individual who addresses you. Laugh once again. The fact is, I am engaged. I can fancy I see you reeling under this blow! I have been reeling under it for thirty-six hours.

"It's partly your fault. Coming over the Saint Gothard a week ago, I fell in with a family party, Herapath by name; father, mother, boy and girl. They had come part of the way by train, and were driving over the top. The boy and I walked, and I discovered he was at Grandcourt, and of course knew you, though he's not in your house, but Moss's. That's how *you* come to be mixed up in it. During the last hour or so Miss H   walked with us, and before we reached the Devil's Bridge my fate was sealed.

"The ladies were in great distress about some lost luggage—lost by the kind offices of the boy—and I went back to Como to look for it. It lost me two days, and I never found it. However, I found the brightest pair of blue eyes when I got back. I will draw you no portraits, you old scoffer; but I challenge you to produce out of your own imagination anything to match it. I don't mind confessing to you that I feel half dazed by it all at present, and have to kick myself pretty often to make sure it is not a dream. The father, whom I bearded yesterday, nods his head and will say 'Yes' as soon as he's looked into my credentials. Meanwhile I am tolerated, and dread nothing except the premature turning up of the lost luggage.

"But, to be practical for once in my life. Amongst much that is delightfully vague and dreamy, one thing stands out very clear in my own mind at present. I must do something. My loafing days are over. The profession of a gentleman at large, with which you twit me, I hereby renounce. She will back me up in any honest work—she says so. I've confessed the way I wasted the last three years. She said she is glad she did not know me then. Oh my, William, it is all very well for you to scoff. I'm not ashamed to tell you what it is that has brought me to my senses. Don't scoff, but help a lame dog over a stile. My object in life is to have an object in life at present. Give me your counsel, and deserve the benediction of someone besides your friend, M.R."

The patient reader must infer what he can from these five letters. They are copied word for word from the original documents, and speak for themselves. I am unable to say whether the luggage was found—whether Miss Daisy got her sleeves altered to her liking—whether Arthur found any "fun" left on his arrival, a fortnight late, at Grandcourt, or how soon Mr Blake's reply to the father's letter reached Lucerne. All these momentous questions the reader can settle for himself as well as I can for him. He will at any rate be able to understand that when one day in October a telegram reached Railsford from Grandcourt with the brief announcement—"Vacancy here; see advertisement *Athenaeum*! am writing"—it created no small stir in the manly breast of the worthy to whom it was directed.

He went at once to Westbourne Park and held a cabinet council with his chief adviser, and again, on returning home, called his sisters into consultation. He wrote to his college tutor, drew up a most elegant letter to the governors, read a few chapters of *Tom Brown's Schooldays*, and then waited impatiently for Grover's promised letter.

"You will have guessed," said that letter, when it arrived, "from my telegram that Moss has resigned, and that there will be a vacancy for a house-master and Master of the Shell here at Christmas. You know how I would like to see you appointed. But—"

"But what?" inquired someone who read the letter over the reader's shoulder.

"I should not be your friend if I represented this place as a bed of roses, especially Moss's house. You'll have hard work to hold your own with the boys, and harder still with some of the masters. You will get more criticism than backing-up from head-quarters. Still it is a splendid opening for a man of courage like you; and all the school would profit by your success. Talk to Podmore about it; he'll give you good advice. So will Weston. Of course I can do nothing at all but look on sympathetically, and, if you try for the place and succeed, promise you at least one hearty welcome."

"It seems pretty clear it won't be child's play," said Railsford, folding up the letter.

"It would not suit you if it was," replied his adviser.

This brave speech went far to make up Railsford's mind.

In the house at Westbourne Park, particularly, the career opening before our hero was hailed with eager enthusiasm. "Dear Arthur" was in Moss's house, and at Christmas he would get his remove to the Shell. In both capacities he would have the protecting interest of his prospective brother-in-law, spread like an aegis over his innocent head. "It really seems almost a providential arrangement," said Mrs Herapath.

"I am sure it will be a great thing for Arthur," said Daisy.

"It makes one believe there's some truth in the saying that every man has his niche waiting for him somewhere in life," moralised Mr Herapath.

That evening a letter came from Arthur to Daisy. The boy, of course, knew nothing of Railsford's candidature.

"Such a flare-up!" wrote the youth. "Moss has got kicked out! He's jacked it up, and is going at Christmas. Jolly good job! He shouldn't have stopped the roast potatoes in the dormitories. Bickers's fellows have them; they can do what they like! Dig and I did the two mile spin in 11.19, but there was too much slush to put it on. All I can say is, I hope we'll get a fellow who is not a cad after Moss, especially as he will be Master of the Shell, and I'll get a dose of him both ways after Christmas. We mean not to let him get his head up like Moss did; we're going to take it out of him at first, and then he'll cave in and let us do as we like afterwards. Dig and I will get a study after Christmas. I wish you'd see about a carpet, and get the gov. to give us a picture or two; and we've got to get a rig-out of saucepans and kettles and a barometer and a canary, and all that. The room's 15 feet by 9, so see the carpet's the right size. Gedge says Turkey carpets are the best, so we'll have a Turkey. How's Railsford? Are you and he spoons still? Dig and the fellows roared when I told them about catching you two that time at Lucerne in the garden. You know, when I thought the window was being smashed? Could you lend me a bob's worth of stamps till Christmas? I'll pay you back. Dig says he once had a cousin who went spoons on a chap. He says it was an awful game to catch them at it. So, you see, we've lots to sympathise about. Love to all.

"I am, yours truly,—

"Arthur.

"P.S.—Don't forget the stamps. Two bob's worth will do as well."

Daisy laughed and cried over this outrageous epistle, and hesitated about showing it to Mark. However, that happy youth only laughed, and produced half a crown, which he begged Daisy to add to her own contribution.

"That's the sort of Young England I like!" said he. "It will be like a canter on a breezy moor to come in contact with fresh life and spirit like this, after wasting my time here for three years."

"I expect you will find it breezy," said Daisy, recovering her smiles. "Arthur is a dreadful boy; it *will* be so good for him to have you."

At the end of a fortnight came a summons to Railsford, as one of six selected candidates, to appear and show himself to the governors. He had expected thus much of success, but the thought of the other five rendered him uncomfortable as he leaned back in the railway carriage and hardened himself for the ordeal before him. Grover had deemed it prudent not to display any particular interest in his arrival, but he contrived to pay a flying visit to his hotel that evening.

"There's only one fellow likely to run you close—an Oxford man, first-class in classics, and a good running-man in his day. I think when they see you they'll prefer you. They will have the six up in alphabetical order, so you'll come last. That's a mercy. Take a tip from me, and don't seem too anxious for the place, it doesn't pay; and keep in with Ponsford."

"Will he be there? Oh, of course. What sort of men are the governors?"

"Very harmless. They'll want to know your character and your creed, and that sort of thing, and will leave all the rest to Ponsford."

Next morning at 11.30 Railsford sat with his five fellow-martyrs in the ante-room of the governors' hall at Grandcourt. They talked to one another, these six unfortunates, about the weather, about the Midland Railway, about the picture on the wall. They watched one another as, in obedience to the summons from within, they disappeared one by one through the green baize door, and emerged a quarter or half an hour later with tinged cheeks, and taking up their hats, vanished into the open-air. Railsford was the only one left to witness the exit of the fifth candidate. Then the voice from within called, "Come in, Mr Railsford," and he knew his turn was come. It was less terrible than he expected. Half a score of middle-aged gentlemen round a table, some looking at him, some reading his testimonials, and one or two putting questions. Most of them indulgent to his embarrassment and even sharing it. Dr Ponsford, however, massive, stern, with his shaggy eyebrows and pursed mouth, was above any such weakness.

"What have you been doing since you left college?" demanded he, presently fixing the candidate with his eyes.

It was a home question. Railsford answered it honestly, if hesitatingly.

"I was unfortunately not under the necessity of working," he added, after going through the catalogue of his abortive studies, "that is, not for my livelihood." Some of the governors nodded their heads a little, as though they recognised the misfortune of such a position.

"And what places you under that necessity now?"

"I do not expect to remain a bachelor always, sir."

Here a governor chuckled.

"Ha, ha! Hymen comes to the rescue. Wonderful the revolutions he makes in young fellows' lives."

The governor had left school fifty-five years ago, and was rather proud to have remembered who Hymen was. The doctor waited with chilling patience till the interruption was over.

"You feel yourself competent to take charge of a house of forty to fifty boys, do you? as well as to conduct a class of seventy?"

"I have thought over the matter, and tried to realise the duties, and think I can succeed."

"Quite right; I like that. No brag," said another of the governors, in an aside.

"Your temper is good, is it? you are not likely to fall out with your fellow-masters, are you?"

"Yes, that's important," interjected a governor.

"I believe I am good-tempered and patient."

"Well, Mr Railsford, you may retire. If you are not busy elsewhere, you can remain a short time in the outer room."

Railsford retired, and for an interminable half-hour kicked his heels in the ante-chamber. He got to hate the picture on the wall and the ruthless ticking of the clock in the hall outside. Presently the door opened and his name was called. This time the spokesman was the chairman of the governors.

"We have been through your testimonials a second time, Mr Railsford, and are satisfied with them, both those which refer to your scholarship and those which relate to your character and other qualifications. We are also glad to know from you that you have fully considered the responsibilities of this very important post, and are prepared to enter upon them in a firm yet conciliatory spirit. The governors and head-master agree with me in considering that, taken as a whole, your qualifications are higher than those of the other candidates, and they, therefore, have agreed to appoint you to the vacant post. I trust it may result in our mutual satisfaction and the good of the school."

Chapter Two.

"Veni, Vidi, —"

If a light heart and faith in one's own good luck are omens of success, Mark Railsford undoubtedly entered on his new duties at Grandcourt under the most favourable of auspices. It would not have been to his discredit if his light heart had acknowledged even slightly the weight of the responsibility it was undertaking. But, as a matter of fact, it was all the lighter for that very responsibility. The greater the task, he argued, the greater the achievement; and the greater the achievement, the greater the triumph. A less sanguine hero might have been daunted by the pictures with which his nervous friends did their best to damp his ardour. Grover, delighted as he was at the success of his friend's application, took care to keep the rocks ahead well above the surface in all his letters and conversations. Railsford laughed him pleasantly to scorn.

Grover's was not the only attempt made to intimidate our hero. A week or so before he entered upon his duties, a nervous-looking man called to see him. It was Mr Moss, the late master.

"I hear you have been appointed to my house," he said, by way of explanation, "and I thought it would be only friendly to call and tell you the sort of thing you are to expect when you go there."

"Thanks, very much," said Railsford, with a smile of the corner of his mouth.

"You may be made of cast iron, or be possessed of the patience of a Job," began this cheery adviser. "If so, you're all right. I wasn't either."

"Did you find the boys unmanageable?"

"No—not more than other boys—all boys, of course, are the sworn foes of law and order, and nobody imagines anything else. No, your difficulties, if you have anything like my luck, will be more with your colleagues than your subjects."

"And how do they make themselves objectionable?" asked the new master, rather contemptuously.

Mr Moss did not miss the tone of this question, and fired up himself.

"Of course, if *you* don't mind being systematically snubbed at head-quarters—thwarted and slandered by your fellow-masters—baulked in every attempt to improve the condition either of your house or the school—and misrepresented and undermined in your influence among your boys, you may go up and enjoy it. I didn't. That's why I left."

"At any rate, I have one friend among the masters—Grover."

"Oh, poor Grover. He is the only master who can get on at all, and he does so by effacing himself on every possible occasion, and agreeing with everybody."

"Not a very noble character to hear of one's friend," said Railsford, who was beginning to get tired of this jeremiad.

"I don't blame him; he can stand more than you or I can."

"That, I suppose, is meant for a compliment to me?" said Railsford, laughing. "You think, then, I would be wise to back out before it is too late?"

"I don't say that, only—"

"Only you pity me. Thanks, very much."

That evening Railsford sent a line to Grover:—

"Tell me in two words why Moss left Grandcourt."

A telegram came next morning, "Incompatibility of temper."

Whereat the new master chuckled, and dismissed the lugubrious ex-master and his friendly warnings from his mind. But although the gloomy prognostications of his Job's comforters failed in the least to depress his spirits, one very small cloud hovered occasionally on the horizon. This was the attitude of his worthy and respected prospective pupil and brother-in-law, Arthur Herapath. That young gentleman, who had been prudently kept in the dark while term lasted, was, as may be imagined, considerably astounded on arriving home to be met with the news that the new master of the Shell at Grandcourt was to be Mark Railsford.

"What a lark!" he exclaimed.

Now, genial as the remark was, the tone in which it was uttered was not calculated to inspire confidence in the breasts of those to whom it was addressed. There was more of enjoyment in it than respect. Yet boys will be boys, and who can gauge the depths of a nature below the smiles that ripple on the surface?

It was little incidents like these which occasionally suggested to Railsford, far more forcibly than the lugubrious warnings of his officious friends, that the task before him at Grandcourt would tax his powers considerably. But, on the whole, he rejoiced that all would not be plain-sailing at first, and that there was no chance of his relapsing immediately into the condition of a humdrum pedagogue.

The Christmas holidays slipped away only too fast for Arthur and for Daisy. Mark, much as he felt the approaching separation from his betrothed, could not suppress a slight feeling of exultation as the day drew near when he was to "go, see, and conquer" at Grandcourt. His three idle years made the prospect of hard work now welcome; and the importance which everyone else attached to his new duties made him doubly keen for a fray on which so many eyes were turned.

Dr Ponsford had suggested, in terms which amounted to a mandate, that the new master might find it convenient to arrive at Grandcourt a day before the school returned, in order to take possession of his quarters and acquaint himself with the details of his coming duties. This arrangement was not altogether satisfactory, for it deprived Mark of the pleasure of his future brother-in-law's escort, which was a great loss, and also of the prospect of finding Grover at his journey's end, on which he had reckoned with some confidence. However, it was only the difference of a day, and during that day he would at least do his utmost to make a favourable impression on his chief. So, with a heart full of confidence, and a cab full of luggage, he set out gaily on his new career.

"Good-bye, Mark. You'll be good to my son, I know," said Mrs Herapath.

"Good-bye, my boy; take care of your health," said Mr Herapath.

"Good-bye, Mark," said Daisy.

"Ta-ta, old man," called Arthur. "See you to-morrow."

This last greeting, strange as it may seem, recurred to Railsford's memory more frequently than any of the others during the course of the long railway journey to Grandcourt. It took all sorts of forms as the day wore on. At first it seemed only a fraternal *au revoir*, then it became a rather serious promise, and finally sounded in his ears rather like a menace.

Here was he, going down like a prince to his coronation, and his subjects would "see him to-morrow." It had never occurred to him before that these subjects might have something to say to the ordering of the new kingdom, and that he should have to reckon with them, as well as they with him. The idea was not altogether comfortable, and he tried to shelve it. Of course he would get on with them. They would look up to him, and they would discover that his interests and theirs were the same. He was prepared to go some way to meet them. It would be odd if they would not come the rest to meet him. He turned his mind to other subjects. Still he wished he could be quite sure that Arthur's innocent "see you again to-morrow" had no double meaning for him.

The railway took him as far as Blankington Junction, about five miles from Grandcourt; and, as it would be some time before a Grandcourt train came up, he decided, after seeing his effects into a cab, to take advantage of the fine, frosty afternoon, and complete his journey on foot. He was, in fact, beginning to grow a little depressed, and the exercise would brace him up. He had, foolishly enough, looked forward to a somewhat different kind of advent, dropping, perhaps, with some little *éclat* on a school where Arthur had already proclaimed his fame among the boys, and where Grover had prepared him a welcome among the masters. Compared with that, this solitary backstairs arrival seemed tame and dispiriting, and he half regretted that he had not postponed his coming till to-morrow, even in the face of Dr Ponsford's suggestion.

A mile from Grandcourt he caught sight of the square red ivy-covered brick tower of the school among the trees. Even in winter it looked warm and picturesque. It was growing dark when he passed the lodge, and crossed the playing-field towards the school-house. The cabman was awaiting him in the square.

"Never gave me your name," explained he, "and nobody knows nothink about you here. Five miles is seven-and-six, and luggage is two bob more, and waiting another 'alf-hour's a crown,—namely, twelve shillings, and thank you, mister."

Railsford rang the bell at the porter's lodge. A small child of eight appeared.

"Where's your father?" asked the new master.

"Yout," replied the girl.

"Well, your mother?"

"Please, she's—she's in the churchyard along of my Aunt Sally."

"Well, run and— You mean she's dea—?"

The child nodded before he had finished his sentence.

"Is there anyone about?" inquired the perplexed new-comer.

"There's Mrs 'Astings, doing the floors in Bickers's."

Mrs Hastings was duly summoned, and arrived with her broom and kneeling-pad.

"My good woman, can you tell me the fare from Blankington here?"

The lady looked perplexed, then embarrassed, then angry.

"And you fetched me over from Bickers's—me, with my lame foot, over the cobbles—to ask me that! You oughter be ashamed of yerself, young man. Ask the cabman; he knows."

It was hopeless. Railsford assisted to unload the cab, and meekly gave the cabman the fare demanded.

"I am Mr Railsford, the new master," said he presently, overtaking Mrs Hastings, as she hobbled back in dudgeon to her work; "which are my rooms?"

"I'm sure I don't know. You're a day too early. All the rooms is up, and it will take us all our times to get them done against the school comes back to-morrow."

"It is an extraordinary thing," said Railsford, who began to feel his dignity somewhat put upon, "that Dr Ponsford should tell me to come to-day, and that no preparations—"

"'Tain't got to do with me. You'd best go to the doctor's house, out of that gate, across the little square, the house on the far side of the chapel."

Railsford, leaving his luggage stacked on the pavement outside the porter's lodge, started off with flushed cheeks to the lion's den. The doctor, said the maid, was in, but was at dinner. The gentleman had better call again in half an hour.

So Railsford, in the closing twilight, took a savage walk round the school precincts, in no mood to admire the natural beauties of the place, or to indulge in any rhapsodies at this near view of the scene of his coming triumphs. In half an hour he returned, and was shown into the doctor's study.

"How do you do, Mr —;" here the doctor took up his visitor's card to refresh his memory—"Mr Railsford?"

"I was afraid, sir," said Mark, "I had mistaken your letter about coming to-day; there appears to be no one—no one who can—I have been unable to ascertain where I am to go."

The doctor waited patiently for the end of this lucid explanation.

"I rather wonder it did not suggest itself to you to call on me for information."

Railsford wondered so too, and felt rather sheepish.

"Your train must have been late. I expected you an hour ago."

"I think we were up to time. I walked from Blankington here."

"Really—I wish I had known of your intention."

"I trust," said Railsford, struck by a horrible suspicion, "you were not waiting dinner for me."

"Not in the least," said the doctor, with a grim smile; "but I had calculated on taking you round before nightfall. We must defer our visit till the morning. Talking of dinner," he added, "you will be ready for something after your journey, will you not?"

As Railsford was nearly famishing, he could only colour up and reply—

"Thank you."

The doctor rang the bell.

"See that Mr Railsford gets dinner. I have to go out," he added, "but you will, no doubt, make yourself at home;" and the great man withdrew, leaving the new master in a very crestfallen and disturbed state of mind.

If this was a sample of the sympathy he might expect at head-quarters, Moss's prognostications, after all, were not quite baseless. He made the best of his solitary dinner, and then sallied out in the dark to try to find the porter's lodge once more and rescue his luggage. That functionary was still absent, and Mark was compelled himself to haul his belongings in under cover, and leave word with the little girl that they were to be taken over to Mr Railsford's rooms as soon as her father came in. Then taking with him a bag which contained what he wanted for the night, he returned to the head-master's house and made a point of retiring to rest before his host reappeared on the scene.

Once more luck was against him.

"You vanished early last night," said the doctor, blandly, at breakfast next morning. "I brought Mr Roe in to supper, thinking you and he might like a chat about the work in the Shell, about which he could have given you some useful hints. However, early hours are very commendable."

"I am extremely sorry," faltered Railsford. "I had no idea you would be home so early. I should have liked to meet Mr Roe so much."

"Take some more coffee?" said the doctor.

After breakfast Mark was conducted in state to his house. The floors were all damp and the carpets up; beds and washstands were piled up in the passages, and nowhere was a fire to be seen.

"There are your rooms," said the doctor, pointing out a suite of three apartments opening one into the other, at the present time reeking of soft-soap and absolutely destitute of furniture. "You will find them comfortable and central. The inner room is the bedroom, the middle your private sitting-room, and this larger one the house-parlour. Now we will go to the dormitories and studies. You understand your head boys—those in the Sixth and Fifth—have a study to themselves; the Shell have studies in pairs, and the junior school-work in the common room. But all these points you will make yourself familiar with very shortly. As a house-master, you will of course be responsible for everything that takes place in the house—the morals, work and play of the boys are under your supervision. You have four Sixth-form boys in the house, who are prefects under you, and in certain matters exercise an authority of their own without appeal to you. But you quite understand that you must watch that this is not abused. The house dame, Mrs Farthing, superintends everything connected with the boy's wardrobes, but is under your direction in other matters. I shall introduce you to her as we go down.

"I refer you to the school time-table for particulars as to rising, chapel, preparation, and lights out, and so forth. Discipline on all these points is essential. Cases of difficulty may be referred to a session of the other masters, or in extreme cases to me; but please remember I do not invite consultation in matters of detail. A house-master may use the cane in special cases, which must be reported through the masters' session to me. So much for your house duties.

"As Master of the Shell, you preside at morning school there every day, and, as you know, have to teach classics, English, and divinity. In the afternoon the boys are taken by the French, mathematical, and chemical masters. But you are nominally responsible for the whole, and any case of insubordination or idleness during afternoon school will be reported to you by the master in charge, and you must deal with it as though you had been in charge at the time.

"Now come and make Mrs Farthing's acquaintance."

Mrs Farthing, a lean, wrathful-looking personage, stood in the midst of a wilderness of sheets and blankets, and received her new superior with a very bad grace. She looked him up and looked him down, and then sniffed.

"Very good, Mr Railsford; we shall become better acquainted, I've no doubt."

Railsford shuddered at the prospect; and finding that his luggage was still knocking about at the porter's lodge, he made further expedition in search of it, and at last, with superhuman efforts, succeeded in getting it transferred to his quarters, greatly to the disgust of Mrs Hastings, who remarked in an audible aside to her fellow-scrubber, Mrs Willis, that people ought to keep their dirty traps to themselves till the place is ready for them.

After which Railsford deemed it prudent to take open-air exercise, and await patiently the hour when his carpets should be laid and Grandcourt should wake up into life for the new term.

Chapter Three.

Opening Day.

The combined labours of Mesdames Farthing, Hastings, Wilson, and their myrmidons had barely reached a successful climax that afternoon, in the rescue of order out of the chaos which had reigned in Railsford's house, when the first contingent of the Grandcourtiers arrived in the great square. Railsford, who had at last been permitted to take possession of his rooms and to unstrap his boxes, looked down from his window with some little curiosity at the scene below.

The solemn quadrangle, which an hour ago had looked so ghostly and dreary, was now alive with a crowd of boys, descending headlong from the inside and outside of four big omnibuses, hailing one another boisterously, scrambling for their luggage, scrimmaging for the possession of Mrs Farthing's or the porter's services, indulging in horseplay with the drivers, singing, hooting, challenging, rejoicing, stamping, running, jumping, kicking—anything, in fact, but standing still. In their own opinion, evidently, they were the lords and masters of Grandcourt. They strutted about with the airs of proprietors, and Railsford began to grow half uneasy lest any of them should detect him at the window and demand what right *he* had there.

The scene grew more and more lively. A new cavalcade discharged its contents on the heels of the first, and upon them came cabs top-heavy with luggage, and a stampede of pedestrians who had quitted the omnibuses a mile from home and run in, and one or two on tricycles, and one hero in great state on horseback. Cheers, sometimes yells, greeted each arrival; and

THE CAB CAME ON APACE, ITS JAUNTY JEHU FLOURISHING HIS
WHIP AND SHOUTING LOUDLY TO HIS OPPONENT

when presently there lumbered up some staid old four-wheeler with a luckless new boy on board, the demonstration became most imposing.

"*See you to-morrow*!" thought Railsford to himself, as he peered down. Suddenly an unwonted excitement manifested itself. This was occasioned by an impromptu race between two omnibuses and a hansom cab, which, having been all temporarily deserted by their rightful Jehus, had been boarded by three amateur charioteers and set in motion. The hero in charge of the hansom cab generously gave his more heavily-weighted competitors a start of fifty yards; and, standing up in his perch, shook his reins defiantly and smacked his whip, to the infinite delight of everyone but the licenced gentleman who was the nominal proprietor of the vehicle. Of the omnibuses, one got speedily into difficulties, owing to the charioteer getting the reins a trifle mixed and thereby spinning his vehicle round in a semicircle, and bringing it up finally in the middle of the lawn, where he abruptly vacated his post and retired into private life.

The other omnibuses had a more glorious career. The horses were spirited, and entered into the fun of the thing almost as much as their driver. Railsford long remembered the picture which this youthful hero presented; with his face flushed, his head bare, his sandy hair waving in the breeze, his body laid back at an obtuse angle, as he tugged with both hands at the reins. The cab behind came on apace, its jaunty Jehu flourishing his whip and shouting loudly to his opponent to keep his right side. The crowd forgot everything else, and flocked across the grass with loud cheers for the champions.

"Wire in, hansom," shouted some.

"Stick to it, Dig," cried others.

How the mad career might have ended no one could tell; but at each corner the cab closed in ominously with its clumsy competitor, whose horses were fast getting beyond the control of their driver, while the vehicle they were dragging rocked and yawed behind them like a tug in a gale. Railsford was meditating a descent on to the scene, with a view to prevent a catastrophe, if possible, when a shout of laughter greeted the appearance on the scene of the lawful master of the omnibus, in headlong pursuit of his property. By an adroit cut across the grass this outraged gentleman succeeded in overtaking the vehicle and boarding it by the step behind; and then, amid delighted shouts of "Whip behind, Dig!" the spectators watched the owner skip up the steps and along the top, just as "Dig," having received timely warning of his peril, dropped the reins and skipped the contrary way along the top and down the back stairs, depositing himself neatly on *terra firma*, where, with admirable *sang-froid*, he joined the spectators and triumphed in the final pulling up of the omnibus, and the consequent abandonment of the race by the indignant hero of the hansom cab, who protested in mock heroics that he was winning hand over hand, and would have licked the 'bus to fits if Dig hadn't funked it.

In the altercation which ensued the company generally took no part, and returned, braced up and fortified by their few minutes' sport, to the serious business of identifying and extricating their luggage from the general *mêlée*, and conveying themselves and their belongings into winter quarters.

The new master was impressed by what he had seen—not altogether unfavourably. True, it upset in a moment all his dreams of carrying Grandcourt by the quiet magic of his own influence to the high level he had arranged for it. Still, the race had been a pretty one while it lasted, and both competitors had handled the ribbons well. They would be the sort of boys to take to him—an old 'Varsity Blue; and he would meet them half-way. Railsford's house should get a name for pluck and *esprit de corps*; and Railsford and his boys should show the way to Grandcourt! How Dr Ponsford and the "session of masters" would follow their lead it did not at present enter into the head of the vain young man to settle.

A knock came at his door as he stood lost in these pleasing reflections, and Grover entered.

"Here you are, then, old man," said he—"an old stager already. It was a great disappointment I could not be here when you got down."

"I wish you had. I have had not exactly a gay time of it."

And he related his experiences. Grover laughed.

"That's Ponsford all over," said he. "He's a fine fellow, but a bear. How do you like your quarters?"

"I've only just got into them, and really haven't had time to look round. And, to tell the truth, for the last ten minutes or so I've been so interested in the scene below that I had forgotten what I was doing. There was a most amusing chariot race between a cab and an omnibus."

Grover looked serious.

"I know," said he. "I'm afraid there will be trouble about that. It's as well, perhaps, you are not expected to know the chief offenders. One or two of them belong to your house."

Railsford looked uncomfortable. It had not occurred to him till now that the proceeding which had so moved his interest and amusement was a breach of discipline.

"I hope I shall not be called upon to deal with it," said he.

"No. I hear Ponsford has the matter in hand himself."

And the friends went on to talk of other matters.

After a while Grover hastened away to his own house, leaving Railsford somewhat uneasy in his mind.

If Dr Ponsford were to question him on the subject of the chariot race, he felt that he would be seriously compromised at the outset of his career. He knew at least the nickname of one of the delinquents; and had actually, by standing and watching the contest without protest, been an accessory to the offence. He busied himself forthwith in his unpacking, and studiously avoided the window until daylight departed, and the court below became silent and deserted.

Just about four o'clock another knock sounded at his door, and Arthur Herapath presented himself, leading by the arm the tawny-haired hero of the chariot race.

"What cheer, Marky?" cried the brother-in-law to be. "Here we are. Had a spiffing spin up from the station, hadn't we, Dig? This it Dig, you know, Sir Digby Oakshott, Baronet, M.P., A.S.S., and nobody knows what else. He and I have bagged Sykes' old room, just over here."

Railsford in his shirt-sleeves, and hemmed round by his luggage, looked up rather blankly at this friendly oration. However, his dignity came to his rescue.

"How are you both? I hope we're to have a good steady term, my boys. Go to your study now—later on we must have a talk."

Arthur looked at his friend and winked; Sir Digby was visibly agitated, and grinned vehemently at a cobweb in the corner of the ceiling.

"All serene," said the former. "By the way, Daisy was all right when I left her, and sent her love and a—"

"Do you hear me, Arthur? Go to your study."

"Oh, all right—but there was a message from the gov. I was to be sure and give you directly I saw you. He says I can have a bob a week pocket-money, and you're to give it to me, and he'll owe it to you at the end of the term. I'd like the first now, please."

"Go immediately to your room," shouted Railsford, as near to losing his temper as his future brother-in-law had ever seen him. "How dare you disobey me?"

"Well, but it was a message from the gov., and—I say, Dig," added he, turning to his friend with a nudge, "you cut when Mark tells you."

Dig departed, and Railsford weakly fell in with the arrangement of the junior, and allowed him to remain and deliver the rest of his domestic messages.

"Now, look here, Arthur," said the master, closing the door and facing his unabashed future kinsman, "we must come to an understanding at once. During term time I forbid you to mention Daisy's name, either to me or anybody else, unless I wish it—"

The boy whistled. "What, have you had a row, then? Is it all broken off? My eye, what will—"

"Rubbish!" said Mark, scarcely able to keep grave; "it's neither one nor the other. But I don't choose you should talk of her, and I insist on being obeyed."

"Jolly rough not to be able to talk about one's own sister!" interposed the innocent.

"Of course, I mean not in connection with me," said Railsford. "And another thing, you must not call me Mark, but Mr Railsford, while term lasts."

"All serene, Mr Railsford, old man! Jolly stiff, though, between brothers, isn't it?"

"You must treat me as if I were merely your master, and no other relative."

"How queer! Mayn't I even be fond of you?"

"Yes, as your master. I count on you, mind, to set a specially good example to the other boys, and back me up in every way you can. You will be able to do a great deal if you only try."

"I'm game! Am I to be made a prefect, I say, Mark—Mr Railsford, I mean?"

"And remember," said Mark, ignoring the question, "that we are here to work, and not to—to drive omnibuses."

Arthur brightened up suddenly.

"You saw the race, then? Stunning spurt round the last lap, only Dig hadn't any stay in him, and the cab had the inside berth. I say, don't let anybody know it was Dig, will you? He'd get in rather a mess, and he's going to put it on hard this term to make up."

Could anything be more hopeless than the task of impressing this simple-minded youth with a sense of his duty and deportment towards the new Master of the Shell?

Railsford gave the attempt up, and the school-bell happily intervened to make a diversion.

"That's for dinner. It's generally at two, you know; but on opening day it's 4.30," said the boy. "We shall have to cut, or we shall be gated, I say."

"Well, you must show me the way," said Mark. "I'm ready."

"You'll have to wear your cap and gown, though," replied Arthur, "or you'll get in a row."

Railsford hastened to rectify the omission, and next moment was standing in the great square beside his lively young pilot, amid a crowd of boys hastening towards the school hall.

"We'd better do a trot," said the boy.

"We shall do it all right, I think," said the master, whose dignity revolted against any motion more rapid than quick walking. Arthur, trotting at his side and encouraging him from time to time to "put it on," detracted a little from the solemnity of the procession. The bell was just ceasing to ring as they entered the hall, and for the first time Railsford found himself in the presence of the assembled school.

Arthur had darted off to his own table, leaving his companion to find his way to the masters' table at the head of the hall, where all his colleagues were already in their places, standing for grace.

Railsford, considerably flurried, slipped into the place which Grover had reserved for him just as the head boy present began to recite the Latin collect, and became painfully aware that his already damaged character for punctuality was by no means enhanced in the severe eyes of Dr Ponsford. The new master glanced round a little nervously at his colleagues. Grover introduced him to a few of the nearest, some of whom received him with a friendly greeting, others eyed him doubtfully, and one or two bristled up grimly. The *éclat* of his first appearance at Grandcourt had paled somewhat, and he was thankful to have Grover to talk to and keep him in countenance.

"Tell me who some of these men are," he whispered. "Which is Roe?"

"On the other side of me. He has the house next to mine. You, I, Roe, and Bickers have the four sides of the Big Square."

"Which is Bickers?"

"The man with the black beard—last but one on the other side."

Railsford gave a furtive look down the table, and encountered the eyes of Mr Bickers fixed discontentedly on him.

A lightning flash at midnight will often reveal minute details of a scene or landscape which in the ordinary glare of day might pass unnoticed by the observer. So it was in this sudden chance encounter of glances. It lasted not a moment, but it was a declaration of war to the knife on one side, hurled back defiantly on the other.

"Not a bad fellow if you don't stroke him the wrong way," said Grover.

"Oh," said Railsford, in a tone which made his friend start. "Who is beyond him?"

"Lablache, the French master; not very popular, I fancy."

And so on, one master after another was pointed out, and Railsford formed his own opinions of each, and began to feel at home with several of them already. But whenever his eyes turned towards the end of the table they invariably encountered those of Bickers.

There was not much general conversation at the masters' table. Dr Ponsford rarely encouraged it, and resented it when it arose without his initiative.

The buzz and clatter at the boys' tables, however, growing occasionally to a hubbub, amply made up for any sombreness in the meal elsewhere; and Railsford, having exhausted his inquiries, and having failed to engage one of his neighbours in conversation, resigned himself to the enjoyment of the animated scene. He was not long in discovering the whereabouts of his youthful kinsman, whose beaming face shone out from the midst of a bevy of particular friends, while ever and again above the turmoil, like a banner in the breeze, waved the tawny mane of Sir Digby Oakshott. It amused Railsford to watch the group, and when now and then they looked his way, to speculate on what was the subject of their conversation. Perhaps Arthur had been telling them of the new master's athletic achievements at Cambridge, and how he had rowed his boat to the head of the river; or possibly he had been describing to them some of the big football-matches which he, Mark, had taken his young friend to see during the holidays; or maybe they were laying down some patriotic plan for the future good of Railsford's house. His heart warmed to the boys as he watched them. It was a pity, perhaps, he could not catch their actual words.

"Seems jolly green," said Dig.

"So he is. Blushes like a turkey-cock when you talk about spoons. Never mind, he's bound to be civil to us this term, eh, Dig? We've got the whip hand of him, I guess, over that summer-house business at Lucerne."

Here Dig laughed.

"Shut up! He'll hear!"

"What's the joke?" demanded a bullet-headed, black-eyed boy who sat near.

"What, didn't I tell you, Dimsdale? Keep it close, won't you? You see that chap with the eyeglass next to Grover. That's Railsford, our new master—Marky, I call him. He's engaged to Daisy, you know, my sister. Regular soup-ladles they are."

Here Dig once more laughed beyond the bounds of discretion.

"What an ass you are, Dig!" expostulated Arthur; "you'll get us in no end of a mess."

"Awfully sorry—I can't help. Tell Dimsdale about—you know."

"Don't go spreading it, though," said Arthur, shutting his eyes to the fact that he was confiding his secret to the greatest gossip in Grandcourt, and that one or two other heads were also craned forward to hear the joke. "I caught them going it like one o'clock in the hotel garden at Lucerne—it was the first time I twigged what was up; and what do you think he called my sister?"

"What?" they all demanded.

"Keep it close, I say. Ha, ha!—give you a guess all round; Dig knows."

"Pussy cat," suggested one.

"Jumbo," suggested another.

"Cherubim," suggested a third.

Arthur shook his head triumphantly.

"Out of it, all of you. You can tell 'em, Dig."

Dig composed his features once or twice to utter the word, but as many times broke down. At last in high falsetto he got it out,—

"Chuckey!"

The laugh which greeted this revelation penetrated to the upper region, and caused Dr Ponsford to rise on his seat and look in the direction of the uproar.

At the same moment the Sixth-Form boy at the head of the table left his place and bore down on the offenders.

"*Cave!*" muttered Arthur, purple in the face; "here's Ainger."

Instantly the party was thoroughly buried in its bread and cheese.

"Was that you, Oakshott, making that row?"

"I was only saying something to Herapath," replied the innocent; "I'm sure *I* didn't make a row."

"Don't tell falsehoods. Do fifty lines, and next time you'll be sent up."

"That's a nice lark," muttered the baronet as the senior retired. "It was you chaps made the row, and I get potted for it. But I say," added he, as if such a mishap were the most common of incidents, "that isn't a bad joke, is it? Fancy calling Herapath's sister—"

"*Cave*, shut up!" exclaimed Arthur, dealing his friend a ferocious kick under the table; "they've got their eyes on us. Don't play the fool, Dig."

Railsford was aroused from the pleasant contemplation of this little comedy by a general rising, in the midst of which the doctor, followed by his staff, filed out of the hall into the governor's room adjoining, which was ordinarily used as a masters' withdrawing-room. Here Railsford underwent the ordeal of a series of introductions, some of which gave him pleasure, some disappointment, some misgivings, and one at least roused his anger.

"Mr Bickers," said Dr Ponsford, "let me introduce Mr Railsford. You will be neighbours, and ought to be friends."

"I am proud to know Mr Railsford," said Mr Bickers, holding out his hand; "Grandcourt, I am sure, is fortunate."

Railsford flushed up at the tone in which this greeting was offered; and touching the proffered hand hurriedly, said, with more point than prudence—

"I heard of Mr Bickers from my predecessor, Mr Moss."

It was some satisfaction to see Mr Bickers flush in his turn, as he replied, with a hardly concealed sneer—

"Ah, poor Moss! He was a great flatterer. You must not believe half he says about his absent friends."

"Railsford," said Grover, taking his friend by the arm, and anxious to interrupt what promised to be an uncomfortable dialogue, "I must introduce you to Roe. He had charge of the Shell for some years, and can give you some hints which will be useful to you. You'll like him."

Railsford did like him. Mr Roe was one of the best masters at Grandcourt, and his university career had been as brilliant in athletics, and more brilliant in scholarship, than his younger colleagues. He had a quiet voice and manly bearing, which bespoke a vast fund of power latent beneath the surface; and Railsford, for once in his life, experienced the novel sensation of standing in the presence of a superior. Mr Roe accepted Mark's apologies for his non-appearance the evening before with great good-humour, and invited him to his rooms to spend an evening and talk over school-work.

"You are not likely to have much leisure at first. I wish you had a quieter house; but a little good government and sympathy will go a long way towards bringing it up to the mark. As to the Shell, you will find that pretty easy. It wants more management than teaching—at least, I found so. If once the boys can be put on the right track, they will go pretty much of their own accord. It's easier to guide them than drive them; don't you think so?"

"I have no experience yet; but that is my idea, certainly."

"Then you'll succeed. Have you been introduced to Monsieur Lablache? This is Mr Railsford, the new Master of the Shell, monsieur."

Monsieur shrugged himself ceremoniously. He had a big moustache, which curled up in an enigmatical way when he smiled; and Railsford was at a loss whether to like him or dislike him.

"We shall be friends, Meester Railsford, I hope," said the foreigner; "I have much to do wiz ze young gentlemen of the Sell. Hélas! they try my patience; but I like them, Meester Railsford, I like them."

"I only wish I knew whether I liked you," inwardly ejaculated the new master, as he smiled in response to the confession.

A bell put an end to further conference, and Mark went off in a somewhat excited state of mind to his own house.

Mr Roe's few words stuck in his mind—especially one of them.

What did he mean by classing sympathy and good government together in the way he had? How can you reduce a disorderly house to order by sympathy?

However, he had no leisure for guessing riddles that night.

Chapter Four.

A Friendly Chat.

If Mark Railsford had been left with no better guide to his new duties and responsibilities than the few hurried utterances given by Dr Ponsford during their tour through the premises that morning, his progress would have been very slow and unsatisfactory. It was part of the doctor's method never to do for anyone, colleague or boy, what they could possibly do for themselves. He believed in piling up difficulties at the beginning of an enterprise, instead of making smooth the start and saving up the hard things for later on. If a master of his got through his first term well, he would be pretty sure to turn out well in future. But meanwhile he got as little help from head-quarters as possible, and had to make all his discoveries, arrange his own methods, reap his own experiences for himself.

Grover had good reason to know the doctor's peculiarity in this respect, and took care to give his friend a few hints about starting work, which otherwise he might never have evolved out of his own consciousness.

Amongst other things he advised that he should, as soon as possible, make the acquaintance of the head boys of his house, and try to come to a good understanding with them as to the work and conduct of the term. Accordingly four polite notes were that evening handed by the house-messenger to Messrs Ainger, Barnworth, Stafford, and Felgate, requesting the pleasure of their company at 7.30 in the new master's rooms. The messenger had an easy task, for, oddly enough, he found the four gentlemen in question assembled in Ainger's study. They were, in fact, discussing their new house-master when his four little missives were placed in their hands.

"What's the joke now, Mercury?" asked Barnworth.

The messenger, who certainly was not nicknamed Mercury on account of the rapidity of his motions or the volatility of his spirits, replied, "I dunno; but I don't see why one letter shouldn't have done for the lot of yer. He's flush with his writing-paper if he isn't with his pounds, shillings and pence!"

"Oh, he's not tipped you, then? Never mind, I'm sure it wasn't your fault!"

Mercury, in private, turned this little sally over in his mind, and came to the conclusion that Mr Barnworth was not yet a finished pupil in manners. Meanwhile the four letters were being opened and perused critically.

"'*Dear Ainger*'—one would think he'd known me all my life!" said Ainger.

"'*I shall be so glad if you will look in at my rooms*,'" read Barnworth. "He evidently wants my opinion on his wall-paper."

"'*At 7.30, for a few minutes' chat*'—nothing about tea and toast, though," said Stafford.

"'*Believe me, yours very truly, M. Railsford*.' So I do believe you, my boy!" said Felgate. "Are you going, you fellows?"

"Must," said Ainger; "it's a mandate, and there's no time to get a doctor's certificate."

"What does he want to chat about, I wonder?" said Stafford.

"The weather, of course!" growled Barnworth; "what else is there?"

Stafford coloured up as usual when anyone laughed at him.

"He wants to get us to take the oath of allegiance, you fellows," said Felgate. "'Will you walk into my parlour? said the spider to the fly,' that's what he means. I think we'd better not go."

Ainger laughed rather spitefully.

"It strikes me he'll find us four fairly tough flies. I mean to go. I want to see what he's like; I'm not at all sure that I like him."

"Poor beggar!" murmured Barnworth. "Now my doubt is whether he likes me. He ought to, oughtn't he, Staff?"

"Why, yes!" replied that amiable youth; "he doesn't look as if he was very particular."

"Oh, thanks, awfully!" replied Barnworth.

The amiable coloured up more than ever.

"I really didn't mean that," he said, horrified at his unconscious joke. "I mean he doesn't seem strict, or as if he'd be hard to get on with."

"I hope he's not," said Ainger, with a frown. "We had enough of that with Moss."

"Well," said Felgate, "if you are going, I suppose I must come too; only take my advice, and don't promise him too much."

Railsford meanwhile had transacted a good deal of business of a small kind on his own account. He had quelled a small riot in the junior preparation room, and intercepted one or two deserters in the act of quitting the house after hours. He had also gone up to inspect the dormitories, lavatories, and other domestic offices; and on his way down he had made glad the hearts of his coming kinsman and the baronet by a surprise visit in their study. He found them actively unpacking a few home treasures, including a small hamper full of ham, a pistol, some boxing-gloves, and a particularly fiendish-looking bull-dog. The last-named luxury was the baronet's contribution to the common store, and, having been forgotten for some hours in the bustle of arrival, was now removed from his bandbox in a semi-comatose state.

"Hullo!" said Railsford, whose arrival coincided with the unpacking of this natural history curiosity, "what have you got there?"

Oakshott's impulse, on hearing this challenge, had been to huddle his unhappy booty back into the bandbox; but, on second thoughts, he set it down on the mat, and gazing at it attentively, so as not to commit himself to a too hasty opinion, observed submissively that it was a dog.

It is melancholy to have to record failure, in whatever sphere or form; but truth compels us to state that at this particular moment Mark Railsford blundered grievously. Instead of deciding definitely there and then on his own authority whether dogs were or were not *en règle* in Railsford's house, he halted and hesitated.

"That's against rules, isn't it?" said he.

"Against rules!" said Arthur, crimson in the face—"against rules! Why, Dig and I had one a year ago, only he died, poor beast; he had a mill with a rat, and the rat got on to his nose, and punished him before—"

"Yes," said the master; "but I shall have to see whether it's allowed to keep a dog. Meanwhile you must see he does not make a noise or become a nuisance."

"All serene," replied Dig, who had already almost come to regard the new master as a sort of brother-in-law of his own; "he's a great protection against rats and thieves. My mother gave him to me—didn't she, Smiley?"

Smiley was at that moment lying on his back all of a heap, with his limp legs lifted appealingly in the air, and too much occupied in gasping to vouchsafe any corroboration of his young master's depositions.

Railsford departed, leaving the whole question in an unsettled condition, and not altogether satisfied with himself. He knew, the moment he was outside the door, what he ought to have said; but that was very little consolation to him. Nor was it till he was back in his own room that he remembered he had not taken exception to the pistol. Of course, having looked at it and said nothing, its owner would assume that he did not disapprove of it. And yet he really could not sit down and write, "Dear Grover,—Please say by bearer if pistols and bull-dogs are allowed? Yours truly, M.R." It looked too foolish. Of course, when he saw them written down on paper he knew they were not allowed; and yet it would be equally foolish now to go back to the study and say he had decided without inquiry that they were against rules.

He was still debating this knotty point when a knock at the door apprised him that his expected guests had arrived. Alas! blunder number two trod hard on the heels of number one! He had no tea or coffee, not even a box of biscuits, to take off the edge of the interview and offer a retreat for his own inevitable embarrassment and the possible shyness of his visitors. The arrangements for that reception were as formal as the invitations had been. Was it much wonder if the conference turned out stiff and awkward? In the first place, as all four entered together, and none of them were labelled, he was quite at a loss to know their names. And it is a chilling beginning to a friendly chat to have to inquire the names of your guests. He shook hands rather nervously all round; and then, with an heroic effort at ease and freedom, said, singling out Felgate for the experiment—

"Let me see, you are Ainger, are you not?"

It was a most unfortunate shot; for nothing could have been less complimentary to the jealous and quick-tempered captain of the house than to be mistaken for his self-conceited and unstable inferior, with whom, he was in the habit of congratulating himself, he had little or nothing in common.

"No, sir," said Felgate, omitting, however, to confess his own name, or point out the lawful owner of the name of Ainger.

The master tried to smile at his own dilemma, and had the presence of mind not to plunge further into the quicksands.

"Which of you is Ainger?" he inquired.

"I am, sir," replied the captain haughtily.

"Thank you," said Mark, and could have eaten the word and his tongue into the bargain the moment he had spoken. This was blunder number three, and the worst yet! For so anxious was he to clear himself of the reproach of abasing himself before his head boys, that his next inquiries were made brusquely and snappishly.

"And Barnworth?"

"I am, sir."

"And Stafford?"

"I am, sir."

"And Felgate?"

"I am, sir."

That was all over. The master smiled. The boys looked grave.

"Won't you sit down?" said the former, drawing his own chair up to the hearth and poking the fire.

Ainger and Felgate dropped into two seats, and Stafford, after a short excursion to a distant corner, deposited himself on another. Barnworth—there being no more chairs in the room—sat as gracefully as he could on the corner of the table.

"I thought it would be well," began Railsford, still dallying with the poker—"won't you bring your chair in nearer, Stafford?"

Stafford manoeuvred his chair in between Ainger and Felgate.

"I thought it would not be a bad thing—haven't you a chair, Barnworth? dear me! I'll get one out of the bedroom!"

And in his flurry he went off, poker in hand, to the cubicle.

"What a day we're having!" murmured Barnworth.

Stafford giggled just as Railsford re-entered. It was awkward, and gave the new master a very unfavourable impression of the most harmless boy in his house.

"Now," said he, beginning on a new tack, "I am anxious to hear from you something about the state of the house. You're my police, you know," he added with a friendly smile.

Stafford was the only one who smiled in response, and then ensued a dead silence.

"What do you think, Ainger? Do things seem pretty right?"

"Yes," said Ainger laconically.

"Have you noticed anything, Barnworth?"

"There's a draught in the big dormitory, sir," replied Barnworth seriously.

"Indeed, we must have that seen to. Of course, what I mean is as to the conduct of the boys, and so on. Are the rules pretty generally obeyed?"

It was Stafford's turn, and his report was disconcerting too.

"No, sir, not very much."

The new master put down the poker.

"I am sorry to hear that; for discipline must be maintained. Can you suggest anything to improve the state of the house?"

"No, sir," replied Felgate.

This was getting intolerable. The new master's patience was oozing away, and his wits, strange to say, were coming in.

"This is rather damping," he said. "Things seem pretty right, there's a draught in the big dormitory, the rules are not very much obeyed, and nothing can be suggested to improve matters."

The four sat silent—the situation was quite as painful to them as to Mark.

The latter grew desperate.

"Now," said he, raising his voice in a way which put up Ainger's back. "You four boys are in the Sixth, and I understand that the discipline of the house is pretty much in your hands. I shall have to depend on you; and if things go wrong, of course I shall naturally hold you responsible."

Ainger flushed up at this; while Stafford, on whom the master's eyes were fixed, vaguely nodded his head.

"I am very anxious for the house to get a good name for order, and work—and," added he, "I hope we shall be able to do something at sports, too."

Here, at least, the master expected he would meet with a response. But Ainger, the boy chiefly interested in sports, was sulking; and Barnworth, who also was an athlete, was too absorbed in speculating what remark was maturing itself in Felgate's mind to heed what was being said.

"I suppose the house has an eleven—for instance?"

"Yes, generally," said Stafford.

Felgate now came in with his remark.

"Something ought to be done to prevent our house being interfered with by Mr Bickers," said he; "there are sure to be rows while that lasts."

"Oh," said Railsford, who had heard rumours of this feud already; "how are we interfered with?"

"Oh, every way," replied Ainger; "but we needn't trouble you about that, sir. We can take care of ourselves."

"But I should certainly wish to have any difficulty put right," said the new master, "especially if it interferes with the discipline of the house."

"It will never be right as long as Mr Bickers stays at Grandcourt," blurted Stafford; "he has a spite against everyone of our fellows."

"You forget you are talking of a colleague of mine, Stafford," said Railsford, whom a sense of duty compelled to stand up even for a master whom he felt to be an enemy. "I can't suppose one master would willingly do anything to injure the house of another."

Ainger smiled in a manner which offended Railsford considerably.

"I am sorry to find," he said, rather more severely, "that my head boys, who ought to aim at the good of their house, are parties to a feud which, I am sure, can do nobody any good. I must say I had hoped better things."

Ainger looked up quickly. "I am quite willing to resign the captaincy, sir, if you wish it."

"By no means," said Railsford, a little alarmed at the length to which his protest had carried him, and becoming more conciliatory. "All I request is that you will do your best to heal the feud, so that we may have no obstacle in the way of the order of our own house. You may depend on me to co-operate in whatever tends in that direction, and I look to you to take the lead in bringing the house up to the mark and keeping it there."

At this particular juncture further conference was entirely suspended by a most alarming and fiendish disturbance in the room above.

19

It was not an earthquake, for the ground beneath them neither shook nor trembled; it was not a dynamite explosion, for the sounds were dull and prolonged; it was not a chimney-stack fallen, for the room above was two storeys from the roof. Besides, above the uproar rose now and then the shrill yapping of a dog, and sometimes human voices mingled with the din.

Railsford looked inquiringly at his prefects.

"What is that?" he said.

"Some one in the room above, sir," replied Barnworth. "It was Sykes' study last term," added he, consulting Ainger. "Who's got it this time?"

"Nobody said anything to me about it," said the house-captain.

"The room above this is occupied by Herapath and Oakshott," interposed Railsford.

The captain made an exclamation.

"Did they get your leave, sir?"

"Not exactly; they told me they were going to have the study this term, and I concluded it was all right. Is it not so?"

"They are Shell boys, and have no business on that floor. All the Shell boys keep on the second floor. Of course, they'll say they've got leave."

"I'm afraid they will think so. Is there any other claimant to the study?"

"No; not that I know of."

"Perhaps they had better remain for the present," said the master. "But I cannot imagine what the noise is about. Will you see, Ainger, as you go up?"

This was a broad hint that the merry party was at an end, and no one was particularly sorry.

"Wait a second in my room, you fellows," said Ainger, on the stairs, "while I go and shut up this row."

The mystery of this disorder was apparent as soon as he opened the door. The double study, measuring fifteen feet by nine, was temporarily converted into a football field. The tables and chairs were piled on one side "in touch"; one goal was formed by the towel-horse, the other drawn in chalk on the door. The ball was a disused pot-hat of the baronet's, and the combatants were the two owners of the study *versus* their cronies and fellow "Shell-fish"—Tilbury, of the second eleven, and Dimsdale, the gossip. There had been some very fine play on both sides, and a maul in goal at the towel-horse end, in which the dog had participated, and been for a considerable period mistaken for the ball. *Hinc illae lacrymae.*

At the moment when Ainger looked in, Herapath's side had scored 35 goals against their adversaries' 29. The rules were strict Rugby, and nothing was wanted to complete the sport but an umpire. The captain arrived in the nick of time.

"Offside, Dim!—wasn't he, Ainger? That's a place-kick for us! Hang the dog! Get out, Smiley; go and keep goal. See fair play, won't you, Ainger?"

To this impudent request Ainger replied by impounding the ball. "Stop this row!" he said peremptorily. "Tilbury and Dimsdale, you get out of here, and write fifty lines each for being off your floor after eight."

"We only came to ask Herapath what Latin we've to do this term; and there's no preparation for to-morrow."

"Well, if this is your way of finding out about your Latin, you know just as much up-stairs as down here. Be off; and mind I have the lines before dinner to-morrow."

The two champions retired disconcerted, leaving the captain to deal with the arch offenders.

"First of all," said he, "what business have you in this study?"

"Oh, Railsford knows we're here; we told him, and he didn't object."

"Don't you know you ought to come to the prefects about it?"

Oddly enough, both the boys had completely forgotten.

"Besides," explained Dig, "as Railsford and Herapath are sort of brother-in-laws, you know, we thought it was all right."

The reason did not appear very obvious; but the information was interesting.

"Oh, that's it, is it?" asked the captain. "What relation is he to you?"

"He's spoons on my sister Daisy."

The captain laughed.

"I hope she's like her brother," said he.

The two culprits laughed vociferously. It was worth anything to them to get the captain in a good-humour.

"Well, if that's the case," said Ainger, "I shan't have anything to do with you. You've no right on this floor; you know that. If he chooses to let you be, he'll have to keep you in order. I don't pity him in the room underneath."

"I say, do you think he could hear us easily—when we were playing?"

"Oh, no, not at all," said the captain, laughing.

"Really! I say, Ainger, perhaps we'd better have a study up-stairs, after all."

"Thanks; not if I know it. You might pitch over my head instead of his. I suppose, too, he's allowed you to set up that dog?"

"Yes; it's a present from Dig's mother. I say, he's not a bad-looking beast, is he?"

"Who? Dig? Not so very," said the captain, quite relieved to be able to wash his hands of this precious couple.

He departed, leaving the two worthies in a state of bewildered jubilation.

"What a splendid lark!" exclaimed Arthur. "We shall be able to do just what we like all the term. There! we're in luck. Mark thinks Ainger's looking after us; and Ainger will think Mark's looking after us; and, Diggy, my boy, nobody will look after us except Smiley—eh, old dog?"

Smiley, who had wonderfully recovered since an hour ago, here made a playful run at the speaker's heels under the belief that the football had recommenced; and the heart-rending yelps which Railsford heard in the room below a few moments later were occasioned by an endeavour to detach the playful pet's teeth from the trouser-ends of his owner's friend.

The Master of the Shell retired to bed that night doubtful about his boys, and doubtful about himself. He was excellent at shutting stable doors after the abstraction of the horses, and could see a blunder clearly after it had been committed. Still, hope sprang eternal in the breast of Mark Railsford. He would return to the charge to-morrow, and the next day, and the next. Meanwhile he would go to sleep.

The discussion in the captain's room had not been unanimous.

"Well," said Felgate, when Ainger returned, "how do you like him?"

"I don't fancy I shall get on with him."

"Poor beggar!" drawled Barnworth. "I thought he might have been a good deal worse, myself."

"So did I," said Stafford. "He was quite shy."

"No wonder, considering who his visitors were. We were all shy, for the matter of that."

"And I," said Felgate, "intend to remain shy. I don't like the animal. He's too fussy for me."

"Just what he ought to be, but isn't. He'll let things go on, and make us responsible. Cool cheek!" said Ainger. "However, the row overhead will wake him up now and then. Fancy, young Herapath, unless he's making a joke, which isn't much in his line, says Railsford's engaged to his sister; and on that account the young beggar and his precious chum get leave to have Sykes' study and do what they like. They may, for all I shall interfere. If it's a family affair, you don't catch me poking my nose into it!"

"Engaged, is he?" cried Felgate, laughing. "What a joke!"

"It's nothing to do with us," said Barnworth, "whether he is or not."

"Unless he goes in for favouritism; which it seems he is doing," said Ainger.

"Well, even so, you've washed your hands of young Herapath, and he's a lucky chap. But having done so, I don't see what it matters to us how many wives or sweethearts he has."

"It seems to me," said Ainger, who was still discontented, "we shall get no more backing from him than we did from Moss. I don't care twopence about that young ass Herapath; but if the house is to go on as it was last term, and we are to be interfered with by Bickers and nobody to stand up for us, we may as well shut up at once, and let him appoint new prefects."

"Yes, but are you sure he won't back us up?" drawled Barnworth. "I'm not a betting man, like Stafford, but I have a notion he'll come out on our side."

Ainger grunted sceptically, and announced that he had to unpack; whereat his comrades left him.

Few persons at Grandcourt gave the captain of Railsford's house credit for being as honest as he was short-tempered, and as jealous for the honour of his house as he was short-sighted as to the best means of securing it. And yet Ainger was all this; and when he went to bed that night Railsford himself did not look forward more anxiously to the opening term than did his first lieutenant.

Chapter Five.

Arthur and the Baronet settle down for the Term.

The reader is not to imagine that Railsford's house contained nobody but the four prefects of the Sixth-form and the sedate tenants of the study immediately over the master's head, who belonged to the Shell. On the contrary, the fifty boys who made up the little community were fully representative of all grades and classes of Grandcourt life. There was a considerable substratum of "Babies" belonging to the junior forms, who herded together noisily and buzzed like midges in every hole and corner of the house. Nor were Herapath and Oakshott, with their two cronies, by any means the sole representatives of that honourable fraternity known as the Shell, too mature for the junior school, and yet too juvenile for the upper forms. A score at least of Railsford's subjects belonged to this noble army, and were ready to wage war with anybody or anything—for a consideration.

Still ascending in the scale, came a compact phalanx of Fifth-form heroes, counting some of the best athletes of the second eleven and fifteen, and yet not falling in with the spirited foreign policy so prevalent in the rest of the house. On an emergency they could and would turn out, and their broad backs and sturdy arms generally gave a good account of themselves. But as a general rule they grieved their friends by an eccentric habit of "mugging," which, as anybody knows, is a most uncomfortable and alarming symptom in a boy of a house such as Railsford's. True, there were among them a few noble spirits who never did a stroke of work unless under compulsion; but as a rule the Fifth-form fellows in Railsford's lay under the imputation of being studious, and took very little trouble to clear their characters. Only when the school sports came round, or the house matches, their detractors used to forgive them.

The four prefects, to whom the reader has been already introduced, divided among them the merits and shortcomings of their juniors. Ainger and Felgate, though antagonistic by nature, were agreed as to an aggressive foreign policy; while Barnworth and of course the amiable Stafford considered there was quite enough work to do at home without going afield. Yet up to the present these four heroes had been popular in their house—Barnworth was the best high jumper Grandcourt had had for years, and Ainger was as steady as a rock at the wickets of the first eleven, and was reported to be about to run Smedley, the school captain, very close for the mile at the spring sports. Stafford, dear fellow that he was, was not a particularly "hot" man at anything, but he would hold the coat of anyone who asked him, and backed everybody up in turn, and always cheered the winner as heartily as he condoled with the loser. Felgate was one of those boys who could do better than they do, and whose unsteadiness is no one's fault but their own. His ways were sometimes crooked, and his professions often exceeded his practice. He meant well sometimes, and did ill very often; and, in short, was just the kind of fellow for the short-tempered, honest Ainger cordially to dislike.

Such was the miscellaneous community which Mark Railsford found himself called upon to govern. It was not worse than a good many masters' houses, and had even its good points.

And yet just now it was admitted to be in a bad way. The doctor had his eye on it, and there is nothing more adverse to reform than the consciousness that one has a bad name. The late master, Mr Moss, moreover, had notoriously found the place too hot for him, and had given it up. That again tells against the reputation of a house. And, lastly, although it had a few good scholars and athletes, who won laurels for the school, there seemed not enough of them to do anything for the house, which had steadily remained at the bottom of the list for general proficiency for several terms.

If you inquired how all this came about, you would hear all sorts of explanations, but the one which found most favour in the delinquent house itself was summed up in the single word "Bickers." The origin of the deadly feud between the boys of Railsford's and the master of the adjoining house was a mystery passing the comprehension even of such as professed to understand the ins and outs of juvenile human nature. It had grown up like a mushroom, and no one exactly remembered how it began. Mr Bickers, some years ago, had been a candidate for the Mastership of the Shell, but had been passed over in favour of Mr Roe. And ever since, so report went, he had been actuated by a fiendish antipathy to the boys who "kept" in the house of his rival. He had worried Mr Moss out of the place, and the boys of the two houses, quick to take up the feuds of their chiefs, had been in a state of war for months. Not that Mr Bickers was a favourite in his own house. He was not, any more than Mr Moss had been in his. But any stick is good enough to beat a dog with, and when Mr Bickers's boys had a mind to "go for" Moss's boys, they espoused the cause of Bickers, and when Mr Moss's boys went out to battle against those of Bickers's house, their war-cry was "Moss."

Much legend had grown up round the feud; but if anyone had had patience to examine it to the bottom he would probably have found the long and short to be that Mr Bickers, being unhappily endowed with a fussy disposition and a sour and vindictive temper, had incurred the displeasure of the boys of his rival's house, and not being the man to smooth away a bad impression, had aggravated it by resenting keenly what he considered to be an unjust prejudice against himself.

This little digression may enable the reader, if he has had the patience to wade through it, to form an idea of the state of parties in that particular section of Grandcourt which chiefly came under Railsford's observation. With Roe's and Grover's houses on the other side of the big square, his boys had comparatively little to do as a house, while with the remote communities in the little square they had still less in common.

But to return to our story. The first week of the next term was one of the busiest Mark Railsford ever spent. His duties in the Shell began on the second day, and the opening performance was not calculated to elate his spirit. The sixty or seventy prodigies of learning who assembled there came from all houses. A few were bent seriously on work and promotion, the majority were equally in different about the one and the other, and the remainder were professional idlers—most successful in their profession.

Such were the hopeful materials which Railsford was expected to inspire with a noble zeal in the pursuit of classics, history, and divinity. It would have bets as easy—at least, so it seemed to the master—to instruct he monkey-house at the Zoological

Gardens. The few workers (scarcely one of whom, by the way, was in his own house) formed a little *coterie* apart, and grabbed up whatever morsels of wisdom and learning their master could afford to let drop in the midst of his hand-to-hand combat with the forces of anarchy and lethargy. But he had little to say to them. His appeals were addressed to the body of gaping, half-amused, half-bored loungers in the middle of the room, who listened pleasantly and forgot instantaneously; who never knew where to go on, and had an inveterate knack of misunderstanding the instructions for next day's work. They endured their few morning hours in the Shell patiently, resignedly, and were polite enough to yawn behind their books. They were rarely put out by their own mistakes, and when occasionally the master dropped upon them with some penalty or remonstrance, they deemed it a pity that anyone should put himself so much about on their account.

Railsford was baffled. There seemed more hope in the turbulent skirmishers at the back of the room, who at least could now and then be worked upon by thunder, and always, in theory, acknowledged that lessons were things to be learned. On the first day the "muggers" knew their task well, and Railsford glowed with hope as he expressed his approbation. But when he came to the gapers his spirits sunk to zero. They had unfortunately mistaken the passage, or else the page was torn out of their book, or else they had been prevented by colds or sprained wrists or chilblains from learning it. When told to construe a passage read out not two minutes before by one of the upper boys, they knew nothing about it, and feared it was too hard for their overwrought capacities; and when pinned down where they sat to the acquirement of some short rule or passage, they explained sorrowfully that that had not been Mr Moss's method. In divinity they raised discussions on questions of dogma, and so subtly evaded challenge on questions of Greek Testament construction and various readings. In history they fell back on a few stock answers, which rarely possessed the merit of having any connection with the questions which they pretended to satisfy. But the gapers were men of peace, after all. They rarely insisted upon their own opinion, nor did it offend them to be told they were wrong.

The noisier element were less complacent; it is true, they never did a lesson through, or construed a sentence from one end to the other. Still, when they took the trouble to "mug" a question up, they expected to be believed. It hurt them a good deal to be informed that they knew nothing; and to detain them or set them impositions because of a difference of opinion on an historical, classical, or theological question seemed grossly unjust. When, for instance, Sir Digby Oakshott, Baronet, on an early day of the term, publicly stated that the chief features of Cromwell's character was a large mouth and a wart on the nose, he was both hurt and annoyed to be ordered peremptorily to remain for an hour after class and write out pages 245 to 252, inclusive, of the School History. He had no objection, as he confided to his friend and comforter, Arthur Herapath, Esquire, to the Master of the Shell entertaining his own opinions as to the character of the personage in question. But he believed in the maxim "give and take," and just as he would cheerfully have received anything Mr Railsford might have to say on the subject, he at least expected that his own statement should be received in an equally candid spirit, particularly (as he was anxious to point out) since he had personally inspected a portrait of Cromwell not long ago, and verified the existence of the two features alleged.

Sir Digby, indeed, deserved some little commiseration. He had come up to Grandcourt this term pledged to the hilt to work hard and live virtuously. He had produced and proudly hung in a conspicuous place in his study a time-table, beautifully ruled and written in red and black ink, showing how each hour of every day in the week was to be spent in honest toil and well-earned sport. He had explained to his friend the interesting fact that a duplicate of this table had been presented to his mother, who thereby would be able to tell at any moment how her dear son was occupied.

"Let's see," said he, proudly, taking out his watch. "7.15. Now what am I doing at 7.15 on Thursdays? French preparation. There you are! So if she's thinking about me now she knows what I'm up to."

"But you're not doing French preparation," suggested Arthur.

"Of course I'm not, you ass. How could I when I lent Dimsdale my book? Besides, we've not started yet. I've got about a million lines to write. Do you know, I'm certain it was Bickers got me into that row about the omnibus; I saw him looking on. I say, that was a stunning lark, wasn't it? I'd have won too if Riggles had kept his right side. Look here, I say, I'd better do some lines now; lend us a hand, there's a good chap. Wouldn't it be a tip if old Smiley could write; we could keep him going all day long!"

Master Oakshott had, in fact, become considerably embarrassed at the beginning of the term by one or two accidents, which conspired to put off the operation of the time-table for a short period.

The doctor had received information through some channel of the famous chariot race on opening day, and had solaced the defeated champion with a caning (which he did not mind) and five hundred lines of Virgil (which he greatly disliked). In addition to that, Digby had received fifty lines from Ainger for pea-shooting, which, not being handed in by the required time, had doubled and trebled, and bade fair to become another five hundred before they were done. And now he had received from Railsford—from his beloved friend's future brother-in-law—seven pages of School History to write out, of which he had accomplished one during the detention hour, and had solemnly undertaken to complete the other six before to-morrow. It spoke a good deal for the forbearance and good spirits of the unfortunate baronet that he was not depressed by his misfortunes.

Arthur, too, had come up with every idea of conducting himself as a model boy, and becoming a great moral support to his future brother-in-law. It had pained him somewhat to find that relative was not always as grateful for his countenance as he should have been. Still, he bore him no malice. The time would come when the elder would cry aloud to the younger for aid, and he should get it.

Meanwhile, on this particular evening, Arthur found himself too busy, getting the new study into what he termed ship-shape order, to be able to adopt his friend's suggestion about the lines. His idea of ship-shape did not in every particular correspond with the ordinary acceptation of the term. He had brought down in his trunk several fine works of art, selected chiefly from the sporting papers, and representing stirring incidents in the lives of the chief prize-fighters. These, after endeavouring to take out a few of the creases contracted in the journey, he displayed over the fireplace and above the door, attaching them to the wall by means of garden nails, which had an awkward way of digging prodigious holes in the plaster and never properly reaching the laths behind. Most of the pictures consequently required frequent re-hanging, and by the end of the evening looked as if they, like the shady characters painted on them, had been in the wars.

Then Arthur had produced with some pride a small set of bookshelves, which packed away into a wonderfully small space, but which, when fitted together, were large enough to accommodate as many books as he possessed. The fitting together, however, was not very successful. Some of the screws were lost, and had to be replaced by nails, and having used the side-pieces for the shelves, and the shelves for the sides, he and Dig had a good deal of trouble with a saw and a cunningly constructed arrangement of strings to reduce the fabric into the similitude of a bookcase. When at last it was done and nailed to the wall, it exhibited a tendency to tilt forward the moment anything touched it, and pitch its contents on to the floor.

After much thought it occurred to Herapath that if they turned it upside down this defect would operate in the other direction, and hold the books securely against the wall. So, having wrenched the nails out, and been fortunate enough to find a space on the wall not gaping with wounds in the plaster, they re-erected it inversely. But, alas! although the top shelf now tilted back at the wall, the bottom shelf swung forward an inch or two and let its contents out behind with the same regularity and punctuality with which it had previously ejected them in front.

Dig pronounced it a rotten concern, and voted for smashing it up; but Herapath, more dauntless, determined on one further effort.

BURYING THE TWO MECHANICS UNDER A CASCADE OF BOOKS, PLASTER, AND SHATTERED TIMBER

He began to drive a large nail vehemently into the floor immediately under the refractory bookcase, and then, tying a string round the bottom shelf, he hitched the other end round the nail and drew the fabric triumphantly into the wall. It was a complete success. Even Dig applauded, and cried out to his friend that another inch would make a job of it.

Another inch did make a job of it, for just as the bottom shelf closed in the top gave a spring forward, pulling the nail along with it, and burying the two mechanics under a cascade of books, plaster, and shattered timber. Arthur and Dig sat on the floor and surveyed the ruin stolidly, while Smiley, evidently under the delusion that the whole entertainment had been got up for his amusement, barked vociferously, and, seizing a *Student's Gibbon* in his teeth, worried it, in the lightness of his heart, like a rat. At this juncture the door opened, and Railsford, with alarm in his face, entered.

"Whatever *is* the matter?" he exclaimed.

It was an excellent cue for the two boys, who forthwith began to rub their arms and shoulders, and make a demonstration of quiet suffering.

"This horrid bookcase won't stick up!" said Arthur. "We were trying to put the things tidy, and it came down."

"It's a pretty good weight on a fellow's arm!" said the baronet, rubbing his limb, which had really been grazed in the downfall.

"It is a very great noise on the top of my head," said the master. "I dare say it was an accident, but you two will have to be a great deal quieter up here, or I shall have to interfere."

"We really couldn't help it, Mark—I mean Rails—I mean Mr Railsford," said Arthur, in an injured tone. "There's Dig will get into no end of a row, as it is. He was writing out that imposition for you, and now he's hurt his arm through helping me— brick that he is! I suppose you won't mind if I finish the lines for him?"

Arthur was staking high, and would have been sadly disconcerted had his kinsman taken him at his word.

"Is your arm really hurt, Oakshott?" inquired the master.

"Oh no; not much," said Digby, wincing dramatically, and putting on an air of determined defiance to an inward agony. "I dare say I can manage, after a rest. We had taken some of the books out, so I only had the bookcase and three shelf-loads of books on the top of me! That wasn't so much!"

25

"How much have you written?" demanded the master.

"Two pages, please, sir."

"This time I will let that do."

"Thanks, awfully!" broke in Arthur; "you're a brick! Dig'll never do it again, will you, Dig?"

"I could do it, you know, if you really wanted," said Dig, feeling up and down his wounded limb.

"That will do!" said Mark, who had already begun to have a suspicion that he had been "done." "Clear up this mess, and don't let me hear any more noise overhead."

When he had gone, the friends embraced in a gust of jubilation.

"No end of a notion of yours!" said Dig. "That leaves the lines for the doctor and the others for Ainger. He'll keep. We'll have him in to tea and dose him with marmalade, and square him up. But, there, I must do the doctor's lines, or I shall catch it!"

And so, despite his wounded arm, he set to work, aided by his friend, and worked off about half the penalty, by which time his arm and elbow were very sore indeed. Dimsdale, who came in later, was bribed with an invitation to jam breakfast in the morning, to help with the remainder, and the same inducement prevailed upon Tilbury. So that by a fine co-operative effort Dig stood clear with the doctor before night was over, and considered himself entitled to a little rest, which he forthwith proceeded to take.

The breakfast-party next morning was a great success on the whole. It was a little marred by the fact that whereas covers were laid for four, just fourteen guests turned up. This was partly Arthur's fault, for, having sallied forth with an invitation in his pocket to anyone who would help his friend out with a few lines, he had dropped them about in a good many other quarters. He had secured the attendance of Simson and Maple of the Shell, and of Bateson and Jukes of the Babies, and, with a view to ingratiate himself with some of his neighbours on the first floor, he had bidden to the banquet Wake, Ranger, Wignet, and Sherriff of the Fifth, and actually prevailed upon Stafford to lend the dignity of a Sixth-form patronage to the *reunion*.

These heroes were naturally a little disgusted on turning up at the rendezvous to find the room crowded, with scarcely standing space to space, by a troop of hungry and noisy juniors. The good hosts perspired with the heat of the room, and, as guest after guest crowded in, began to look a little anxious at the modest fare on the table, and speculate mentally on how far one loaf, one pot of jam, four pats of butter, a pint coffee-pot, and three-and-a-half tea-cups would go round the lot. At length, when Stafford arrived, and could not get in at the door for the crush, despair seized them.

"You kids had better hook it," said Arthur, to half a dozen of the juniors, who had squeezed themselves into a front rank near the table. "There's not room to-day. Come to-morrow."

Loud were the complaints, not unmingled with threatenings and gibes, of these disappointed Babies.

"What a horrible shame!" exclaimed Jukes, in a very audible voice. "We were here first."

"Do you hear?—cut!" repeated the host.

"Come, along," said Bateson; "what's the use of bothering about a crumb and a half a-piece? I never saw such a skinny spread in all my days."

And in the ten years which comprehended Master Bateson's "days" he had had a little experience of that sort of thing.

The company being now reduced to eight, to wit, Stafford, the four Fifth-form boys, the two hosts, and Dimsdale, assumed more manageable proportions. There was room at least to move an arm or a leg, and even to shut the door. But when it came to taking seats, it still became evident that the table could by no possibility hold more than six. Another crisis thereupon arose. Dimsdale was regretfully dismissed, and departed scarlet in the face, promising, as he slammed the door, to show "up" his hosts. These amiable worthies, much distressed, and not a whit cooler that the room was now comparatively empty, smiled feebly at this threat, and arranged to sit on one another's laps, so as to bring the company finally down to the capabilities of the table. But at this juncture Stafford, who had grown tired of waiting, and evidently saw little prospect of conviviality in the entertainment, remembered that he had some work to do before morning school, and rose to leave.

"Why, we've not begun yet," gasped his hosts.

"I really must go. Thanks for asking me. I've enjoyed it so much," said the amiable prefect, departing.

"Look here, I say," expostulated Arthur, "you might stay. I'll get some eggs, or a herring, if you'll stop."

But the guest of the morning was beyond reach of these blandishments, and with muttered reflections on human depravity generally, the hosts took a seat at each end of the festive board, and bade the four Fifth-form fellows fall to.

They had already done so. One had cut the loaf, another had meted out the jam, another had poured out the coffee, and another had distributed the butter.

"Have some coffee?" said Wake, pleasantly, to Dig; "very good stuff."

"Thanks," said Dig, trying to look grateful. "I'll wait till there's a cup to spare."

"If you're putting on the eggs," said Ranger, confidentially, to Arthur, "keep mine on an extra fifteen seconds, please. I like them a little hardish."

"Awfully sorry," said Arthur, with a quaver in his voice; "jolly unlucky, but we're out of eggs. Got none in the place."

"Oh, never mind," said Ranger, reassuringly. "The herrings will do quite as well. Stafford may not fancy them, but we do, don't we, you chaps?"

"Rather," said Sheriff, thoughtfully scooping out the last remnants of the jam from the pot.

Arthur looked at the baronet and the baronet looked at Arthur. Things were growing desperate, and at all risks a diversion must be made. What could they do? Dig had a vague idea of creating a scare that Smiley had gone mad; but as the animal in question was at that moment peacefully reposing on the hearth, there seemed little probability of this panic "taking." Then he calculated the possibilities of secretly cutting away one leg of the table, and so covering the defects of the meal by an unavoidable catastrophe. But he had not his penknife about him, and the two table-knives were in use.

Arthur at this point came gallantly and desperately to the rescue.

"I say, you fellows," began he, ignoring the hint about the herrings, "do you want to know a regular lark?"

"Ha, ha!" laughed Oakshott, not having the least idea what his friend was going to say, but anxious to impress upon his guests that the joke was to be a good one.

"What is it?" asked Wignet, who never believed in anyone else's capacities for story-telling.

"Why," said Arthur, getting up a boisterous giggle, "you know Railsford, the new master?"

"Of course. What about him?"

"Well—keep it dark, you know. Shut up, Dig, and don't make me laugh, I say—there's such a grand joke about him."

"Out with it," said the guests, who were beginning to think again about the herrings.

"Well, this fellow—I call him Marky, you know—Mark's engaged to my sister, and—"

"Ha ha ha!" chimed in Dig.

"And—he calls her '*Chuckey*,' I heard him. Oh, my wig!"

This last exclamation was caused by his looking up and catching sight of Railsford standing at the door.

The Master of the Shell had in fact called up in a friendly way to ask how Sir Digby Oakshott's arm was after the accident of the previous night.

Chapter Six.

When the Cat's away the Mice will play.

If Railsford had entertained any lurking hope that his private affairs were sacred in the hands of his prospective kinsman, the little incident recorded at the close of the last chapter did away with the last remnant of any such delusion. He did not say anything about it. He was punctilious to a degree in anything which affected his honour; and as what he had overheard on the occasion in question had been part of a private conversation not intended for his ears, he felt himself unable to take any notice of it. Still, it was impossible for him to regard the faithless Arthur with quite as brotherly an eye as before; and the manner in which that young gentleman avoided him for the next few days, and hung out signals of distress in his presence, showed pretty plainly that these silent reproaches were not being thrown away.

Of course Arthur did every imaginable thing to make matters worse in the house, by way of proving his contrition. He besought Wake not to let the story go about, greatly to the amusement of that young humourist, who had already heard it from half a dozen sources since the beginning of the term. He threatened Dimsdale with all sorts of penalties if he spread the secret any further. Dimsdale, who had long ago informed everyone of his acquaintance, cheerfully promised it should go no further. So anxious was Arthur to make up for his offence, that when one or two fellows spoke to him about it, and asked him if it was true that Railsford and his sister were going to be married, he prevaricated and hedged till he got hopelessly out of his depth.

"Married!" he would reply, scornfully, "fiddlesticks! I tell you there's nothing in it—all jaw! Who told you they were going to be married?"

From utterances like these an impression got abroad in some quarters that Railsford wanted to marry "Chuckey," but "Chuckey" wouldn't have him. So the last end of the story was worse than the first.

Railsford, however, did not hear this latest version of his own romance; and, indeed, had plenty of other things just at this time to occupy his attention.

Much to his own satisfaction, he received a polite note from Smedley, the captain of the school, to inform him that he had been elected a vice-president of the Athletic Union, and expressing a hope that he would favour the treasurer with the annual subscription now due, and attend a committee on Saturday evening in Mr Roe's house to arrange about the spring sports.

Both requests he gladly complied with. Previous to the meeting he had been present as umpire at a football-match in the meadows between the first twelve against the next twenty. It was a finely-contested battle, and his opinion of Grandcourt rose as he stood and looked on.

It had not occurred to him till he was about to start that his two principal prefects would of course be members of the committee in whose deliberations he was to take part. But he considered he might safely leave the control of the house during his short absence to the keeping of Stafford and Felgate, who, though neither of them the kind of boy to inspire much confidence, had at least the title to be considered equal to the task. After all, it was only for an hour. Possibly no one would know of his absence, and on this the first occasion of his being present at a meeting in whose objects he had so much interest, he felt that his duty to the school had as much claim on him as his duty to his house. So he ran the risk, and went quietly out at the appointed time, in the comfortable assurance that his house was absorbed in preparation, and would never miss him.

The meeting came up to his expectations. He was the only master present, and as such was voted to the chair. He made a little speech he had got ready in case of need, lauding up athletics to the skies, and confessing his own sympathy and enthusiasm for whatever tended towards the physical improvement of Grandcourt. The boys cheered him at every sentence, and when Smedley afterwards welcomed him in the name of the boys, and said they were all proud to have an old "Blue" among their masters, he received quite a small ovation. Then the meeting went heartily to work over the business of the sports.

After an hour and a half's steady work the programme was arranged, the date was fixed, the expenses were estimated, and the vote of thanks was given to the chairman.

"Would you mind umpiring again next Saturday, sir?" asked Smedley, as they parted.

"With all the pleasure in the world—any time," said the master, only wishing he could play in the fifteen himself.

Railsford's house, meanwhile, had celebrated the temporary absence of its ruler in strictly orthodox fashion. Scarcely had he departed, flattering himself that the deluded mice were still under the spell of the cat's presence in their neighbourhood, when the word went round like wildfire, "Coast's clear!" Arthur and the baronet heard it in their study, and flung their books to the four winds and rushed howling down to the common room. The Babies heard it, and kicked over their forms, and executed war-dances in the passages. The Fifth-form "muggers" heard it, and barricaded their doors and put cotton-wool in their ears. Stafford and Felgate heard it, and shrugged their shoulders and wondered when the other prefects would be back.

"There's nobody about. Come on. We can kick up as much row as we like!" shouted the high-principled Arthur. "Who cares for my spooney old brother-in-law, Marky?"

The shout of laughter which followed this noble appeal suddenly dropped into a deadly silence as the lank form of Mr Bickers appeared in the doorway. Arthur rapidly lost himself in the crowd. The two prefects, with flushed faces, elbowed their way into the room as though just arrived to quell the uproar. A few boys snatched up books and flopped down at their desks. But Mr Bickers had too keen an eye to let himself be imposed upon. He had witnessed the scene from a window in his own house, and surmising by the noise that no authority was present to deal with the disorder, had taken upon himself to look in in a friendly way and set things right.

"Silence!" he cried, closing the door behind him, and walking two steps into the room. "Where is Mr Railsford?"

"Out, sir," said Stafford.

"And the prefects?"

"Felgate and I are prefects, sir. The other two are out."

"And you two have allowed this noise and disorder to go on for half an hour?"

"We were going to stop it," said Felgate, faltering.

"By looking on and applauding?" responded the master. "You forget that from one of my windows everything that goes on here is plainly visible, including those who stand at the door and look on when they ought to know better. Go to your rooms, you two."

"We are in charge of the house, sir," mildly protested Felgate.

"*I* am in charge of the house," thundered Mr Bickers. "Obey me, and go."

They withdrew, chafing, crestfallen, and very uncomfortable.

"Now," said Mr Bickers, when the door was again closed, "Arthur Herapath, come here."

Mr Bickers's knowledge of the names of the boys in other houses was quite phenomenal. Arthur, with hanging head and thumping heart, slunk forward.

"So, sir," said Mr Bickers, fixing him with his eye, "you are the model boy whom I heard proclaiming as I came in that you could make as much noise as you liked, and called your absent master by an insulting name."

"Please, sir," pleaded the unlucky Arthur, "I didn't mean it to be insulting. I only called him Marky, because he's my brother-in-law—I mean he's going to be."

"That's right, Mr Bickers," said the baronet, nobly backing up his friend; "he's spoo— I mean he's engaged to Daisy, Herapath's sister."

"Silence, sir," said the master with a curl of his lips. "Herapath, come here, and hold out your hand."

So saying, he took up a ruler from a desk close at hand.

"Please, sir," expostulated Arthur—he didn't mind a cane, but had a rooted objection to rulers—"I really didn't—"

"Hold out your hand, sir!"

There was no denying Mr Bickers. Arthur held out his hand, and was there and then, before half his house, admonished six times consecutively, with an emphasis which brought the tears fairly into his hardened eyes.

"Now go, all of you, to your studies, and continue your preparation. I shall remain in the house till Mr Railsford returns, and report what has occurred to him."

When half an hour later the Master of the Shell, full of his athletic prospects, returned to his quarters, he was gratified as well as surprised by the dead silence which reigned, His astonishment was by no means diminished when on entering the common room he encountered Mr Bickers pacing up and down the floor amidst the scared juniors there assembled.

Railsford, with all his follies, was a man of quick perception, and took in the whole situation at a glance. He understood why Mr Bickers was there, and why the place was so silent. Still more, he perceived that his own authority in the house had suffered a shock, and that a lesson was being read him by the man whom, of all his colleagues, he disliked the most.

"Good-evening," said Mr Bickers, with a show of friendliness.

Mark nodded.

"I am glad to be able to render up your house to you in rather better order than I found it. If you'll take my advice, Railsford, you will not venture out, in the evening specially, leaving no one in authority. It is sure to be taken advantage of."

Railsford bit his lips.

"I ought to be much obliged to you," said he coldly. "As it happens, I did not venture out without leaving anyone in authority."

"If you mean Stafford and—what is his name?—Felgate—I can't congratulate you on your deputies. They were, in fact, aiding and abetting the disorder, and I have sent them to their rooms as incompetent. I would advise you to relieve them of their office as soon as you can."

"Thank you for your advice," said Railsford, whose blood was getting up. "I will make my own arrangements in my own house."

"Of course, my dear fellow," replied Bickers, blandly, "but you should really find two better men than those. There was no attempt to stop the disorder (which had been going on for half an hour) when I arrived. I had to castigate one of the ringleaders myself—Herapath by name, claiming kinship with you, by the way. I'm not sure that you ought not to report him to Dr Ponsford."

It was all Railsford could do to listen quietly to this speech, drawled out slowly and cuttingly by his rival. He made a desperate effort to control himself, as he replied—

"Don't you think, Mr Bickers, you might with advantage go and see how your own house is getting on in your absence?"

Mr Bickers smiled.

"Happily, I have responsible prefects. However, now you are back—and if you are not going out again—I will say good-night."

Railsford said "Good-night," and disregarding the proffered hand of his colleague, walked moodily up to his own room.

He may be excused if he was put out and miserable. He was in the wrong, and he knew it. And yet the manner in which the rebuke had been administered was such as no man of spirit could cheerfully endure. The one idea in his mind was, not how to punish the house for its disorder, but how to settle scores with Bickers for restoring order; not how to admonish the incompetent prefects, but how to justify them against their accuser.

He sent for the four prefects to his room before bed hour. Ainger and Barnworth, it was plain to see, had been informed of all that had happened, and were in a more warlike mood even than their two companions.

"I hear," said Railsford, "that there was a disturbance in the house while I was away for a short time this evening. Ainger and Barnworth of course were out too, but I should like to hear from you, Stafford and Felgate, what it was all about."

Stafford allowed Felgate to give his version; which was, like most of Felgate's versions, decidedly apocryphal.

"There was rather a row, sir," said he, "among some of the juniors. Some of them were wrestling, I fancy. As soon as we saw what was going on, Stafford and I came to stop it, when Mr Bickers turned up and sent us to our rooms. We told him we had been left in charge by you, but he would not listen."

"Very annoying!" said the master.

"It's rather humiliating to our house, sir," said Ainger, "if our prefects are not to be allowed to deal with our own fellows."

"I agree with you," said Mark, warmly. "I have no reason whatever for doubting that they can and will do their duty when—"

He had intended to say "when they are not interfered with," but deemed it more prudent to say, "when occasion requires."

"We could easily have stopped the row, sir," said Stafford, "if we had been allowed to do so."

"I have no doubt of it," said the master. "I am glad to have had this little explanation. The honour of our house is of common interest to all of us."

A week ago this speech would have seemed a mere commonplace exhortation, but under present circumstances it had a double meaning for those present.

"He's a brick," said Ainger, as they returned to their studies. "He means to back us up, after all, and pay Bickers out."

"What surprises me," said Barnworth, "is that Stafford, the bull-dog, did not invite the intruder out into the square and impress the honour of our house with two black marks on each of his eyes."

"I'm just as glad," said Felgate, "it's all happened. We shouldn't have got Railsford with us if—"

"If you'd done your duty, and stopped the row the moment it began," said Ainger; who, with all his jealousy for his house, had no toleration for humbug, even in a prefect whose cause he espoused. So Railsford's house went to bed that night in a warlike mood.

Chapter Seven.

The Session of Masters and an Outrage.

It is to be feared that Mark Railsford, Moral Science man though he was, had yet to learn the art of applying his philosophy to his own circumstances, or he would never have committed the serious error, on the day following the event recorded in the last chapter, of writing the following foolish note to Mr Bickers:—

"*February* 1.

"Sir,—Referring to the unpleasant topic of our conversation last night, I have since consulted my prefects on the matter, and made other inquiries as to what took place here during my temporary absence at the athletic meeting. The report I have received, and which I am disposed to credit, differs materially from your own version. In any case, allow me to say that I require no assistance in the management of my house. When I do, I shall ask for it. Meanwhile I shall continue to consider the interference of anyone, whatever his motives, as an impertinence which I, although the junior master at Grandcourt, shall have no hesitation in resenting to the utmost of my power. I trust these few lines may obviate any future misunderstanding on a point about which I feel very strongly.

"Yours, etcetera,

"M. Railsford."

Mr Bickers was hardly the man to neglect the opportunity afforded by this letter for a crushing reply; and accordingly he spend a pleasant hour that same afternoon in concocting the following polite rejoinder:—

"*February* 1.

"Dear Railsford,—Many thanks for your note just to hand. I can quite believe that the version of yesterday's proceedings which you are disposed to credit, given by your prefects (two of whom were absent, and the other two participators in the disturbance), differs materially from my own. Such diversities of opinion are not uncommon in my experience. As to the management of your house, I assure you in what I did yesterday I had no intention of assisting you. In fact, you were not there to assist. It was because you were not, that my duty to the school suggested that I should attempt to do what you would have done infinitely better, I am aware, had you been on the spot. Under similar circumstances I should do the same again, in face of the uncomfortable knowledge that thereby I should be guilty of an impertinence to the junior master at Grandcourt. It is kind of you to take steps to make your meaning quite clear on this matter.

May I suggest that we refer the matter to the session of masters, or, if you prefer it, to Dr Ponsford? I believe the masters meet to-night. Unless I hear from you, I shall conclude you are as anxious as I am to have the matter thoroughly gone into by a competent tribunal, to obviate any future misunderstanding on a point on which you naturally feel strongly.

"Believe me, my dear Railsford,

"Yours, very truly,

"T. Bickers."

Mark was entertaining company when this uncomfortable letter arrived, in the person of Monsieur Lablache, the French master. It would be difficult to say what there was in the unpopular foreigner which attracted the Master of the Shell. It may have been a touch of Quixotic chivalry which led him to defy all the traditions of the place and offer his friendship to the best-hated person in Grandcourt; or it may have been a feeling that monsieur was hardly judged by his colleagues and pupils. However it was, during the short time the term had run, the two men had struck up an acquaintance which perplexed a great many spectators and displeased a great many more.

"I think you should be careful with Lablache," said Grover to his friend. "Not that I know anything against him, but his reputation in the school is rather doubtful."

"I suppose the reputation of all detention masters is doubtful," said Railsford, laughing; "yours or mine would be if we had his work to do. But a man is innocent till he is proved guilty in England, isn't he?"

"Quite so," said Grover. "I don't want to set you against him, for, as I say, I know nothing of him. All I mean, is, that you must be prepared to share a little of his unpopularity if you take up with him. That's all."

"I'll take my chance of that," said Railsford.

The first time Monsieur Lablache appeared in Railsford's house, in response to an invitation from the new master to come and take coffee, there was considerable excitement in the house. The juniors considered their liberty was at stake, and hissed their master's guest down the corridors. The Shell boys presumed still further, and raised a cry of "Turn him out!" and some even attempted to hustle him and trip him upon the stairs.

But the most curious incident of that untriumphal progress was when Munger, the cad of the Fifth, confronted monsieur in the lobby outside Railsford's room with the shout, "He's going to raise money on his old clothes at last!" The brutal words (for monsieur was very shabbily attired) were scarcely uttered when Railsford's door suddenly opened and Munger was sent reeling across the lobby under a blow which echoed through the house. The Master of the Shell, white with rage, stood there with a look on his face which sent the few loiterers packing to their dens, and made Munger only sorry the wall against which he staggered did not open and let him through.

"Come here, you—you boy!"

Munger advanced, scarcely less pale than his master.

"Apologise to Monsieur Lablache—here, down on your knees—for behaving like a blackguard, and saying what you did!"

"No, it is no matter," began monsieur, with a shrug, when Mark checked him by a gesture almost as intimidating as that by which he had just summoned the offender.

"You hear me?" he said to the boy.

Munger went down on his knees and repeated whatever he was told; and would have called himself by still worse names, had he been requested. It didn't matter much to Munger!

"Now tell me your name?"

"Munger."

"Your form?"

"Fifth."

The master turned on his heel and ushered his guest into the room, leaving Munger to rub his cheek, and wonder to himself how he ever came to stand being knocked about in the way he had been that afternoon.

This had happened a day or two ago. Since then, whatever the house thought, no one was bold enough to molest the French master publicly in Railsford's, unless it was perfectly certain Mr Railsford was out of the way.

It would be a mistake to say the two masters had become devoted friends. Monsieur Lablache's chief attraction in Railsford's eyes was that he was looked down upon by the other masters, and persecuted by the boys; while the French master was so unused to notice of any kind, that he felt a trifle suspicious that the kindness of his new acquaintance might be in some way a snare. However, a little mutual mistrust sometimes paves the way to a good deal of mutual confidence; and after a few days the two men had risen considerably in one another's esteem. When Railsford, on the evening in question, crushed Mr Bickers's note up in his hand, with an angry exclamation, monsieur said—

"*Voilà, mon cher* Railsford, you do not get always *billets-doux*?"

Monsieur had heard, of course, as everyone else had, of the new master's matrimonial prospects.

"No," said Railsford, gloomily; "not always," and he pitched Mr Bickers's letter into the grate as he spoke.

"Perhaps," said monsieur, "you do not always write them. I advise you to not answer that letter."

"Why?" said Railsford, "how do you know what that letter is?"

"I do not know; but I think that it does need no answer."

Railsford laughed. "You are setting up as a soothsayer, monsieur. Suppose I tell you that letter does need an answer, quickly?"

"Then, I say, somebody else will answer it better than you will."

Railsford picked the crushed-up letter off the coals just in time to save it from the flames.

"How should you answer it, monsieur?"

Monsieur slowly unfolded the paper and smoothed it out.

"Meester Beekaire!" said he, with a twist of his moustache, as he recognised the writing. "You mean that I read it?"

"Certainly, if you like."

The Frenchman read the document through, and then pitched it back into the fire.

"Well?" said Railsford.

"Well, my good friend, it seems you do not know Meester Beekaire as well as others."

"Is that all?" said Railsford, a little nettled.

"The masters' meeting is to-night, is it not?"

"So he says."

"You shall go?"

"Of course."

"It will not be pleasant times for you, for you will need to make speeches, my good friend."

"Look here," said Railsford, who was getting a little impatient of these enigmatical utterances, "I fancied you could give me some advice; if you can't, let us talk about something more pleasant."

"I do give you advice. I say to you, go to the meeting, and say you did wrong, and will not do it again—"

"What!" thundered Mark, in a voice which made Arthur and the baronet in the room overhead jump out of their chairs.

"My kind Railsford, it is only my advice. You have been in the wrong. I say to you, as a brave man, do not make yourself more wrong. Meester Beekaire would help you very much to make yourself more wrong. Do not let him help you, I say."

Unpalatable as it was, there was some force in his visitor's advice, which Railsford was bound to admit. Poor monsieur was not a shining example of successful dealing with his fellow-masters. Still, out of the mouth of the simple one may sometimes hear a home truth.

The masters' session was a periodical conference of the Grandcourt masters, half social, half business, for the purpose of talking over matters of common school interest, discussing points of management, and generally exchanging ideas on what was passing in the little world of which they were the controllers. Dr Ponsford rarely, if ever, put in an appearance on such occasions; he had the greatest faith in holding himself aloof from detail, and not making himself too accessible either to master or boy. Only when the boys could not settle a matter for themselves, or the masters could not settle it for them, he interfered and settled it without argument and without appeal. It was never pleasant when the doctor had to be called in, and the feeling against such a step contributed very largely to the success of the school's self-government.

Railsford by this time knew most of his fellow-masters to speak to, but this was the first occasion on which he had met them in their corporate capacity, and had he not been personally interested in the proceedings he would felt a pleasant curiosity in the deliberations of this august body.

Mr Bickers was already there, and nodded in a most friendly way to the Master of the Shell on his arrival. Grover and Mr Roe welcomed their new colleague warmly, and began at once to compare notes as to school-work. A few minutes later Monsieur Lablache, a little smarter than usual, came in, and having bowed to the company generally—a salute which no one seemed to observe—subsided on a retired seat. Railsford, to the regret perhaps of some of his friends, presently walked across and took a seat beside him, and the meeting began.

"Before we come to business," began Mr Roe, who by virtue of his seniority occupied the chair, "I am sure the meeting would wish me to express their pleasure at seeing Mr Railsford among us for the first time, and to offer him a hearty welcome to Grandcourt."

"Hear, hear," said Grover and others, amongst whom Mr Bickers's voice was conspicuous.

Railsford felt uncomfortable thus to become an object of general notice, and coloured up as he nodded his acknowledgments to the chairman.

"They do not know of your scrape," said monsieur, cheerfully. "I would tell them about it, my good friend, before Meester Beekaire makes his little speech."

Railsford glared round at his companion, and felt his heart thumping at the prospect of the task before him.

"There are one or two matters," began Mr Roe, "to bring before—"

Railsford rose to his feet and said, "Mr Roe, and gentlemen—"

There was a dead silence at this unexpected interruption, broken only by an encouraging cheer from Mr Bickers.

Supposing the new master was about to acknowledge the compliment just paid him by a set speech, Mr Roe put down his agenda paper and said, "Mr Railsford."

"If you will allow me," began Mark, rather breathlessly, "I would like to refer to a matter which personally concerns myself. I should not venture to do it in this way, immediately after your kind welcome, if I did not feel it to be my duty. Yesterday, gentlemen, an unfortunate incident occurred in my house—('Hear, hear,' and a smile from Mr Bickers). I went—"

"Excuse me," said the chairman, "may I explain to Mr Railsford, as he is a new member here, that our practice is invariably to take up any questions in order of the seniority of the masters present. Mr Smith, I believe, has a motion on the paper—"

Poor Railsford subsided, full of confusion, stripped of his good resolutions, abusing himself for his folly, and wishing Monsieur Lablache and his advice at the bottom of the sea.

What Mr Smith and the other masters who followed had to say he neither heard nor cared. His determination to admit his own error had oozed away, and he resolved that if his story was to be kept waiting, it should be none the sweeter, when it did come, for the delay.

Several topics were discussed pleasantly, with a view to elicit the opinion of the meeting on small questions of policy and discipline.

Presently Mr Roe turned to Bickers. "I think you said you had some question to ask, Mr Bickers?"

"Oh, well, yes. Mine's quite a hypothetical point, though," began Mr Bickers, airily. "I just wanted to ask, supposing one of us becomes aware of a riot in a neighbouring house, during the absence of the master of that house, and ascertains, moreover, that the prefects on duty, so far from making any attempt to control the disorder, are participating in it, I presume there can be no question that it would be the duty of anyone of us to interfere in such a case? It's quite a hypothetical case, mind, but it might occur."

"Certainly, I should say, if you were quite sure the proper house authorities were not there to enforce order," said Mr Roe.

"Of course," said Grover; "but it's rather an unlikely case, isn't it?"

"It occurred in my house last night," broke in Railsford, hotly. "I was at the Athletic Union, and two of my prefects; the other two were left in charge. Mr Bickers took upon himself to interfere in my absence, and I have written to tell him that I consider his action impertinent, and resent it. In reply, he writes—"

"A *private* letter," interposed Mr Bickers hurriedly, evidently not relishing the prospect of having his effusion read.

"It was not marked 'private,' but I can quite understand the writer would not like to hear it read aloud here. All I wish to say is that his hypothetical case is no more hypothetical than his interference was in the affairs of my house; and that if he asks my opinion on the matter, I shall tell him he would do better to mind his own business!"

Railsford sat down, very hot, and painfully conscious that he had not exhibited the moderation and temper which he had promised himself to observe.

An embarrassed silence ensued. Mr Roe, a man of peace, frowned, and turned inquiringly to Bickers.

Bickers stroked his beard and smiled, and said nothing.

"Do you wish to say anything?" asked the chairman.

"By no means. Mr Railsford has said all I could wish said far more eloquently than I could. Shall we go on to the next business, Mr Chairman?"

As for Railsford, the further proceeding had no interest for him, and he vanished the moment the meeting was over, without speaking to anyone.

As Mr Bickers walked off towards his house, he really felt a little sorry for his fellow-master, who had let himself down by so paltry an exhibition of temper thus early in his career. However, no doubt he would take to heart to-night's lesson, and do himself more justice in future. Mr Bickers, in the fulness of his heart, took a little round of the big square on his way home, with the double intent of giving himself the air, and perchance intercepting, for the good of the school, one or more youthful night-birds in their truant excursions. This was a kind of sport in which Mr Bickers was particularly successful, and which, therefore (as became a successful sportsman), he rather enjoyed. To his credit be it said, he was strictly impartial in his dealings; whether the culprit belonged to his own house (as often happened) or to another's, he was equally down upon him, and was never known to relax his penalties for the most plausible excuse set up by his ingenious victims.

To-night it seemed as if he would return without a "bag" at all, and he was about to resign himself to his disappointment, when his quick eyes detected in the darkness a hovering shadow moving ahead of him in the direction of Railsford's house. It vanished almost immediately, but not before the master had caught a faintly uttered "Hist!" which betrayed that he had to deal with more than one truant. He quickened his pace a little, and came once more in view of the phantom slinking along by the wall at a pace which was not quite a run. Rather to Mr Bickers's surprise the fugitive passed the door of Railsford's, and made straight on towards the chapel, slackening pace as he did so.

"A decoy," said the knowing master to himself. "Employed to draw me on while the rest make good their retreat. There is a touch of generosity in the decoy which one is bound to admire; but on this occasion, my young friend, you are dealing with rather too aged a bird to be caught—"

At this moment he had come up to the door of Railsford's, and before his soliloquy had been able to advance by another word he seemed to see sparks before his eyes, while at the same moment his feet went from under him, and something was drawn over his head. The bag, or whatever it was, was capacious; for the neck of it descended to his waist, and closed by the magic of a slip-knot round his mouth and elbows before he had the presence of mind to shout or throw out his arms. To complete his misfortune, as he tried to raise himself, another noose was snugly cast around his feet, and thus gagged and pinioned, silently, rapidly, and dexterously, Mr Bickers found himself in a situation in which, he could positively aver, he had never stood—or lain—before.

The thought did flash through his sack-enveloped head, that his assailants, whoever they were, must have rehearsed this little comedy carefully and diligently for a day or two, in order to arrive at the perfection displayed in the present performance. He also made a mental calculation that three, possibly four, fellow-beings were engaged on the job, of whom two were strong, and two were small; one of the latter possibly being the decoy whom he had so lately apostrophised.

Not a syllable was uttered during the ceremony; and the victim recognising his position, had the good sense to remain cool and not waste his time and dignity in a fruitless struggle.

The pinioning being complete, and a small hole being considerately opened in the sack in the region of the nose for purposes of respiration, he was hauled up one or two steps, dragged one or two feet, deposited on the board floor of the shoe-cupboard, and, after a few mild and irresolute kicks, left to his own meditations, the last sound which penetrated into the sack being the sharp turning of a key on the outside of his dungeon door.

"So," soliloquised Mr Bickers, after discovering that he was unhurt, though uncomfortably cramped, "our friend Railsford is having one lodger more than the regulation number to-night. This will make another hypothetical case for the next session of masters!"

Chapter Eight.

The Doctor has a Word or Two with Railsford's House.

Railsford's house was not famous for early risers. The chapel-bell in winter began to ring at 7.30, and "call-over" was at 7.45. Between these two periods, but chiefly at the 7.45 end, most of the rising in the house was accomplished. Master Simson, the Shell-fish, was in for the hundred yards under fourteen at the sports; and being a shy youth who did not like to practise in public, he had determined to rise before the lark and take a furtive spin round the school track while his schoolfellows and enemies slept. It was a cold, raw morning, and before he was fully arrayed in his flannels he had had more than one serious idea of relapsing into bed. Be it said to his credit, he resisted the temptation, and gallantly finished his toilet, putting on an extra "sweater" and pea-jacket to boot—for he had seven pounds to run off between now and the sports. He peered out of the window; it was dark, but a patter on the panes showed him that a light sleet was falling outside. If so, being of a frugal mind, he would not run in his new shoes, but in his old boots.

Now, his old boots were in the cupboard under the staircase by the front door. And the reader understands at last why it is I have taken so much trouble to describe Master Simson's movements on this particular morning.

It was so rare an event for any boy to be up at six o'clock on a winter morning in Railsford's, that no one had ever thought about making a rule to prevent the early birds leaving the house at that hour, if they could succeed in getting out. Simson, who had interest with the cook, believed he could get an *exeat* through the kitchen window; meanwhile he must get his boots. He armed himself with a match—the last one in the box—and quietly felt his way along the corridor and down the stairs. There was a glimmer of light from under the maids' door as he passed, which told him they were up and that he would not have long to wait downstairs. At the foot of the stairs he turned sharp round, and following the wall with his hand, came at length on the familiar handle of the "boot-box." To his surprise the door was locked, but the key was on the outside.

"A sell if I hadn't been able to get in," said he to himself, opening the door.

Now Simson, like a cautious youth, aware of the frailty of matches, wisely resolved to penetrate as far as possible into the interior of the cupboard, in the direction in which he knew his particular boots to be, before striking a light.

But at the first step he tripped on something and fell prostrate over a human carcase, which emitted a muffled gasp and moved heavily as he tumbled upon it. Then there went up a yell such as curdled the blood of half Railsford's as they lay in their beds, and made the domestics up-stairs cling to one another in terror, as if their last moment had come.

Simson, with every hair on his head erect, made a frantic dive out of that awful den, banging the door and locking it behind him in a frenzy of fright. Then he dashed up-stairs, and plunged, as white as his shirt, into the dormitory.

Another yell signalised his arrival. Not his, this time, but the joint performance of the other occupants of the room, who, sitting up with their chins on their knees, half petrified by the horror of the first shriek, now gave themselves up for lost when the door broke open in the dark, and a gasping something staggered into the room.

"There's some—bo—dy been mur—dered," gasped Simson, "in the bo—ot-box!"

Everybody was on his feet in a moment.

"Murdered?"

"Yes," said Simson, wonderfully comforted by the noise and general panic. "I got up early, you know, to have a grind on the track, and went to get my boots, and—I—I fell over it!"

"Over what?"

"The bo—od—y," whispered Simson.

"Has anybody got a light?" shouted Arthur.

But at that moment a light appeared at the door, and Ainger came in.

"What's all this row—what's the matter?"

"Simson says somebody's been murdered in the boot-box," replied Arthur. "I say, hadn't we better go and see?"

It was a practical suggestion. The corridor was already full of half-dressed inquirers, and a moment later Mr Railsford's door opened. The story was repeated to him.

"Come with me, Ainger," said he, quietly; "the rest of you return to your dormitories, and remain there."

Arthur, seized by a noble desire not to leave his future kinsman unprotected in such an hour of peril, elected to disregard this last order, and, accompanied by his henchman, followed the candle at a respectful distance down the stairs.

"There's no blood on the stairs," observed the baronet, in a whisper.

"They've left the key in the door," muttered Arthur.

"Hold the light," said Railsford, turning the key, and entering.

Prostrate on the ground, bound hand and foot, and enveloped down to the waist in a sack, lay the figure of a man, motionless, but certainly not dead, for sounds proceeded from the depths of the canvas. In a moment Railsford had knelt and cut the cords round the prisoner's feet and hands, while Ainger drew the sack from the head.

Arthur gave a whistle of consternation as the features of Mr Bickers came to light, pale and stern. The sudden sight of Medusa's head could hardly have had a more petrifying effect. The victim himself was the first to recover. Stretching his arms and legs in relief, he sat up, and coolly said,—

"Thank you."

"Whatever does all this mean?" exclaimed Railsford, helping him to rise, for he was very stiff and cramped.

"That I cannot say. Kindly reach my hat, Ainger."

"Who has done this?"

"That, too, I cannot say. I can walk, thank you."

"Won't you come to my room and have something? You really must," said Railsford, taking his arm.

Mr Bickers disengaged his arm, and said coldly, "Thank you, no; I will go to my own, if you will open the door."

Arthur at this moment came up officiously with a glass of water, which Mr Bickers drank eagerly, and then, declining one last offer of assistance, went slowly out towards his own house.

Railsford retired to his room and threw himself into his chair in a state of profound dejection. Mysterious as the whole affair was, one or two things were clear. The one was that his house was disgraced by this criminal and cowardly outrage, the other was that the situation was made ten times more difficult on account of the already notorious feud between himself and the injured master. His high hopes were once more dashed to the ground, and this time, it almost seemed, finally.

Mark Railsford was no coward, yet for half an hour that morning he wished he might be well out of Grandcourt for ever. Then, having admitted cooler counsels, he dressed and went to the captain's study.

"Call the other prefects here, Ainger. I want to talk to you."

The seniors were not far off, and speedily assembled.

"First of all," said the master, who perceived at a glance that it was not necessary for him to explain the gravity of the situation, "can any of you give me any information about this disgraceful affair?"

"None, sir," said Ainger, a little nettled at the master's tone; "we have talked it over, and, as far as we are concerned, it's a complete mystery."

"Have you any reason to suspect anybody?"

"None at all, sir."

"You know, all of you, I needn't tell you, that the credit of the house is at stake—in fact, it's gone till we find the offenders. Mr Bickers will naturally report the matter to Dr Ponsford, and I am going to the doctor for the same purpose. I wished to consult you before taking any step, because this is a matter in which we must work together."

"Certainly, sir," said Ainger, speaking for the rest.

"What I mean is, that no personal feeling must come between us and the duty we all owe to Grandcourt to see this wrong put right; you understand me?"

"Yes," said the downright Ainger; "we none of us like Mr Bickers, but we must find out the fellows who scragged him, all the same."

"Exactly; and I am glad to hear you say that. There is one other matter. Two of you, Stafford and Felgate, recently felt specially aggrieved by something which Mr Bickers said to you. You must forget all that now, and remember only that your duty to the whole school requires that you should do everything in your power to help to put an end to this scandal."

"Of course we shall," said Felgate, curtly, in a tone which Railsford did not consider particularly encouraging.

However, having opened his mind to his lieutenants, he went away straight to the doctor's. Mr Bickers was leaving just as he entered, and Railsford read in his looks, as he brushed past, no great encouragement to hope that things would soon be made right.

"Mr Bickers," said he, advancing almost in front of his colleague, "I *must* tell you how distressed I am at what has occurred. I—"

"Yes, it *is* trying for you," said the injured master, drily. "Excuse me, though; I want my breakfast."

It was not easy to feel cordial sympathy with a man like this. However, there was nothing for it but to go and lay his case before the doctor, and Railsford entered accordingly.

Dr Ponsford was at breakfast, and asked his visitor to take a seat.

"You have come to tell me that Mr Bickers's assailants are discovered?" said he.

"I wish I could," said Railsford. "I have only had time to speak to my prefects."

"Two of whom are not to be trusted, and profess a personal spite against Mr Bickers."

This was just like the doctor. He gave other people information and never wanted any himself.

"I know, of course, what you refer to. I have not myself found any reason to consider Felgate or Stafford untrustworthy. Mr Bickers says—"

"I know what Mr Bickers says; but what do you say?"

"Well, sir, frankly, I do not feel quite sure of Felgate; and Stafford is too amiable to say 'no' to anybody."

"Now let me hear about the affair this morning."

Railsford gave a careful account of the discovery of Mr Bickers in the boot-box, and was conscious that the doctor, although he gave little sign of it, was not quite blind to the unfortunate position in which he, as the new master of the offending house, was placed.

"Have a call-over of your house at ten o'clock, Mr Railsford. I will come."

This announcement was about as cheerful a one in Grandcourt as an appointment made by the Court of the Inquisition would have been, once upon a time, in Spain, Railsford rose to go.

"You had better stop and have breakfast here," said the doctor, ringing the bell for another cup. During the meal no further reference was made to the event of the morning, but Railsford was drawn out as to his work and the condition of his house generally, and was painfully aware that the doctor was making the best of his time to reckon him up. He only wished he could guess the verdict. But on this point he received no light, and went off presently charged with the unpleasant task of summoning his house to answer for themselves at the bar of the head-master.

It was a curious spectacle, the crowd of boys which assembled in the common room that morning at Railsford's. Some were sulky, and resented this jumbling of the innocent and guilty. Some were so anxious to appear guileless and gay, that they overdid it and compromised themselves in consequence. Some were a little frightened lest an all-round flogging should be proposed. Some whispered mysteriously, and looked askance at one or two fellows who had been "mentioned" as possibly implicated. Some, like Arthur and the baronet, with Simson squeezed in between them, looked knowing and important, as though horses and chariots would not drag their secret out of them. Ainger looked pale, and his big chest went up and down in a manner which those who knew him felt to be ominous. Stafford looked alternately solemn and sneering, according as he turned to the captain or Felgate. And Barnworth alone looked comfortable, and, apparently, had not an idea what all the excitement was about.

At ten o'clock Railsford entered in his cap and gown, and Ainger immediately began to call over the roll. Every one answered to his name except Maple of the Shell, who was away at his father's funeral, and Tomkins the Baby, who had been so scared by the whole affair, that he had turned sick during breakfast, and retired—with the dame's permission—to bed.

During the call-over the doctor had entered and seated himself at the master's desk. His quick eye took in each boy as he uttered his "Adsum," dwelling longer on some than on others, and now and then turning his glance to the master and senior prefect. When it was all over and Ainger had handed in the list, the head-master took his eyeglass from his eye, laid the list on the desk before him, and said—

"Boys, this is an unusual and unpleasant visit. You know the object of it; you know the discredit which at present lies on your house and on Grandcourt, and you know what your duty is in the matter. If any boy here does not know what I mean, let him stand up."

It was as much as the life of anybody present was worth to respond to this challenge. One or two who could never hear a good story too often would not have objected if somebody else had demanded further information. But for their own part, their discretion outdid their curiosity, and they retained their seats amidst a dead silence.

"Very well. Now I will put a question to you as a body. It is a very serious question, and one which no honest boy here, if he is able to answer it, can afford to evade. A great deal more depends on your answer than the mere expulsion of one or more wrong-doers. You boys are the guardians of the honour of your house. The only honourable thing at a time like this is to speak the truth, whatever the consequences. The question I ask is this— Was any boy here concerned in the outrage on Mr Bickers? or does any boy know who was? I will wait for two minutes, that you may understand the importance of the question, before I call for an answer."

Dead silence. The boys for the most part looked straight before them with heightened colour, and watched the slow progress of the minute-hand of the clock.

"I repeat the question now," said the doctor, when the allotted time had run—"Was any boy here concerned in the outrage on Mr Bickers? or does any boy know who was? If so, let him stand up."

The silence which followed was broken to some by the thumping of their own hearts. But no one rose; and a sense of relief came to all but Railsford, who felt his spirits sink as the prospect of a near end to his trouble receded.

"Every boy here," said the doctor, slowly, "denies all knowledge of the affair?"

Silence gave consent.

"Then," continued the head-master, more severely, putting up his eyeglass, and handing the list to Ainger, "I shall put the question to each boy separately. Call over the list, and let each boy come up and answer."

Ainger began by calling out his own name, and forthwith walked up to the master's desk.

"Do you know anything whatever of this affair?" asked the doctor, looking him full in the face.

"No, sir," said Ainger, returning the look, after his fashion, half defiantly.

The next name was called, and its owner marched up to the desk and uttered his denial. Railsford, as he stood scanning keenly the face of each boy in turn, felt that he was watching the action of some strange machine. First Ainger's clear voice. Then the short "Adsum," and the footsteps up to the desk. Then the doctor's stern question. Then the quick look-up and the half-defiant "No, sir," (for they all caught up the captain's tone). And, finally, the retreating footsteps, and the silence preceding the next name.

There was no sign of faltering; and, wherever the secret lurked, Railsford saw little chance of it leaking out. A few boys, indeed, as was natural, gave their replies after their own fashion. Barnworth looked bored, and answered as though the whole performance was a waste of time. Arthur Herapath was particularly knowing in his tone, and accompanied his disclaimer with an embarrassing half-wink at his future kinsman. Felgate said "No" without the "sir," and swaggered back to his place with an ostentatious indifference which did not go unnoted. The baronet, who was nothing if not original, said nothing, but shook his head.

"Reply to the question, sir!" thundered the doctor, ominously.

Whereat Sir Digby, losing his head, said, "No, thank you, sir," and retired, amid some confusion.

Simson, when interrogated, mildly added to his "No, sir" the explanatory sentence, "except finding him there when I went for my boots"; and Munger, the cad, added to his answer, "but I'll try to find out," with a leer and an oily smile, which Ainger felt strongly tempted to acknowledge by a kick as he passed back to his place. Stafford, painfully aware that he was one of the "mentioned" ones, looked horribly confused and red as he answered to his name, and satisfied several of the inexpert ones present that it was hardly necessary to look further for one of the culprits.

So the call-over passed, and when once more Ainger handed in the list Railsford seemed further than ever from seeing light through the cloud which enveloped it. The doctor's brow darkened as he took once more his glass from his eye.

"This is very serious," said he, slowly. "When I came here it was with the painful feeling that the house contained boys so cowardly and unprincipled as to waylay a defenceless man in the dark, and to treat him as Mr Bickers has been treated. But it is tenfold worse to believe that it contains boys cowardly enough to involve the whole house in their own disgrace and punishment. (Sensation.) I will not mince matters. Your house is deeply disgraced, and cannot pretend to rank any longer with the other houses, who at least have a good name, until you have yourselves made this matter right. It rests with you to retrieve your credit. Meanwhile—"

Everybody took a long breath. The occasion was as when the judge puts on the black cap before passing sentence of death.

"Meanwhile the house will cease to dine in Hall, but will dine in this room at one o'clock daily; and on Saturdays, instead of taking the half-holiday in the afternoon, you will take it in the morning, and assemble for school at twelve o'clock. I still trust that there may be sufficient self-respect among you to make this change only of slight duration; or that," and here the doctor's tone grew bitter, and his mouth gathered sarcastically—"at least self-interest may come to your assistance, and make it possible to return to the old order."

And he stalked from the room.

"Let us off easy, eh?" said the baronet.

"Easy?" fumed Arthur; "he might as well have given us a bit of rope a-piece and told us to go and hang ourselves! Look at Ainger; do you suppose *he* thinks we've been let off easy?"

The captain's face left no doubt on that question.

Chapter Nine.

Ainger has a Crumpet for Tea, and Smedley sings a Song.

Railsford for a brief moment had shared the opinion of his distinguished pupil, that the doctor had let the house off easily. But two minutes' reflection sufficed to undeceive him. The house was to dine daily at one o'clock in Railsford's. That meant that they were to be cut off from all association with the rest of the school out of school hours, and that just when all the rest turned out into the playing-fields they were to sit down at their disgraced board. The half-holiday regulation was still worse. For that meant nothing short of the compulsory retirement of his boys from all the clubs, and, as far as athletics went, their total exclusion from every match or contest open to the whole school.

The house was slower at taking in the situation of affairs than the master. With the exception of Ainger, on whom the full significance of the doctor's sentence had flashed from the first, there was a general feeling of surprise that so big a "row" should be followed by so insignificant a retribution.

"Who cares what time we have dinner," said Munger to some of his admirers, "as long as we get it after all? Now if old Punch (this was an irreverent corruption of the head-master's name current in certain sets at Grandcourt)—if old Punch had stopped our grub one day a week—"

"Besides," broke in another, "we'll get things hotter than when we dined in hall."

"A precious sight hotter," said Arthur, wrathfully. "What are we to do at beagle-time to-morrow? Just when the hounds start we've got to turn in to dinner. Bah!"

This was the first practical illustration of the inconvenience of the new *régime*, and it instantly suggested others.

"We'll be stumped," said Tilbury, "if this goes on after cricket starts—it'll be all up with any of us getting into one of the School matches."

"I suppose," said Ranger of the Fifth, "this will knock all of us out of the sports, too?"

Fellows looked blank at the suggestion. Yet a moment's reflection showed that Ranger was right. One o'clock was the daily training hour in the playing-fields, and Saturday afternoon four weeks hence was the date fixed for the School sports.

It took some days for Railsford's house to accommodate itself to the new order of things imposed upon it. Indeed, it took twenty-four hours for Grandcourt generally to comprehend the calamity which had befallen the disgraced house. When one o'clock arrived on the first afternoon, and neither Ainger, Wake, Wignet, Tilbury, Herapath, nor the other familiar frequenters of the playing-field, put in an appearance, speculation began to pass about as to the cause of their absence. Some of Bickers's boys knew there had been a "howling shine" about something. But it was not till Smedley, impatient to settle some question relating to the sports, sent his fag to fetch Ainger that it became generally known what had happened. The fag returned with an important face.

"Such a go!" said he, in reply to his chief's inquiry; "there's a feast going on at Railsford's! Smelt fine! I saw them through the door, but couldn't go in, because Railsford was there. Ainger and all the lot were tucking in. The beef was just going in, so they've only just started."

"Jolly shame!" said someone who overheard this announcement; "we never get feasts in our house! I suppose Railsford thinks he'll get his chaps in a good-humour by it. It's not fair unless everybody does it."

"It'll be hall-time before they've done. We'd better not wait," said one of the Sixth. "I wonder what it all means?"

"I heard Ponsford had been down rowing them about something this morning—something some of them had been doing to Bickers, I believe."

"Very likely; Bickers looked as green as a toad this morning, didn't he, Branscombe?"

"He did look fishy," said Branscombe, shortly, "but I say, Smedley, hadn't we better measure off without Ainger, and get him to see if he approves afterwards?"

So the work went on without the representatives of Railsford's house, and the bell rang for school-dinner before any of the missing ones had put in an appearance.

The mystery was heightened when in Hall the fifty seats usually occupied by Railsford's boys stood empty; and no inquiry was made from the masters' table as to the cause of the defection. It was noticed that Mr Railsford himself was not present, and that Mr Bickers still looked upset and out of sorts.

"Have you any idea what the row is?" said Smedley to Branscombe as the company stood round the tables, waiting for the doctor.

"How should I know? You'd better go and ask up there."

Smedley did. As the doctor entered, he marched up to meet him, and said,—

"None of Mr Railsford's house are here yet, sir."

"Quite right. Call silence for grace and begin," said the doctor, slowly.

For the rest of the day Railsford's seemed to be playing hide and seek with the rest of the school, and it was not till late in the evening that the mystery was cleared up.

"Come and let's see what it's all about," said Smedley to Branscombe.

Both the seniors had been fretting all the afternoon with a sense of something gone wrong at Grandcourt, the former with just a little indignation that he, the captain of the school, should be kept in the dark, along with everybody else, on the subject.

"I ought to work," said Branscombe; "you go and *tell* me what's up."

"Why, I thought you were as anxious as anyone to know?"

"So I am," said Branscombe, who to do him justice looked thoroughly worried; "but you know while there's this row on between the two houses I—I don't care to go over there without being asked."

"*I* asked you, didn't I?" said Smedley. "You're not afraid of being eaten up, are you? Never mind. I'll brave the wild beasts myself, and let you know how I get on."

It was the rule at Grandcourt that after dark no boy from one house might enter another without permission. Smedley therefore went straight to Railsford.

"May I go and see Ainger, please, sir?"

"Certainly. And, Smedley," said the master, as the captain retired, "look in here for a moment as you go out. I want to see you about the sports."

Smedley found Ainger alone, and heard from him a full, true, and particular account of the day's events.

The captain's wrath was unbounded.

"What!" he exclaimed, "cut all of you out of the sports and everything! I say, Ainger, it must be stopped, I tell you. I'll go to the doctor."

"Might as well go to the unicorn over the gate," said Ainger.

"Can't you find the fellows?"

"That's just it. There's not even a fellow in the house I can suspect so far."

"You feel sure it's one of your fellows?"

"It couldn't be anyone else. Roe's and Grover's fellows never come over our side, and never have anything to do with Bickers. And it's hardly likely any of Bickers's fellows would have done it. In fact, ever since Bickers came in here the other night and thrashed one of our fellows, the two houses have been at daggers drawn."

"So Branscombe said. He didn't seem to care about coming in with me. I asked him."

"I don't wonder. Some of the young fools down there would give him a hot reception for no other reason than that he belongs to Bickers's house."

"I don't fancy he's proud of that distinction," said Smedley, laughing. "But, I say, can't anything be done?"

"Nothing; unless Railsford can do anything."

"Railsford asked me to go in and see him. Come, too, old man."

But Railsford had nothing to suggest. He explained dejectedly the effect of the doctor's sentence. It meant that his house was out of everything in the playing-fields; and that, as for himself, he was as much excluded as his boys. And he confirmed Ainger's opinion that it was utterly useless to appeal further to the doctor.

"It would be only fair, sir," said Smedley, "for you to take back the prize and subscription you offered for the sports."

"Certainly not, my dear fellow," said the master. "If I cannot take part in the sports in person, at least I would like to have some finger in the pie."

That was all that passed.

"I like Railsford," said Smedley; "he's genuinely cut up."

"It's awfully rough on him," replied Ainger.

The two friends said good-bye.

"By the way, Smedley," said Ainger, calling the captain back, "I may as well tell you, we are going to have our revenge for all this."

"What!" said Smedley, rather alarmed. "Surely you're not going to—"

"To roast the doctor? No. But we're going to make this the crack house of the school in spite of him."

Smedley laughed.

"Good! You've a busy time before you, old man. I'll promise to keep it dark—ha! ha!"

"You may think it a joke, dear old chap," said Ainger, standing at the door and watching his retreating figure, "but even the captain of Grandcourt will have to sit up by-and-by."

Smedley, the brave and impetuous, walked straight from Railsford's to the doctor's. He knew his was a useless mission, but he wasn't going to shirk it. The doctor would snub him and tell him to mind his own affairs; "but"—so said the hero to himself—"what do I care? I'll tell him a piece of my mind, and if he like to tell me a piece of his, that's only fair. Here goes!"

The doctor was engaged in his study, said the servant; but if Mr Smedley would step into the drawing-room he would come in a few minutes. Smedley stepped into the dimly-lighted drawing-room accordingly, which, to his consternation, he found already had an occupant. The doctor's niece was at the piano.

Smedley, for once in a way, behaved like a coward, and having advanced a step or two into the room, suddenly turned tail and retreated.

"Don't go, Mr Smedley," said a pleasant voice behind him. "Uncle will be here in a minute."

"Oh, I—good-evening, Miss Violet. I'm afraid of—"

"Not of me, are you? I'll go if you like," said she, laughing, "and then you'll have the room to yourself."

"Oh no, please. I didn't mean that. Won't you play or sing something, Miss Violet?"

So Miss Violet sang "Cherry Ripe," and then, the doctor not having yet put in an appearance, Smedley asked if she would mind playing the accompaniment of "Down among the Dead Men," as he would like to try it over.

The young lady cheerfully complied, and when presently the head-master stalked into the room he was startled, and possibly a little amused, to be met with the defiant shout of his head boy,—

"And he that will this health deny,

Down among the dead men—down among the—"

He was shaking his fist above his head, after the fashion of the song at the school suppers, when he suddenly stopped short at the sight of the doctor, and realised the horror of the situation.

"Go on, Mr Smedley," said Miss Violet, "finish the verse. We shan't be a moment, uncle."

But Smedley could as soon have finished that verse as fly up the chimney. So the doctor's niece finished it for him, and then, with a "Good-night, Mr Smedley; thank you very much for the song," she tripped out of the room, leaving the hero to his fate.

It was not a very terrible fate after all.

"You and my niece have been having quite a concert," said the doctor.

"I hope I did not disturb you, sir. Miss Violet was so kind as to play some accompaniments for me while I was waiting for you."

"You want to see me. What is it, Smedley?"

Smedley till this moment had forgotten the object of his delicate mission, and now, suddenly recalled to business, felt less taste than ever for his task. Still he must go through with it.

"It was about Mr Railsford's house, sir."

"That, Smedley, is not a subject for discussion."

"I know, sir. All I mean is that the whole school will suffer."

"That increases the responsibility of those who can rectify all by owning their misconduct."

"Won't it be possible to make some exceptions, sir? Our School sports will go all to pieces without Ainger and Barnworth and some of their fellows."

"You must see they do not go to pieces, Smedley," said the doctor; "it would be unworthy of the school if they did. As for Mr Railsford's boys, I have said what I had to say to them, and have nothing more to add."

"But Mr Railsford himself, sir," began the captain, desperately playing his last card; "we hoped he—"

"It is a most unfortunate thing for everyone," said the doctor—"I include myself and you and Mr Railsford. We are called upon to make a sacrifice, and there should be no question about our being willing, all of us, to make it for the good of the school. Good-night, Smedley, good-night."

Smedley walked back, humming "Cherry Ripe" to himself, and feeling decidedly depressed about things in general.

Chapter Ten.

Arthur puts two and two together.

Sir Digby Oakshott, of Oakshott Park, Baronet, was down on his luck. His heart had been set on saving his house single-handed by a brilliant discovery of the miscreants to whom it owed its present disgrace.

It had been a busy week for him. He had had three or four fights a day with outraged suspects, and had not invariably got the best of them. Besides, in his devotion to the public service his private duties had been neglected, and the pile of impositions had grown with compound interest. Worst of all, his own familiar friend had lifted up his heel against him, and had openly gibed at his efforts. This was "the most unkindest cut of all," and Sir Digby felt it deeply.

"What's the use of going on fooling?" said Arthur, one evening, when the tension was becoming acute. "Why can't you shut up making an ass of yourself?"

"Look here, Arthur, old man," said the baronet deprecatingly, "I don't want to be jawed by you. It's no business of yours."

"What I can't make out," pursued his friend sarcastically, "is why you haven't tried to smell the chaps out by means of Smiley. Now, if you let Smiley have a good sniff of that bit of rope on your watch-chain, and then turn him out into the square, he'd ferret them out for you."

"I tell you what, old man, if it's coming to a regular row between us two, hadn't you better say so at once, and get done with it?"

"Who says anything about a row? All I say is, you're in a precious good way of getting yourself kicked round the house, the way you're going on; and I don't much mind if I'm asked to lead off."

"You'd better try to kick me, that's all," said Dig.

"I'll see what I can do for you some day. But, I say, Dig, can't you see what a howling ass you're making of yourself?"

"No, I don't know so much about asses as you do," responded Dig.

"Daresay not. If you were in the company of one all day long, as I am, you'd soon throw it up. I tell you, my—"

Here the speaker suddenly broke off and looked affectionately at the troubled face of his old chum.

"Look here, Dig, old man, I don't want to have a row with you, no more do you. I vote we don't."

"Hang a row," said Dig. "But it seems to me, Arthur, you don't care twopence whether the chap's found out or not."

Arthur's face clouded over.

"Perhaps I do, perhaps I don't. I don't see we're called upon to show them up."

"But look what a mess the house is in till they're bowled out. We'll never get hold of a bat all the season."

"Jolly bad luck, I know, but we must lump it, Dig. You must drop fooling about with your clues. Don't get in a wax, now. I've got my reasons."

"Whatever do you mean? Do you know who it was, then? Come in! Who's there?"

The intruder was the Baby Jukes, who carried half a dozen letters in his hand, one of which he presented to the two chums.

"One for you," said he. "They're all the same. Wake gave Bateson and me a penny a-piece for writing them out, and we knocked off twenty. He says he'd have sent you one a-piece, only he knows you've not two ideas between you. Catch hold."

And he departed, smiling sweetly, with his tongue in his cheek, just in time to avoid a Caesar flung by the indignant baronet at his head.

"Those kids are getting a drop too much," said Dig. "They've no more respect for their betters than Smiley has. What's this precious letter?"

The letter was addressed to "Messrs Herapath and Oakshott," and was signed by Wake of the Fifth, although written in the inelegant hand of Master Jukes the Baby.

"'Central Criminal Court, Grandcourt. The assizes will open this evening in the forum at 6.30 sharp. You are hereby summoned on urgent business. Hereof fail not at your peril.'"

"What do that mean?" again inquired Dig. "What right has Wake to threaten us?"

"Don't you see, Wake, whose father is a pettifogging lawyer, is going to get up a make-believe law court—I heard him talk about it last term—instead of the regular debating evening. The best of it is, we kids shall all be in it, instead of getting stuck on the back bench to clap, as we generally are."

"He's no business to tell us to fail not at our peril," growled Dig. "What will they do?"

"Try somebody for murder, perhaps, or—why, of course!" exclaimed Arthur, "they'll have somebody tried for that Bickers row!"

"By the way," said Dig, returning to the great question on his mind, "you never told me if you really knew who did it."

Arthur's face clouded again.

"How should I know?" said he shortly. "What's the use of talking about it?"

There was something mysterious in Herapath's manner which disturbed his friend. It was bad enough not to be backed up in his own schemes, but to feel that his chum knew something that he did not, was very hard on Sir Digby.

Now he recalled it, Arthur had all along been somewhat reserved about the business. He had made sport of other fellows' theories, but he had never disclosed his own. Yet it was evident he had his own ideas on the subject. Was it come to this, that after all these terms of confidence and alliance, a petty secret was to come between them and cloud the hitherto peaceful horizon of their fellowship?

Digby, perhaps, did not exactly put the idea into these poetical words, but the matter troubled him quite as much.

Now, it is my intention, at this place, generously to disclose to the reader what was hidden from Sir Digby Oakshott, Baronet, and from everyone else at Grandcourt—namely, that Arthur Herapath was fully persuaded in his own mind that he knew the name of the arch offender in the recent outrage, and was resolved through thick and thin to shield him from detection. He was perfectly aware that in so doing he made himself an accessory after the fact, but that was a risk he was prepared to run. Only it decided him to keep his knowledge to himself.

Arthur was not a particularly sharp boy. His qualities were chiefly of the bull-dog order. He did not take things in with the rapidity of some fellows, but when he did get his teeth into a fact he held on like grim death. So it was now. In the first excitement of the discovery he had been as much at sea and as wild in his conjectures as anybody. But after a little he stumbled upon a piece of evidence which gave him a serious turn, and had kept him serious ever since.

On the morning of the discovery, Arthur, being in the neighbourhood of the "boot-box," thought he would have a look round. There was no fear of his mistaking the place; he had been there before, and seen Mr Bickers come out of the sack. Everything was pretty much as it had been left. The sack lay in the corner where it had been thrown, and the cord, all except the piece which the baronet had secured, was there too. On the dusty floor could clearly be perceived the place where Mr Bickers had rolled about in his uncomfortable shackles during the night, and on the ledge of the dim window which let light into the boot-box from the lobby still stood the tumbler which Arthur himself had officiously fetched an hour or two ago.

One or two things occurred to Arthur which had not previously struck him. One was that the door of the boot-box was a very narrow one, and, closing-to by a spring, it would either have had to be held open or propped open while Mr Bickers was being hauled in by his captors. He found that to hold it open wide he would have to get behind it and shut himself up between it and the stairs. Most likely, all hands being required for securing the victim, the captors would have taken the precaution to prop the door open by some means, so as to be ready for their deep-laid and carefully prepared scheme.

So Arthur groped about and discovered a twisted-up wedge of paper, which, by its battered look and peculiar shape, had evidently been stuck at some time under the door to keep it from closing-to. He quietly pocketed this prize, on the chance of its being useful, and after possessing himself of the sack and cord, and two wax vestas lying on the floor, one of which had been lit and the other had not, he prepared to quit the scene. As he was going up-stairs he caught sight of one other object— not, however, on the floor, but on the ledge of the cornice above the door. This was a match-box of the kind usually sold by street arabs for a halfpenny. Arthur tried to reach it, but could not get at it even by jumping.

"The fellow who put that there must have been over six feet," said he to himself.

With some trouble he got a stick and tipped the box off the ledge, and as he did so it occurred to him that, whereas the dust lay a quarter of an inch thick on the ledge, and whereas the match-box had no similar coating of dust, but was almost clean, it must have been put up there recently. He opened the box and looked inside. It contained wax vestas, with curiously coloured purple heads, which on examination corresponded exactly with the matches he had picked up on the floor of the boot-box.

"Oh," said Arthur to himself, very red in the face, "here's a go!" and he bolted up to his room.

Dig, as it happened, was out, not altogether to his chum's regret, who set himself, with somewhat curious agitation, to examine his booty.

First of all he examined once more the match-box, and satisfied himself that there was no doubt about the identity of its contents with the stray vestas he had picked up. The result was decisive. The box had been placed above the door very recently by someone who, unless he stood on a form or climbed on somebody else's back, must have been more than six feet high. No one puts matches above doors by accident. Whoever put it there must have meant it—and more than that, must have opened it and dropped one out inside the boot-box.

"Now," considered the astute Arthur, "it was pitch dark when Bickers was collared; lights were out, and the fellows thought they'd have a glim handy in case of need. They struck one and spilt one, and shoved the box up there, in case they should want it again. I say! what a clever chap I am! The tall chap this box belongs to did the job, eh?"

An expert might possibly find a flaw in this clue, but Arthur was a little proud of himself.

Next he spread out the sack and inspected the cord. There was not much to help him here, one would suppose, and yet Arthur, being once on a good tack, thought it worth his while to look closely at these two relics.

The sack was not the ordinary type of potato-sack which most people associate with the term, but more like a large canvas pillow-case, such as some article of furniture might be packed in, or which might be used to envelop a small bath and its contents on a railway journey. Arthur perceived that it had been turned inside out, and took the trouble to reverse it. It was riddled with holes, some of them to admit the running cords which had closed round the neck and elbows of the unfortunate Mr Bickers, and some, notably that in the region of the nose, made hastily, with the motive of giving the captive a little ventilation.

Arthur could not help thinking, as he turned the sack outside in, that it would have been nicer for Mr Bickers to have the comparatively clean side of the canvas next to his face instead of the very grimy and travel-stained surface which had fallen to his lot.

But these speculations gave place to other emotions as he discovered two black initials painted on the canvas, and still legible under their covering of dirt and grease. There was no mistaking them, and Arthur gave vent to a whistle of consternation as he deciphered an "M.R."

Now, as Arthur and everybody else knows, "M.R." *may* mean Midland Railway, but the Midland Railway is not six feet two inches, and does not carry wax vestas about him, or drop them on the floor of the boot-box.

Arthur gaped at those initials for fully three minutes, and then hurriedly hid the sack away in the cupboard.

He had still one more point to clear up. He pulled the wedge of paper out of his pocket and began nervously to unroll it. It was frayed and black where the door had ground it against the floor; but, on beginning to open it, it turned out to be a portion of a torn newspaper. It was a *Standard* of February 4—two days ago—and Arthur whistled again and turned pale as he saw a stamp and a postmark on the front page, and read a fragment of the address—"...ford, Esquire, Grandcourt."

"That settles it clean!" he muttered to himself. "I say! who'd have thought it!"

Then he sat down and went over the incidents of the last twenty-four hours.

Last night—it is sad to have to record it—Arthur had been out in the big square at half-past nine, when he should have been in bed. He had been over to find a ball which he had lost during the morning while playing catch with Dig out of the window. On his way back—he remembered it now—he had had rather a perilous time. First of all he had nearly run into the arms of Branscombe, the captain of Bickers's house, who was inconveniently prowling about at the time, probably in search of some truant of his own house. Then in doubling to avoid this danger he had dimly sighted Mr Bickers himself, taking a starlight walk on Railsford's side of the square. Finally, in his last bolt home, he had encountered Railsford stalking moodily under the shadow of his own house, and too preoccupied to notice, still less to challenge, the truant.

All this Arthur remembered now, and, carrying his mind a day or two further back, he recalled Mr Bickers's uninvited visit to the house—Arthur had painful cause to remember it—and Railsford's evident resentment of the intrusion, and the threatenings of slaughter which had been bandied about between the two houses ever since.

"Why," said Arthur to himself, "it's as clear as a pikestaff. I see it all now. Bickers said it was about a quarter to ten when he was collared. No fellows would be about then, and certainly no one would know that he would be passing our door, except Marky. Marky must have been actually hanging about for him when I passed! What a pity I didn't stop to see the fun! Yes, he'd got his sack ready, and had jammed the door open with this paper, and got his matches handy. Bickers would never see him till he came close up, and then Marky would have the sack on in two twos before he could halloa. My eye! I would never have believed it of Marky. Served Bickers right, of course, and it'll be a lesson to him; but it'll be hot for Marky if he's found out. Bickers says there may have been more than one fellow on the job, but I don't fancy it. If Mark had had anybody, he'd have got me to help him, because it would be all in the family, and I'd be bound to keep it dark. Wouldn't he turn green if he knew I'd twigged him! Anyhow, I'll keep it as close as putty now, and help him worry through. Very knowing of him to go with a candle and let him out this morning, and look so struck all of a heap. He took me in regularly."

43

Arthur said this to himself in a tone which implied that if Mark had been able to take *him* in, it was little to be wondered at that all the rest of the house had been hoodwinked.

"Hard luck," thought he condescendingly. "I daren't tell Dig. He's such a gossip, it would be all over the place in a day. Wonder if I'd best let Marky know I've spotted him? Think not. He wouldn't like it, and as long as he's civil I'll back him up for Daisy's sake."

Then, having stumbled on to the thought of home, it occurred to him that since the opening day, when he had sent a postcard to announce his arrival, he had not yet troubled his relatives with a letter this term. It was a chance, while he was in the humour, to polish them off now; so he took up his pen, and thus discoursed to his indulgent sister:—

"Dear Da,—Mark's all right so far. He doesn't hit it with a lot of the chaps, and now and then we hate him, but he lets Dig and me alone, and doesn't interfere with Smiley. I hope you and he keep it up, because it would make me look rather foolish if it was all off, especially as Dimsdale and one or two of the chaps happen to have heard about it, and have bets on that it won't last over the summer holidays.

"I'm getting on very well, and working hard at French. *Je suis allant à commencer translater une chose par Molière le prochain term si je suis bon.* There's a howling row on in the house just now. Bickers got nobbled and sacked the other night, and shoved in the boot-box, and nobody knows who did it. I've a notion, but I'm bound to keep it dark for the sake of a mutual friend. It would be as rough as you like for him if it came out. But I believe in *assistant un boiteux chien au travers de la stile*; so I'm keeping it all dark. Ponsford has been down on us like a sack of coals. They've shoved forward our dinner-hour to one o'clock, so we're regularly dished over the sports, especially as Saturday afternoon has been changed into morning. The house will go to the dogs now, *mais que est les odds si longtemps que vous êtes heureuses?* Dig sends his love. He and I remember the loved ones at home, and try to be good. By the way, do you think pater could go another five bob? I'm awfully hard up, my dear Daisy, and should greatly like not to get into evil ways and borrow from Dig. Can you spare me a photograph to stick up on the mantelpiece to remind me of you always? You needn't send a cabinet one, because they cost too much. I'd sooner have a *carte-de-visite* and the rest in stamps, if you don't mind. I'm doing my best to give Marky a leg-up. I could get him into a row and a half if I liked, but for your sake I'm keeping it all dark. I hope you'll come down soon. It will be an awful game if you do, and I'll promise to keep the fellows from grinning. *Maintenant, il faut que je close haut. Donnez mon amour à mère et père, et esperant que vous êtes tout droit, souvenez me votre aimant frère*, Arthur Herapath. *Dig envoie son amour à tous.*"

Daisy might have been still more affected by this brotherly effusion than she was, had not she received a letter by the same post from Mark himself, telling her of his later troubles, and containing a somewhat more explicit narrative of recent events than had been afforded in the letter of his prospective brother-in-law.

"I am, I confess, almost at a loss," said he. "I do not like to believe that anyone in the house can have the meanness to involve us all in this misfortune by his own guilty silence. ... Much depends now on the spirit which my prefects show. I believe, myself, that if they take a proper view of the situation, we may weather the storm. But the new order of things hits them harder than anyone else, for it excludes them from football, cricket, and the sports; and I fear it is too much to expect that they will even try to make the best of it! I begin to feel that a master, after all, if he is to do any good, must be a sort of head boy himself, and I would be thankful if my seniors let me into their confidence, and we were not always dealing with one another at arm's length. All this, I fear, is uninteresting to you; but it means a good deal to me. The flighty Arthur does not appear to be much cast down by our troubles. I wish I could help him to a little of the ballast he so greatly needs. But, although I am the master of this house, I seem scarcely ever to see him. I hear him, though. I hear him this minute. He and his chum occupy the room over me, and when they execute a war dance—which occurs on an average six times a day—it makes me tremble for my ceiling. I have a notion Arthur spends his weekly allowance rather recklessly, and am thinking of suggesting to your father that a reduction might be judicious," etcetera, etcetera.

Had Railsford guessed, as he wrote these rather despondent lines, that his youthful kinsman in the room above was hugging himself for his own astuteness in tracking out his (Railsford's) villainy, he might perhaps have regarded the situation of affairs as still less cheerful. As it was, after the first discovery, the hope had begun to dawn upon the Master of the Shell, as it had already dawned on Barnworth, that some good might even result from the present misfortunes of the house. And as the days passed, he became still more confirmed in the hope, and, with his usual sanguine temper, thought he could see already Railsford's house starting on a new career and turning its troubles to credit.

Alas! Mark Railsford had rough waters still to pass through. And the house, before it was to start on its new career, had several little affairs to wind up and dispose of.

Among others, the Central Criminal Court Assizes were coming on, and the boys were summoned, "at their peril," not to fail in appearing on the occasion.

Chapter Eleven.

A "Cause Célèbre."

Wake, of the Fifth, was one of those restless, vivacious spirits who, with no spare time on their hands, contrive to accomplish as much as any ordinary half-dozen people put together. He formed part of the much-despised band of fellows in his form contemptuously termed "muggers." In other words, he read hard, and took no part in the desultory amusements which consumed the odd moments of so many in the house. And yet he was an excellent cricketer and runner, as the school was bound to acknowledge whenever it called out its champions to do battle for it in the playing-fields.

More than that, if anyone wanted anything doing in the way of literary sport—in the concoction of a squib or the sketching of a caricature—Wake was always ready to take the work upon himself, and let who liked take the credit. He had a mania for verses and epigrams; he was reputed a bit of a conjuror, and no one ever brought a new puzzle to Grandcourt which Wake, of Railsford's, could not, sooner or later, find out.

Among other occupations, Wake had for some time past acted as secretary for the House Discussion Society—an old institution which for years had droned along to the well-known tunes—"That Wellington was a greater man than Napoleon," "That Shakespeare was a greater poet than Homer," "That women's rights are not desirable," "That the execution of Charles the First was unjustifiable," etcetera, etcetera. But when, six months ago, Trill, of the Sixth, the old secretary, left Grandcourt, and Wake, at the solicitation of the prefects (who lacked the energy to undertake the work themselves), consented to act as secretary, the society entered upon a new career. The new secretary alarmed his patrons by his versatility and energy. The old humdrum questions vanished almost completely from the programme, and were replaced by such interesting conundrums as "Is life worth living?" "Ought the *Daily News* to be taken in at the school library?" "What is a lie?" and so on. Beyond that, he boldly appropriated evenings for other purposes than the traditional debate. On one occasion he organised a highly successful reading of *Coriolanus*, in which the juniors, to their vast delight, were admitted to shout as citizens. Another evening was given to impromptu speeches, every member who volunteered being called upon to draw a subject out of a hat and make a speech upon it there and then. And more than once the order of the day was readings and recitations, in which the younger members were specially encouraged to take part, and stood up gallantly to be shot at by their critical seniors.

Whatever might be said of this novel departure from old tradition, no one could deny that the Discussion Society had looked up wonderfully during the last six months. The forum was generally crowded, and everyone, from prefect to Baby, took more or less interest in the proceedings. No one, after the first few meetings, questioned Wake's liberty to arrange what programme he liked, and the house was generally kept in a pleasant flutter of curiosity as to what the volatile secretary would be up to next.

The "Central Criminal Court" was his latest invention, and it need scarcely be said the idea, at the present juncture, was so startling that a quarter of an hour before the hour of meeting the forum was packed to its fullest extent, and it was even rumoured that Mr Railsford had promised to look in during the evening. It was evident directly to the juniors that the proceedings had been carefully thought out and settled by the secretary, in consultation with some of the wise heads of the house. The room was arranged in close imitation of a court of justice. The bench was a chair raised on two forms at one end; the witness-box and the dock were raised spaces railed off by cord from the rest of the court. Rows of desks represented the seats of the counsel, and two long forms, slightly elevated above the level of the floor, were reserved for the accommodation of the jury. The general public and witnesses-in-waiting were relegated to the rear of the court.

The question was, as everyone entered, Who is who? Who is to be the judge, and who is to be the prisoner, and who are to be the counsel? This natural inquiry was answered after the usual style of the enterprising secretary. Every one on entering was asked to draw out of a hat a folded slip of paper, which assigned to him the part he was to play, the only parts reserved from the lot being that of judge, which of course was to be filled by Ainger, and that of senior counsels for the prosecution and defence, which were undertaken respectively by Barnworth and Felgate. It was suspected later on that a few of the other parts were also prearranged, but no one could be quite sure of this.

"What are you?" said Dig, pulling a long face over his piece of paper.

"I'm junior counsel for the defence," said Arthur proudly. "What are you?"

"A wretched witness," said the baronet.

"What a spree! Won't I pull you inside out when I get you in the box, my boy!"

There was a call for order, and Ainger, mounting the bench, said,—

"This is quite an experiment, you fellows. It may be a failure, or it may go off all right. It depends on how we do our best. The idea is that a prisoner is to be tried for murder (delight among the juniors). Barnworth, who is the counsel for the prosecution, has prepared the story, and Felgate has been told what the line to be taken against the prisoner is, so that he might prepare his defence. These are the only two who know exactly what they are to do beforehand. All the rest will have to act according to the papers they have drawn. Who has drawn prisoner?"

Amid much laughter Stafford blushingly owned the soft impeachment, and was called upon to enter the dock, which he did, looking rather uncomfortable, and as if he half repented his consent to take a part in the proceedings.

"Now," proceeded Ainger, consulting a paper, "the twelve jurymen are to go into the box there."

The twelve boys with "Jury" on their papers obeyed. They were a motley crew, some being Fifth-form boys, some Shell-fish, and some Babies. And by the odd irony of fate, the one who had drawn the "foreman's" ticket was Jukes, the Baby.

"Now the witnesses go to the back seats there. You'll find on each the name you will be called by, and a short note of what your evidence is to be. You will have to listen very carefully to Barnworth's story, so as to know exactly what it's all about."

There was a laugh at this. Some thought it a trifle queer that witnesses should have to learn what their evidence was to be from notes given them in court and from counsel's speech. But they were young, and did not know much of law courts.

"Of course you must not show one another your notes," said Ainger; "that would spoil all."

"Ta-ta," said the baronet rather dismally to his chum; "they call me Tomkins!"

"The junior counsel for the prosecution, of course, are to sit behind Barnworth, and for the defence behind Felgate. You must listen carefully, as you may have to help in the cross-examination. The rest of the public go to the back; and now we are ready to begin. Usher, call silence in the court."

Tilbury, whose proud office it was to act in this capacity, shouted, "Order, there! shut up!" in a loud voice.

Wake, who acted as clerk, read out the name of the case, "Regina *versus* Bolts." The jury answered to their names and promised to bring in a true verdict. The prisoner was called upon to plead guilty or not guilty, and answered, "Not guilty"; and then Barnworth rose and opened the case for the prosecution.

"My lord, and gentlemen of the jury," he began; "the prisoner at the bar is charged with the wilful murder of John Smith, on the night of Tuesday, February 4."

This was interesting, for Tuesday, February 4, was the date of the Bickers affair.

"I shall, as briefly as possible, narrate the circumstances of this unfortunate affair. The prisoner, Thomas Bolts, is a workman in the employ of a large firm of engineers in this neighbourhood, in which the murdered man was also engaged as a foreman and overseer. It is unnecessary, gentlemen of the jury, to explain to you that the works in question are divided into several distinct departments, or shops. I need not describe them all, but two of them were the screw department and the boiler department. Smith was foreman and overseer of the screw department, while the prisoner was one of the skilled workmen in the boiler department. For some time past ill-feeling had existed between the men of the boiler department and the deceased on account of his interference with them; and this ill-feeling appears to have culminated a few days before the murder, on account of an intrusion made by Smith into the boiler department, and the alleged assault of one of the men there employed."

Every one saw now what was coming, and pricked up his ears in anticipation. Ainger, who had had as little idea of the turn things were going to take as anybody else, grew fidgety, and wished Wake had shown more discretion. But it was too late to stop the case now.

"This assault occurred, I believe, on the 2nd of February."

"No, the 3rd—the day before," whispered Ranger, who acted as junior counsel for the prosecution.

"I am obliged to my learned friend for correcting me. This occurred on the 3rd, the day before the murder. Now, gentlemen of the jury, I ask your attention to the occurrences which followed. At the time of the assault the prisoner, in the absence of the head foreman, was acting as overseer of his shop, and witnesses will prove that he protested against the behaviour of the deceased, and was in consequence insulted by Smith. I mention this to show that a personal grudge existed between the two men."

Stafford, whose *rôle* as prisoner may or may not have been the result of mere accident, began not to like the turn things were taking.

"On the 4th everything went well till the evening, although, it is stated, a formal complaint of Smith's interference was made through the regular, foreman of the boiler-shop, as will appear in evidence. In the evening of that day—that is, about eight o'clock—a meeting of the heads of the various departments was held in a distant part of the works, which was attended by Smith as well as the other foremen. The meeting lasted till 9.30, and Smith was last seen proceeding to his own quarters, in the neighbourhood of the boiler-shop.

"On the morning of the 5th, a workman named Simple, on entering the coal-cellar under the stairs of the boiler-shed, stumbled against a human body, and being frightened, gave an alarm. The foreman of the boiler department, accompanied by the prisoner and one or two other men, proceeded to the spot, and found the body of the deceased lying on the floor among the coals, enveloped in a sack, and bound hand and foot. He was alive at the time, and on being released stated that on passing the door of the boiler-shed, on the previous evening, he had been seized from behind by some person unknown, and after being bound in the sack had been dragged into the cellar and shut up there for the night. He was much exhausted when found, and on the evening of the 5th succumbed to the injuries he had received."

Some of the juniors breathed again. It was *very* like the story of Mr Bickers, only Mr Bickers was alive and kicking still. It was much more satisfactory for the present purposes to have the fellow out of the way.

"Now, gentlemen of the jury," proceeded Barnworth, putting his hands in his pockets and addressing himself particularly to Jukes, the Baby, "I ask your particular attention to a few facts. At the time of the murder the prisoner, who is usually working in his own shop, was observed to be absent, and no satisfactory account can be given of his whereabouts. Further than that, a witness will prove to you that after the quarrel on the previous day he was heard to say that he would pay the deceased out. It will also be proved that on the same afternoon he procured several yards of cord from a neighbouring shop, which the maker will identify as very like the cord used for binding the murdered man. Finally, on an inquiry made by the head of the firm, on a question being put to each man in the boiler department in succession, it was observed that the accused gave his replies with evident confusion and alarm. For these reasons, gentlemen of the jury, and others which will come out in evidence, I shall ask you by your verdict to find the prisoner guilty of the wilful murder of John Smith."

This seemed a very strong case, and one or two of the jury rather wondered that the judge did not at once direct them to bring in a verdict of "Guilty." However, as it appeared to be the usual thing to hear evidence, they waited.

The first witness called was Job Walker, and, in response to the call, Blyth of the Fifth stepped into the box.

His evidence related to the feud between the murdered, man and the men in the boiler-shop; and he gave an account of the intrusion of Smith on the night of the 3rd and of the quarrel which ensued. Blyth, in fact, related what had happened in the common room at Railsford's that evening, only changing names and places in accordance with Barnworth's story.

When his examination in chief was concluded, Felgate rose and said,—

"I have one or two questions to ask you, Mr Job Walker. You say you were in the boiler-shop during the whole of the evening in question. Where was the proper foreman of the shop at the time?"

"He was out."

"Was work going on as usual in his absence?"

"Pretty much."

"What do you mean by pretty much? Were *you* working yourself?"

Great delight of the juniors, for Blyth had been one of the chief rioters.

"Well," said he, "perhaps I was a little slack." (Laughter.)

"Who was in charge of the shop at the time?"

"The prisoner and another workman called Flounders."

"And pray were they 'slack,' too, as you call it?"

"Yes—they were no good at all." (Laughter.)

"Were you present when the proper foreman returned?"

"Yes, I was."

"Did he say anything to the prisoner?"

"He seemed in a great rage."

"Did they come to blows?"

"No—but I shouldn't have been surprised if they had."

"That will do, Mr Job Walker."

Barnworth asked another question before Mr Walker stepped down.

"Did you notice what took place between the prisoner and the deceased?"

"Yes. The deceased, when he came in, told the prisoner he was no good, and sent him to his place and took charge of the shop. The prisoner was very angry, and said he would like to pay Smith out."

The general opinion was that Blyth had acquitted himself well, and he was cheered by the public as he stood down.

Timothy Simple was next called, and Simson, rather pale and scared-looking, answered to the name.

The examination of this witness was left to Ranger, who got him to narrate the circumstances of his finding the body of the "deceased" on the morning of the 5th. The unfortunate youth seemed to forget that the trial was a mock one, and coloured up and stammered and corrected himself, as if the life of a fellow-being actually depended on his evidence.

Felgate, after a hurried communication from his junior, only asked a very few questions in cross-examination.

"Did you observe if the body was lying with its head to the door or its feet?"

"I really couldn't say. It was so dark, and I was so horrified."

"Was the key of the cellar always on the outside of the door?"

"Yes, generally; it must have been, because I locked it behind me when I ran out."

"Who would be the last person at night to go to the cellar? Would the foreman go round and lock up?"

"I don't know; I suppose so."

"You wouldn't swear that the foreman did not usually keep the key at night in his own room?"

"No—that is, yes. Do you mean I wouldn't swear he did, or didn't?"

"You would not swear he did not keep it?"

"I don't know."

"But you wouldn't swear he didn't?"

"I couldn't, because if I don't know—"

"If you don't know you couldn't swear he didn't do it. Come, tell the jury, Yes, or No, Mr Simple; it is an important question."

Simson looked up and down. Half a dozen friends were winking at him suggestively from different parts of the court, and he couldn't make out their meaning. At length he perceived Munger nodding his head, and as Munger had lent him a crib to Ovid the day before, he decided to refer to him.

"Yes," he said.

"I thought so," said Felgate. "Why could you not say that before, Mr Simple?"

And Simson descended from his perch amid laughter and jeers, not quite sure whether he had not committed a crime beside which the offence of the prisoner at the bar was a trifle.

"Call William Tomkins," said Barnworth.

William Tomkins was called, and Dig, with his tawny mane more than usually dishevelled, and an excited look on his face, entered the box. He glared round him defiantly, and then dug his hands into his pockets and waited for his questions.

"Your name is William Tomkins?" began Barnworth.

"Sir William Tomkins, Baronet," said the witness, amidst laughter.

"To be sure, I beg your pardon, Sir William. And what are you, pray?"

"A baronet." (Loud laughter.)

"A baronet in reduced circumstances, I fear. You work in the boiler department of this factory?"

"All right, go on."

Here the judge interposed.

"The witness must remember that he is bound to answer questions properly. Unless he does so I shall order him to be removed."

This somewhat damped the defiant tone of Digby, and he answered the further questions of counsel rather more amiably. These had reference to the discovery of the body on the morning of the 5th, with the details of which the reader is already acquainted. The public began to get a little tired of this constant repetition of the same story, and were about to vote the proceedings generally slow, when a double event served to rouse their flagging attention.

Mr Railsford entered the court as a spectator, and was accommodated with a seat on the bench, beside the judge. At the same moment, Barnworth, having ended his questions, Arthur Herapath, junior counsel for the defence, rose to his feet, and said,—

"Now, Sir William Tomkins, Baronet, have the goodness to look at me and answer a few questions. I would advise you to be careful."

The baronet replied by putting his tongue in his cheek, and giving a pantomimic wave of his fist in the direction of the learned counsel.

"Now, Sir William Tomkins, Baronet, how old are you, my lad?"

"Find out," said Sir William hotly.

"That's what I mean to do. Answer me, sir, or I'll get the beak to run you in for contempt of court."

"Come and do it," said the witness, red in the face.

Here the judge again interposed.

"The learned junior must confine himself to the case before us, or I shall have to ask Mr Felgate to conduct the cross-examination."

"All serene, my lord," rejoined the learned junior, who was thoroughly enjoying himself. "Of course, if your lordship think the question's not important I won't press it against your lordship's desire. I'm obliged to your lordship for your lordship's advice, and I'll pull your nose, Dimsdale"—this was in a parenthesis—"if you don't shut up. Now, Sir William Tomkins, Baronet, you say you saw the prisoner pulled out of the sack?"

"I never said anything of the sort."

"My lord, I must ask your lordship to commit this man for perjury. He's telling crackers."

"I think he said he saw the murdered man pulled out of the sack," said the judge.

"That's what I said. How came you to say you didn't, eh, sir? Didn't I tell you to be careful or you'd get your hair combed a way you don't fancy? Now, what I want to know is, what's the width of the door of the cellar?"

"Look here," said the witness, "if you want to make an ass of yourself you'd better shut up. What's that got to do with it?"

"It's quite a proper question," said the judge.

"There you are!" said Arthur, delighted. "I'm obliged to your lordship for your lordship's remarks. Now, Sir William Thingamy, what do you mean, sir, by refusing to answer the question? I've a good mind to ask his lordship to send you to penal servitude. Now, what about the door?"

"I don't know anything about it, and I don't care."

"Ha! ha! You'll *have* to care, my boy. Could two chaps go through it together?"

"Come and try," said the baronet, snorting with wrath.

"You must answer the question, witness," said the judge.

"No; *he* knows two chaps couldn't. He measured it himself and found it was only twenty-eight inches wide."

"Who measured it?" asked one of the jury.

"Why, Herapath, that idiot there."

Arthur was somewhat sobered by this piece of evidence, as well as by a significant consultation on the bench, which he rather feared might relate to his conduct of the case.

"That's what I wanted to get at," said he. "Now, Sir William, what's the *height* of that door, eh?"

"What's the good of asking me when you measured it yourself, you duffer? Didn't you tell me yourself it was seven feet two to the top of the ledge?"

"There you are! Keep your hair on! That's what I wanted! Seven foot two. Now suppose you were told a box of wax lights was found stuck upon that ledge, and that two of the matches out of it were found on the floor of the boot-box—cellar, I mean—what should you think?"

"It is hardly evidence, is it, to ask a witness what he would think?" suggested Barnworth.

"Oh, isn't it? Easy a bit, and you'll see what we're driving at, your lordship! I'll trouble your lordship to ask the learned chap not to put me off my run. Come, Mr What's-your-name, what should you think?"

Dig mused a bit, and then replied, "I should think it was a little queer."

"Of course you would! So it *is* a little queer," said Arthur, winking knowingly at his future brother-in-law. "Now, could *you* reach up to the top of that ledge, my little man?"

"You be blowed!" responded the baronet, who resented this style of address.

"That means you couldn't. When you're about four feet higher than you are you'll be able to do it. Now could the prisoner reach up to it?"

"No, no more could you, with your boots and three-and-sixpenny Sunday tile on!"

"Order in the court! Really, your lordship, your lordship ought to sit on this chap. Perhaps your lordship's friend on your lordship's right would kindly give him a hundred lines when next he comes across him. Now, Mr Baron, and Squire, and Knight of the Shire, and all the rest of it, I want to know if there's any chap in our house—I mean the boiler-shop—could reach up there? Mind your eye, now!"

"Ainger could by jumping."

"I didn't ask you anything about jumping, you duffer! How tall would a chap need to be to reach up there?"

"About double your measure—over six foot."

"There you are! Now is there any chap in our boiler-shop over six feet?"

"No."

"I knew you'd say that. Think again. What about the foreman?" and he gave a side inclination of his head towards the unconscious Railsford.

"Oh, him! Yes, *he's* over six foot."

"Go down two places, for saying *him* instead of *he*. There you are, my lord, we've got it at last. Bowled the chap out clean, first ball. That's our case, only there's plenty more to be got out first. We'll trouble your lordship to bring the chap in not guilty, when it's all done." And he nodded knowingly to the jury.

Railsford had sat and listened to all this in a state of the completest mystification. Not having heard Barnworth's opening statement, he had no glimmer of a suspicion that the *cause célèbre* occupying the attention of this august assembly was anything but a pleasant fiction from beginning to end, and he had been wondering to himself whether such performances, conducted in the irregular style which he had witnessed, could be of any good. However, coming as a guest (for the master of the house was always a visitor on such occasions), he deemed it best not to interfere just then. He would give Arthur a little friendly advice as to the conduct of a junior counsel later on.

But he was the only unconscious person in the court. The listeners had been quick to pick up the drift of Barnworth's opening story, and equally quick to detect the line of defence taken up by Felgate and his vivacious junior. They kept their eyes fixed most of the time on Railsford, to note how he took it; and when Arthur reached his triumphant climax, some among the juniors fully expected to see their master fall on his knees and plead guilty before the whole court.

Instead of that he laughed, and, turning to the judge, said, in an audible voice,—

"This seems very amusing, but it's all Hebrew to me. Is this the end?"

"I think we've had nearly enough for to-night," said Ainger, who himself felt rather uneasy lest matters should go any further. Not that he laid any stress on Arthur's wonderful discovery—that merely amused him; but he foresaw a danger of the tone of the proceedings becoming offensive, and considered it better to interpose while yet there was time.

"Gentlemen," he said, "as far as the case has gone I think I may say it has been ably conducted and patiently listened to. As our time is nearly up I adjourn the hearing till a future occasion."

"Jolly hard luck," said Arthur to his senior. "I'd got plenty more to come out."

"You've done quite enough for one evening," said Felgate, grinning, "the rest will keep."

Chapter Twelve.

Throwing down the Gauntlet.

Arthur's great hit at the Central Criminal Court was the topic in the junior circles at Railsford's for some days. It was hardly to be expected that Sir Digby Oakshott would share in the general admiration which fell to his friend's lot. That young baronet had a painful sense of having come off second best at the trial, and the relations between the friends became considerably strained in consequence. What made it harder for Dig was that Arthur had suddenly gained quite a prestige among the lower boys of the house, who, without being too curious, arrived at the conclusion that he knew a thing or two about Railsford in connection with the row about Bickers, and was keeping it dark.

Strangely enough, from the same cause, Railsford himself leapt into sudden popularity with his juniors. For if he, argued they, was the man who paid out Bickers for them, then, although it put them to a little inconvenience, they were resolved as one man to back their hero up, and cover his retreat to the best of their ability. The master himself was considerably surprised at the sudden outburst of affection towards himself. He hoped it meant that his influence was beginning to tell home on the minds of his youthful charges; and he wrote cheerfully to Daisy about it, and said he had scarcely hoped in so short a time to have made so many friends among his boys.

"Tell you what," said Arthur one evening, after discussing the virtues of his future kinsman with some of the Shell, "it wouldn't be a bad dodge to get up a testimonial for Marky. I know a stunning dodge for raising the wind."

"Good idea," said Tilbury, "I'm game."

"Let's give it him soon, to get him in a good-humour, next week," suggested someone.

"No, we'd better do it just before the Easter holidays," replied Arthur; "that'll start him well for next term."

That evening the differences between the two friends were patched up. Dig, under a pledge of secrecy, was initiated into the whole mystery of the sack, and the wedge of paper, and the wax vestas, promising on his part to respect his friend's reputation in the matter of the "fifty-six billion Snowball."

The baronet was fully impressed with the importance of his friend's disclosures.

"It's a regular case," said he. "I never thought it of him. We must keep it dark and give him a leg out."

"I fancy so," said Arthur. "It's a sort of family affair, you see. It's half a pity he can't know that we've bowled him out and are sticking to him. But I suppose it's best not to let him suspect it."

"No—better keep it all dark. He'll know all about it some day."

And the two confederates went to bed happy that night, in the consciousness that they were restored to one another's confidence, and that they were standing between their miscreant "kinsman" and the punishment which properly belonged to his crime. On the following morning a notice appeared on the common room door, signed by Ainger, summoning the house to meet after tea on particular business. The important business had no connection with the *affaire Bickers*, but was the captain's first move towards pulling up the house to the proud position he designed for it.

"Now, you fellows," said he, in the course of a short spirited speech, "I needn't tell you that our house is down on its luck this term. (Cheers.) We are in the black books of the doctor, as you know—and we can't well help it. Somebody in the house thinks fit to tell a lie, and gets us all into trouble; but we aren't going down on our knees to that person or any other sneak to help us when we mean to help ourselves. (Loud cheers.) Now this is one way I propose we help ourselves. We are, you all know, cut out of the sports, and school cricket, and all that sort of thing. (Shame!) Very well; but they can't prevent our getting up house sports of our own, and a house eleven, and showing that we aren't going to be put down. (Applause.) I mean to train hard myself, and run the mile if I can in quicker time than Smedley or anyone else in the School sports; and unless I'm mistaken Barnworth means to show that Railsford's house can jump an inch higher than any other house at Grandcourt, even though we don't get a prize for it (tremendous cheers); and I am not so sure if Wake doesn't press their second man pretty close. (Bravo, Wake!) You youngsters will have to do your share. We want a Railsford's fellow to lick the time of every event in the School sports. (Loud cheers.) We may not be able to do it in all; but we'll know the reason why, if we don't. (So we will!) You'll have to sit up, some of you, if you're going to do it. But of course you'll do that. (Rather!) Railsford's sports will be held this day three weeks—just a week after the School sports. So we shall know what we've got to beat. That's one thing I've got to say. Every boy here should enter for some event or other, and see he wins it. (Applause.) The next thing is this. Cricket is coming on; it begins the Saturday after the sports. We aren't going to be done out of our cricket to please anybody! (Tremendous enthusiasm and waving of caps.) We intend to turn out as stiff a house eleven as ever played in the fields, and some fine day you fellows will see Railsford's play the School and win. (Applause.) Yes, and we'll have a second eleven, too. (Rather! from the juniors.) Mr Railsford is going to back us up. (Cheers.) He played in his college eleven at Cambridge, and he's promised to give up all his Saturdays to the end of the term to coach us. (Three cheers for Railsford.) Now the last thing—"

"Whatever else can there be?" said the baronet, in a perspiration of fervour.

"Some of you may open your eyes when I mention it, but I know you won't funk it. We mean to get hold of all the School prizes at Grandcourt this term, if we can. (Sensation.) Yes, you may gape, but it's a fact! Of course, I can't beat Smedley for the gold medal. (Yes, have a try!) Rather! I mean to try; and Smedley will have to put on steam. (Loud cheers.) Then Stafford is going to cut out Branscombe—(Boo-hoo!)—for the Melton Scholarship, and Barnworth will get the vacant Cavendish Scholarship, and Wake and Ranger and Sherriff and Wignet are going to walk off with all the Fifth-form prizes; and Herapath will pull off the Swift Exhibition, and Sir Digby Oakshott, Baronet.—(tremendous cheers)—will win the Shell History medal."

"I say!" said the baronet, mopping his face vehemently; "that's the first I've heard about that!"

"Yes, and our Babies are going to show the way, too!" continued the captain; "and on prize-day we'll crowd up and cheer them when they toddle up to take their prizes. (Laughter and cheers.) That's all I want to say. (Laughter and applause.) Some of you will say I'm cracked. (No!) I'm not! Railsford's is going in and going to win, and if you all back up—(So we will I)— we shall do it easily. (Cheers.) Don't let us brag too much. The school will find out what we are up to soon enough without our blowing trumpets. Oh, there's one thing more," continued the captain—"positively the last—(laughter)—about this row we're all in. It was a caddish thing, whoever did it, to maul a man about in the dark when he couldn't defend himself— (cheers)—and a low thing, whoever did it, to tell a lie about it. (Cheers.) But my advice is, let the beggar alone. He's an enemy to our house, but we aren't going to make ourselves miserable on his account. Let him alone. Don't go poking and sniffing about to try to smell him out. (Arthur blushed violently here.) Think of something better. In spite of him we're going to make Railsford's the cock house at Grandcourt! That will be the best way to pay him out, and it will take us all our time to do it, without dirtying our fingers over him."

Ainger concluded amidst a burst of cheers which quite took him aback, and the meeting dispersed enthusiastically to talk over the wonderful programme, and take the first steps towards carrying it out.

The captain's words came upon most of the fellows as a surprise that there could be any other way out of their present misfortunes than by submitting to them tamely and giving up the glory of their house as a bad job. The audacious proposal first took their breath away, and then took possession of them. They would have their revenge; and here was a way open to them. It scarcely occurred to any but the experienced seniors that there would be any difficulty in making Ainger's bold predictions true. Arthur for instance, having heard it publicly announced that he was about to win the Swift Exhibition, thought and behaved as if the prize were already in his hands.

"Twenty pounds a-year for three years," said he complacently, to his ally. "Not a bad pot. Tell you what, Dig, we'll get a tandem tricycle, my boy, with the first year's money. Hope they'll pay it in advance, don't you? then we can get it after break-up, and have some ripping spins in the summer holidays. Better fun than fooling about in Switzerland with Marky and Daisy. We'll either get that, or I know a jolly little boat Punter has for sale at Teddington, with a towing-line and double sculls, and a locker under the stern seat for grub. He wanted £22 for it, but I expect he'll come down the £2 for ready money. Perhaps it would be better to buy it this summer, and get the tricycle with next year's money. I've a good mind to write to Punter to-night."

"Hadn't you better get the Exhibition first?" suggested the baronet.

"Of course I mean to get it," said Arthur, rather nettled; "I fancy Ainger's as good a judge of what a chap can do in that line as you are."

"I don't know," replied Dig; "he said *I* was going to get the History Medal, but I'm not so sure if I shall."

"Well, I did think he was letting out a bit when he said that," replied Arthur, with a chuckle. "Never mind, we'll go halves in the Exhibition."

It must be admitted that the prospect of his coming academical success did not appreciably affect Arthur Herapath's studies during the present term. Four-and-a-half months is a long time to look ahead in a schoolboy's career; and, as it happened, the captain's speech had suggested other matters in the immediate future, which for the time being absorbed not only Arthur's attention but everyone else's.

That evening, a list of events for the House sports was exhibited on the common room door, with space below each for the names of intending competitors. It was noticed that the list corresponded in every particular with the list of the School sports to be held a week earlier, and that the compiler (who was detected by the handwriting to be Barnworth) had already written in brackets the names of those who had entered for each of the events in the School sports. Every one, therefore, in Railsford's, could see, not only what he was going in for, but who the competitors were whom he was expected to beat.

A good beginning had already been made before the list came under the notice of the juniors. For the High Jump, which this year, for some reason or other, had been looked forward to as one of the principal events, the signature of Barnworth stood boldly underneath the dreaded names of Smedley and Clipstone. More than that, Wake, too, had entered himself in the lists against these great competitors. The entries for the Mile were scarcely less interesting. Smedley was to run for the School, and, still more formidable, the long-legged Branscombe. Against them now appeared the names of Ainger and Stafford, and the plucky Ranger of the Fifth, and so on down the list, for all the big events, the prefects and the redoubtable Fifth-form "muggers" of Railsford's had set their challenge, and the hearts of the juniors swelled big within them as they crowded round the board to write their names against the lesser contests.

Arthur and the baronet adopted the simple and modest method of entering themselves for everything; and it was not till Maple hinted something about the entrance fees mounting up to about a sovereign a-piece that they drew in their horns and limited their ambitions to the long jump under fifteen, the junior hurdle race, and the quarter-mile under sixteen. The other Shell-fish followed suit. Tilbury, of course, put himself down for throwing the cricket-ball under fifteen. Indeed, some of his admirers thought he might even venture to throw against the seniors; only Felgate already had his name down for that event. Dimsdale undertook the hundred yards under fifteen against several strong opponents; and, on the whole, among them, the boys of the Shell contrived to make a strong show on the list for every event within their reach. When the turn came for the Babies, they evinced equal spirit, and divided the list among them with a fierceness which augured ill for the Babies of the other houses whose claims they challenged.

Ainger and Barnworth strolled down later on to examine the list, and now suggested a few alterations. The baronet for instance, was called upon to enter for the second class of kicking the football contest, and Arthur was moved from the quarter-mile to the half-mile, because a good man was wanted there to beat Smythe, of the School-House, whereas Sherriff could very well be trusted to take care of the quarter-mile for Railsford's house.

Mr Railsford presently arrived on the scene, and went into the whole programme enthusiastically, and in a way which won him friends among the boys, more even than his reputed authorship of the Bickers outrage had lately done. He invited any boys who chose during the next few days to try over their event in his presence, and suggested that a record of the times should be carefully kept, with a view to ensure that each trial should beat the last.

More than that, he offered a prize for the best all-round record in the house; and proposed that, although they were not rich enough to give prizes for each event, any boy who beat the School record in his competition should receive back his entrance fee. This practical suggestion gave much satisfaction.

"Of course," said he, to one or two of those round him, "it is harder to run against time than against another fellow. You must make up your minds for that; and I would advise you to try to get the two best in our house to enter for each event, so as to get the spur of a close race. Our times are sure to be the better for it."

Boys liked him for that word "our." It sounded like a common cause, and they were quick to hail the first symptom of such feeling in a master.

The next fortnight witnessed a smart athletic fever in the house. Of course, it soon spread abroad what Railsford's was up to, and the School form generally improved in consequence. In fact, when the day arrived for the School sports, it was generally felt that Grandcourt had rarely come on to the ground better up to the mark. Alas! Grandcourt came on to the ground in two halves, and on two different days. When the boys of the school-House, Roe's, Bickers's, and Grover's turned out to the starting-post, Railsford's, chafing like greyhounds in the leash, turned in to their penitential dinner.

"Never mind," said Ainger, as the distant shouts were wafted from the playing-fields into the common room, "it will be our turn to-day week!"

Chapter Thirteen.

A Fly in the Ointment.

Ainger's prediction that the house was not likely to get much backing-up in its new efforts from Felgate, looked likely enough to be fulfilled. While everyone else was full of athletic and scholastic fervour, he remained listless and even sulky. Some said it was because Ainger had proposed the great scheme, and Felgate disdained to play second riddle even to the captain. Others said it was because he could not win anything even if he tried. Others darkly hinted that he was one of the authors of the house's present disgrace; and others whispered that there was no love lost between Railsford and his fourth prefect. In this last conjecture the gossips were right. Felgate and the Master of the Shell had not hit it from the first day of their acquaintance; and within the last few days an occurrence had taken place which had brought the two into violent collision.

Railsford on leaving his room one afternoon had been attracted by the noise of groans and weeping at the far end of the passage. Going in the direction of the melancholy sounds, he discovered Bateson, the Baby, with a face as white as a sheet, huddled up all of a heap, the picture of misery and tribulation.

"What is the matter?" inquired the master.

The sufferer did not hear him at first; but on a repetition of the question he looked up and groaned.

"Oh, I'm dying! I'm so ill! Oh, what *shall I* do?"

Railsford was alarmed. The boy looked so white, and trembled all over. He stooped down to lift him up; but Bateson blubbered.

"Don't touch me, please. Oh, I'm dying!" and rolled over, groaning.

It was no time for parleying. Railsford lifted him up in his arms and looked at him. There were beads of perspiration on his face, and a flavour of strong tobacco about his jacket. Bateson had been smoking. The master carried him downstairs and out into the square, where he set him on his feet. The cool air instantly revived the unhappy boy, and what it left undone a short and sharp fit of sickness completed.

"You're better now," said Railsford, when this little ceremony was over.

Bateson was fain to admit it.

"How many more cigars have you got about you?" inquired the master, as he stalked with the delinquent at his heels into his room, and closed the door.

The Baby was pale this time with terror, not with tobacco. He tremblingly turned out his trousers pockets, and produced a big cigar of which about a quarter had been consumed.

"That's all, really, sir," he faltered.

Railsford took the cigar and sniffed it. In his old college days he would not like to say he had not smoked as good a one himself.

"Very well," said he, handing it back to the astonished Baby. "Now, Bateson, sit down on that chair. Here are some matches. You must finish this cigar to the end before you leave this room."

The wretched Bateson turned green and began to howl.

"Oh no, please sir! Don't say that, sir! It will kill me! Please, Mr Railsford!"

Railsford quietly lit a match, and handed it to the boy. Bateson fairly went down on his knees, and grovelled at the master's feet.

"Oh, Mr Railsford! I'll promise never to touch one again—I really will if you'll only let me off. I should die if you made me. Oh, please!"

Railsford blew out the match and told the boy to get up.

"I never did it before," whimpered Bateson—it was hardly necessary to say that. "I didn't know it was any harm. Felgate said it would do me good. Please, Mr Railsford, may I put it in the fire? I'll never touch such a beastly thing again."

And as Railsford said nothing to prevent it, he flung the origin of his evils into the fire.

"Now go to your room," said the master. "And don't be so foolish again."

Bateson departed, marvelling that he had not been thrashed for his crime, but pretty effectually cured of any ambition to renew his narcotic experiments. Railsford, had he been anyone else but Master of the House, would have enjoyed this little adventure. As it was, he did not like it, for it could scarcely end where it had. He astonished Felgate that evening by a visit to his study.

"Felgate," said he, "I wish to know your reason for giving Bateson a cigar to smoke."

"I give Bateson a cigar, sir?"

"Do you deny it, Felgate?" demanded the master sternly.

"Oh," said the prefect, with a forced laugh, "I believe there was some joke about a cigar. He had a great fancy to try one."

A scornful look came into Railsford's face as he said, "Do you really suppose, Felgate, any good is gained by not telling the truth at once?"

"The truth, sir?" said Felgate, firing up as uncandid persons always do when their veracity is questioned. "I don't understand you, sir."

"You understand me perfectly," said Railsford. "You know that it is against rules for boys to smoke here."

"I wasn't smoking," said Felgate.

"No. You encouraged another boy to do what you dared not do yourself; that is hardly creditable in a prefect."

Felgate shifted his ground.

"There's nothing wrong in smoking," said he; "lots of fellows do it."

"I do it myself," said Railsford bluntly, "but what has that to do with this matter? You, as a monitor, are on your honour to observe the rules of the school, and see that others observe them. You break them yourself, and encourage others to break them. Is there nothing wrong in that?"

Felgate said nothing, and jauntily took up a book.

"Put down that book, and bring me all the cigars or tobacco you have, at once."

Railsford said this quietly and firmly. He had lost his shy, hesitating manner with his prefects; and now, when, for the first time, he was in collision with one of their number, he showed himself a stronger man than Felgate, at any rate, had given him credit for being. The prefect looked for a moment as if he would resist. Then he sullenly went to his locker and produced a case containing four cigars.

"These are all you have?"

Felgate nodded.

"They are confiscated by the rules of the school," said Railsford. "They will be returned to you after breaking-up. I wish I were able to return them to you now, and rely on your honour not to repeat your offence."

"I don't want them back," said Felgate, with a sneer. "You may smoke them yourself, sir."

He repented of the insult before it had left his lips. Railsford, however, ignored it, and quietly taking the cigars from the case, took them away with him, leaving the case on the table. Felgate's impulse was to follow him and apologise for his ill-bred words. But his evil genius kept him back; and before bed-time arrived he not only repented of his repentance, but reproached himself for not saying a great deal more than he had. Felgate had a wonderful gift of self-delusion. He knew he had acted wrongly and meanly. "And yet," he argued, "smoking is no crime, and if the school rules make it one, it doesn't follow that I'm a sinner if I have a whiff now and then. He admits he smokes himself. He doesn't call himself a sinner. Easy enough for him to be high and mighty. One law for him and another for me."

Poor young Bateson had a sorry time of it for the next week. In his terror at the prospect of having to smoke that awful cigar to the bitter end, he had scarcely known what he was saying; and it was not until Felgate charged him with being a sneak that he realised he had said anything to compromise his senior. Felgate was not one of the vulgar noisy sort of bullies, but a good deal worse. He made the wretched Baby's life miserable with all sorts of exquisite torture. He hounded him on to break rules, and then caught him red-handed, and held over his head threats of exposure and punishment. He passed the word round the house that the boy was a tell-tale, and little was the mercy poor Bateson got either from friend or foe when that became known. Nor did Felgate, in his revengeful whims, omit the orthodox functions of the bully. Only he took care to perform such ceremonies in private, for fear of a mishap. But in these precautions he unluckily reckoned without his host.

Railsford, after what had happened, was hardly likely to consider Bateson's lot a happy one, and kept a sharp look-out to prevent any mischief coming to the luckless Baby on account of his confessions. For some days, no sign of any such trouble came under the master's notice; and he was beginning to congratulate himself that Felgate had taken a proper view of his delinquencies, and was taking the only manly course of making amends, when the smouldering fires broke out unexpectedly and fiercely. Master Bateson was one of those practical young gentlemen who believe in having a shilling's worth for a shilling; and when after a day or two he heard himself called a sneak from every corner of the house, it occurred to him, "What's the use of being called a sneak if I'm not one?" Whereupon he marched off to Railsford, and informed him that Felgate had twice screwed his arm; once made him catch hold of a poker at the hot end—the proof whereof he bore on his hand—had once made him stand in the corner on one foot for the space of an hour by the clock; and had half a dozen times threatened him that unless he did something wrong he would accuse him of theft or some other horrible crime to the doctor. By reason of which ill-usage and threats, he, the deponent, went in bodily fear of his life.

"Oh, and please, Mr Railsford, be sure and not let him know I told you, or he'll kill me!"

Railsford had another uncomfortable interview with Felgate after this. Felgate as usual began by impugning the junior's veracity, but on the master's proposing to send for the boy, and let him repeat his story there and then, he sullenly admitted that he might have played practical jokes on his tender person of the kind suggested. When Railsford said the matter was a serious one, the prefect smiled deprecatingly, and said it was not pleasant to him to be spoken to in this manner, and that if Mr Railsford wished to punish him he would be glad to have it over and done with. Railsford said that the question in his mind was whether he would allow Felgate to continue a prefect of the house. Whereupon Felgate promptly changed colour and dropped his sneer entirely.

"I'm sure," said he, "I had no intention of hurting him. I may have been a trifle inconsiderate, but I didn't suppose—he didn't complain to me, so I could hardly know he minded it."

"I can have very little confidence in a prefect who acts as you have done, Felgate."

"You may depend on me, sir, not to touch him again."

"I want to depend on more than that," said the master. "As a prefect, you hold a position of influence in the house. If that influence is badly used—"

"I don't think you will have to complain any more," said Felgate.

"I sincerely hope not—for you may be sure another offence of this kind could not possibly be passed over. For the present I shall say no more about this, and shall do my best to treat you with the same confidence as heretofore. Just now we need all to work together for the good of our house and the school; and the boys are sure to look to the prefects to help them. Good-night, Felgate."

The grimace with which the prefect returned the salute, after the door closed, might have convinced Railsford, had he seen it, that he had done no good either to himself, the house, or the prefect by his leniency. As it was, he was destined to make the discovery later on. Felgate, to all appearances, resumed his old ways in the house. He let young Bateson alone, and kept to himself his feud with the master. He even attempted to pretend a languid interest in the new ambitions of his fellow-prefects, and at Ainger's request entered his name for one of the events in the sports list. Railsford observed with some relief that he appeared to recognise the force of the rebuke which had been administered him, and with characteristic hopefulness was tempted to look upon the incident as ended.

It was by no means ended. Felgate, to all appearance docile and penitent, nursed his wrath within him, and kept his eye open, with all the keenness of a sportsman, to the slightest opening for a revenge. In a quiet way he continued to do a great deal in the house to thwart the spirit of enterprise which was at present knitting all factions together. He sneered in a superior way at the enthusiasm all round him, and succeeded in making one or two of the fellows a little ashamed of their own eagerness.

The funds for Railsford's testimonial came in slowly. The result of a fortnight's hard work was only four shillings and threepence, and to get even that wretched sum Arthur had made himself temporary enemies all over the house. He wrote an urgent letter to Daisy, to "shell out" something, and strove to work on the feelings of his parents to assist him to do honour to their future son-in-law. Meanwhile he conceived the wild project of approaching the prefects on the subject. Unluckily for everybody, he made his first attempt with Felgate.

"A testimonial for Marky?" inquired that worthy. "What for?"

"Well, you know he's been pretty civil since he came, and he's backed us up in that row about Bickers, you know. We thought we'd get him a ring, you know. He's spoons on my sister Daisy, and Dig and I thought it would fetch him if we stuck 'Chuckey'—that's the pet name he calls her—on it. Don't you think it would be a good dodge? He'd be sure to be pleased if he saw your name on the list of subscribers, Felgate."

"I'm certain of that," said Felgate, laughing, "and if only I'd got any tin I'd be delighted. By the way, I fancy I did see a sixpence kicking about somewhere."

"Thanks, awfully. That'll be a stunning lift. He's sure to be extra civil to you after it."

"Oh, I see. Bribery, is it?" said Felgate, laughing. "And what particular reason have you for getting Mr Chuckey a testimonial?"

"Ha, ha!" said Arthur, who felt bound to laugh at the senior's joke. "Jolly good name for him. Oh, some of the fellows think he's backed us up, you know, about Bickers and all that. Thanks awfully for the sixpence, Felgate. I'll be sure and stick your name at the top of the list. I say, when's that trial adjourned to?"

"I don't know. By the way, youngster, what a smart barrister you made that evening. Where did you pick it all up?"

"Oh, I don't know," said Arthur, feeling rather flattered. "Dig and I went and heard a chap tried at the Old Bailey once. It was rather slow. But, I say, do you really think I doubled up Dig well? He was awfully wild."

"I don't wonder. You did it splendidly. Whatever put all the things into your head?"

"Oh, I don't know," said Arthur, getting a little "tilted" with all this flattery from a senior. "It was a notion I had."

"Not half a bad notion," said Felgate, beginning to think the game was worth following up. "Not one fellow in a dozen would have thought about that match-box up on the ledge."

"That's just it. It must have been a tall chap to put it up there."

"Of course, unless someone got on a chair."

"I thought of that," responded Arthur grandly; "only there were one or two other things to come out if I'd had time. I say, do you know when it's adjourned to?"

"I don't know. I hope not for long. I'd like to hear what else you've got. I could never make up such things to save my life."

"Perhaps I didn't make them up," said Arthur, who felt that for once in a way thorough justice was being done to his own cleverness.

"You don't mean you can produce the actual match-box? Why, you ought to be made Attorney-General or Lord Chancellor."

"Can't I, though, I can!" said Arthur, "and something else too. Suppose we'd found the door was kept open with a wedge of paper addressed in a certain handwriting to a certain name—eh? and suppose the sack had the initials on it of the same fellow that the paper and match-box belonged to—eh? That would make a pretty hot case for our side, wouldn't it?"

"My word, youngster; you're a sharp one. But I suppose it's all make-up!"

"Not a bit of it," said Arthur, flushed by his triumph.

"I'll believe it when I see it," said Felgate sceptically.

"I'll show it you now," said Arthur, "if you'll promise to keep it dark. I'm not making up a bit of it."

"If you aren't, all I can say is—Where are they?"

"Come and see," said Arthur, leading the way to his study.

Dig was out on leave in the village.

"There you are," said Arthur, when he had opened his locker and produced the precious relics. "There's the match-box. Have you ever seen any others of the same kind? I have."

"I fancy I saw one once," said Felgate.

"Belonging to a fellow six foot two who could reach up to the ledge?"

Felgate nodded.

"Now look at that paper—a bit of the *Standard*: there's part of the address. I fancy I know my sister Daisy's fist when I see it. There you are! That was screwed up to jam open the door to keep it from sliding-to. Six foot two again. Then there's the sack—precious like an M and an R those two letters, aren't they? and M R is precious like the initials of six foot two again. I don't blame him if he did scrag old Bickers—very good job; and as it happens, it don't hurt our house very much now we're going to get all the sports; and I'm booked for the Swift Exhibition—£20 a-year for three years. We mean to back him up, and that's one reason why we're going to give him the testimonial—though none of the chaps except Dig knows about these things. I say, be sure you keep it quiet, Felgate, won't you? I trust you not to tell anybody a word about it."

"Don't you be afraid of me, youngster," said Felgate. "I'd advise you to take good care of those things. We'll have some fun with them when the trial comes on again. Don't go saying too much about it till then. Did I give you the sixpence? No? There it is. Put it down from 'A Friend.' I must go now, young 'un."

He departed, leaving Arthur to pack up his treasures, amid some misgivings lest the sixpence in his hand was after all hardly worth the secret he had bought it with.

Chapter Fourteen.

Challenging the Record.

On the Monday before Railsford's sports, Ainger and Barnworth sat rather dismally conning a document which lay on the table between them.

It was Smedley's report of the School sports held the Saturday before, and was sufficiently alarming to dishearten any ordinary reader.

"'The Mile Race. Smedley 1, Branscombe 2. Time 4 minutes 50 seconds.' Whew!" said Ainger, "I can't beat that; 4.52 is the shortest I've done it in, and I doubt if I could do that again."

"Fiddlesticks! If you don't do it in 4.48 you deserve to be sent home to the nursery. But do you see Branscombe gave up before the end? That's odd. I rather thought he was the better man of the two."

"Branscombe seems to be down on his luck altogether this term," said Ainger. "I fancy he hasn't a very sweet time at Bickers's."

"But he ought to have won the mile, for all that. He's got the longest legs in Grandcourt, and used to have the best wind."

"Gone stale," said Ainger, "and growing too fast. Why, he must be as tall as Railsford already; and he's good for an inch or so more."

"Poor beggar! But what about the high jump?"

"High jump? Smedley and Clipstone a tie, 5 feet 4½."

"Thank you," said Barnworth. "I may as well scratch at once. I once jumped that, but that was in the days of my youth."

"Fiddlesticks! If you don't clear 5 feet 5, you deserve to be sent home to a daily governess," said Ainger, laughing. "And, by the way, I hear Wake has been jumping finely lately. Mind he doesn't do it for you."

"Wake had better mind his own business," responded Barnworth. "I, a prefect and a very great person in this house, should greatly resent it if a Fifth-form fellow beat me at the jump. Upon my word I'd give him 100 lines."

"'Cricket-ball. Clipstone 77 yards.' What a poor throw! Felgate is sure to beat that, at any rate."

"Not if he can help," said Barnworth. "In fact, if I were you, I would either scratch him, or see someone else is in too, to make sure of it. Unless you do, we lose it."

"Do you mean he'd throw short on purpose?"

"My dear fellow, you are just beginning to perceive what anybody who isn't a born simpleton would have seen for himself a week ago."

Ainger's brow clouded. "I'll enter myself, then," said he.

"No you won't; enter Stafford. Stafford won't get the mile, which you will. A little success may keep him with us; otherwise the odds are he may go over to the enemy—*alias* your friend Felgate."

Ainger wrote Stafford's name down there and then.

In this way the two friends went through the list. It was a strong record to beat, and if they were doubtful of themselves they were still more doubtful of some of their juniors.

For instance, Arthur, if he meant to win the long jump under sixteen, would have to clear 15 feet 8 inches; and Dimsdale, to secure the 100 yards under fifteen, would have to do it in 13 seconds. Tilbury was safe for the cricket-ball in his class; and Arthur, if he took care, might beat Smith's record for the Shell half-mile. Most of the other events were decidedly doubtful, and it was evident the week which remained would need to be used well, if the ambitious attempt of Railsford's house was to succeed. By no means the least interested peruser of the list when presently it was posted up on the common room door Railsford himself.

For a week or two past he had been as nearly happy as he could be in the congenial work of training and encouraging the youthful athletes of his house. He had felt drawn to them and they to him by quite a new bond of sympathy. He spared himself in nothing for the common cause, and his enthusiasm was, as might be expected, contagious.

"There are one or two of these records we shall not beat," said the master to Ainger; "but the majority of them we should be able to manage."

He spoke so hopefully that Ainger's spirits went up decidedly. A final overhaul of the list was made, and the times registered compared with the times on the School list. In one or two cases Railsford advised that a second man should be run with a good start, in order to force the pace, and through one or two names belonging to hopeless triflers or malcontents he quietly passed his pencil.

"I see Stafford has entered for the cricket-ball," said he, "as well as Felgate; how is that?"

"We should lose the cricket-ball otherwise," said Ainger. "Felgate may do his best if someone is against him, but he won't if he's the only man in for us. He has no interest in sports."

Railsford's face clouded.

"Is Stafford the best man to enter? Should not you or Barnworth go in?"

"I think not, sir. Stafford made some good practice yesterday, and can beat the School record as it is."

During the next few days every spare moment at Railsford's house was used in preparing for the great trial of Saturday. Nor, strange to say, did the school-work suffer in consequence. The idlers in the Shell, being in the way of spurts, took a sudden spurt of interest in class—partly for fear of being excluded by detention or otherwise from Saturday's celebration, and partly because the healthy condition of their bodies had begotten for the time being a healthier condition of mind. Arthur and the baronet actually knew their syntax for two days running, and the astounding phenomenon of a perfectly empty detention-room occurred on both the Friday and the Saturday. The latter event was specially satisfactory to Railsford, as he was able to secure the services of Monsieur Lablache as assistant-judge—not exactly a popular appointment, but, failing any better, one which fellows had to make the best of.

The house rose that Saturday morning with a full sense of the crisis which was upon it. Despite Felgate's sneers, and the jealous ridicule which floated in from outside on their efforts, they felt that they stood face to face with a great chance. Their reputation as a house was on its trial; they were boycotted by the doctor, and held up as a warning to evil-doers. They resolved to make themselves a warning to good and evil-doers alike that day, and show the doctor and everyone else that the spirit was not yet knocked out of them.

The half-holiday at Railsford's, as we have said, began under the new *régime* immediately after breakfast, and ended at one o'clock, so that the farce of morning school did not interpose to chill the ardour of the combatants. The whole house assembled in flannels in honour of the occasion. The weather was very much like what the School had had a week ago; if anything, the ground was hardly in quite as good condition. At any rate, it was felt that, as far as externals went, the test between the two days' performances would be a fair one. True, there was something a little chilly about the empty field. The usual inspiriting crowd of partisan spectators was absent, and the juniors of Railsford, who usually had to fight for front places, felt it a little dismal when they discovered that they could occupy any position they liked—even the ladies' stand.

Arthur was very angry with himself for not getting Daisy down for the occasion. Her presence would have lent undoubted prestige both to himself and Dig, as well as to Railsford; and if she could have given the prizes afterwards it would have been a magnificent family affair. He bemoaned this omission to Railsford himself as he walked down with him to the fields. However, just before proceedings begun, the wished-for excitement was supplied by three most unexpected arrivals on the course. The first was that of the doctor's niece, who, having watched the School sports a week ago with great interest, and being secretly rather sorry for the misfortunes which had over taken Railsford's house, saw no reason why she should not take her accustomed place in the stand to-day. The boys were just in the mood to appreciate this little act of chivalry, and as she shyly walked up to the pavilion, they welcomed her with a cheer which brought the blushes to her cheeks and a smile of half-frightened pleasure to her lips. Boys who had seen her every day for the last three months in chapel suddenly discovered that she was simply charming; they greeted her much as mortals in distress would greet the apparition of the good fairy, and fifty champions there and then were ready to do battle for her, and only wished they had the chance.

The excitement of this arrival was hardly passed when another figure appeared on the scene, hardly less important or less popular. This was no other than Smedley, the School captain, who had asked and obtained special leave from Mr Roe to be present as representing the school on the occasion. He was still indignant at the disabilities imposed upon the rival house; and though he by no means wished it success in its ambitious project of beating the School record, his sense of fair play told him that if no one was on the ground to represent the other houses, they would compete at a disadvantage. If it went out that the School captain had been present, everyone, at any rate, would have to admit there had been fair play and no opening for dispute, whatever the result might be. So Smedley, although it might be to see his own record beaten, came down to the fields that morning. There was a little uncertainty as to his reception at first, for Railsford's was in an Ishmaelitish mood, and was ready to call everybody an enemy who wasn't on its side.

But when Ainger was heard to say—

"Hurrah! he's a regular brick to come and back us up like this!" everybody jumped to the correct view of Smedley's motives, and cheered him scarcely less enthusiastically than they had just now cheered their "Queen of Love and Beauty."

"I only wish he was in his flannels," said Arthur, "and would run the mile against us. It would be something like to lick him off his own stride."

Arthur was rather proud of his athletic slang. What he meant was that he would sooner see Ainger win the mile against Smedley himself than against Smedley's time.

"Never mind, he's going to be the judge, do you see? I say, old man, you and I'll have to sit up now."

This was the universal effect of the captain's presence. Perhaps he hardly realised himself what an advantage his presence was conferring on his rivals.

The first event on the programme was the Babies' hundred yards, for which our friends Bateson and Jukes were entered, with the serious record of twenty-two seconds to beat. They were both a little pale and nervous with the excitement of opening the ball, and looked round wistfully, first at Railsford, then at Smedley, where he stood, watch in hand, at the winning-post, and then up at the ladies' stand.

"Now, youngsters," said Railsford, "do your very best. You ought both of you to run it under twenty seconds. Are you ready now? Off!"

The flood-gates were opened now; and from this moment till the end of the sports Railsford's kept up a continual roar. Both Bateson and Jukes had little difficulty in registering a double victory for their house. Bateson covered the ground in nineteen seconds and Jukes in twenty-one. While the cheers for this initial victory were in full cry, the third of that morning's apparitions came upon the scene. This was no other than Mr Bickers, at sight of whom a chill fell upon the assembly. What did he want there? Hadn't he done them harm enough? Who asked him to come? Why wasn't he making his own fellows miserable instead of coming here and spoiling their fun?

Mr Bickers, after looking round him, and taking in the scene generally, walked up to the ladies' stand. Fellows dropped back sullenly to make room for him, although one or two pretended not to notice him and continued to stand and shout "Bateson!" "Jukes," until he pushed them aside.

"Good-morning, Miss Violet," said he, lifting his hat. "I did not expect to see you here."

"Didn't you, Mr Bickers? I'm going to see all the events. They have just run the first race, and Bateson and Jukes have both beaten the boy in your house who won last week. Haven't you a programme? Mr Railsford will give you one."

"Thank you. I'm not staying long. It will be rather dull for you, will it not?"

"Dull!" said Miss Phyllis, laughing. "*I* don't think it dull, thank you."

Mr Bickers walked slowly into the enclosure, watched by everyone. Railsford greeted him with a nod, and then walked off to the starting-post to prepare for the next race. The prefects of the house looked another way, and Smedley was busy comparing his watch with that of monsieur.

"Smedley," said Mr Bickers, "how come you to be here? You ought to be in your house."

"I have an *exeat*, sir," said the captain.

"From the doctor?"

"From Mr Roe."

"Mr Roe can scarcely be aware that I have refused a similar application to boys in my own house."

Smedley made no reply to this observation, about which he had nothing to say.

"You had better go in, Smedley. I will explain to Mr Roe."

Smedley looked at him in blank astonishment. It sounded more like a jest than sober earnest.

"I have my master's *exeat*" he said; "if he or the doctor cancels it I shall go in at once, sir."

It was Mr Bickers's turn to stare now. He had overdone it for once in a way. His genius for interference had carried him a step too far; and with a "Very good, Smedley," in terms which were meant to be ominous, he turned away and proceeded to where Railsford was.

It was to speak to Railsford that he had come out into the fields that morning. His interviews with Miss Violet and the captain had been by the way. Railsford was busy marshalling the competitors for the Shell quarter-mile, of whom there was an unusual number. He was too much engrossed to notice Mr Bickers until that gentleman called him by name.

"I want a word with you, Railsford," said Mr Bickers.

"Now then, toe the line and be ready. Be careful about fouling. Are you ready?"

"Railsford, I want a word with you."

Railsford looked sharply round and perceived who the intruder was.

"I can't speak to you now, Mr Bickers, I'm busy. Now, boys, are you all ready? Off!"

And he started to run beside the race. Mr Bickers put as cheerful a face on this little rebuff as he could, and presently walked across to the winning-post to make another attempt. The race had been well won by Tilbury, who had beaten the School record hollow, and shown himself a long way ahead of his fellow-runners. He of course came in for an ovation, which included a "Well run" from Smedley, and a "Bravo, indeed" from Railsford, which he valued specially. It was while he was receiving these friendly greetings that Mr Bickers once more approached Railsford.

"Now you have a moment or two to spare," he began.

"I've not a moment to spare," said Railsford, irritated. "What do you want?"

"I want you to look at this letter. It concerns you."

And he produced an envelope from his pocket.

"Give it to me," said Railsford. "I'll read it when I have time."

"No, thank you. I want you to—"

"Ring the bell for the high jump," said Railsford, turning his back. At the signal the whole company closed in a solid phalanx round the poles. For the high jump was one of the great events of the day. Mr Bickers became mixed up in the crowd, and saw that it was hopeless to attempt further parley. He turned on his heel, and the fellows made a lane for him to pass out. As he got clear, and began slowly to retreat to his own house, the boys raised a loud defiant cheer. But whether this was to hail his departure or to greet the appearance of Barnworth and Wake, ready stripped for the fray, it would be difficult to say. But whichever it was, Mr Bickers seemed by no means discomfited. He turned and caught sight of the head and shoulders of his rival towering among his boys, and he smiled to himself and tapped the letter in his hand.

"Not a moment to spare!" said he to himself. "Good. We can wait. You may not be in such a hurry to get rid of me when you do read it; and your dear boys may change their minds about their hero, too," added he, as a fresh cheer, mingled with a "Huzza for Railsford," was wafted across the fields.

Chapter Fifteen.

Mr Bickers prefers the Door to the Window.

The history of the great events of Railsford's sports were so faithfully chronicled at the time by Arthur Herapath in a long letter to his sister Daisy, that it would be presumption on my part, with that valuable document lying before me, to attempt to narrate in my own words what has been so much more vivaciously described by my young friend. Arthur was great at letter-writing, especially to his sister. And there is small doubt that, with the aid of a slang dictionary and a little imagination on her own part, that sympathetic young person was usually able to catch the drift of her young brother's rollicking lucubrations.

"Dear Da. Thanks awfully for the bob."

A good many of Arthur's letters began with this curious observation. Whether this particular "bob" had reference to Railsford's testimonial or not, the writer cannot speak positively.

"We had a ripping time at our sports, and licked all the records but three. No end of a crow for us. The School's tearing its hair all over the place, and our fellows have been yelling for two days without stopping. It's a jolly good job that row about Bickers came on when it did, as our chaps would never have pulled themselves together as they did without it. Nobody wants to find the chap out now; so your particular is all serene up to now, and I don't mean to drip and spoil his game." (We wonder what Daisy made of this curious sentence when she read it!) "Dig and I were awfully riled we hadn't got you down for the sports, and I wanted Marky to wire up for you and put them off till you came. As it was, it didn't matter a bit, for Miss Violet showed up like a trump as she is, and backed us up; so it's just as well you hadn't come. Violet nodded to me! She's the most beautiful girl in the world. Smedley turned up too; brickish, wasn't it? Bickers of course came, and tried to spoil our sports, but Marky gave him a flea in his ear, and Dig and I howled; so he didn't stay long.

"Bateson and Jukes pulled off the kids' hundred yards; and jolly cocky they were, I can tell you. Bateson's the sneak I told you of.

"Tilbury won the Shell quarter-mile. Dig and I were in for it, but we wanted to save ourselves for the long jump and hurdles, so we ran easy, and Tilbury did it hands down.

"Ah, Da, really you should have been there to see the high jump! Smedley and Clipstone tied 5 4½ last week for the School. No end of a jump to beat; and Dig and I were in a blue funk about our men. Barnworth and Wake were the only two entered;—dark horses both; at least *I* didn't know what either of them could do. I heard Ainger tell Violet he thought we'd pull it off, so I perked up. They started at 4 foot 10. Wake muffed his first jump, and we gave ourselves up for gone 'coons. However, he hopped over second try. They went up by inches to five feet. My word! you should have seen the way Violet clapped! They'd have been cads if they hadn't gone over, with her backing them up like that. Wake's got the rummiest jump you ever saw. He runs sideways at the bar, and sort of lies down on his back on it as he goes over. You'd think he'd muff it every time, but just as he looks like done for, he kicks up his foot and clears. Barnworth takes it straight—skips up to the bar and goes over like a daisy, without seeming to try.

"At 5 foot 1, Wake mulled twice, and we thought he was out of it. But the third time he got over finely with a good inch to spare. It got precious ticklish after this; and no one said a word till each Jump was done: and then we let out. Violet stood up and looked as if she'd got a ten-pound note on the event. At 5 foot 3 Barnworth came a cropper; and I fancy he must have screwed his foot. Anyhow, he had to sit a minute before he tried again. Then he went over like a shot—and you may guess we yelled. Five foot 3½. Both of them mulled the first—but Barnworth cleared easily second shot. We fancied Wake would too, but he missed both his other chances, and so got out of it. Awfully good jump this for a Fifth-form chap.

"Barnworth pulled himself together after that, and cleared the 5 foot 3½ and 5 foot 4 first go. Then came the tug. The bar went up to 5 4½, Smedley's jump, and you might have heard a fly cough. We were pretty nervous, I can tell you, and it would have done you good to see Violet standing up and holding her breath. Barnworth was the only chap that didn't seem flurried. Smedley and Marky both looked blue, and poor Froggy looked as if he was going to blubber.

"My wig! Daisy, if you'd heard the yell when the beggar cleared the bar first shot! Dig and I went mad; and somebody had to clout us on the head before we could take it in that the fun wasn't over. Of course it was not. *Pas un morceau de il*—we'd tied them; but we'd still to lick them.

"'Bravo, Barnworth,' yells Violet. 'Go it, old kangaroo,' howls Dig. 'Take your time and tuck in that shoe-lace,' says Marky. 'A million to one on our man,' says I; and then up goes the bar to 5 foot 5; and then you could have heard a caterpillar wink. Old Barnworth looked a little green himself this time; and didn't seem in a hurry to begin. He muffed his first jump, and we all thought the game was up. But no! The beggar hopped over second time as easily as I could hop 3 feet. My word, it was a hop! Dig stood on his head and I could have done so too, only Violet was looking. She was no end glad. *Elle est une brique et une demie!* So's Smedley; for though it was his jump was beaten, he cheered as loud as anybody. I forgive him the licking he gave me last term. Marky made a regular ass of himself, he was so pleased. Every one wanted Barnworth to go on, but he wouldn't, as he had a race to come on.

"Then came the Shell hurdles, 120 yards, ten flights. Dig and I were in, and had to beat 19½ seconds. I felt jolly miserable, I can tell you, at the start, and that ass Dig made it all the worse by fooling about just to show off, and making believe to spar at me, when he was shaking in his shoes all the time; Marky wasn't much better, for he came and said, 'You'll have to run your very best to win it.' As if we didn't know that! He don't deserve a testimonial for doing a thing like that. Next that ass Smedley went and made up to Violet just when she wanted to back us up, and I don't believe she saw a bit of the race till the finish. It was enough to make any chap blue. Then monsieur started us, and kept us waiting a whole minute (it seemed like an hour) while the second hand of his wretched watch was getting round. And then he started us in such a rotten way that it wasn't till I saw Dig running that I took in we were off, and coming up to the first hurdle. But soon the fellows began to yell, and I felt better.

"Dig had the pull of me at the start, but I got up to him at the third hurdle. He missed a step in landing, and that put him out, and we went over the fourth and fifth neck and neck. Then I saw Violet stand up, out of the corner of my left eye; and Smedley began to look at us too. After that it was all right. At the sixth hurdle we both rose together, and then I heard a crack and a grunt behind me, and knew poor old Dig had come a cropper. Of course I had no time to grin, as I had my time to beat. But it was very lonely doing those next three hurdles. I didn't know how I was going, only I could swear I'd been twenty seconds long before I got to the eighth. I nearly mulled the ninth, and lost a step after the jump. That made me positive I'd not beaten my time; and I had half a mind to pull up, I was so jolly miserable. However, the fellows were still yelling, so I pulled myself together and went at the last hurdle viciously and got clean over, and then put it on all I could to the winning-post. I guessed I'd done it in thirty seconds, and wished there was a pit I could tumble into at the end.

"Then Marky came and patted me on the back. 'Splendid, old fellow,' said he. 'How do you mean?' said I; 'ain't I licked into a cocked hat?' 'You've done it in nineteen seconds,' said he. 'Go on!' said I. And then the other fellows came up and cheered, and then Violet called out, 'Bravo, Herapath,' and Ainger said, 'Run indeed, young 'un.' So I had to believe it; and I can tell you I was a bit pleased. *J'étais un morceau plaisé.*

"I was sorry for old Dig, but he won the Shell wide jump directly afterwards. I made a mess of the half-mile. I ought to have got it from Smythe, of the School-house; but all I could do was to dead heat his time. I suppose I was fagged after the hurdles. Tilbury had it all his own way with the Shell cricket-ball, and Stafford got the senior throw. Felgate was in against him—rather a decent chap, one of our prefects; had me to tea in his room the other day. He and Marky don't hit it. He was lazy, and didn't bother himself. Fellows said he could easily have licked the School record if he'd tried; but he didn't; and Stafford missed it by a few inches. So that event we lost. Jolly sell, *joli vendre.*

"Never mind, we got the mile, and that was the crackest thing of all. We had to beat Smedley and Branscombe, both—only Branscombe—he's Bickers's prefect—didn't run it out last week. Smedley's time was 4.50. Ainger and Stafford ran for us; and Ranger was put on the track with 200 yards start to force the pace.

"Stafford was out of it easily; but Ranger stuck to it like a Trojan. The first lap he was still a hundred yards to the good, and going like steam. Ainger ran finely, and overhauled him gradually. Still he had about twenty yards to the good at the beginning of the last lap. Then it was fine to see Ainger tuck in his elbows and let himself out. A quarter of a mile from home Ranger was clean out of it, regularly doubled up; but Ainger kept on steadily for a couple of hundred yards.

"Then, my word, he spurted right away to the finish! You never saw such a rush up as it was! The fellows *yelled*, I can let you know. Every one knew that it was our event the second the spurt began, and when he got up to the tape and '4.42' was shouted out, it was a sight to see the state we were in. It's the best mile we ever did at Grandcourt, and even Smedley, though he was a bit riled, I fancy, at his licking, said he couldn't have done it in the time if he'd tried.

"I send you Dig's programme, with the times all marked. You'll see we won them all except the senior cricket-ball, half-mile, and senior hundred. It's a rattling good score for us, I can tell you; and we cheered Marky like one o'clock. It was an awful sell Violet couldn't give away our prizes; but she shied at it. I suppose old Pony would have gruffed at her. She is the most beautiful girl in the world.

"You needn't go telling the *mater*, but I was off my feed a whole day after the sports. How soon do fellows get money enough to marry? If I get the Swift Scholarship I shall have £20 a-year for three years—something to start with. I wish you'd come down and give me a leg-up. I'm afraid that cad Smedley's got his eye on her. His father's only a doctor. We're better off than that, besides being chummy with a baronet. Hullo! there's the bell for cubicles. Ta, ta. *Je suis très miserable.* Your aff. A.H."

Little dreaming of the sad blight which had come over his future young kinsman's life, Railsford was sitting in his room that Sunday evening, feeling rather more than usually comfortable. He had some cause to be pleased. His house had done better than anyone expected. They had beaten all the records but three, and, without being specially conceited, Railsford took to himself the credit of having done a good deal to bring about this satisfactory result.

"Curious," said he to himself, "that in all probability, if that affair of Bickers's had not happened, we might never have risen as a house; indeed, it's almost a mercy the culprit has never been discovered, for we should have then been plunged back into the current, and the work of pulling ourselves together might never have been done. It's odd that, as time goes on, there is not even a hint or a suspicion who did it. There's only one boy in the house I'm not sure of, and he is too great a coward to be a ruffian. Well, well, we have the cricket season and the exams, coming on. If only we do as well in them as we've done in the sports, it will not be altogether against us if the mystery remains a mystery a little longer."

Whereupon the door opened and Mr Bickers stepped in. Railsford had completely forgotten the episode in the fields the previous day; he scarcely recollected that Mr Bickers had been present at the sports, and was delightfully oblivious to the fact that he, Railsford, had either slighted or offended his colleague. He wondered what was the occasion of the present visit, and secretly resolved to keep both his temper and his head if he could.

"Good-evening," said he, with a friendly smile. "I'm just going to have my coffee; won't you have a cup too, Bickers?"

Mr Bickers took no notice of this hospitable invitation, but closed the door behind him and said, "I want a few words with you, Mr Railsford."

"Certainly? I've nothing to do— Won't you take a seat?"

Mr Bickers took a seat, a little disconcerted by Railsford's determined good-humour. He had not counted upon that.

"The last time I saw you you were hardly so polite," said he, with a sneer.

"When was that? I'm very sorry if I was rude; I had no intention, I assure you."

Railsford began to feel a little like the lamb in the fable. This wolf had evidently come bent on a quarrel, and Railsford, lamb and all as he was, would have liked to oblige him. But he was quick enough to see—with the memory of more than one failure to warn him—that his only chance with Mr Bickers was, at all costs, not to quarrel.

"You are fortunate in your short memory; it is a most convenient gift."

"It's one, at any rate, I would like to cultivate with regard to any unpleasantness there may have been between you and me, Bickers," said Railsford.

This was not a happy speech, and Mr Bickers accepted it with a laugh.

"Quite so; I can understand that. It happens, however, that I have come to assist in prolonging your memory with regard to that unpleasantness. I'm sorry to interfere with your good intentions, but it cannot be helped this time."

"Really," said Railsford, feeling his patience considerably taxed, "all this is very perplexing. Would you mind coming to the point at once, Bickers?"

"Not at all. When I saw you yesterday I asked you to look at a letter I had with me."

"Oh, yes; I remember now. I was greatly taken up with the sports, and had no time then. I felt sure you would understand."

"I understood perfectly. I have brought the letter for you now," and he held it out.

Railsford took it with some curiosity, for Mr Bickers's manner, besides being offensive, was decidedly mysterious.

"Am I to read it?"

"Please."

The letter was a short one, written in an evidently disguised hand:

"Sir,—The name of the person who maltreated you lately is perfectly well-known in Railsford's house. No one knows his name better than Mr Railsford himself. But as the house is thriving by what has occurred, it is to nobody's interest to let out the secret. The writer of this knows what he is speaking about, and where to find the proofs.—A Friend."

Railsford read this strange communication once or twice, and then laughed.

"It's amusing, isn't it?" sneered Mr Bickers.

"It's absurd!" said Railsford.

"I thought you would say so," said Bickers, taking back the letter and folding it up. "For all that, I should like to know the name of the person referred to."

"You surely do not mean, Bickers, that you attach any importance to a ridiculous joke like that?"

"I attach just the importance it deserves, Railsford."

"Then I would put it in the fire, Bickers."

Mr Bickers's face darkened. Long ere now he had calculated on reducing the citadel of his adversary's good-humour, and now that it still held out, he felt his own self-possession deserting him.

"Allow me to tell you, Railsford, that I believe what that letter states!"

"Do you really? I hope when I tell you that every word of it which relates to myself is a grotesque falsehood, you will alter your opinion."

"Even that would not convince me," said Bickers.

Railsford stared at him blankly. He had surely misunderstood his words.

"I said," he repeated, and there was a tremor of excitement in his voice, which afforded his enemy the keenest pleasure—"I said that every word in that letter which refers to me is false. You surely don't believe it after that?"

"I said," repeated Mr Bickers, with a fine sneer, "that even that would not convince me."

Surely the longed-for explosion would come now! He saw Railsford's face flush and his eyes flash. But before the furious retort escaped from his lips, a wise whisper from somewhere fell between them and robbed the wolf of his prey.

"Then," said the Master of the Shell, forcing his lips to a smile, "there is not much to be gained by prolonging this interview, is there?"

Mr Bickers was deeply mortified. There was nothing for it now but for him to assume the *rôle* of aggressor. He would so much have preferred to be the aggrieved.

"Yes, Railsford," said he, rising from his chair and standing over his enemy. "I dare you to say that you neither know nor suspect the person who assaulted me!"

Railsford felt devoutly thankful he had kept his head. He now dug his hands into his pockets, stretched himself, and replied,—

"You may very safely do that, Bickers."

It was hard lines for poor Bickers, this. He had worked so hard to get himself an adversary; and here was all his labour being lost!

"You're paltering," snarled he. "I dare you to say you did not do the cowardly deed yourself!"

Railsford could not imagine how he had ever been so foolish as to be in a rage with the fellow. He laughed outright at the last piece of bluster. Bickers was now fairly beside himself, or he would never have done what he did. He struck Railsford where he sat a blow on the mouth, which brought blood to his lips. This surely was the last card, and Railsford in after years never knew exactly how it came about that he did not fly there and then at his enemy's throat, and shake him as a big dog shakes a rat. It may have been he was too much astonished to do anything of the sort; or it may have been that he, the stronger man of the two, felt a sort of pity for the poor bully, which kept him back. At any rate, his good genius befriended him this time, and saved him both his dignity and his moral vantage. He put his handkerchief to his lips for a moment, and then said quietly—

"There are two ways of leaving this room, Bickers: the door and the window. I advise you to choose the door."

Mr Bickers was too cowed by his own act to keep up the contest, and hating himself at that moment almost as much—but not quite—as he hated his enemy, he slunk out of the door and departed to his own house. Railsford sat where he was, and stared at the door by which his visitor had left, in a state of bewildered astonishment.

The more Railsford thought the matter over, the less he liked it. For it convinced him that there was someone desirous of doing him an injury by means of the very master who was already predisposed to believe evil of him. It was rather a damper after the glorious result of the sports, and Railsford tried to laugh it off and dismiss the whole matter from his mind.

"At least," said he to himself, "if the accusation comes in no more likely a form than I have seen to-night, I can afford to disregard it. But though Bickers made a fool of himself for once in a way, it does not at all follow that he will not return to the attack, and that I may actually have to answer to Grandcourt the charges of that precious letter. It's too absurd, really!"

Chapter Sixteen.

The Testimonial.

As the reader may suppose, the sympathetic soul of Miss Daisy Herapath was considerably moved by the contents of her brother's letter, which we gave in the last chapter. She naturally took an interest in the welfare and doings of Railsford's house; and as she heard quite as often from the master as she did from his pupil, she was able to form a pretty good, all-round opinion on school politics.

Arthur's lively account of the House sports had delighted her. Not that she understood all the obscure terms which embellished it; but it was quite enough for her that the house had risen above its tribulations and rewarded its master and itself by these brilliant exploits in the fields. But when Arthur passed from public to personal matters, his sister felt rather less at ease. She much disliked the barefaced proposal for the testimonial, and had told her brother as much more than once. On the whole, she decided to send Arthur's letter and its enclosure to Railsford, and confide her perplexities to him.

Railsford perused the "dear boy's" florid effusion with considerable interest, particularly, I grieve to say, certain portions of it, which if Daisy had been as wise as she was affectionate, she would have kept to herself. When people put notes into circulation, it's not the fault of those into whose hands they come if they discover in them beauties unsuspected by the person for whose benefit they were issued. Railsford saw a great deal more in Arthur's letter than Daisy had even suspected. A certain passage, which had seemed mere mysterious jargon to her, had a pretty plain meaning for him, especially after the interview last Sunday with Mr Bickers.

"It's a jolly good job that row about Bickers came on when it did. ... Nobody wants to find the chap out now, so your particular is all serene up to now, and I don't mean to drip and spoil his game."

63

What could this mean except that Arthur, somehow or other, knew a secret respecting the Bickers affair which he was keeping to himself, presumably in the interests of Railsford? Could this mysterious hint have any connection with the false rumour which had reached Bickers and magnified itself in his mind to such an uncomfortable extent? Railsford resolved to delight the heart of his young relative by a friendly visit, and make a reconnaissance of the position. He had a very good pretext in the anxious solicitude expressed in Daisy's letter for the health and appetite of her love-tossed brother. He would make it his business to inquire how the sufferer did.

Waiting, therefore, until a preternatural stillness in the room above assured him that Dig was out of the way, the Master of the Shell went up-stairs and ushered himself into Arthur's study.

"Hard at work, I see," said Railsford cheerily. "How are you getting on?"

"All serene, thanks," replied Arthur. "That is, not very well."

"Have you stuck fast in your translations? Let me look."

"Oh no. I'm not doing my exercise," said Arthur, in alarm. "I'm only looking up some words. Do you want to see Dig? He's gone to Wake's room."

"No, I came to see you. I heard you'd been out of sorts. Are you all right now? Was it the sports knocked you up?"

"No—that is, yes, they did a bit, I think," said Arthur. It was the sports which had done it, though not in the way "Marky" fancied.

"Well, we mustn't have you laid up, must we? We want you for the Swift Scholarship, you know."

"Oh, all right, sir, I'm going to mug hard for that after Easter, really."

"Why put it off till then? You may come to my room any evening you like. I shall generally have time enough."

This invitation did not fascinate the boy as it deserved to do.

"I fancy I'd work steadier here," said he. "Besides, Dig and I use the same books."

"Well, the first thing is to get yourself all right. What's troubling you, Arthur?"

This was a startling question, and Arthur felt himself detected.

"I suppose you've heard. Keep it quiet, I say."

"What is it? Keep what quiet?"

"Why, about *her*, you know. I say, Marky—I mean Mr Railsford—could you ever give me a leg-up with her? If you asked her to your room one day, you know I could come too, and do my work."

Railsford laughed.

"I thought you could do your work better here; besides, you and Oakshott use the same books."

"Oakshott be hanged! I mean—I say, Marky, do you think I've a chance? I know Smedley's—"

Railsford's experience in cases of this sort was limited, but he was philosopher enough to know that some distempers need to be taken seriously.

"Look here, Arthur," said he gravely, "the best thing you can do is to go straight over to Dr Ponsford's and ask to see him, and tell him exactly how matters stand. Remind him that you're just fifteen, and in the Shell, and that your income is a shilling a week. You need not tell him you were detained two afternoons this week, because he will probably find that out for himself by looking at monsieur's books. If he says he will be delighted to accept your offer, then I promise to back you up. Let me see, I know the doctor's at home this evening; it's not 7.30 yet, so you'll have time, if you go at once, to catch him before his tea. I'll wait here till you come back."

Arthur's face underwent a wonderful change as the master quietly uttered these words. It began by lengthening, and growing a little pale; then it grew troubled, then bewildered, then scarlet, and finally, when he had ended, it relaxed into a very faint smile.

"I think I'll wait a bit," said he gravely.

"Very well, only let me hear the result when you do go."

"I think I may as well start work for the Swift to-night," said he, "if you don't mind."

"By all means, my boy. Come along to my room and we'll look through the list of subjects."

Arthur, before the task was half over, had recovered his spirits and advanced far in the esteem of his future kinsman.

"Awfully brickish of you, sir," he said. "It wouldn't be a bad score for our house if we got all the prizes at the exams, would it?"

"Not at all. But we mustn't be too confident."

"Jolly lucky we're cut off from the rest of the chaps, isn't it? It makes us all sit up."

"That state of things may end any time, you know," said the master. "But we must 'sit up' all the same."

"Oh, but it won't come out till the exams, are over, will it?"

"How do I know?"

Arthur glanced up at his kinsman, and inwardly reflected what a clever chap he was to ask such a question in such a way.

"Oh, all right. All I meant was, it wouldn't suit our book, would it, to let it out just yet?"

"It's not a question of what suits anyone. It's a question of what is right. And if anybody in the house knows anything I don't, he ought to speak, whatever it costs."

"There's an artful card," thought Arthur to himself, and added aloud—

"I don't fancy any fellow knows anything you don't, Marky—I mean Mr Railsford. *I* don't."

"Don't you? Do you know," said the master, "I have sometimes had an impression you did. I am quite relieved to hear it, Arthur."

"Oh, you needn't be afraid of me," said Arthur, lost in admiration for the cleverness of his future brother-in-law. "I'm safe, never you fear."

"It's a strange mystery," said Railsford, "but sooner or later we shall know the meaning of it."

"Later the better," put in Arthur, with a wink.

"I don't envy the feelings of the culprit, whoever he is; for he is a coward as well as a liar."

"No, more do I, Perhaps you're too down on him, though. Never mind, he's safe enough, for you and me."

"You have an odd way of talking, Arthur, which doesn't do you justice. As I said, you have more than once made me wonder whether you were not keeping back something about this wretched affair which I ought to know."

"Honour bright, I know a jolly lot less about it than you; so you really needn't be afraid of me; and Dig's safe too. Safe as a door-nail."

Railsford was able to write home on the following Sunday that Arthur had quite recovered his appetite, and that the "low" symptoms to which Dig had darkly referred had vanished altogether. Indeed, Arthur on this occasion developed that most happy of all accomplishments, the power of utterly forgetting that he had done or said anything either strange in itself or offensive to others. He was hail-fellow-well-met with the boys he had lately kicked and made miserable; he did not know what you were talking about when you reminded him that a day or two ago he had behaved like a cad to you; and, greatest exploit of all, he had the effrontery to charge Dig with being "spoons" on Violet, and to hold him up to general ridicule in consequence!

"How much have you really got for the testimonial?" said Dig one morning.

"Eleven and six," said Arthur dismally; "not a great lot, but enough for a silver ring."

"Not with Daisy's name on it."

"No, we'll have to drop that, unless we can scratch it on."

"We'll have a try. When shall we give it?"

"To-morrow's Rag Sunday, isn't it? Let's give it him to-night—after tea. I'll write out a list of the chaps, and you can get up an address, unless Felgate will come and give him a speech."

"Think he will? All serene. We'll give the fellows the tip, and do the thing in style. Hadn't you better cut and get the ring, I say?"

Arthur cut, armed with an *exeat*, and made the momentous purchase. The fancy stationer of whom he bought the ring assured him it was solid silver, and worth a good deal more than the 10 shillings 6 pence he asked. The other shilling Arthur invested in a box wherein to put it, and returned to school very well satisfied with his bargain. He and Dig spent an anxious hour trying to scratch the letters with a pin on the inner surface; and to Arthur belonged the credit of the delicate suggestion that instead of writing the term of endearment in vulgar English they should engrave it in Classic Greek, thus: *chuki*. The result was on the whole satisfactory; and when the list of contributors was emblazoned on a sheet of school paper, and Sir Digby Oakshott's address (for Felgate declined the invitation to make a speech) had been finally revised and corrected, the prospects of the ceremonial seemed very encouraging.

Arthur and Dig, once more completely reconciled, went through the farce of house tea that evening in the common room with considerable trepidation. They had a big job on hand, in which they were to be the principal actors, and when the critical time comes at last, we all know how devoutly we wish it had forgotten us! But everything had been carefully arranged, and everyone had been told what to expect. It was therefore impossible to back out, and highly desirable, as they *were* in for it, to do it in good style.

As the clock pointed to the fatal hour, Dig sharply rattled his spoon against the side of his empty cup. At the expected signal, about a dozen boys, the contributors to the testimonial, rose to their feet, and turned their eyes on Arthur. Railsford, at the head of the table, mistook the demonstration for a lapse of good manners, and was about to reprimand the offenders, when by a concerted movement the deputation stepped over their forms and advanced on the master in a compact phalanx. Arthur and Dig, both a little pale and dry about the lips, marched at their head. "What is all this?" inquired Railsford. Arthur and Dig replied by a rather ceremonious bow, in which the deputation followed them; and then the latter carefully cleared his throat.

"We, the undersigned, boys in your house," he began, reading from the paper before him in a somewhat breathless way, "beg to present you with a small token of our esteem—(Go on, hand it up, Arthur), and hope you will like it, and that it will fit, and trust that the name graven within will suggest pleasant memories in which we all join. The letters are in the Greek character. We hope we shall all enjoy our holidays, and come back better in mind and body. You may rely on us to back you up, and to keep dark things you would not like to have mentioned.—Signed, with kind regards, Daisy Herapath (a most particular friend), J. Felgate (prefect), Arthur Herapath (treasurer), Sir Digby Oakshott, Baronet (secretary), Bateson and Jukes (Babies), Maple, Simson, Tilbury, and Dimsdale (Shell), Munger (Fifth), Snape (Baby in Bickers's house)."

It spoke a good deal for Mark Railsford that under the first shock of this startling interview, he did not bowl over the whole deputation like so many ninepins and explode before the assembled house. As it was he was too much taken aback to realise the position for a minute or so; and by that time the baronet's address was half read. He grimly waited for the end of it, studiously ignoring the box which Arthur held out, opened, to fascinate him with its charms.

When the reading was done, he wheeled round abruptly in his chair, in a manner which made the deputation stagger back a pace; and said—

"You mean it kindly, no doubt; but I don't want a present and can't take one. It was foolish of you to think of such a thing. Don't let it occur again. I'm vexed with you, and shall have to speak to some of you privately about it. Go to your rooms."

"What's to become of the ring!" said Dig disconsolately, as he and Arthur sat and cooled themselves in their study. "Mr Trinket won't take it back. He'd no business to cut up rough like that."

"Fact is," replied Arthur, "Marky's got to draw the line somewhere. He knows he's in a jolly row about that business, you know, and he doesn't want a testimonial for it. I don't blame him. I'll get Daisy to buy the ring in the holidays, and we can have the fellows to a blow-out next term with the money."

Chapter Seventeen.

The Secret Out.

"If you please, sir, would you mind coming to see one of the young gentlemen in our house before you start? He don't seem himself."

The speaker was Mrs Phillips, the dame of Bickers's house, and the individual she addressed was Mark Railsford, who, with his portmanteau on the steps beside him, was impatiently awaiting the cab which should take him from Grandcourt for the Easter holidays. The place was as empty and deserted as on that well-remembered day when he came down—could it be only the beginning of this present term?—to enter upon his new duties at the school. The boys, as was their wont, had almost without exception left by the eight o'clock train, Arthur and Dig being among the foremost. The few who had remained to finish their packing had followed by the ten o'clock. The doctor and his niece had left for town last night; the other masters had made an early start that morning; and Railsford, junior master, and consequently officer of the guard for the day, imagined himself, as he stood there with his portmanteau about two o'clock, the "last of the Mohicans."

"Who is it?" he said, as the cab rumbled through the gateway.

"It's Mr Branscombe, sir. He overslep' hisself, as the way of speaking is, and as there was no call-over, and all the young gentlemen were in a rush, nobody noticed it. But when I went to make the beds, I finds him still in 'is, and don't like the looks of 'im. Anyhow, sir, if you'd come and take a look at him—"

Railsford looked up at the school clock. He could catch the 2.30 train if he left in five minutes. If he lost that train he would have to wait till six. He told the cabman to put the portmanteau on the top, and wait for him at the door of Bickers's house, and then walked after Mrs Phillips, rather impatiently.

He had never set foot in Mr Bickers's house before, and experienced a curious sensation as he crossed the threshold of his enemy's citadel. Suppose Mr Bickers should return and find him there—what a pretty situation!

"Up-stairs, sir, this way," said Mrs Phillips, leading him up to the prefects' cubicles. She opened the door at the end, and ushered him into the house-captain's study.

On his low narrow camp bed lay Branscombe, flushed, with eyes closed, tossing and moaning, and now and then talking to himself, Railsford started as his eyes fell on him.

"He's ill!" he whispered to Mrs Phillips.

"That's what I thought," observed the sagacious dame.

Railsford knew little enough about medicine, and had never been ill himself in his life. But as he lifted the hot hand which lay on the coverlet, and marked the dry parched lips, and listened to the laboured breathing, he knew that he was in the presence of a grave illness of some kind.

"Go and fetch Dr Clarke at once, Mrs Phillips," said he, "and tell the cabman on your way down not to wait."

Branscombe opened his eyes and clutched greedily at the tumbler Railsford offered. But his throat was too sore to allow him to drain it, and he gave it back with a moan. Then he dozed off fitfully, and recommenced his tossing.

"Where are they all?" he asked, again opening his eyes.

He scarcely seemed to take in who Railsford was.

"They went by the ten o'clock train," said Railsford.

"Why didn't they call me? Where's Clipstone?"

"You weren't very well. You had better lie quiet a little," said Railsford.

The invalid made no attempt to get up, but lay back on the pillow and moaned.

"Open the window," said he, "the room's so hot."

Railsford made believe to obey him, and waited anxiously for the doctor. It seemed as if he would never arrive.

It was a strange position for the Master of the Shell, here at the bedside of the captain of his rival's house, the only occupant with him of the great deserted school. He had reckoned on spending a very different day. He was to have seen Daisy once more that afternoon, and the foolish young couple had been actually counting the minutes till the happy meeting came round. By this time he would have been in the train whizzing towards her, with all the troubles of the term behind him, and all the solaces of the vacation ahead. To-morrow, moreover, was the day of the University Boat-Race, and he, an old "Blue," had in his pocket at that moment a ticket for the steamer which was to follow the race. He was to have met scores of friends and fought again scores of old battles, and to have dined with the crews in the evening!

What was to become of all these plans now? He was absolutely a prisoner at this poor fellow's bedside. He did not know his address at home, or where to send for help. Besides, even if he could discover it, it would be twenty-four hours at least before he could hand over his charge into other hands.

These selfish regrets, however, only flashed through Railsford's mind to be again dismissed. He was a brave man, and possessed the courage which, when occasion demands, can accept a duty like a man. After all, was it not a blessing his cab had not come five minutes earlier than it had? Suppose this poor sufferer had been left with no better guardian than the brusque Mrs Phillips, with her scruples about "catching" disorders?

The doctor's trap rattled up to the door at last. He was one of those happy sons of Aesculapius who never pull long faces, but always say the most alarming things in the most delightful way.

"Ah," said he, hardly glancing at the patient, and shaking hands airily with Railsford, "this is a case of the master being kept in, and sending to the doctor for his *exeat*, eh? Sorry I can't give it to you at present, my dear fellow; rather a bad case."

"What is it?" asked Railsford.

"Our old friend, diphtheria; knowing young dog, to put it off till breaking-up day. What an upset for us all if he'd come out with it yesterday! Not profitable from my point of view, but I daresay the boys will have it more comfortably at home than here, after all. This must have been coming on for some time. How long has he been feverish?"

"I don't know. I only found him like this half an hour ago, and want your advice what to do."

The doctor, almost for the first time, looked at the restless invalid on the bed and hummed.

"Dr Ponsford has gone to the Isle of Wight, I hear," said he.

"I really don't know where he's gone," said Railsford impatiently.

"I wish *I* could get a holiday. That's the worst of my kind of doctor—people take ill so promiscuously. As sure as we say we'll go off for a week, some aggravating patient spits blood and says, 'No, you don't.' I think you should send for this boy's mother, do you know."

"I don't know her address. Is he so very ill, then?"

"Well, of the two, I think you should telegraph rather than write. It might be more satisfaction to you afterwards. Have you no way of finding where he lives? Looked in his pockets? There may be a letter there."

It was not an occasion for standing on ceremony, and Railsford, feeling rather like a pickpocket, took down the jacket from the peg and searched it. There was only one letter in the pocket, written in a female hand. It was dated "Sunday," but bore no address further than "London, N." on the postmark.

"Pity," said the doctor pleasantly. "Of course you have had diphtheria yourself?"

"No."

"H'm, I can hardly advise you to leave him till somebody comes to relieve guard. But it's doubtful whether he will be well in time to nurse you. You should send for your own folk in time."

If this doctor had not been Railsford's only support at present, he would have resented this professional flippancy more than he did.

"I'm not afraid," said he. "I shall try to find out where his people live. Meanwhile would it be well to send a trained nurse here; or can I manage myself?"

"Quite straightforward work," said the doctor, "if you like it. I've known cases no worse than this finish up in three days, or turn the corner in seven. You mustn't be surprised if he gets a great deal worse at night. He's a bit delirious already."

Then the doctor went into a few details as to the medicine and method of nursing.

The most important thing was to discover, if possible, the address of the patient's parents, and summon them. He approached the bed in the vague hope that Branscombe might be able to help him. But the sufferer, though he opened his eyes, seemed not to know him, and muttered to himself what sounded more like Greek verse than English. In desperation Railsford summoned Mrs Phillips. She, cautious woman, with a son of her own, would by no means come into the room, but stood at the door with a handkerchief to her mouth.

"Have you any idea where his home is?"

"No. Hasn't he labelled his box?"

"He does not seem to have begun to pack at all. Do you know the doctor's address?"

"No, he said no letters were to be forwarded. You'll excuse me, Mr Railsford, but as you are taking charge, I should like to be spared away an hour or so. I feel so upset, like. A bit of fresh air would be the very thing for me."

She was evidently in such a panic on her own account, and so nervous of her proximity even to Railsford, that he saw it was little use to object.

"You must be back in two hours, without fail," said he; "I may want you to go for the doctor again."

She went; and Railsford, as he listened to the clatter of her boots across the quadrangle, felt more than ever utterly alone. He set himself to clear the room as far as possible of all unnecessary furniture. The poor fellow's things lay about in hopeless confusion. Evidently he had had it in his mind to pack up yesterday; but had felt too ill to carry out his purpose, and gone to bed intending to finish in the morning.

Flannels, running-shoes, caps, books, linen, and papers lay scattered over the room, and Railsford, as he gathered them together and tried to reduce the chaos to order, felt his heart sink with an undefined apprehension.

Yesterday, perhaps, this little array of goods and chattels meant much to the young master who called them his. To-day, what cared he as he lay there tossing feverishly on his bed, muttering his Greek verses and moaning over his sore throat, whose they were, and who touched them? And to-morrow—?

Railsford pulled himself together half angrily. A nice fellow, he, for a sick nurse?

Suddenly he came upon a desk with the key in the lock. Perhaps this might contain the longed-for address. He opened it and glanced inside. It was empty. No. There was only a paper there—a drawing on a card. Railsford took it up and glanced at it, half absent. As his eyes fell on it, however, he started. It was a curious work of art; a sketch in pen and ink, rather cleverly executed, after the model of the old Greek bas-reliefs shown in the classical dictionaries. It represented what first appeared to be a battle scene, but what Railsford on closer inspection perceived was something very different.

The central figure was a man, over whose head a sack had been cast, which a tall figure behind was binding with cords round the victim's neck and shoulders. On the ground, clutching the captive's knees with his arms, and preparing to bind them, sat another figure, while in the background a third, with one finger to his lips, expressive of caution, pointed to an open door, evidently of the dungeon intended for the prisoner. It was an ordinary subject for a picture of this kind, and Railsford might have thought nothing of it, had not his attention been attracted by some words inscribed in classic fashion against the figures of the actors in this little drama.

Under the central figure of the captive he read in Greek capitals the legend BIKEROS; over the head of his tall assailant was written BRANSKOMOS. The person sitting and embracing the captive's knees was labelled KLIPSTONOS, while the mysterious figure in the rear, pointing out the dungeon, bore the name of MUNGEROS. Over the door itself was written BOOTBOX. Below the whole was written the first line of the Iliad, and in the corner, in minute characters, were the words, "S. *Branscombe, inv. et del.*"

Railsford stared at the strange work of art in blank amazement. What could it mean? At first he was disposed to smile at the performance as a harmless jest; but a moment's consideration convinced him that, jest or not, he held in his hand the long-sought clue to the Bickers mystery which had troubled the peace of Grandcourt for the last term.

Here, in the hand of the chief offender himself, was a pictorial record of that grievous outrage, and here, denounced, by himself in letters of Greek, were the names for which all the school had suffered. The Master of the Shell seemed to be in a dream. Branscombe and Clipstone, the head prefects of Bickers's own house! and Munger, the ill-conditioned toady of Railsford's!

His first feelings of excitement and astonishment were succeeded by others of alarm and doubt. The murder was out, but how? He knew the great secret at last, but by what means? His eyes turned to the restless sufferer on the bed, and a flush of crimson came to his face as he realised that he had no more right to that secret than he had to the purse which lay on the table. He had opened the desk to look for an address, and nothing more. If, instead of that address, he had accidentally found somebody else's secret, what right had he—a man of honour and a gentleman—to use it, even if by doing so he could redress one of the greatest grievances in Grandcourt?

He thrust the picture back into the desk, and wished from the bottom of his heart he had never seen it. Mechanically he finished tidying the room, and clearing away to the adjoining study as much as possible of the superfluous furniture. Then with his own hands he lit the fire and carried out the various instructions of the doctor as to the steaming of the air in the room and the preparation of the nourishment for the invalid.

Branscombe woke once during the interval and asked hoarsely, "What bell was that?"

Then, without waiting for an answer, he said,—

"All right, all right, I'll get up in a second," and relapsed into his restless sleep.

Mrs Phillips did not return till eight o'clock; and the doctor arrived almost at the same time.

"Has he taken anything?" he inquired.

"Scarcely anything; he can hardly swallow."

"You'll have a night with him, I fancy. Keep the temperature of the room up to sixty, and see he doesn't throw off his clothes. How old is he—eighteen?—a great overgrown boy, six feet one or two, surely. It goes hard with these long fellows. Give me your short, thick-set young ruffian for pulling through a bout like this. Have you found out where he lives?"

"No, I can't discover his address anywhere."

"Look in his Sunday hat. I always kept mine there when I was a boy, and never knew a boy who didn't."

Branscombe, however, was an exception.

"Well," said the doctor, "it's a pity. A mother's the proper person to be with him a time like this. She'll never— What's this?"

It was an envelope slipped behind the bookcase, containing a bill from Splicer, the London cricket-bat-maker, dated a year ago. At the foot the tradesman had written, "Hon. sir, sorry we could not get bat in time to send home, so forward to you direct to Grandcourt School, by rail."

"There we are," said the doctor, putting the document in his pocket. "This ought to bring mamma in twenty-four hours. The telegraph office is shut now, but we'll wake Mr Splicer up early, and have mamma under weigh by midday. Good-night, Railsford—keep the pot boiling, my good fellow—I'll look round early."

He was gone, and Railsford with sinking heart set himself to the task before him. He long remembered that night. It seemed at first as if the doctor's gloomy predictions were to be falsified, for Branscombe continued long in a half-slumber, and even appeared to be more tranquil than he had been during the afternoon.

Railsford sat near the fire and watched him; and for two hours the stillness of the room was only broken by the lively ticking of the little clock on the mantelpiece, and the laboured breathing of the sufferer.

He was nearly asleep when a cry from the bed suddenly roused him.

"Clip!" called the invalid.

Railsford went to his side and quietly replaced the covering which had been tossed aside.

"Clip! look alive—he's coming—don't say a word, hang on to his legs, you know—*En jam tempus erat*—Munger, you cad, why don't you come? *Italiam fato profugus*. Hah! got you, my man. Shove him in, quick! Strike a light, do you hear? here they come. What are you doing, Clip?—turn him face up. That's for blackguarding me before the whole house! Clip put me up to it. Don't cut and leave me in the lurch, I say. You're locking me in the boot-box!—let me out—I'm in for the mile, you know. Who's got my shoes? *Pastor cum traheret per freta navibus*. Well run, sir! He's giving out! I say, I say. I can't keep it up. I must stop. Clip, you put me up to it, old man. It'll never come out—never—never. He thinks it was Railsford, ho, ho! I'll never do such a thing again. Come along—sharp—coast's clear!"

Then he began to conjugate a Greek verb, sometimes shouting the words and sitting up in bed, and sometimes half whimpering them as Railsford gently laid him back on the pillow. There was not much fear of Railsford dropping asleep again after this. The sick lad scarcely ceased his wild talk all the night through. Now he was going over again in detail that dark night's work in the boot-box; now he was construing Homer to the doctor; now he was being run down in the mile race; now he was singing one of his old child's hymns; now he was laughing over the downfall of Mr Bickers; now he was making a speech at the debating society. It was impossible for the listener to follow all his wild incoherent talk, it was all so mixed up and jumbled. But if Railsford harboured any doubts as to the correctness of his surmise about the picture, the circumstantial details of the outrage repeated over and over in the boy's wild ravings effectually dispelled them.

69

He knew now the whole of the wretched story from beginning to end. The proud boy's resentment at the insult he had received in the presence of his house, the angry passions which had urged him to the act of revenge, the cowardly precautions suggested by his confederate to escape detection, and the terrors and remorse following the execution of their deep-laid scheme. Yet if the listener had no right to the secret locked up in the desk, still less had he the right to profit by these sad delirious confessions.

Towards morning the poor exhausted sufferer, who during the night had scarcely remained a moment motionless, or abated a minute in his wild, wandering talk, sunk back on his pillow and closed his eyes like one in whom the flame of life had sunk almost to the socket. Railsford viewed the change with the utmost alarm, and hastened to give the restoratives prescribed by the doctor in case of a collapse. But the boy apparently had run through his strength and lacked even the power to swallow.

For two terrible hours it seemed to Railsford as if the young life were slipping through his hands; and he scarcely knew at one time if the prayer he sent up would reach its destination before the soul of him on whose behalf it rose. But soon after the school clock had tolled eight, and when the clear spring sun rising above the chapel tower sent its rays cheerily into the sick-chamber, the breathing became smoother and more regular, and the hand on which that of Railsford rested grew moist.

The doctor arrived an hour later, and smiled approvingly as he glanced at the patient.

"He's going to behave himself after all," said he. "You'll find he will wake up in an hour or two with an appetite. Give him an egg beaten up in milk, with a spoonful of brandy."

"What about his parents?" asked Railsford.

"They will be here by the four-o'clock train. What about your breakfast? you've had nothing since midday yesterday; and if you're going to have your turn at that sort of thing," added he, pointing to the bed, "you'd better get yourself into good trim first. Get Mrs Phillips to cook you a steak, and put yourself outside it. You can leave him safely for twenty minutes or so."

Branscombe slept steadily and quietly through the forenoon, and then woke, clear in mind, and, as the doctor anticipated, with an appetite.

He swallowed the meal prepared for him with considerably less pain than yesterday, and then, for the first time, recognised his nurse.

"Thank you, sir," said he; "have I been seedy long?"

"You were rather poorly yesterday, old fellow," said Railsford, "and you must keep very quiet now, and not talk."

The patient evinced no desire to disobey either of these injunctions, and composed himself once more to sleep.

Before he awoke, a cab had driven into the courtyard and set down three passengers. Two of them were Mr and Mrs Branscombe, the third was a trained nurse from London.

As they appeared on the scene, joined almost immediately by the doctor, Railsford quietly slipped away from the room and signalled to the cabman to stop and pick him up. Five minutes later, he and his portmanteau were bowling towards the station, a day late for the boat-race. But in other respects Mark Railsford was a happy man, and a better one for his night's vigil in the Valley of the Shadow of Death.

Chapter Eighteen.

Rods in Pickle for Railsford.

Grandcourt assembled after the holidays in blissful ignorance of the episode narrated in our last chapter. Branscombe's illness had been an isolated case, and apparently not due to any defect in the sanitary arrangements of his house. And as no other boy was reported to have spent his holidays in the same unsatisfactory manner, and as Railsford himself had managed to escape infection, it was decided by the authorities not to publish the little misadventure on the housetop. The captain of Bickers's house was absent on sick leave, and the Master of the Shell (who had been nursing a stubborn cold during the holidays) would not be in his place, so it was announced, for a week. That was all Grandcourt was told; and, to its credit, it received the news with profound resignation.

True, some of the more disorderly spirits in Railsford's house were disposed to take advantage of his absence, and lead the much-enduring Monsieur Lablache, who officiated in his place, an uncomfortable dance. But any indications of mutiny were promptly stamped upon by Ainger and the other prefects, who, because they resented monsieur's appointment, were determined that, come what would, he should have no excuse for exercising his authority. Monsieur shrugged himself, and had no objection to the orderly behaviour of the house, whatever its motive, nor had anyone else whose opinion on such a matter was worth having.

Arthur and Sir Digby, as usual, came back brimful of lofty resolutions and ambitious schemes! Dig had considerably revised his time-table, and was determined to adhere to it like a martyr to his stake.

Arthur, though he came armed with no time-table, had his own good intentions. He had had one or two painful conversations with his father, who had hurt him considerably by suggesting that he wasted a great deal of time, and neglected utterly those principles of self-improvement which had turned out men like Wellington, Dickens, Dr Livingstone, and Mr Elihu Burritt. Arthur had seldom realised before how odious comparisons may become. No doubt Wellington, Dickens, and Company were good fellows in their way, but he had never done them any harm. Why should they be trotted out to injure him?

He thought he *was* improving himself. He was much better at a drop-kick than he had been last year, and Railsford himself had said he was not as bad at his Latin verses as he had been. Was not that improvement—self-improvement? Then he was conscious of having distinctly improved in morals. He had once or twice done his Caesar without a crib, and the aggregate of lines he had had to write for impositions had been several hundred less than the corresponding term of last year.

Thus the son gently reasoned with his parent, who replied that what he would like to see in his boy was an interest in some intellectual pursuits outside the mere school routine. Why, now, did he not take up some standard book of history with which to occupy his spare time, or some great poem like the *Paradise Lost*, of which he might commit a few lines to memory every day, and so emulate his great-uncle, who used to be able to repeat the whole poem by heart?

Both Arthur and Dig had landed for the term with hampers more or less replete with indigestible mementoes of domestic affection. Arthur had a Madeira cake and a rather fine lobster, besides a small box of figs, some chocolate creams, Brazil nuts, and (an enforced contribution from the cook) pudding-raisins.

Dig, whose means were not equal to his connections, produced, somewhat bashfully, a rather "high" cold chicken, some gingerbread, some pyretic saline, and a slab or two of home-made toffee. These good things, when spread out on the table that evening, made quite an imposing array, and decidedly warmed the cockles of the hearts of their joint owners, and suggested to them naturally thoughts of hospitality and revelry.

"Let's have a blow-out in the dormitory," proposed Arthur. "Froggy will let us alone, and we can square Felgate with a hunk of this toffee if he interferes."

Felgate was the prefect charged with the oversight of the Shell dormitory in Railsford's—a duty he discharged by never setting foot inside their door when he could possibly get out of it.

From a gastronomic point of view the boys would doubtless have done better to postpone their feast till to-morrow. They had munched promiscuously all day—during the railway journey especially—and almost needed a night's repose to enable them to attack the formidable banquet now proposed on equal terms. But hospitality brooks no delays. Besides, Dig's chicken was already a little over ripe, and it was impossible to say how Arthur's lobster might endure the night.

So the hearts of Maple, Tilbury, Dimsdale, and Simson were made glad that evening by an intimation that it might be worth their while at bed-time to smuggle a knife, fork, and plate a-piece into the dormitory, in case, as Arthur worded it, there should be some fun going.

Wonderful is the intuition of youth! These four simple-minded, uncultured lads knew what Arthur meant, even as he spoke, and joyfully did him and Dig homage for the rest of the evening, and at bed-time tucked each his platter under his waistcoat and scaled the stairs as the curfew rang, grimly accoutred with a fork in one trouser pocket and a knife in the other.

But whatever the cause, the Shell-fish in Railsford's presented a very green appearance when they answered to their names next morning, and were in an irritable frame of mind most of the day. Their bad temper took the form of a dead set on the unhappy Monsieur Lablache, who, during the first day of his vicarious office, led the existence of a pea on a frying-pan. They went up to him with difficulties in Greek prose, knowing that he comprehended not a word of that language; they asked his permission for what they knew he could not grant, and on his refusal got up cries of tyranny and despotism wherewith to raise the lower school; they whistled German war songs outside his door, and asked him the date of the Battle of Waterloo. When he demanded their names they told him "Ainger," "Barnworth," "Wake"; and when he ordered them to stay in an hour after school, they coolly stopped work five minutes before the bell rang and walked under his very nose into the playground.

Poor monsieur, he was no disciplinarian, and he knew it. His backbone was limp, and he never did the right thing at the right time. He shrugged when he ought to have been chastising; and he stormed when he ought to have held his tongue. Nobody cared for him; everybody wondered why he of all men worked at the trade of schoolmaster. Perhaps if some of my lords and baronets in the Shell had known that far away, in a tiny cottage at Boulogne, this same contemptible Frenchman was keeping alive from week to week, with his hard-earned savings, a paralysed father and three motherless little girls, who loved the very ground he trod on, and kissed his likeness every night before they crept to their scantily-covered beds—if they had known that this same poor creature said a prayer for his beloved France every day, and tingled in every vein to hear her insulted even in jest—perhaps they would have understood better why he flared up now and then as he did, and why he clung to his unlovely calling of teaching unfeeling English boys at the rate of £30 a term. But the Grandcourt boys did not know all this, and therefore they had no pity for poor monsieur.

However, as I have said, monsieur shrugged his shoulders, and accepted the help of the prefects to keep his disorderly charges within bounds.

71

From one of the prefects he got very hide help. Felgate had no interest in the order of the house. It didn't matter to him whether it was monsieur who had to deal with the rioters or Ainger. All he knew was, he was not going to trouble his head about it. In fact, his sympathies were on the side of the agitators. Why shouldn't they enjoy themselves if they liked? They didn't hurt anybody—and if they did break the rules of the house; well, who was to say whether they might not be right and the rules of the house wrong?

Arthur Herapath, for instance, had set up with a dog—puppy to his friend's dog, Smiley. Everybody knew live animals were against rules, and yet Railsford had winked all last term at Smiley; why shouldn't Arthur have equal liberty to enjoy the companionship of Smiley minor?

He met master and puppy in the passage one afternoon.

"Hullo, young 'un," said he, "another dog? How many's that?"

"Two," said Arthur, a little doubtful as to the prefect's reception of the news. "You see it would be rough to take him from his mother while he is so young. It's not as if he was no relation."

"Of course not. What have you been doing with Marky these holidays?"

"Oh, he was seedy—sore throat. I fancy he was shamming a bit to get a week extra. You see, he's spoons on my sister Daisy."

"I fancy I've heard that before," observed Felgate.

"What I mean is, he hangs about our place a lot; so it's a good excuse for him to be laid up, you know."

"Quite so. Perhaps he's not in a hurry to come back here for another reason we know of, eh, youngster?"

"Ha, ha! but keep that mum, you know. We must back him through that business. It's nearly blown over already."

"Has it? But, I say—"

Here Ainger came up and detected the puppy.

"You'll have to get rid of that, Herapath," said he.

"What, Smiley's pup? Why? Felgate's given me leave."

"Felgate may do as he pleases. I tell you you must send him home, and Smiley too."

"What!" said Arthur aghast. "Smiley too! why, Railsford knows all about Smiley, and let us have him all, last term."

"But you are not going to have them this term. Two other fellows have started dogs on the strength of Smiley already, and there's to be a clean sweep of the lot."

"Oh, rot! you can't interfere with fellows' rights like that," said Felgate.

"I tell you Railsford gave us leave," repeated Arthur.

"Very well," said Ainger; "unless both of them are packed off home by this time to-morrow, or sent down to the school farm, you'll go up to the doctor and settle the question with him."

"Rubbish!" said Felgate. "Until Railsford—"

"Shut up," said the captain; "I'm not talking to you."

It was hardly to be wondered at if he was out of temper. He was having any amount of extra work to do; and to be thus obstructed by one of his own colleagues was a trifle too much for his limited patience.

Felgate coloured up at the rebuff, knowing well enough that the captain would be delighted to make good his words at any time and place which might be offered him. He remained after he had gone, and said to Arthur—

"That's what I call brutal. You're not going to care two straws what he says?"

"All very well," said Arthur, stroking his puppy; "if he sends me up to Pony, what then?"

"Bless you, he won't send you up to Pony."

"Think not? If I thought he wouldn't, I'd hang on till Marky comes back. He'd square the thing."

"Of course he would. It's a bit of spite of Ainger's. He thinks he's not quite important enough, so he's going to start bullying. I'll back you up."

"Thanks, awfully," said the ductile Arthur. "You're a brick. I'd take your advice."

He did, and prevailed upon Dig to do the same.

The consequence was, that when next afternoon the captain walked into their study to see whether his order had been complied with, he was met by an unceremonious yap from Smiley herself, echoed by an impertinent squeak from her irreverent son.

"You've got them still, then?" said Ainger. "Very well, they can stay now till after you've been to the doctor. Nine o'clock sharp to-morrow morning, both of you."

The friends turned pale.

"Not really, Ainger? You haven't sent up our names, have you? We'll send them off. We thought as Felgate said—oh, you cad!"

This last remark was occasioned by Ainger departing and shutting the door behind him without vouchsafing any further parley.

They felt that the game was up, and that they had been done. In their distress they waited upon Felgate and laid their case before him. He, as is usual with gentlemen of his type, said it was very hard and unjust, and they would do quite right in resisting and defying everybody all round. But he did not offer to go instead of them to the doctor, so that his general observations on the situation were not particularly comforting.

Arthur proposed telegraphing to Railsford something in this form:

"Ainger says Smiley's against rules. Wire him you allow."

But when the form was filled up and ready to send, the chance of it succeeding seemed hardly worth the cost.

Finally they went down sadly after tea to the school farm and hired a kennel, and arranged for the board and lodging of their exiled pets at so much a week.

Next morning, in doleful dumps, they presented themselves before the doctor. Arthur could hardly help remembering how, a short time ago, he had pictured himself standing in that very room, demanding the hand of Miss Violet. Now, Smiley minor, squeaking and grunting, as he hung by his one tooth to his mother's tail, down there in the school farm, was worth half a dozen Miss Violets to him.

And his once expected uncle—!

The doctor dealt shortly and decisively with the miscreants. He caned them for defying their house-captain, and reprimanded them for imagining that dogs could be permitted under the school roof.

On being told that Mr Railsford had known all about Smiley last term, he declined to argue the matter, and concluded by a warning of the possible consequences of a repetition of the offence.

They went back to their place, sore both in body and mind. To be caned during the first week of the term was not quite in accordance with their good resolutions, and to be bereft of the Smileys was a cruel outrage on their natural affections. They owed both to Ainger, and mutually resolved that he was a cad of the lowest description. For all that they attended to his injunctions for the next few days with wonderful punctuality, and decided to defer, till Railsford's return, their own revenge and his consequent confusion.

Altogether, it was getting to be time for Railsford to turn up. The evening before, the first master's session for the term had been held, and the doctor, for a wonder, had been present. Towards the end of the meeting, after the discussion of a great deal of general business, Mr Bickers rose and asked leave to make a statement. The reader can guess what that statement was.

He begged to remind the meeting that Grandcourt still lay under the cloud of the mystery which enveloped the assault which had been made upon himself last term. For himself, it mattered very little, but for the honour of the school he considered the matter should not be allowed to drop until it was properly cleared up. With a view to assisting in such a result, he might mention that towards the end of last term a rumour had come to his ears—he was not at liberty to say through what channel—that the secret was not quite as dead as was generally supposed. He had heard, on what he considered reliable authority, that in Mr Railsford's house—the house most interested in this painful question—the name of the culprit or culprits was generally known, or, at least, suspected; and he believed he was not going too far in mentioning a rumour that no one could make a better guess as to that name than Mr Railsford himself.

Here Mr Grover and Monsieur Lablache both rose to their feet. Monsieur, of course, gave way, but what he had meant to say was pretty much what Mr Grover did say. He wished to point out that in his friend's absence such an insinuation as that just made by the speaker was quite unjustifiable. For his own part, he thought it a great pity to revive the unfortunate question at all. At any rate, in Mr Railsford's absence, he should certainly oppose any further reference being made to it at this meeting.

"That," echoed monsieur, "is precisely my opinion."

"Very well," said Mr Bickers pleasantly. "What I have to say will keep perfectly well until Mr Railsford comes back."

Whereupon the meeting passed to the next order of the day.

Chapter Nineteen.

Felgate, the Champion of the Oppressed.

It spoke well for Railsford's growing influence with his boys that as soon as he returned to his post every sign of mutiny disappeared, and the house seemed to regain that spirit of ambition and self-reliance which had characterised the last days of the previous term. A few knotty questions, as the reader knows, were awaiting the Master of the Shell on his arrival, but he took them one at a time, and not having been involved in the previous altercations respecting them, disposed of them a great deal more easily than had been expected.

Things had been coming to a climax rather rapidly between Felgate and Ainger. Not that Felgate had committed any unusual offence, or that Ainger had discovered anything new about him which he had not known before; but during the last few weeks of last term, and the opening days of the present, the two had crossed one another's paths frequently, and with increasing friction. Ainger was one of those fellows who, when their mind is set on a thing, seem to lose sight of all but two persons—the person who can help them most and the person who can hinder them most.

In the present case Ainger's heart was set on making his house the crack house of Grandcourt. The person who could help him most was Railsford, and the person who could hinder him most was Felgate. The captain had been shy of the new Master of the Shell for a long time, and the mistrust had not been all on one side, but as last term had worn on, and a common cause had arisen in the temporary disgrace of the house, master and head prefect had felt drawn together in mutual confidence, and Railsford now, though he still did not always realise it, had no more loyal adherent than Ainger. Ainger, on his part, was quite ready to acknowledge that without Railsford the house stood a poor chance of fulfilling the ambitious project he and Barnworth had marked out for it, and he only hoped, now, that the master might not rest on the laurels of last term, but would help to carry through the still more important exploits of this.

The great obstacle to whatever good was going on in Railsford's at present was Felgate. He had nearly succeeded last term in sowing discontent among the juvenile athletes, and he had, in the most unmistakable manner, not done his best in the one competition at the sports for which he had entered. That was bad enough, and the quick-tempered Ainger wrote up a heavy score against him on those two items. But now he had begun on a new line. Although a prefect himself, he not only evinced no interest in the order of the house at a time when the prefects were specially on their mettle, but he had taken pains to undermine the discipline of the place and set his authority up in antagonism to that of his own colleagues.

Felgate laid his plans deeply and cleverly. Ainger, as he knew, was popular because he had won the mile, and was upright, and meant what he said, and said what he meant. No boy of whom the same can be said could help being popular.

"But," said Felgate to himself, "there are other ways of being popular. I haven't won the mile or anything else; I'm not particularly upright, and I shouldn't like to assert I always either say what I mean or mean what I say. Still I can make myself pleasant to a parcel of kids when I choose; I can let them off some of their little rows, and I can help them to some better sport than all this tomfoolery about getting up a crack eleven and winning all the school prizes. Ainger won't like it, but I fancy I can sail close enough to the wind not to give him a chance of being down on me. And as for Railsford—the snob—if he interferes, well, I can take it out of him in a way he don't suspect. What a hypocrite the fellow must be to do a thing like that, and come here smiling and talk about making this the crack house of Grandcourt! Bah!"

And the righteous soul of Felgate waxed hot within him, and he set himself to consider how, with least risk to himself, and most mischief to everyone else, he could drive a wedge into the project of his colleagues, and make to himself a party in Railsford's. He passed in review the various rules of the house, to discover someone on which he might possibly found a grievance. For your man who sets himself to make a party must have a grievance. He fancied he had discovered just what he wanted in the time-honoured rule about compulsory cricket. Every boy was obliged to show up in the cricket-field three times a week, whether he liked it or not. There were very few boys in Railsford's, as Felgate knew, who did not like it; but he fancied for all that he could make something out of the rule.

He began by breaking it himself. He knew that no one would be particularly concerned on his account, for he was an indifferent player, and also a prefect might on a pinch excuse himself. After a week's abstention, during which, rather to his disappointment, no notice was taken of his defection, he began to talk about it to one and another of the more studious boys of the house, boys very keen on winning the school prizes at the end of the term for which they were entered. Sherriff of the Fifth was one of these, and, much as he liked cricket, he was bemoaning one day having to turn out into the fields just when he wanted to finish a knotty problem in trigonometry.

"Don't go," said Felgate. "Surely no one has a right to spoil your chance of a scholarship for a musty old school rule that ought to have been abolished a century ago."

"It's not a bad rule on the whole, I fancy," said Sherriff; "but it comes a little rough on me just now."

"My dear fellow, we're not quite slaves here; and if it doesn't suit you to go down on your knees to an antiquated rule of this kind, then you're not the fellow I take you for if you do it. It hasn't suited me often enough, and I've not been such a muff as to think twice about it."

"What happened to you when you didn't turn up?"

"Nothing, of course. I should have been rather glad if something had, for the sake of fighting the thing out. It's enough to make some fellows loathe the very name of cricket, isn't it?"

"Some of the fellows who can't play don't like it, certainly."

"I don't blame them. If only a few of them would stand out, they'd soon break down the system. But I'm keeping you from your work, old man; you'll think me as bad as the rule. They say you'll have a jolly hard fight for your exam, so you're right to waste no time."

The result of this conservation was that Sherriff, one of the steadiest second-rate bats in the house, was absent from the practice, and a hue-and-cry was made after him. He was found working hard in his study.

"I really can't come to-day. I'm in for the exam, you know, and it'll take me a tremendous grind to lick Redgrave."

"But," said Stafford, who was the ambassador, "it's all the same for all of us. If every fellow said the same, it would be all up with house cricket; and we wanted to turn out such a hot team this year, too. Come on. You'll do your work twice as well after it; and the ground's just in perfect condition for batting to-day."

Sherriff was not proof against this wily appeal. It had been an effort to him to break the rule. It was no effort now to decide to keep it. So he jumped into his flannels and took his beloved bat, and made a long score that morning against Wake's bowling, and was happy. Felgate mentally abused him for his pusillanimity, but saw no reason, for all that, for not turning the incident to account. He proclaimed poor Sherriff's wrongs to a few of the other malcontents.

"It's hard lines," said he, "that just because of this wretched rule, Sherriff is to lose his scholarship. He can't possibly win it unless he's able to read every moment of his time; and that our grave and reverend seniors don't mean to allow."

"Brutal shame," said Munger, "hounding him down like that I've half a mind to stick out."

"That's what Sherriff said," sneered Felgate, "but he had to knuckle under."

"Catch me knuckling under!" said Munger.

He stayed away the next practice day, and, much to his mortification, nobody took the slightest notice of his absence.

"You see," said Felgate, "if only one or two of you stand steady, they can't compel you to play. It's ridiculous."

Next day, accordingly, three fellows stayed away; who, as they were the three premier louts in Railsford's, were never missed or inquired after. But when the next day the number swelled to five, and included Simson, who at least knew one end of a bat from the other, and had once tipped a ball to leg for two, the matter was no longer to be overlooked. The captain's attention was called to the fact that one fellow in the Fifth, three in the Shell, and one Baby, besides Felgate, were not down on the ground.

"Fetch them, then," said Ainger, "and tell them to look sharp, or they'll catch it."

Wake was the envoy this time, and duly delivered his message to the deserters, whom, rather suspiciously, as it seemed to him, he found together.

"You'd better go, you youngsters," said. Felgate, with a sneer; "you'll have to do it sooner or later—you'd better cave in at once."

"I'm hanged if I go," said Munger.

"I fancy that's a safe fixture, whether you go or not," drily observed Wake. "Look sharp, are you coming or not?"

"I'm not coming, I tell you," said Munger.

"No more am I," said Simson.

"No more am I," said each of the others.

"Are you coming, Felgate?" demanded Wake.

This was an irreverent question for a Fifth-form boy to ask a prefect, and Felgate naturally rebuked it.

"It's no business of yours, and you'd better not be impudent, I can tell you. As it happens, I've got some work to do, and can't come. Cut away, you needn't stay."

Wake departed cheerfully, and announced that the whole thing was a "put-up job," as Arthur would have called it, and that Felgate was at the bottom of it. Whereupon Ainger's face grew dark, and he walked, bat in hand, to the house. The mutineers, with the exception of Felgate, who, with the usual prudence of a professional "patriot," had retired to his study, were loafing about the common room just where Wake had interviewed them.

"What's the meaning of all this?" demanded the captain; "what do you mean by not turning up to cricket and sending word you weren't coming when Wake came for you?"

It was much easier defying Ainger in his absence than in his presence, and now that he stood there and confronted them, the delinquents did not quite feel the hardy men of war they had been five minutes ago. Munger, however, tried to carry the thing off with a bluster.

"We don't see the fun of being compelled to go every time. We don't care about cricket; besides—we don't mean to go. Felgate doesn't go; why don't you make him?"

The captain put down his bat.

"Munger, go and put on your flannels at once."

"What if I don't?" asked Munger.

Ainger replied by giving him a thrashing there and then, despite his howls and protests that he had just been going, and would never do it again. The captain replied that he didn't fancy he *would* do it again in a hurry; and as the remainder of the company expressed positive impatience to go to the cricket-field, he let them off with a caution, and, after seeing them started, walked moodily up to Felgate's study.

Felgate was comfortably stretched on two chairs, reading a novel. But as he held the book upside down, Ainger concluded that he could not be very deeply engrossed in its contents.

"You're working, I hear?" said the captain.

"Is that all you've come to tell me?" replied Felgate.

"No, only most fellows when they're reading—even if it's novels, read the right way up. It's bad for the eyes to do it upside down."

Felgate looked a little disconcerted and shut up his book.

"You've missed the last two weeks at cricket," said the captain. "We have managed to get on without you, though, and one of the things I looked in to say now was that if you choose to stay away always you are welcome. Don't think it will put us out."

This was unexpected. Felgate was prepared to hear a peremptory order to go to the field, and had laid his plans for resisting it.

"I've just been seeing one or two other louts down below who hadn't turned up. I'm glad to hear you advised them to go when I sent Wake to fetch them. It's a pity they didn't take your advice, for I've had to thrash Munger. And if you happen to know where I can find the coward who put him and the rest up to breaking the rule, and didn't dare to show face himself, I'll thrash him too."

Felgate was completely disconcerted by this speech, and gnashed his teeth to find himself made a fool of after all.

"Why on earth can't you get out of my study and go down to your cricket? I don't want you here," he snarled.

"I dare say not. But I thought you ought to know what I have been doing to enforce the rule, and what I mean to do. I hope you will tell that coward I spoke of what he may expect."

"Look here," said Felgate, firing up—for a baulked bully rarely talks in a whisper—"you may think yourself a very important person, but I don't." (This was the speech Felgate had prepared in case he had been ordered down to cricket.) "I consider the cricket rule is a bad one, and I'm not surprised if fellows kick against it. I've something better to do than to go down to the field three times a week; and I shall certainly sympathise with any fellows who complain of it and try to get it abolished, and I've told them so. You can do what you like with me. I've told you what I shall do."

"And I," said the captain, whose temper was extinguished, "have told you what I shall do. Is this room large enough, or shall we come outside?"

Felgate stared at him in consternation.

"Whatever do you mean?"

"To fight."

"Rot! I'm not going to fight."

"Very well. Then I give you your choice—a thrashing like that I gave Munger just now; or you can go and put on your flannels and come down to the field."

Felgate hesitated. He had rarely been in such an awkward fix. He knew that a thrashing from the captain, besides being painful, would mean the extinction of any influence he ever had at Grandcourt. On the other hand—

But he had not time to argue it out. Ainger had already laid down his bat.

"You shall have it your *own* way," snarled he; "I'll come to the field."

Chapter Twenty.

The Little Sweep.

Ainger's victory over the rebels had a great moral effect on the house. There was no further question as to the hardship of compulsory cricket; indeed, everyone became so keen on the prospect of turning out a "crack" eleven, that if the rule had required the attendance of every boy daily instead of thrice a week the fellows would have turned up.

The prospects brightened rapidly after a week or two's practice. Railsford put his shoulder to the wheel with his usual energy. He would bowl or bat or field with equal cheerfulness, if thereby he might smarten up the form of any player, however indifferent, who really wanted to improve. He specially devoted himself to the candidates for a place in the second eleven; and it presently began to be rumoured that Railsford's would be able to put two elevens in the field, able to hold their own against any other two in Grandcourt. It was rather a big boast, but after the exploits of the house at the sports nobody could afford to make too little of its ambitious projects.

Arthur, Dig, and their *coterie*—most of them safely housed already in the second eleven—caught a regular cricket fever. They lived in an atmosphere of cricket. They thought in cricket, and dreamed of nothing else. Any question which arose resolved itself into a cricket match in their minds, and was mentally played out to bring it to a decision. Their ordinary talk betrayed their mania, and even their work was solaced by the importation of cricket into its deepest problems.

Here, for instance, is an illustration of the kind of talk which might been have overheard one evening during the first part of the term in the study over Railsford's head.

Arthur was groaning over his Euclid.

"I'm clean bowled by this blessed proposition," said he. "Here have I been slogging away at it all the evening and never got my bat properly under it yet. You might give us a leg-up, Dig."

"Bless you," said Dig, "I'm no good at that sort of yorker. I'm bad enough stumped as it is by this Horace. He gets an awful screw on now and then, and just when you think you've scored off him, there you are in among the slips, caught out low down. I vote we go and ask Marky."

"Don't like it," said Arthur. "Marky served us scurvily over poor old Smiley, and I don't mean to go over his popping-crease, if I can help it, any more."

"That was an underhand twist altogether," said Dig. "Bad enough for Ainger to bowl us out, without him giving it out, too, the way he did. You know, I really think we ought to tell him what a nice way we can stump him out if we like. He just thinks we've caved in and put off our pads."

"I don't like it, Dig. It would be an awfully bad swipe, and Daisy would be knocked over as much as he would. We're not forced to play up to him any more; but I don't like running him out."

"You're a jolly decent brother-in-law, you are," said Dig admiringly, "and it's a pity Marky don't know what he owes you."

At this point Tilbury burst into the room. If Dig and Arthur were a little crazed about cricket, Tilbury was positively off his head.

"How's that, umpires?" cried he, as he entered. "Did you see me playing this afternoon? Went in second man, with Wake and Sherriff bowling, my boys. I knocked up thirty-two off my own bat, and would have been not out, only Mills saw where I placed my smacks in between the two legs, and slipped up and got hold of me low down with his left."

"All right," said Arthur. "Why don't you put on side? I was watching you, and saw you give three awfully bad chances in your first over. Never mind, stick to it, and we'll make a tidy player of you some day. I hear they're going to get up a third eleven. I dare say Ainger will stick you in it if we ask him."

Tilbury laughed good-humouredly; for it was all on the cards that he might get a place in the first eleven before very long.

"I fancied Ainger had knocked you two over the boundary a little while ago. I heard someone say, by the way, if you two could be thrown into one, and taught to hold your bat straight and not hit everything across the wicket, you could be spared to play substitute in Wickford Infant School eleven at their next treat. I said I fancied not, but they're going to try you, for the sake of getting rid of you for half a day."

"Get along. You needn't bowl any of your mild lobs down to us. By the way, is it true you've been stuck in the choir?"

"Yes; awful sell. I tried to scratch, but Parks said they were hard up for a good contralto; so I had to go in the team. I'm to be third man up in the anthem to-morrow—got half a line of solo."

"All serene," said Arthur, "we'll look out for squalls. Tip us one of your low A's, and we'll sky it from our pew. Who's there?"

It was Simson, also infected with the fever, although with him, being of the weak-minded order, it took the form of a craze for "sport" generally. For Simson, as we have mentioned, once tipped a ball to leg for two, and consequently was entitled to be regarded as an authority on every subject pertaining to the turf generally.

He looked very important at present, as he began:

"I say, you chaps, I've got something to tell you—private, you know. You know Mills? His father's brother-in-law lives at Epsom, and so gets all the tips for the races; and Mills says he's put his father up to no end of a straight tip for the Derby. And Mills says he wants to get up a little sweep on the quiet. No blanks, you know. Each fellow draws one horse, and the one that wins gets the lot. Jolly good score, too."

"Oh yes," said Arthur, "I know all about that! I once put a sixpence in a sweep, and never saw it again. Catch me fielding in that little game."

"Oh, but Mills says it's not to be for money, for that's not allowed. He suggested postage-stamps, and then whoever won would be able to write lots of letters home, you know."

"Who wants to write lots of letters home?" said Dig, whose correspondence rarely exceeded two letters a term.

"Well, of course, you're not obliged," explained Simson seriously. "If I drew Roaring Tommy—I mean," said he, correcting himself with a blush, "if I drew the favourite, you know, and potted the sweep, I should turn the stamps into tin."

"Is Roaring Tommy the favourite, then?" asked Tilbury.

"Yes. I oughtn't to have let it out. I told Mills I wouldn't; because it might get his father into a row. Mills says he's dead certain to win. I say, shall you fellows go in?"

"I don't mind," said Tilbury, "as it's not money. Any fellow sell me six stamps?"

"Yes, for sevenpence," said Arthur. "I'm not going in, young Simson. My governor said to me the chances were some young blackleg or other would be on to me to shell out something for a swindle of the kind; and he said, 'Don't you do it.' Besides, I've not got the money."

"I could lend you six stamps," said Simson, who was very keen on the scheme, and failed to see any point in Arthur's other remarks.

"Not good enough," said Arthur.

"Not much chance of scoring, either," said Dig, "if there's about twenty go in and only one wins."

"Just as likely you win it as anybody else," said Simson.

"Come on, you needn't funk it. Lots of fellows are in—Felgate's in."

Arthur whistled.

"He's a prefect," said he.

"Of course he is, and he doesn't see any harm in it."

"Who else?" asked Arthur.

"Rogers, and Munger, and Sherriff."

"A first eleven chap," ejaculated Dig.

"Lots of others. There's twelve names already out of twenty-one. No! thirteen, counting Tilbury. It'll be too late to do it to-morrow."

Arthur looked at Dig and Dig looked at Arthur. Twenty-one sixpences were ten shillings and sixpence, and ten shillings and sixpence would buy a new bat,—at a cost of six stamps. His father had warned him against gambling with money, but had said nothing about postage-stamps. And the cautions Dig had received against all "evil ways" did not even specify gambling at all.

Simson took out his list and wrote Tilbury's name, and then waited for Arthur's decision.

"May as well," said Dig.

"Wait till to-morrow," said Arthur, who still felt qualms.

"You'll be too late then," said Simson.

"All right—that'll settle it then," said Arthur.

"Felgate said he thought you'd be sure to go in," urged the tempter.

"Did he?" said Arthur, a good deal impressed.

"Yes," said Dig jocularly, already fumbling the ten-and-six in anticipation in his pocket. "Any muff can get round Arthur."

It was an unlucky jest, if the baronet's object was to decide his friend in favour of the proposal. For Arthur coloured up and took his hand out of his pocket.

"Wait till to-morrow," said he again.

"Dig, you'll give your name now, won't you?" said Simson.

"Don't know," said Dig evasively; "better not stick it down, that is, not unless the list gets full up, you know."

Simson treated this evasive reply as a consent, and wrote Digs name down, there and then, in his presence.

"Come on, Herapath," said he, making a last appeal. "Don't desert your old friends."

"I tell you I can't say anything till to-morrow," said Arthur, a little crusty.

Simson gave it up and departed.

"Felgate seems to be bowling wide just now," observed Dig. "I shouldn't have fancied he'd have gone in for this sort of thing."

"Why shouldn't he, just as much as you?" growled Arthur.

"I? I haven't gone in for it yet."

"Oh yes, you have; your name's down."

"Only as last man in, though, in case he should get filled up."

"Doesn't matter whether you go in first or last, you're in the game."

"Well," said Dig resignedly, "I don't think I am, really; but if I am, I hope I get Roaring Tommy."

Simson had not much difficulty in filling up his list. The specious pretext of the postage-stamps did not delude many, but Felgate's name worked wonders. Felgate had had no intention of allowing his name to be used, and was indeed in blissful ignorance that his support was generally known. He had in a reckless way expressed his sympathy with what he chose to term a very innocent "round game," and had given practical proof of his sympathy by buying a ticket. That was yesterday, and he had since forgotten the whole affair, and was quietly looking about him for some new way of wiping off the rapidly-accumulating score against Railsford and his lieutenant Ainger.

After his rebuff about the compulsory cricket—which, fortunately, no one but the captain (who was not the man to say much about it) had witnessed—Felgate had retired for a time into comparative seclusion. He believed in his lucky star, and hoped there was a good time coming. He still had his trump card in hand, but if he could win his trick without it he would be so much to the good.

Arthur, when, on the day after Simson's visit, he heard that the list was closed without him, kicked Simson, and felt on the whole rather glad. He had thought the matter over, and did not like breaking his promise to the people at home. Besides, he still felt sore at the loss of his former sixpence in a similar venture, and looked upon the whole business as more or less of a "plant." Further than that, he now had a delightful opportunity of tormenting Sir Digby, who had weakly yielded to the tempter, albeit with a few qualms and prickings of conscience.

"Just like you!" bragged Arthur; "anybody can do you! A precious lot of your six stamps you'll see back! *I* know Mills—a regular shark!—and if there's a row, he'll back out and leave you and the rest of them to catch it; then who'll be Roaring Tommy, eh?"

Digby did not like this sort of talk; it offended him—besides, it frightened him.

"Stuff and nonsense!" said he. "Who's to care about a few postage-stamps? I wouldn't gamble with money, not if I was paid for it. Why, I should fancy if Felgate goes in for it it's not much harm."

"Felgate knows what he's up to, and can look after himself," said Arthur. "You can't; you swallow everything any ass tells you!"

"I don't swallow all *you* tell me, for one!" retorted Dig.

Arthur coloured; he did not like being pulled up short like that, especially when he was doing the high moral business.

"All serene!" said he testily; "do as you please. I've warned you to keep out of it, young Oakshott. Don't blame me if you burn your fingers."

Thus said his prigship, and undid all the credit his little act of self-denial had earned him. He is not the only boy who gets his head turned now and then by the unexpected discovery that he is virtuous. Is he, reader?

But, without being a prophet, his prigship managed on the present occasion to make a pretty near prediction, for Sir Digby Oakshott did burn his fingers.

He was summoned one evening to Mills's study to draw his horse. The twenty-one names were shaken up in a hat, and those present each drew out one. To Dig's disgust, he drew Blazer—a horse whom everybody jeered at as a rank outsider. Simson was the fortunate drawer of Roaring Tommy. Mills got the second favourite, and Felgate—for whom, in his absence, Mills drew—got another outsider called Polo.

Dig scarcely liked to tell Arthur of his bad luck, but his chum extracted the secret from him.

"I'm jolly glad!" said Arthur sententiously; "the worst thing that could happen to you would be to win. I'm glad you'll have a good lesson."

"Thanks," said Dig, and went out to try to sell Blazer for three stamps. But no one would look at him, and Dig finally crushed the paper into his waistcoat-pocket in disgust, and wished he had his stamps safe there instead.

A fortnight later, just as he and Arthur were marching down proudly to the cricket-field, in order to take part in a great match—the first of the season.—between an eleven of Ainger's and an eleven of Barnworth's, he was struck all of a heap by the amazing announcement, conveyed by Simson, that Blazer had won the Derby! Dig turned pale at the news, and convulsively dug his hand into his pocket to see if he had his paper safe.

"Not really?" he exclaimed.

"Yes, he has! Roaring Tommy was nowhere. Jolly lucky for me I sold my ticket to Tilbury for eight-and-six! I wish I'd bought yours for threepence when you asked me."

Dig laughed hysterically.

"Then I've got the ten-and-six?" he asked.

"Rather."

Dig made two duck's eggs, and missed every ball that came in his way that afternoon, and was abused and hooted all round the field. What cared he? He had Blazer burning a hole in his pocket, and ten-and-six in postage-stamps waiting for him in Mills's study. As soon as he could decently quit the scene of his inglorious exploits, he bolted off to claim his stakes. Mills was not at home, so he took a seat and waited for him, glancing round the room carefully, in case the stamps should be lying out for him somewhere. But they were not.

In due time Mills returned.

"Hullo, kid! what do you want?"

Dig grinned and pulled out his paper.

"How's that, umpire?" demanded he.

Mills stared at the document.

"What on earth is the row with you? What are you driving at?"

"Ten-and-sixpence, please," said the beaming baronet; "I've got Blazer."

Mills laughed.

"You're not in much of a hurry. Has Blazer won, then?"

"Yes; a rank outsider, too. Do you know, I tried all I knew to sell my ticket for threepence. Just fancy if I had."

"It's a pity you didn't," said Mills, taking a chair, "The fact is, there's been a bit of a muddle about Blazer. That ass Simson, when he wrote out the tickets, wrote Blazer twice over instead of Blazer and Catterwaul. They were both such regular outsiders, it didn't seem worth correcting it at the time. I'm awfully sorry, you know, but your's—let's see," said he, taking the cadaverous baronet's ticket and looking at it, "yours has got one of the corners torn off—yes, that's it. Yours should be Catterwaul."

Dig gasped, and tried to moisten his parched lips. It was a long time before the words came.

"It's a swindle!" cried he, choking. "I've won it—I—I—give me the 10 shillings 6 pence."

"Don't make an ass of yourself," said Mills. "I tell you you've got the wrong paper; isn't that enough?"

"No, it's not enough, you thief, you!" roared Dig, tossing his tawny mane. "Everybody said you were a blackleg—I know it's all lies you're telling, and I—I—I don't care if you do lick me."

As he didn't care, of course it didn't so much matter, but Mills cut short further argument by licking him and ejecting him neck and crop from the room.

In the passage he pitched head-first into the arms of Mr Railsford.

"What's wrong?" asked the master, looking down at the miserable face of the small savage before him.

"It's a swindle!" shouted Dig. "It's a swindle, Mr Railsford. I won it fairly—and he's a thief—he's stolen 10 shillings 6 pence of mine."

"Don't make all that noise," said Railsford quietly, for the luckless baronet was almost out of his wits. "I can hear you without shouting. Who has robbed you?"

"Why, that blackleg swindler in there!" said Dig, pointing at Mills's door. "Ten-and-six, ten-and-six—the thief!"

"Come with me," said the master, and he led Dig back into Mills's study.

"Mills," said he, "Oakshott says you have robbed him. What does it mean?"

"I've not done anything of the kind," said Mills, himself rather pale and scared. "I told him—it was all a mistake. It wasn't my fault."

"What was a mistake? Just tell me what it is all about."

Here Dig took up the parable.

"Why, he got up a sweep on the Derby, and got us each to shell out six stamps, and there were twenty-one fellows in, and I drew Blazer, the winner; and now he won't give me the stakes, and says my Blazer is a mistake for Catterwaul!"

Railsford frowned.

"This is a serious matter. You know the rule about gambling."

"Oh, please, sir," said Mills, who had dropped all his bravado, as he realised that he stood a good chance of being expelled, "I really didn't mean it for gambling; it wasn't for money, only stamps; and I thought there was no harm. I'll never do such a thing again, sir, really." And he almost went on his knees.

"The doctor must deal with this matter, Mills," said Railsford sternly. "You must go to him to-morrow evening."

"Oh, Mr Railsford, he'll expel me!" howled the culprit.

"Good job, too," ejaculated Dig, *sotto voce.*

"Possibly," said the master. "Where is the money?"

Dig's spirits rose. He knew he would get his rights!

"The stamps—here, sir," said the wretched Mills, going to his desk.

"And where is the list of names?"

Mills produced it, tremulously. Railsford's brows knit as he glanced down it.

"Each of these boys gave you six stamps?"

"Twenty-one sixpences, ten-and-six," said Dig, rehearsing his mental arithmetic.

"Yes, sir. I really didn't mean to cheat, sir."

"Yes, you did," yapped Dig, who now that he was to finger his winnings had perked up wonderfully.

"Silence, Oakshott," said Railsford angrily. "Your name is here, last on the list. Take back your six stamps, and write me out one hundred lines of Livy by Thursday morning."

Poor Dig turned green, and staggered back a pace, and stared at the six stamps in his hand.

"Why!" gasped he. "I had Blazer—I—"

"Be silent, sir, and go to your study, and tell Tilbury to come here."

In due time Tilbury came, and received back his six stamps, and a hundred lines of Livy, and an order to send the next boy on the black list to receive a similar reward for his merits. And so the tedious process went on, and that afternoon, in Mills's study, twenty boys sadly took back six stamps each, and received among them two thousand lines of Livy, to be handed in on Thursday morning. One name remained: the first on the list, and consequently the last in the order in which Railsford had taken it.

"I will return these," said he, taking up the six remaining stamps, "to Felgate myself."

Mills made one more appeal.

"Do let me off going to the doctor, sir!" implored he. "Why, sir, I never thought it could be wrong if Felgate went in for it, and they've all got their stamps back, sir. Please let me off."

"I cannot do that. If the doctor treats you less severely than you deserve, it will be because you have made this reparation, instead of carrying out the act of dishonesty you had it in your mind to perpetrate."

And he left him there, and proceeded, with a heart as heavy as any he had worn since he came to Grandcourt, to Felgate's study.

Chapter Twenty One.

The Naturalists' Field Club.

Felgate, as we have said, had almost forgotten the existence of the sweep or the fact that he had given his name to the venture. When therefore Railsford unexpectedly walked into his study, he did not in any way connect the visit with that trivial incident. He conjured up in his mind any possible motive the master could have for this interview. He could only think of one, and perceiving a paper in Railsford's hands, concluded that he had discovered the authorship of a certain anonymous letter addressed to Mr Bickers, and had looked in for a little explanation.

Felgate was quite prepared to gratify him, and promised himself a cheerful quarter of an hour over so congenial an occupation. He was, in consequence, considerably mortified when the real object of the visit unfolded itself.

"Felgate," said Railsford, "I have come to you on very unpleasant business. This is not the first time I have had to caution you that your example in the house is neither worthy of a prefect nor a senior boy."

"Thank you, sir," said Felgate, with ostentatious indifference. He had better have remained silent, for Railsford dismissed whatever of mildness he had come armed with, and stood on his dignity.

"Don't be impertinent, Felgate; it will do you no good. I want to know how it comes that your name appears here at the head of a list of entries for a sweepstake on a horse race, when you as a prefect know that gambling in any shape or form is strictly prohibited here?"

Felgate, taken back by this unexpected indictment, looked at the paper and laughed.

"I really don't know how my name comes there. I can't be supposed to know why anybody who likes should write my name down on a piece of paper."

"You mean to say that you never entered your name?" asked Railsford, beginning to feel a sense of relief.

"Certainly not."

"You were asked to do so? What did you reply?"

"I haven't a notion. I probably said, don't bother me—or do anything you like, or something of that sort."

"Did you point out that it was against the rules?"

"No. Is it against the rules? There doesn't seem any harm in it, if fellows choose to do it. Besides, it wasn't for money."

"Did you give six stamps?"

"Stamps? I fancy someone came to borrow some stamps of me a week or so ago. I forget who it was."

"Felgate," said the master with a tone of scorn which made the prefect wince, "it is hardly worth your while to tell lies when you can satisfy me of your guilt quite as easily by telling the truth. I won't ask you more questions, for I have no wish to give you more opportunities of falsehood. Here are your six stamps. Go to Doctor Ponsford to-morrow at 8 p.m."

Felgate looked blank at this announcement.

"What!" he exclaimed. "Go to the doctor? Are you going to tell him about a trifle like this?"

"It is no trifle for a prefect deliberately to break the school rules and encourage others to do so. I have said the same thing to you before."

"Look here, Mr Railsford," said Felgate, with a curious mixture of cringing and menace. "It's not fair to send me to the doctor about a thing like this. I know you have a spite against me; but you can take it out of me without bringing him into it. I fancy if you knew all I know, you'd think twice before you did it."

Railsford looked at him curiously.

"You surely forget, Felgate, that you are not speaking to a boy in the Shell."

"No, I don't. I know you're a master, and head of a house, and a man who ought to be everything that's right and good—"

"Come, come," interrupted Railsford, "we have had enough of this. You are excited and forget yourself to talk in this foolish way."

And he quitted the study.

What, he wondered, could be the meaning of all this wild outbreak on the part of the detected prefect? What did he mean by that "If you knew all I know"? It sounded like one of those vague menaces with which Arthur had been wont to garnish his utterances last term. What did Felgate know, beyond the secret of his own wrong-doings, which could possibly affect the Master of the Shell?

It flashed across Railsford suddenly—suggested perhaps by the connection of two ideas—that Arthur himself might be in some peril or difficulty. It was long since the master had attempted to control the secret of his prospective relationship with the vivacious young Shell-fish. Everybody knew about it as soon as ever he set foot in Grandcourt, and Daisy's name was common property all over the house. Arthur had contrived to reap no small advantage from the connection. The prefects had pretty much left him alone, and, as a relative of the master, he had been tacitly winked at in many of his escapades, with a leniency which another boy could not have hoped for.

What if now Arthur should lie under the shadow of some peril which, if it fell, must envelop him and his brother-in-law both? If, for instance, he had committed some capital offence, which if brought to light should throw on him (Railsford) the terrible duty of nipping in the bud the school career of Daisy's own brother? It seemed the only solution to Felgate's mysterious threat, and it made him profoundly uncomfortable.

He felt he had not done all the might for the boy. He had been so scrupulously careful not to give any pretext for a charge of favouritism, that he had even neglected him at times. Now and then he had had a chat; but Arthur had such a painful way of getting into awkward topics that such conferences were usually short and formal. He had occasionally given an oversight to the boy's work; but Arthur so greatly preferred to "mug," as he called it, in his own study, that opportunities for serious private coaching had been quite rare.

Recently, too, a difference had sprung up between Arthur and Marky about the Smileys; and Railsford felt that he had not done all he might to smooth over that bitter memory and recover the loyalty and affection of the bereaved dog-fancier. It may have been some or all of these notions which prompted the master to invite his young kinsman to accompany him on the following day—being the mid-term holiday—on an expedition into the country.

The occasion had been chosen by the Grandcourt Naturalists' Field Club for their yearly picnic. This club was a very select, and, by repute, dry institution, consisting partly of scientific boys and partly of masters. Its supposed object was to explore the surrounding country for geological, botanical, and historical specimens, which were, when found, deposited in a museum which nobody in the school on any pretext ever visited.

Every member had the privilege of introducing a friend, but no one took advantage of the invitation, except once a year, on the occasion of the annual picnic, when there was always a great rush, and a severe competition to be numbered among the happy participants of the club's hospitality.

It was long since Arthur had given up all idea of joining these happy parties. Great therefore was his astonishment and delight when on the evening before the term holiday Railsford put his head into the study and said—

"Arthur, would you like to come to-morrow to the Field Club picnic at Wellham Abbey?"

"Rather," said Arthur.

"Very well; be ready at ten. I've ordered a tandem tricycle."

Arthur was in ecstasy. If there was one kind of spree he liked it was a picnic at an abbey; and if there was one sort of conveyance he doated on it was a tricycle. He wiped off every score on his mental slate against Marky, and voted him the greatest brick going, and worthy to be backed up to the very end—especially if they had oysters at the picnic!

"Wish *you* could come, old man," said he to Dig, who was groaning over his 100 lines of Livy.

"I wouldn't go with him if he asked me, the cad!" growled Dig.

"No, he's not a cad. If it hadn't been for him you wouldn't have seen one of your stamps back; and you might have been expelled straight away into the bargain. Tell you what, Dig, you've been scouting for Stafford all the last week; he ought to do something for you. Why don't you ask him to take you? He'll do it, like a shot. He's always civil to us."

Dig thought it over.

"If he says Yes, will you help me polish off my lines?"

"All right. I say, go soon, or somebody else may have asked him."

Dig went, and to his satisfaction was informed that Stafford would take him, if he promised to be steady. Which of course he did promise. So between them the two chums polished off the Livy—never was the great historian made such mincemeat of before or after—and then gave themselves over to delightful anticipations of the Field Club picnic.

One misgiving disturbed Arthur's peace of mind. Railsford might make a base use of his opportunity as partner on the tricycle to corner him about his misdeeds and generally to "jaw" him. Besides, as Dig was going too, it would be ever so much jollier if Dig and he could go to Wellham together and let the masters go by themselves.

"We must work it somehow, Dig," said Arthur. "If we go we must have a high old time—and not be let in for a lot of rot about old bones and fossils and that sort of thing."

"Rather not," said Dig, "though I wouldn't mind if we could get hold of a skull. It would look prime on the mantelpiece."

"Gammer, who went last year, says it was an awful go-to-meeting turn-out. Top-hats, and service at the abbey, and scarcely a bit of grub; but I hear the spread's to be rather good this year, down by the river's edge."

"Hooroo!" said Dig, "I guess you and I will be about when they call over for that part of the spree."

The morning was dull and cloudy, and Dig and Arthur as they stood on the hall steps and looked up at the sky, debated with themselves whether the day would hold up long enough to allow of the picnic at the water's edge. To their relief, the other excursionists who gradually assembled took a hopeful view of the weather and predicted that it would be a fine afternoon, whatever the morning might be.

As they were Naturalist Field Club people, our boys supposed they knew what they were saying, and dismissed their qualms in consequence.

Wellham Abbey was ten miles off. Most of the party proposed to reach it on foot. Mr Roe was driving with the doctor and his niece, and one or two others, like Railsford, preferred to travel on wheels.

Dig was standing somewhat lugubriously beside Arthur, inspecting the tandem, and wondering how he was to get to Wellham, when Mr Grover came up and said to Railsford—

"How are you going, Railsford? Not in that concern, are you? Come and walk with me, I've not had a chat with you for ages."

Arthur felt a violent dig in his ribs from the delighted baronet. There was a chance for the "high old time" yet.

"Well, the fact is, I'd promised one of my boys to give him the ride," said the Master of the Shell.

"Oh, please don't mind me," said Arthur. "Oakshott and I can bring the machine for you to Wellham, if you'd sooner walk."

"Is Oakshott going?"

"Yes, sir. Stafford's asked him, hasn't he, Dig?"

"Yes, sir. I've scouted for Stafford at cricket this term, so he's asked me to-day; and I've done my lines, sir."

"Oh, very well," said Railsford, to whom the temptation of a walk with Grover was even greater than that of a *tête-à-tête* ride with Arthur Herapath; "but can you manage it?"

"Manage it?" exclaimed they, in tones as if they could scarcely believe they heard aright, "rather, sir."

"Well," said the master, tickled with the evident delight of the pair to be together, "take care how you go. You had better take the Grassen Road, so as to avoid the hill. Come along, Grover."

So these two artful young "naturalists" had it their own way after all.

"Come on, sharp," said Arthur, "and get out of the ruck."

"Jolly good joke telling us not to go by Maiden Hill," said Digby; "that'll be the best part of the lark."

Luckily a tandem tricycle of the type provided for them is not a machine which requires any very specially delicate riding. Had it been, Arthur and Dig might have been some time getting out of the "ruck," as they politely termed the group of their pedestrian fellow-naturalists. For they were neither of them adepts; besides which, the tricycle being intended for a pair of full-grown men, they had some difficulty in keeping their saddles and working their treadles at one and the same time. They had to part company with the latter when they went down, and catch them flying as they came up; and the result was not always elegant or swift. However, they managed to pass muster in some sort, as they started off under the eye of their master, and as speedily as possible dodged their vehicle up a side lane, where, free from embarrassing publicity, they were at leisure to adapt their progress to their own convenience.

It wasn't quite as much fun as they had expected. The machine was a heavy one, and laboured a good deal in its going. The treadles, as I have said, were very long; the brake did not always act, and the steering apparatus was stiff. Even the bell, in whose music they had promised themselves some solace, was out of tune; and the road was very like a ploughed field. The gaiety of the boys toned down into sobriety, and the sobriety into silence, and their silence into the ill-humour begotten of perspiration, dust, fatigue, and disappointment. Their high old time was not coming off!

At length, by mutual consent, they got off and began viciously to shove the machine up the hill.

"They'll all be there already," said Arthur, looking at his watch. "We've been two hours."

"I wish I'd walked with them," said Dig.

"Pity you didn't," growled Arthur, "you aren't very lively company."

"Anyhow, I've done my share of the fag. You and Marky may bring the beast home."

This altercation might have proceeded to painful lengths, had not a diversion occurred in their arrival at the crest of the hill.

Any ordinary traveller would have stood and admired the beautiful view—the finest, it was said, in the county. But Arthur and Dig were in no humour for artistic raptures. The sight of the abbey towers peeping cut in the valley among the trees, and of the silver river which curled past it, suggested to them no thoughts of historic grandeur—no meditations on the pathetic beauty of ruin. It made them smell oysters and hear the popping of lemonade corks, and reminded them they had still two long miles to go before lunch.

"Get on, sharp," said Arthur, climbing into his saddle, "it won't take us long to go down the hill."

It didn't! They did the distance, a mile and a half, in about three minutes. The brake came to grief the moment they started, and they had nothing for it but to hold on and let her fly. As to attempting to control the speed with their feet, they were thankful enough to get those members up on the rest out of reach of the treadles, which plunged up and down like the pistons of a steam-engine. Luckily there was nothing on the road; luckily, too, the ruts which had broken the ground on the other side were for the most part absent on this. Once or twice the machine lurched ominously, and they thought all was up, and once or twice a stone or obstacle ahead promised to terminate finally their headlong career. But the gallant tandem cleared them all, and her passengers clutched on to their handles like grim death; and between them they did the distance in some seconds under the record, and ran a clean half-mile on the level at the foot of the hill before they could bring one of the most famous runs of the season to a standstill. Thanks to this rapid performance they were only about a quarter of an hour after the pedestrians at the abbey.

"Well, here you are," said Railsford; "you came by Grassen, I suppose? Rather rough riding, wasn't it?"

"We came by Maiden Hill after all," said Arthur. "It *was* rather rough."

"Did you walk down, then?"

"No, we rode it. We came down in pretty good time. There's something the matter with the brake, so we had to let her go."

Possibly Railsford had a better notion of the narrow escape of the two hare-brained young guests of the club than they had themselves. They forgot all about it the moment they saw a hamper being carried in the direction of the river and heard Mr Roe announce that they might as well have lunch now, and explore the abbey afterwards.

"Hear, hear," whispered Dig to his friend. "Eh?"

"Rather," said Arthur.

And they were invaluable in spreading the repast and hastening the moment when Mr Roe at last announced that they were all ready to begin.

It was rather an imposing company. The doctor was there, and his niece, and Messrs Roe, Grover, Railsford, and one or two other masters. Smedley also was present, very attentive to Miss Violet; and Clipstone was there, as well as our friends Ainger, Barnworth, and Stafford. And all the learned luminaries of the Fifth were there, too, and one or two scientists from the Fourth. Arthur and Dig had rarely been in such good company, and had certainly never before realised how naturalists can eat. It was a splendid spread, and the two chums, snugly entrenched behind a rampart of hampers, drowned their sorrows and laid their dust in lemonade, and recruited their minds and bodies with oysters and cold beef, and rolls and jam tarts, till the profession of a naturalist seemed to them to be one of the most glorious in all this glorious world.

"Now," said Mr Roe, who was president of the club and host, "let us go and see the abbey. I have put together a few notes on its history and architecture, which I thought might be useful. Let us go first to the Saxon crypt, which is unquestionably the oldest portion of the structure."

"Oh, lag all that," said Dig to his friend. "Are you going to hear all that rot?"

"Not if I know it," replied Arthur. "We'd better lie low, and help wash up the plates, and when they're gone we can go for a spin up the big window."

So, when Mr Roe, having collected his little audience round him, began to descant with glowing countenance on the preciousness of some fragments of a reputed Druidical font lately dug up in the crypt, two naturalists, who should have been hanging on his lips, were busy polishing up the plates and the remnants of the repast, at the water's edge, and watching their chance for a "spin" up the ruined arch of the great window. That window in its day must have been one of the finest abbey windows in England. It still stood erect, covered with ivy, while all around it walls, towers, and roof had crumbled into dust. Some of the slender stone framework still dropped gracefully from the Gothic arch, and at the apex of all there still adhered a foot or two of the sturdy masonry of the old belfry.

No boy could look up to that lofty platform, standing out clear against the grey sky, without feeling his feet tingle. Certainly Arthur and Dig were not proof against its fascination.

The first part of the climb, up the tumbled walls and along the ivy-covered buttresses, was easy enough. The few sparrows and swallows bustling out from the ivy at their approach had often been similarly disturbed before. But when they reached the point where the great arch, freeing itself, as it were, of its old supports, sprung in one clear sweep skyward, their difficulties began. The treacherous stones more than once crumbled under their feet, and had it not been for the sustaining ivy, they would have come down with a run too.

"You see," said Mr Roe to his admiring audience below, "the work of dissolution is still rapidly going on. These stones have fallen from the great arch since we came here."

"Regular jerry-builders they must have had in those days," growled Dig, scrambling up the last few yards; "did you ever see such rotten walls?"

Arthur confessed he hadn't; but having gained the top, he forgave the builders. Rarely had Dig and he been so pleased with themselves and one another. It was a genuine feat of climbing, of which very few could boast; and peril and achievement bind friends together as no mortar ever binds bricks.

"That window," said Mr Roe, looking up from below, "is considered inaccessible. It is said to be haunted; but the truth is, I believe, that it is infested by owls."

Here a faint "boo-hoo!" from above bore sudden and striking testimony to the truth of the master's observations.

"Hullo!" said Arthur, peering over, "they're going. Look sharp down, Dig, or we'll be left."

Dig obeyed. It was much more difficult getting down than getting up. Still, by dint of clinging tight hold of the ivy and feeling every step, he managed to descend the perilous arch and get on to the comparatively safe footing of the buttress.

"You cut on," shouted Arthur from above, "I'll be down in a second. Don't wait—I have found an owl's nest up here; and I'm going to collar a young 'un for each of us. Don't tell them. If Railsford asks where I am, tell him I'm walking home. You can go with him on the tandem. I'll be home as soon as you."

At the same moment a shout from below of "Herapath!" "Oakshott!" still further hastened Dig's descent to *terra firma*.

"Come on," said Railsford, who was already seated on the tricycle, "it's coming on to rain. Where's Herapath?"

"Oh, he's walking home. He told me to tell you so. We've been scrambling about. Can I come in the tandem?"

"If he's not coming you can. Has he gone on, then?"

"No—he was just getting a—a specimen," said Dig, hopping up on the saddle, and resolving that Marky should do all the work. "He says he'd sooner walk."

"Dear me! here comes the rain," said Railsford, turning up his collar, "we'd better go on. He'll get wet, whichever way he comes home."

So they departed—as also did Mr Roe and the doctor and all the others.

"There's an owl again," said Mr Roe, looking back at the big window.

He was wrong. The shout he heard was from Arthur; not this time in sport, but in grim earnest. For, having abandoned the idea of capturing the owls, he had started to descend the arch. He had safely accomplished half the distance when a ledge of mortar gave way under him and left him hanging by his arms to the ivy. He felt in vain with his feet for some support, but could find none. Dig's previous descent had knocked away most of the little ledges by which they had come up.

Finally, by a desperate effort, he pulled himself up a few inches by the ivy and managed to get a footing again. But there he stuck. He could not go down further; and to go up would bring him no nearer Grandcourt than he was at present. So it was

Arthur shouted; and everyone thought him an owl, and left him there in the rain to spend a pleasant evening on the top of the great window of Wellham Abbey.

Chapter Twenty Two.

The Haunted Window.

"Let me see," said the doctor, as he and Railsford met once during the day, "I have two of your boys to see this evening. One, a prefect. Was it necessary to send him up?"

"It was, sir. If I saw the slightest prospect of dealing properly with him myself I would have done so. He is an enemy to the order of our house, and, as you know, our house just now cannot afford to have more enemies than it has."

"Your enemies are those of your own house," said the doctor sternly. "I had expected long before this that it would have been possible to restore it to the ordinary rights of Grandcourt. An impenetrable mystery is a bad thing for a school."

"It is," said Railsford, feeling uncomfortable. And here the conservation ended.

Railsford had not been long in his room that evening when Sir Digby Oakshott knocked at the door and entered with a long face.

"Please, sir, have you seen anything of Herapath?" said he. "He's not turned up."

"What—are you sure?"

"I've asked them all. All the others have come. I expect he'll get pretty drenched if he's lost his way."

"He can't have lost the way—it's too simple. What was he doing at the abbey when you last saw him?"

"Going after owls," said Dig.

"Where?"

"On the big window. We got to the top, you know; and I came down as soon as I saw you all starting; and he shouted that he would be down in a second, and was going to walk home; and we weren't to wait. I say, I wonder if he's got stuck up there, or come a cropper?"

Dig's face was pale as the thought flashed across his mind. Railsford was not a bit less concerned.

"Go quickly and see if Mr Roe has sent away his trap, and, if not, keep it. If it has gone, go to Jason's and get one directly, Oakshott."

In five minutes the baronet returned.

"I can't get a trap anywhere," said he dismally, "but I've got Jason to send a horse."

"That will do," said Railsford, hurrying down.

"Will it do?" groaned Dig. "*I* can't go too! Oh, Mr Railsford," shouted he, as the master was jumping into the saddle, "what road shall you come back by?"

"Maiden Hill," said the master, digging his heels into the horse's side.

With a heavy heart Digby watched him start, and then putting on his cap determinedly, followed him on foot into the night and rain.

"I shall do it in two hours and a half," said he to himself, "if I trot part of the way. What a cad I was to leave him up there!"

It was not till bed-time at Railsford's that fellows generally became aware that the master and two of the boys were missing. Railsford and Oakshott had both been seen in the school after their return from the picnic. Railsford had, of course, depended on the boy to explain his sudden absence, and Dig had been too miserable and excited to think of telling anybody as he started on his weary tramp.

The first inquiry for the missing ones came from the doctor, who, after his interview with Felgate, sent a messenger over to the Master of the Shell to request his presence in the head-master's study at once. The messenger returned to report that Mr Railsford was not in, and no one knew where he was gone. Then, the hue and cry being once raised, it appeared that Arthur and Dig's study was also empty and that its owners were nowhere to be found.

Presently the school gatekeeper reported that on coming up from the town just now he had seen Mr Railsford galloping on one of Jason's horses in the direction of the London road! And Munger, who had been out of bounds, reported in private (because the disclosure might get him into trouble if it came to the ears of the authorities) that just as he was sneaking in at the gate he met Sir Digby Oakshott, Baronet, sneaking out.

The doctor, who might never have heard of the affair, had he not chanced to want to see Railsford particularly that evening, walked over to the house about bed-time and interviewed Ainger.

"Have you the slightest idea what it all means?" asked the head-master.

"Not the slightest, sir," said Ainger shortly. If he had had, he would have spoken long ago, as the doctor knew—or should have known.

"No one is to stay up," said the doctor, "and I wish you to take charge of the order of the house in Mr Railsford's absence, Ainger. Circumstances have occurred which may make it necessary to remove Felgate to another house, meanwhile he has forfeited his prefecture here."

And the doctor went away, leaving the captain of Railsford's with a new perplexity piled up on all the others.

Whereupon Ainger sent his house to bed; and threatened them with all sorts of penalties if lights were not out and all quiet by 9.30. It was a sleepless night for a good many in Grandcourt. Mr Roe and Grover sat up together in the rooms of the former, anxious and perplexed about their missing friend. Mr Bickers walked about his room too, and wondered if his game was to slip through his fingers after all. And Felgate lay awake and laughed to himself in the conviction that to him belonged the glory of hunting the scoundrel from Grandcourt. And Maple, Simson, Tilbury, and Dimsdale, in the Shell dormitory lay awake too, and strained their ears at every sound in the court below, and wondered ruefully what had become of their two missing comrades.

Dig, as he ploughed his way footsore and weary through the rain and mud of Maiden Hill, down which he had shot at such a glorious pace not twelve hours before, thought wistfully once or twice of that warm dry bed in the dormitory and the friendly voices of his allies there assembled. But he would never return there without old Arthur! In the times of their prosperity and security those two boys had often quarrelled, often neglected one another, often forgotten all about one another; and a casual onlooker might have said, "They are not friends—they are no more to one another than any other two boys in the school."

Ah, but if the critic could have looked into Dig's heavy heart as he floundered through the mud that night he would have told a different tale. Often enough our friend seems to us like an ordinary friend. We have our little tiffs and our little reconciliations; we have our mutual jokes and our time-honoured arguments. We say good-bye with unruffled spirits, and meet again with an unimpassioned nod. But now and again the testing time comes. The storm breaks over our heads, the thunder rolls round us. Then the grip of our hands tightens, we find that, we are not friends, but brothers; and the lightning flash reveals to us, what we never suspected before, that there is something in the world dearer to us even than life; and as our hearts sink we envy those happy people, who, by their simple trust in their Saviour and in the all-pervading Goodness, are able to face with courage both Life and Death.

Dig stumbled on, dead beat, losing heart, at every step, and stopping sometimes to take breath with a gasp which sounded ominously like a sob. The long hill seemed interminable; there was no glimmer of a light anywhere to cheer him; no clatter of a horse's hoofs to ring hope into his heart. All was black, and wet, and dreary. What if he should find the abbey deserted, and have to walk home—alone! He had nearly reached the ruin when he stumbled against two men conversing in the middle of the road. To his inexpressible relief one of them was Railsford.

"Mr Railsford!" gasped the boy, springing upon the master with a suddenness which made both men start, "is that you? Where's Arthur? Have you found him?"

"He's all right—he's on the top of the window still, and we can't get him down till daylight. I'm just arranging with Farmer White to bring a ladder."

Dig made a dash in the direction of the abbey gate.

"Where are you going?" said Railsford.

"I'm going to hop up beside him," shouted Dig, almost beside himself with relief.

The master caught him firmly by the arm.

"If you think of such a thing, Oakshott, I shall get Farmer White here to cart you straight back to Grandcourt."

This terrible threat sobered Dig at once. He waited impatiently till the two men had made their arrangements, and then, with beating heart, accompanied the master to the ruin.

"He is safe up where he is," said the latter, "and says he has room to sit down and a back of ivy to lean against. But he must be half drowned and frozen. It will do him good to know you are here. Now stay where you are, while I get on the wall and shout to him. He cannot hear us down here." Dig waited, and listened to the master scrambling up the ivy and feeling his way on his hands and knees along the wall to the bottom of the arch.

Then he heard him shout—

"Arthur, are you there, all right?"

And his heart leapt as a shrill reply came back from the heights.

"Oakshott is here with me," shouted the master.

It was all a mistake about not being able to hear from the level ground. Dig heard the "Hallo! what cheer, Dig?" as plainly as he heard Railsford himself.

"What cheer?" he howled in reply. "Keep up your pecker, old man."

"Rather!" yelled Arthur.

Then Dig begged and besought Railsford to allow him to mount at least to where the latter stood, and the master made him happy by consenting. From this point it was easy to carry on a talk; and there in the rain through the dark watches of the night those three had one of the most profitable conversations they had ever enjoyed. A yokel who chanced to pass, hearing those weird, celestial voices, took to his heels and ran a mile straight off, and reported with ashy face and trembling lips that a ghost had appeared on the arch of the abbey as he passed, and called to him thrice, and had shrieked with demoniacal laughter as he hurried from the accursed place.

Towards dawn the rain ceased, and the three watchers, despite all their efforts, became drowsy. When Farmer White and two of his men arrived on the scene with a long ladder and a rope, they had to stand and shout from below for a minute or so before Railsford started into wakefulness and remembered where he was. As for Dig, he lay with his cheek buried in the wet ivy, sleeping as soundly as if he had been in the dormitory at school.

It was no easy task to get Arthur down from his dizzy perch. In the first place, he was so sound asleep that it was impossible to rouse him from below; consequently he could give no assistance in his own rescue. The ladder was far too short to reach within a quarter of the distance of where he was; and for a long time it seemed as if the ropes might as well have been left at home.

At length, however, by a combined effort the ladder was hoisted on to the top of the wall, and so elevated it reached a point on the arch above the place where the stones had given way. The difficulty was to secure it on the narrow ledge in any way so that it could be ascended safely. When, finally, by dint of careful adjustment and rigid holding at the bottom, it was pronounced reasonably safe, Dig was most eager to volunteer the ascent, urging that he was the lightest weight, and that the four men could do more good in holding the ladder.

"The lad's right," said the farmer; "let him go up."

Railsford was forced to consent. It would have been obviously risky for a heavy man to ascend that rickety ladder. Dig rarely felt so proud and happy as when he skipped lightly up the rungs and reached the ivy-covered masonry of the arch.

It was not a difficult climb to the top, and it was as well it was not, for in his eagerness he forgot the admonitions of caution he had received below, and scrambled up as recklessly as if he had been ascending a London tramcar. His heart beat as at last he came upon his dear old friend.

Arthur sat sound asleep, his hands behind his head, his legs hanging over the edge of the arch, and his back propped in the angle formed by the junction of the window and the fragment of the old roof. Lucky for him was that natural armchair; for without it, at the first fall of sleep, he would undoubtedly have rolled from his perch into the depths below. Dig approached him gently and discreetly.

"Nearly time to get up, old chappie," said he, laying his hand on the sleeper's arm to prevent any sudden start.

That "nearly" was a stroke of genius. Had he incautiously announced that the chapel-bell had begun to ring, or that he would be late for call-over, the result might have been fatal.

As it was, Arthur opened his eyes lazily and yawned—

"All serene. Why, hullo, I say! Is that you, Dig, old man?"

"Yes, rather! Sit steady; we've got a ladder and ropes, and Marky's just down there. How are you?"

Arthur rubbed his eyes, and his teeth chattered.

"Pretty cold and stiff, old man. How jolly of you to come! You see, the mortar or something slipped, and I couldn't get up

DIG COULD SUPPORT HIM FROM ABOVE AS HE CAME DOWN

or down. I yelled, but you'd gone. At last I managed to get up again, and there I've stuck. How are we going down now?"

"They've got the ladder up just below us, if you can manage to get down so far."

Arthur began to move his stiff limbs one by one, by way of judging what he could do.

Dig, meanwhile, shouted down that he was safe up, and Arthur was all right.

"Not time for another try at the owls," said the latter, getting one foot up and trying to rise.

"Owls be hanged," said Dig, helping his friend gingerly to his feet.

"I feel like a poker," said Arthur. "Shouldn't care to run a mile just now."

"Nobody wants you to. What you've got to do is to dig hold of the ivy with your hands and let yourself down. I'll go first and take care of your feet."

"Awfully brickish of you, Dig," said Arthur. "I'm sorry I'm such a lout. I feel as if my joints want oiling."

"Come on," said Dig.

The descent was slow, and for poor Arthur painful; but, thanks to the ivy and Dig's steady steering, it was in due time accomplished safely, and the top of the ladder reached.

"Now, then, one at a time," shouted the farmer.

"He can't go alone," called Dig; "he's too stiff. Won't it bear both of us?"

The unanimous opinion below was that it would not. Even Dig's weight as he went up had been as much as they could manage.

Finally Railsford suggested that a rope should be thrown up, which Dig could tie round Arthur's body, and so support him from above as he came down.

The plan was a good one, and Arthur contrived by its help to lower himself down the steps into the arms of his rescuers.

Dig was not long in following; and five minutes later the party was standing, safe and sound and thankful, on the greensward of the abbey floor. The farmer insisted on taking them all to his house, and comforting their souls and bodies with a hot breakfast in front of a blazing fire. After which he ordered out his trap and drove them himself up to Grandcourt.

The first getting-up bell was ringing as they drove into the quadrangle, and at the sound of the wheels half a dozen anxious watchers darted out to welcome their return. Still more shouted down greetings from the dormitory window, and Arthur and Dig, had they been in the mood for lionising, might have had their heads turned by the excitement which their reappearance seemed to produce. But they were neither of them in a mood for anything but going to bed. For, after the excitement of the night and morning, a reaction had set in, and their heads ached and their bodies were done out. They even resisted Railsford's recommendation of a hot bath, and took possession of the dormitory and curled themselves up to sleep, leaving Fate or anyone else to explain their absence for the next few hours to the authorities below.

As for Railsford, after seeing his young charges stowed away in their berths, he shook himself together, took his cold bath, and walked over to breakfast with Grover, none the worse for the fatigues and exposure of that eventful night.

"Have you seen the doctor yet?" inquired Grover, when the meal was over. "I suppose not. He was asking for you particularly last night."

"What for, do you know?"

"I don't. I was wondering if you did, for I imagine from his manner it is something important."

"Oh, I know; I had to report one of my prefects yesterday for gambling. No doubt it is in connection with that."

"Perhaps. You know it seems a great pity you and Bickers hit it so badly. Bickers seems to have a preposterous notion in his head that you are in some way responsible for what happened to him last term. He even wanted to bring the matter up in the last session of masters in your absence; and when we stopped it he promised to return to it at the next."

"Oh, Bickers!" said Railsford scornfully. "I am really tired of him, Grover. It's the greatest pity he wasn't allowed to say what he had to say at that meeting. He will never be happy till he has it off his mind; and it surely wouldn't be necessary for me to take any notice of his rhodomontades."

"I'm glad you are so little concerned about them. I was afraid they might be worrying you."

Railsford smiled.

"I've plenty in my own house to do that, thanks. No, all I ask is to keep the peace with Bickers, and have nothing to do with him. He may then say anything he likes. Well, I suppose I had better go over to the doctor's now and report myself."

The doctor received Railsford coldly, and required a full account of the strange adventures of the preceding night. Railsford felt a little hurt at his evident want of sympathy in his story, and was beginning to look out for a chance of escaping, when Doctor Ponsford said—

"I wanted to see you last night about Felgate, your prefect. I had a very unsatisfactory interview with him. He appears to lack principle, and, as you said, not to recognise his responsibility in the house. He tried to shift the blame for this gambling business wholly upon Mills—who, by the way, I flogged—and could not be brought to see that there was anything wrong in his conduct or unbecoming in a senior boy. I think it may be well to remove him next term, either into my house or Mr Roe's; meanwhile he understands that he does not retain his prefecture in yours."

"I am thankful for such an arrangement," said Railsford.

"That, however, is only part of what I had to say to you. Before he left he brought a most extraordinary charge against you which I should certainly have disregarded, had it not coincided strangely with a similar charge made elsewhere. I only repeat it to you in order to give you an opportunity of repudiating it. It had relation to the outrage which was committed on Mr Bickers last term, for which your house still lies in disgrace. He stated that you knew more about that mystery than anyone else at Grandcourt, and, indeed, gave me the impression, from the language he used, that he actually considers you yourself were the perpetrator of the outrage. That, of course, is the mere wild talk of a revengeful ill-doer."

Railsford laughed a short uneasy laugh. Had the doctor worded the question in slightly different form, it might have been difficult to answer it as decisively as he could now.

"It is; and if he were here to hear me I would say that it is as absolutely and wickedly false as emphatically as I say it to you, sir. I am sorry indeed that you should have thought it necessary to put the question."

"There is never anything lost," said the doctor drily, "by giving the calumniated person an opportunity of denying a charge of this sort, however preposterous. I am myself perfectly satisfied to take your word that you neither had any part in the affair yourself nor have you any knowledge as to who the culprits are."

Railsford coloured and bit his lips. The doctor had now put the question in the very form which he had dreaded. If he could only have held his peace the matter would be at an end, perhaps never to revive again. But could he, an honest man, hold his peace?

"Excuse me," said he, in undisguised confusion; "what I said was that the imputation that I had anything to do with the outrage myself was utterly and entirely false."

"Which," said the doctor incisively, "is tantamount to admitting that the imputation that you are sheltering the real culprits is well-founded."

"At the risk of being grievously misunderstood, Doctor Ponsford," replied Railsford slowly and nervously, yet firmly, "I must decline to answer that question."

"Very well, sir," said the doctor briskly; "this conversation is at an end—for the present."

Chapter Twenty Three.

"After You."

Thanks to youth and strong constitutions, Arthur and Dig escaped any very serious consequences from their night's exposure at Wellham Abbey. They slept like dormice from eight in the morning to six in the afternoon, and woke desperately hungry, with shocking colds in their heads, and with no inclination whatever to get up and prepare their work for the following day. The doctor came and felt their pulses, and looked at their tongues, and listened to their coughs and sneezes, and said they were well out of it. Still, as they assured him with loud catarrhic emphasis that they felt rather bad still, and very shaky, he gave them leave to remain in bed for the rest of the day, and petrified them where they lay by the suggestion of a mustard poultice a-piece. They protested solemnly that the malady from which they suffered was mental rather than physical, and required only rest and quiet to cure it. Whereat the doctor grinned, and said, "Very well." They had leave to stay as they were till the morning; then, if they were not recovered, he would try the mustard poultices. To their consternation and horror, after he had gone, they suddenly remembered that to-night was the night appointed for the first grand rehearsal of a performance proposed to be given by the Comedians of the house on the eve of speech-day at the end of the term.

The Comedians were a time-honoured institution at Grandcourt. Any casual visitor to the school from about the middle of April onwards might at any time have been startled and horrified by finding himself suddenly face to face in a retired corner with some youthful form undergoing the most extraordinary contortions of voice and countenance.

Railsford himself used to be fond of recounting his first experience of this phenomenon. He was going down early one morning to the fields, when on the shady side of the quadrangle he encountered a boy, whom he recognised after a little scrutiny to be Sir Digby Oakshott, Baronet. The reason why he did not immediately grasp the identity of so familiar a personage was because Sir Digby's body was thrown back, his arms were behind his back, his legs were spread out, and his head was thrown into the air, with an expression which the Master of the Shell had never seen there before, and never saw again. There was but one conclusion to come to: the baronet had gone mad, or he would never be standing thus in the public quadrangle at seven o'clock in the morning.

The supposition was immediately confirmed by beholding the patient's face break slowly into a horrible leer, and his mouth assume a diagonal slant, as he brought one hand in front, the index finger close to his nose, and addressed a lamp-post as follows:—

"When Abednego Jinks says a thing, Tommy, my boy, you may take your Alfred David there's more in it than there is in your head."

Railsford, in alarm, was about to hasten for professional assistance for what he considered a very bad case, when Dig, catching sight of him, relieved him inexpressibly by dropping at once into his ordinary sane manner, and saying, with a blush of confusion,—

"Oh, Mr Railsford, I didn't know you were there. I was mugging up my part for the Comedians, you know. I'm Abednego Jinks, not much of a part, only you can get in a little gag now and then."

Railsford, after what he had witnessed, was prepared to admit this, and left the disciple of the dramatic Muse to himself and the lamp-post, and secretly hoped when the performance of the Comedians came off he might get an "order" for the stalls.

Although the Grandcourt House Comedians were an old institution, they had not always been equally flourishing. At Railsford's, for instance, in past years they had decidedly languished. The performances had possibly been comic, but that was due to the actors, not the author, for the scenes chosen were usually stock selections from the tragedies of Shakespeare; such, for instance, as the death of King Lear, the ghost scene in Hamlet, the conspirators' scene in Julius Caesar, and the banquet in Macbeth. But as soon, as the irrepressible Wake got hold of the reins, as of course he did, the old order changed with startling rapidity. The new director made a clean sweep of Shakespeare and all his works.

"What's the fun of doing Roman citizens in Eton jackets and white chokers," said he, "and sending everybody to sleep? Let's give them a change, and make them laugh."

As if everybody hadn't laughed for years at the Roman citizens in Eton jackets!

So he hunted about and made inquiries of friends who were supposed to know, and finally submitted to the company a certain screaming farce, entitled, *After You!* with—so the description informed him—two funny old gentlemen, one low comedian, two funny old ladies, and one maid-of-all-work, besides a few walking gentlemen and others. It sounded promising, and a perusal of the piece showed that it was very amusing. I cannot describe it, but the complications were magnificent; the two old gentlemen, one very irascible the other very meek, were, of course, enamoured of the two old ladies, one very meek, and the other very irascible; the low comedian was, of course, the victim and the plague of both couples, and took his revenge by the usual expedient of siding with each against the other, and being appointed the heir to both. The walking gentlemen were—need it be said?—the disappointed heirs; and the maid-of-all-work, as is the manner of such persons, did everybody's work but her own.

The parts were allotted with due care and discrimination. The two funny old gentlemen were undertaken by Sherriff and Ranger, the two funny old ladies by Dimsdale and Maple, the low comedian by Sir Digby Oakshott, and the maid-of-all-work by Arthur Herapath. As for the walking gentlemen, cabmen, detective, *et hoc genus omne*, they were doled out to anyone who chose to take them. There had been no regular rehearsals yet, but private preparation, of the hole-and-corner kind I have described, had been going on for a week or so. The actors themselves had been looking forward with eagerness—not to say trepidation—to the first rehearsal, which was appointed to take place this evening in the Fourth class-room, in the presence of Wake and Stafford, and a few other formidable critics of the upper school. Great, therefore, was the dismay when it was rumoured that the low comedian and the maid-of-all-work were on the sick list with a doctor's certificate.

The first impulse was to postpone the date, but on Wake representing that there was no evening for ten days on which they could get the use of the room, it was resolved to do the best they could with the parts they had, and read the missing speeches from the book. Although the house generally was excluded from the rehearsals, the Fourth-form boys managed to scramble in on the strength of the class-room in which the performance was to take place being their own. And besides the invited guests named above, it was frequently found, at the end of a performance, when the gas was turned up, that the room was fuller of Juniors and Babies than it had been when the curtain rose.

On the present occasion, not being a full-dress rehearsal, there was no curtain, nor was there anything to distinguish the actors from their hearers, save the importance of their faces and the evident nervousness with which they awaited the signal to begin.

And here let me give my readers a piece of information. A screaming farce is ever so much more difficult to act than a tragedy of Shakespeare. Any—well, any duffer can act Brutus or Richard the Third or the Ghost of Banquo, but it is reserved only to a few to be able to do justice to the parts of Bartholomew Bumblebee or Miss Anastatia Acidrop. And when one comes to compare the paltry exploits and dull observations of the old tragedy heroes with the noble wit and sublime actions of their modern rivals it is not to be wondered at! So it happened on the present occasion.

After You was far too ambitious a flight for the Comedians at Railsford's; they had far better have stuck to *King Lear*. In the first place, none of the characters seemed to understand what was expected of them. Sherriff, the funny, irascible old gentleman, skulked about in the back of the scene, and tapped his fingers lightly on the top of his hat, and stamped his foot gently, with the most amiable of smiles on his countenance. His one idea of irascible humour seemed to be to start every few moments to leave the room, and then stop short half-way to the door, and utter a few additional remarks over his shoulder, and then to make again for the door with a noise which sounded half-way between a sneeze and the bleating of a goat.

Maple also, who personated Miss Olive Omlett, the meek, elderly lady, appeared to have come with a totally erroneous conception of the *rôle* of that inoffensive character. He delivered his speeches in a voice similar to that in which boys call the evening papers at a London railway station, and lost no opportunity of clutching at his heart—which, by the way, Maple wore on his right flank—and of rising up from, and sitting down on, his chair at regular intervals while anybody else was addressing him.

Then, greatly to the chagrin of the director, the jokes which seemed so good in print never came off right in the speaking. Those which were delivered right, nobody—least of all the actors—seemed to see, and the others came to grief by being mauled in the handling. When, for instance, on the meek gentleman observing, "Oh, my poor head!" Miss Acidrop ought to have made a very witty and brilliant point by retorting, "There's nothing in that!" she entirely spoiled the fun by saying, "That's nothing to do with it!" and when loud laughter should have been created by the irascible man walking off with the meek man's hat on his head, they both quitted the scene with no hats on their heads at all.

This was dispiriting, and the absence of the low comedian and the maid-of-all-work tended still further to mar the success of the rehearsal. For Wake had to read these parts from the book, and at the same time coach the other actors. Thus, for instance, in the famous speech of Abednego Jinks the low comedian already cited, it rather broke up the humour of that masterpiece of declamation to hear it delivered thus:—

"When Abednego Jinks—(Oh, that won't do, Ranger! Take your hand out of your waistcoat and look more like a fool. Yes, that's better. Now, where's the place? Oh yes)—when Abednego Jinks says a thing, Tommy, my boy (Oh, no, no, no! Didn't I tell you you needn't start up from your chair as if I was going to cut your throat? Sit steady, and gape at me like an idiot! That's the style!)—Tommy, my boy, Tommy, my boy, To—(Where on earth's the place? Oh yes)—when Abednego Jinks says a thing, Tommy, my boy—"

"Oughtn't you to look funnier than that, yourself?" interposed Ranger, relaxing his own expression to ask the question.

"Oh, of course; only I'm reading just now. Oakshott will have to get that up, of course. Now begin again. Go on; look a fool.—That'll do.—When Abednego Jinks says a thing, Tommy, my boy—(I say, screw your chair round a bit, and face the audience)."

"For mercy's sake," said Stafford, who was getting rather tired of the whole thing, "do tell us what happens when Abednego Jinks says a thing!"

"Tommy, my boy, you may take your Alfred David—(Do look rather more vacant, old man)."

"My dear fellow," once more interposed the prefect, "Ranger could not possibly look a more utter idiot than he looks this minute. What is he to take his affidavit about? I do so want to know."

"You may take your Alfred David, Tommy, my boy (Oh no, that's wrong)—Tommy, my boy, you may take your Alfred David."

"Yes, yes—go on," urged Stafford.

"There's more in it than there is in your head."

"More in what? the affidavit?" asked Ranger solemnly.

"No, that's not what you say; you say, 'You don't say so.'"

"I think," said Stafford, "that what he did say was a good deal funnier than what he ought to say. What's the good of saying, 'You don't say so,' when everyone of us here can swear you did? I don't see the joke in it myself. Do any of you?"

"No; was it meant for one?" asked someone gravely.

"It's not written down in the book that anyone's to grin," said Maple, hastily referring to his copy.

"Oh, that's all right—only I wish you'd look alive and get to some of the jokes. I thought you said it was a funny piece."

"So it is," replied Wake, rather dismally; "it's full of points."

"They must all be crowded up to the end, then," said Stafford.

If Wake had not had a soul above difficulties he might have been tempted to abandon his labour of Hercules on the spot; and, indeed, it is probable his "troupe" would have struck, and so saved him the trouble of deciding, had not an extraordinary and dramatic change suddenly come over the aspect of affairs. The rehearsal was dragging its slow length along, and everybody, even the amiable Stafford, was losing his temper, when the door flew open, and two young persons entered and made their way boldly up to the stage.

As all the room was dark except the part allotted to the actors, it was not till these intruders had mounted the platform and honoured the company with two ceremonious bows that their identity became apparent. Arthur and Dig, after twelve hours in bed, had become weary unto death; and when, presently, from the room below arose the voices and laughter of the Comedians, they kicked the clothes off them, and mutually agreed—colds or no colds—they could stand, or rather lie, it no longer.

"Wouldn't they grin if we turned up?" said Arthur; "I vote we do."

"All serene," said Dig; "we may as well get up."

Dig meant the term "get up" in the professional sense. He accordingly arrayed himself, to the best of his lights, in the garb of a low comedian; that is, he put on a red dressing-gown, flannel drawers, and a very tall collar, made out of cardboard; and blacked a very fine moustache on his lip with a piece of coal. Arthur, meanwhile, had a more delicate task to perform in extemporising the toilet of a maid-of-all-work. An ulster belonging to Tilbury supplied him with a dress, and by turning up the sleeves, and arranging his night-dress apron-wise over the front, he managed to give a fair idea of the kind of character he aimed to personate. He then ruffled up his hair, and brought as much of it as he was able down in the front for a fringe, surmounting it all with a handkerchief shaped to represent a cap. Finally, he smudged his face over with coal dust, and secured one of Mrs Hastings's mops and a pail from the cupboard at the end of the corridor, and pronounced himself ready for the fray.

It need hardly be said that the apparition of these two extraordinary figures created a sensation among the jaded Comedians and their friends. The sudden restoration to health of the two invalids was less astonishing, perhaps, than their strange get-up, or the spirit with which they proceeded to throw themselves into their respective parts.

Wake, with a smile of relief, shut up his book and retired among the audience.

Dig knew his part well, and acted it with such a depth of low comedy that it mattered little what mistakes or blunders the funny irascible and the funny meek gentlemen and ladies made. He uttered the greatest commonplaces a leer and a wink, which imported a vast deal of meaning into the words, and had evidently so well studied his part that he could not even sit down on the chair or walk out of the room without tumbling on all fours or upsetting one or two of the other actors.

Wake suggested mildly that he was overdoing it, but was voted down by an indignant chorus of admirers, who urged the low comedian on to still further extravagance, until, had his part been that of a clown, he could scarcely have thrown more dramatic intensity into it.

He was ably and gallantly backed up by the maid-of-all-work, who was evidently convinced that the main duty and occupation of such functionaries is to upset everything; to clatter up and down the rooms in hob-nail boots; to flourish her mop in her master's and mistress's faces, and otherwise assert her noble independence of the ordinary laws governing domestic servants. In these ambitions she succeeded to a moral; and when, in addition, thanks to the cold in her head, she pronounced all her m's b's and her n's d's, the result was exhilarating in the extreme.

"There's dot bady bed dicer-looking that Bister Tobby and Biss Oblett," said she, flourishing her mop in Miss Omlett's face.

Whereat, although the remark was a serious one, and not meant to be facetious, the audience was convulsed.

The second scene was in full swing: Miss Omlett and the funny, meek old gentleman were taking refuge behind two sofas from the threatened violence of Mr Bumblebee and Miss Acidrop; the low comedian was having a kick-up all round, and the maid-of-all-work was putting her pail on the head of one of the walking gentlemen with the comment—

"Dow, thed, there's goidg to be a dice doise—"

When the door of the room once more opened, and Railsford entered unobserved in the darkness. He had not come to see the performance, although he knew it was about to be held, and had indeed allowed the use of the class-room for the purpose.

But feeling very dejected in the presence of the cloud which had suddenly fallen on him, he had been unable to work that evening, and had decided to pay a visit of condolence to his young kinsman and the baronet, partly in the hope of edifying them by a little quiet talk by the sick bedside, and partly to satisfy himself that no very alarming symptoms had resulted from last night's severe exposure.

Picture his astonishment when he found the two beds in the dormitory empty, and the invalids flown!

He made inquiries of the dame. She had taken them up two eggs a-piece and some tea and hot buttered toast at six o'clock, which they had partaken of, and then, informing her that they felt no better, they had disposed themselves, as she supposed, to sleep.

He looked into their study. They were not there; nor had anyone heard of them in the preparation room. Finally, he peeped into the Fourth class-room, and beheld the two invalids masquerading on the stage, and recognised the voice and sentiments of his kinsman, albeit proceeding through the nose, as he flourished his (or rather her) mop in the air, and announced that there was going to be a "dice doise."

The whole scene was so ridiculous that Railsford deemed it prudent not to discover himself, and withdrew as unobserved as he had entered.

At least he had the satisfaction of knowing that Arthur and Dig were all right after their adventure; and that, thought he, is the main thing.

Poor Railsford had plenty else to occupy his thoughts that evening. The interview with the doctor in the morning had seemed to bring him up short in his career at Grandcourt.

If his enemies had tried to corner him, they could not have done it better. It was true that he knew the culprits, and by not denouncing them was, to that extent, shielding them.

But he had come to that knowledge, as the reader knows, by an accident, of which, as an honourable man, he felt he had no right to take advantage, even to set right so grievous a wrong as the Bickers mystery.

He might explain, without mentioning names, how he had learned the facts; but that would be as good as naming the culprit, for Branscombe had been the only case of serious illness accompanied by delirium at Grandcourt during the last two terms.

He might write to Branscombe, and tell him his dilemma, and beseech him to make a confession. And yet what right had he to take advantage of the boy's unconscious confession to put pressure on him to make it public?

Other persons less fastidious might do it, but Railsford could not.

The alternative, of course, was that he would in all probability have to leave Grandcourt. If the matter had rested only between him and the doctor, he might have made a private communication under pledge of secrecy, and so induced his principal to let the matter drop. But the matter did not rest solely between him and the doctor. Mr Bickers and Felgate, by some means which he was unable to fathom, appeared to have learned the secret, and were not likely to let it drop. Indeed, it was evident that, so far from that, they would like if possible to fix a charge of actual complicity in the outrage on himself.

Railsford laughed contemptuously at the notion, as the wild malice of a revengeful enemy. But he knew that no explanation would be likely to put them off the pursuit short of the actual naming of the culprits, which he was resolved at all risks to refuse.

Was this to be the end of his brilliant school career? After two terms of hard work and honest battle, was he to be turned away, cashiered and mined, just because he had stayed to nurse a sick boy and overheard his delirious confession?

It was no small temptation as he sat in his room that night, to compromise with honour. He could so easily save himself. He could, by a word, sweep away the cloud which hung over his future, and not his future only, but Daisy's. The outrage had been a cowardly one. Two of its perpetrators at least were worthless boys, and the other was away from Grandcourt, and might possibly never come back. Was it worth risking so much for so small a scruple? Did not his duty to Grandcourt demand sacrifices of him, and could he not that very night remove a dark blot from its scutcheon!

So the battle went on, and Railsford fought it out, inch by inch, like a man. He was not single-handed in such matters: he had a Friend who always wins, and He helped Railsford to win that night.

Chapter Twenty Four.

The Strange Adventures of a Brown-Paper Parcel.

Railsford was somewhat surprised at call-over on the following morning to observe that neither Arthur Herapath nor Digby Oakshott answered to their names.

"Why are they not here?" he asked.

"They're still on the sick list," said Ainger.

"Has anyone seen them?"

"Yes, sir," said Tilbury; "they were coughing a good deal in the night, and said they felt too bad to get up this morning, and had the medical doctor's leave to stay in bed till he came round."

"Oh," said Railsford, and walked up-stairs to interview these two unfortunate invalids.

"Well," said he, entering the room just in time to interrupt what he imagined, from the sounds heard outside, must have been a spirited bolster match, "how are you both this morning?"

They both began to cough, wearily, "A little better, I think," said Arthur, with fortitude; "I think we might try to get up later on. But the medical said we'd better wait till he saw us."

And he relapsed into a painful fit of coughing.

"I feel very hot all over," said the baronet, who was notoriously energetic at bolster matches.

"Now, you two," said Railsford sternly, "just get up at once. I shall remain in the room while you dress."

They looked at him in reproachful horror, and broke into the most heart-rending paroxysm of coughing he had ever listened to.

"Stop that noise," said he, "and get up at once."

"Oh, please, Marky—Mr Railsford—we're so bad and—and Daisy would be so sorry if I got consumption, or anything of that sort."

"We shall get into trouble, sir," added the baronet, "for getting up without the medical's leave. He told us to stay in bed, and—"

Here another cough, which, however, was promptly suppressed.

"You will get into no more trouble with him than you have got into already for getting up last night after he had gone, and acting in the farce in the Fourth class-room."

The culprits regarded one another with looks of consternation.

"Did you see us then?" asked Arthur. "You see, Marky—Mr Railsford I mean—we'd promised to—"

"I want no explanations, Arthur; you had no business to get up then, and you've no business not to get up now. Shamming isn't honourable, and that ought to be reason enough why you and Oakshott should drop it."

After this the delinquents dressed in silence and followed their master down to the class-room, where the ironical welcome of their fellows by no means tended to smooth their ruffled plumage.

However, as they *were* down, their colds recovered in ample time to allow of their taking part in the cricket practice in the afternoon; and the exercise had a wonderful effect in reconciling them to their compulsory convalescence.

They were sitting, half working, half humbugging, in their study at preparation-time, when Railsford again looked in. "Herapath," said he, "if you bring your Cicero down to my room presently, I'll show you the passages marked for the Swift Exhibition."

In due time Arthur presented himself. He and Digby between them had smelt a rat.

"He's going to jaw you, you bet," said the baronet.

"Looks like it. I wonder why he always picks on you and me for jawing? Why can't he give the other fellows a turn? Never mind, he was civil to us that night at the abbey—I suppose I'd better let him have his own way."

So, after a fitting interval, he repaired with his books to the lion's den.

These astute boys had been not quite beside the mark in their surmise that the master had ulterior reasons in inviting Arthur to his study. He did want to "jaw" him; but not in the manner they had anticipated.

After going through the Cicero, and marking the portions requiring special getting up for the examination, Railsford put down his pen and sat back in his chair.

"Arthur," said he, "there is something I should like to ask you."

"It's coming, I knew it," said Arthur to himself.

"Do you remember, Arthur, last term, you and I had some talk one evening about what happened to Mr Bickers, and the mysterious way in which that secret had been kept?"

Arthur fidgeted uncomfortably.

"Oh, yes," said he. "That's all done with now, though, isn't it?"

"I think not. Do you remember my asking you if you knew anything about it, which I did not?"

"Oh yes—I didn't. I know nothing more about it than you do."

"How do you know that? What if I knew nothing about it?"

Arthur looked puzzled.

"I want you to be frank with me. It is a matter of great importance to us all to get this affair cleared up—more to me than you guess. All I ask you is, do you know who did it?"

"Why, yes," said Arthur.

"How did you discover? Did anyone tell you?"

"No; I found out."

"Do you consider that you have no right to tell me the name?"

Arthur stared at him, and once more thought to himself what a wonderfully clever fellow this brother-in-law of his was.

"It doesn't much matter if I tell *you*," said he, "only I mean to keep it dark from anybody else."

"Who was it then?" inquired the master, with beating heart. "Tell me."

"Why, you know!"

"I wish to hear the name from you, Arthur," repeated the master.

"All right! Mark Railsford, Esquire, M.A. That's the name, isn't it?"

Railsford started back in his chair as if he had been shot, and stared at the boy.

"What! what do you say?—I?"

Arthur had never seen acting like it.

"All right, I tell you, it's safe with me, I'll keep it as dark as ditch-water."

"Arthur, you're either attempting a very poor joke, or you are making a most extraordinary mistake. Do you really mean to say that you believe it was I who attacked Mr Bickers?"

Arthur nodded knowingly.

"And that you have believed it ever since the middle of last term?"

"Yes—I say, weren't you the only one in it, then?" asked the boy, who could not any longer mistake the master's bewildered and horrified manner for mere acting.

Railsford felt that this was a time of all others to be explicit.

"I did not do it, Arthur, and I had no more connection with the affair than—your father."

Arthur was duly impressed by this asseveration.

"It's a precious rum thing, then, about all those things, you know. They looked awfully fishy against you."

"What things? I don't understand you."

"Perhaps I'd better not tell you," said the boy, getting puzzled himself.

"I can't force you to tell me; but when you know it's a matter of great importance to me to know how you or anybody came to suspect such a thing of me, I think you will do it."

Arthur thereupon proceeded to narrate the history of the finding of the match-box, sack, and wedge of paper, with which the reader is already familiar, and considerably astonished his worthy listener by the business-like way in which he appeared to have put two and two together, and to have laid the crime at his, Railsford's, door.

Nothing would satisfy the boy now but to go up and fetch down the incriminating articles and display them in the presence of the late criminal.

To his wrath and amazement, when he went to the cupboard he found—what it had been the lot of a certain classical personage to find before him—that the "cupboard was bare." The articles were nowhere to be seen. Dig, on being charged with their abstraction, protested that he had never set eyes on them, and when Arthur told him the purpose for which they were wanted, he was scarcely less concerned at the mysterious disappearance than his friend.

Arthur finally had to return to Railsford without the promised evidence.

"I can't make it out," said he; "they're gone."

"Did anyone know about this except yourself?"

"Dig knew," said Arthur, "and *he* must have collared them."

"Who? Oakshott?"

"Oh no; but I happened to say something last term, just after that trial we had, you know; I was talking about it, on the strict quiet, of course, to Felgate."

"Felgate!" exclaimed the master; and the whole truth flashed upon him at once.

"Yes, he promised to keep it dark. I really didn't think there was any harm, you know, as he is a prefect."

"You think he has taken the things, then?"

"Must have," said Arthur. "I don't know why, though; I'll go and ask him."

"You had better not," said Railsford. If Felgate had taken them, he probably had some reason, and there was no occasion to involve Arthur any further in the business.

"The thing is," said Arthur, still sorely puzzled, "if it wasn't you, who was it?"

Railsford smiled.

"That is a question a great many persons are asking. But you are the only boy I have met with who has no doubt in his mind that I was the guilty person."

Arthur winced.

"I'm awfully sorry, sir," said he. "I'll tell them all you had nothing to do with it."

"I think you had better say nothing. How do you know I am not telling you a lie now?"

Arthur winced once more. He would have preferred if Railsford had given him one hundred lines for daring to suspect him, and had done with it.

"I say," said he, "you needn't tell them at home, Marky. I know I was a cad, especially when you were such a brick that night at the abbey, and I'll never do it again. They'd be awfully down on me if they knew."

"My dear boy, you are not a cad, and I shall certainly not tell anyone of your little mistake. But leave me now; I have a lot of things to think about. Good-night."

Arthur returned to his room in dejected spirits.

He had made a fool of himself, he knew, and done his best friend an injustice; consequently he felt, for once in a way, thoroughly ashamed of himself. What irritated him most of all was the loss of the articles he had so carefully treasured up as evidence against somebody.

"Felgate's collared them, that's certain," said he, "and why?"

"He has a big row on with Marky," replied Dig; "I expect he means to bowl him out about this."

"That's it," said Arthur, "that's what he's up to. I say, Dig, we ought to be able to pay him out, you and I; and save old Marky."

"I'm game," said Dig; "but how?"

"Get the things back, anyhow. Let's see, they've got something on at the Forum to-night, haven't they?"

"Yes—two to one he'll be there. Why, of course he will; he's got to second the motion—something about the fine arts."

Arthur laughed.

"We'll try a bit of fine art on him, I vote. Come on, old man; we'll have a look round his rooms for the traps."

So they sallied out, and after peeping into the Forum on their way, to ascertain that their man was safely there, they marched boldly up-stairs to his study. If it had not been for the righteousness of their cause, these boys might have thought twice before entering anyone's room in his absence. But Arthur in his present temper had cast to the winds all scruples, and regarding himself merely as a robbed lioness searching for her whelps, he would have liked to meet the man who would tell him he hadn't a perfect right to be where he was. Dig, for his part, was not prepared to raise any such awkward question.

The boys' instinct had told them right. For one of the first things they beheld, on a corner of the window-sill, apparently put there hurriedly before starting for the Forum, was a brown-paper parcel, corresponding exactly with the missing bundle.

It was carefully tied up, and under the string was thrust an envelope addressed to "Mr Bickers."

Arthur whistled, and Dig ran forward to capture the lost property.

"Steady," said the former warily. "Perhaps it's just a dodge to catch us. See how it lies, in case we have to put it back."

They took the necessary bearings with all precaution, and then hurried back with their prize to their own study.

"How long before the Forum's up?" demanded Arthur, depositing the parcel on the table.

"Twenty minutes," said Dig.

"All serene."

The things had evidently been recently tied up with new string in fresh brown paper, the wedge of paper and the match-box being rolled up in the middle of the sack.

"That seems all right," said Arthur, "now let's see the letter."

He carefully slid a pen-holder under the fold of the envelope, so as to open it without breaking, and extracted the letter, which ran as follows:—

"Dear Sir,—I send you the three things I told you of. The sack has his initials on it; the paper belongs to him, as you will see, and he is the only man in the house who could reach up to put the match-box on the ledge. Please do not mention my name. My only reason is to get justice done.

"Yours, truly,

"T.F."

"Oh, the cad!" was the joint exclamation of the two readers as they perused this treacherous epistle.

"Look alive, now," said Arthur; "cut down as fast as ever you can and fetch one of those turfs lying on the corner of the grass, you know."

"What's that for?" asked Dig, who felt quite out of the running.

"Never mind. Cut away; there's no time to lose. Don't let anyone see you."

Dig obeyed, and selected one of the turfs in question, which he clandestinely conveyed up to his room.

"Now lend a hand to wrap it up," said Arthur. "Don't you see it'll make a parcel just about the size and weight of the sack? Mind how you tie it up—a double knot, not a bow."

Dig began to perceive what the sport was at last, and grinned complacently as he tied up the new parcel into an exact counterfeit of the old.

Arthur overhauled it critically, and pronounced it all right. "Now," said he, "we'll write him a letter."

He sat down and dashed off the following, Dig nudging vehement approval of the contents from behind.

"Sir,—I'm a cad and a liar and a thief. Don't believe a word I say. You can tell anyone you like. Most of them know already. Yours truly,

"Jerry Sneak."

"That's ripping!" exclaimed the admiring Dig, as this elegant epistle was carefully folded into the original envelope, and, after being gummed down, was thrust under the string of the counterfeit parcel. "Oh, I wish I could be there to see it opened!"

"We may get into a row for it," said Arthur. "I don't care. It'll show him up and be a real leg-up for Marky. Look alive now, and come and put it back in his room."

So they sallied up once more and carefully replaced the parcel exactly where they had found it, and then, rejoicing exceedingly, dodged down again. It seemed to them a politic thing just to look in at the Forum on their way down, to witness the end of the debate and take part in the division. They had not the slightest idea what the debate was about, but they made themselves prominent among the "Ays," and cheered loudly when the motion was declared to be carried by two votes.

Felgate nodded to them as he passed out, little guessing the real meaning of the affectionate smile with which they returned the greeting.

"So your cold's better, youngster?" said he to Arthur.

"Looks like it," replied Arthur.

Felgate's first glance as he entered the room was towards the corner in which he had left his parcel.

He had just been cording it up that evening when he suddenly remembered his engagement at the Forum, and in the hurry of the discovery he had carelessly left it out, instead of, as he had intended, locking it up.

"However," thought he to himself, "it's all safe as it happens. I won't send it over to Bickers till to-morrow afternoon, just before the master's session. It will be far more effective if he opens it in the brute's presence; and, after all, I don't care a twopenny-piece if he knows it comes from me or not—the cad!"

He had half a mind to open the letter and tell Mr Bickers to mention his name if he chose; but just as he was about to do so Munger came in to see him. So he abandoned the idea and locked the parcel up safely in his drawer.

Felgate had, as the reader may have judged, come to the conclusion that it was time to play his trump card against his enemy. Railsford's reporting of him to the doctor had been, to mix metaphors a little, the last straw which breaks the patient camel's back.

He had had a very warm and uncomfortable quarter of an hour with the head-master, and, as we know, had defended himself on the plea that Railsford, being a malefactor himself, was not competent to judge of the conduct of his boys. The doctor had severely silenced this covert accusation, although taking note of it sufficiently to suggest the very awkward string of questions which he put the following morning to the unlucky Master of the Shell.

Felgate, however, had an impression that his statement to the doctor had missed fire; and being determined not wholly to cast his trump card away, he had walked across and sought an interview with Mr Bickers.

That estimable gentleman was considerably impressed by discovering, first of all, that this boy was the author of the mysterious letter last term, and secondly, that he possessed such satisfactory evidence of the strange story.

He accepted Felgate's statement that his sole motive was the credit of Grandcourt and the relief of his own conscience, without too particularly inquiring into its value, and undertook not to mention his informer's name in any use he might have to make of the information.

To that end he suggested it would be better for him to have the "evidence" to produce when required. Felgate promised to send it over to him next day, if that would suit. Mr Bickers said it would suit admirably. There was to be a master's meeting in the evening, when no doubt the question would come up, and if Felgate preferred not to appear himself, he might send Mr Bickers the things there with a letter, which the master promised to read without disclosing the name of the writer.

This seemed a satisfactory plan, and Felgate hoped that in return for what he was doing Mr Bickers would intercede with the doctor to restore him to his prefecture. Which Mr Bickers said he would do, and the interview ended.

Felgate had not much difficulty in possessing himself of the "articles." Arthur had himself exhibited them to him last term, and he remembered the corner of the locker in which they had lain. Probably Arthur had never looked at them since, and would be very unlikely to miss them now. Even if he did, Felgate didn't care.

The securing them was easy enough, for on that particular evening Arthur and Dig were roosting on the big arch of Wellham Abbey, in no condition to interfere if all their worldly goods had been ransacked. The remainder the reader knows.

That eventful evening was to witness one more solemnity before the order for "lights out" cut short its brief career.

Arthur and Dig having returned to their study, held a grave consultation over the sack and match-box and wedge of paper.

"We'd better hide them," said Dig, "where he can't find them again."

"Not safe," said Arthur; "we'd better burn them."

"Burn them!" said Dig, astounded by the audacious proposition. "Then we give up all our evidence."

"Good job too; all the better for Marky. They've done us no good so far."

This was true, and Dig, having turned the matter over, said he was "game."

The conspirators therefore locked their door, and piled up their fire. It was long since their study had glowed with such a cheerful blaze. The resin-wheel flared, and crackled, and spat as if it was in the jest and was enjoying it, and the flames blazed up the chimney as though they were racing who should be the first to carry the joke outside.

The match-box and paper wedge vanished almost instantaneously, and the old bone-dry sack itself rose grandly to the occasion, and flared away merrily inch by inch, until, a quarter of an hour after the illumination had begun, the last glowing vestige of it had skipped up after the sparks.

The boys were sitting complacently contemplating this glorious *finale* when a loud knock came at the door, and a shout in Ainger's voice of "Let me in!"

"What's the row?" cried Arthur, shovelling the ashes under the grate, while Dig, with wonderful presence of mind, whipped out the toasting-fork, and stuck half a loaf on the end of it.

"Open the door," cried Ainger, accompanying his demand with a kick which made the timbers creak. "Your chimney's on fire!"

Arthur rushed and opened the door, while Dig, once more with wonderful presence of mind, seized up the bath bucket and emptied it on the fire.

"You young idiots," shouted Ainger as he rushed in, half-blinded with the smoke raised by Dig's *coup de théâtre*, "you'll have the house on fire! Bring a jug with you, both of you, up to the roof."

They each snatched up a jug, and with pale countenances followed the captain up to the skylight. As they emerged on to the roof they were horrified to see the chimney belching forth sparks and smoke with unmistakable fierceness.

Fortunately the roof was flat and the chimney-pot accessible. The contents of the three jugs rapidly damped the ardour of the rising flames, and in five minutes after Ainger's first knock at the door the danger was all over.

"Luckily I happened to see it from Smedley's room opposite," said the captain. "Whatever had you been cooking for supper?" They laughed. It was evident the captain was not going to visit the misadventure severely on their heads.

"Something good," said Arthur. "But I guess it'll be a little overdone now. Thanks awfully, Ainger, for helping us out. We might have got into a jolly row if it hadn't been for you, mightn't we, Dig?"

And they departed peacefully to bed, leaving Ainger to wonder what was the use of being the captain of a house when your main occupation is to put out fires kindled by the juniors, and be patted on the back by them in return!

Chapter Twenty Five.

The Blow falls.

"My good friend," said Monsieur Lablache, "you are in a great trouble. I am sorry for you."

Monsieur had looked in as he sometimes did to breakfast in his friend's study.

The two men, one strong, the other weak, still clung to one another in an odd sort of friendship. Railsford's protection had improved monsieur's position in the school not a little. The boys of his own house were more tolerant of his foreign peculiarities; and some of the other masters, taking to heart the chivalrous example of their junior colleague, had begun to think better of the unpopular detention master, and to recognise good qualities in him to which hitherto they had been blind.

If monsieur could only have got it out of his head that he was a born diplomatist, there would not have been a more harmless master in Grandcourt.

"I am sorry for you, my good friend," repeated he. "But you will be brave."

"Really, Lablache, you don't give a man an appetite for breakfast. Things don't look very cheerful, I know; but what special cause for lamentation have we?"

"Bad lies will be told of you at the masters' meeting to-night," said the Frenchman, "but take courage, *mon ami*, I shall be there."

"Have you any idea what the lies are to be?" asked Railsford, who perhaps was not as jubilant as he might have been at this last cheering promise.

"Meester Beekaire, so I have heard, desires to accuse you of having assaulted him. It is absurd. But no; I overhear him say to Meester Rogers in the masters' hall that he has evidence, he has evidence—ho! ho! it is absurd."

Railsford had not much difficulty after his talk with Arthur last night in guessing where this evidence was likely to be, and whence it proceeded. If that was the whole of the trouble he had to face, he could have afforded to laugh with monsieur. But the doctor's question still rang in his ears. That, he could not get round or avoid.

"Bickers no doubt believes he is right," said he, "but, as you say, monsieur, he is absurd—I wish he had been allowed to say what he wanted at the last meeting, when I wasn't there."

"But, *mon ami*, it would be unfair. Let him say it to your face, and you stand up and say to him to his face, it is one—what you call it, one very big lie."

"Well, I will do my best," said Railsford, smiling. "It is a wretched business altogether."

"It is strange it is a secret still. I have my thoughts often, friend Railsford. I sometimes think of this boy, and sometimes of that boy; I have even said to myself, Why do we look only in Meester Railsford's house? Why could it not be—for I see boys of all the houses—why could it not be perhaps one of Meester Beekaire's own boys? They hate him—I wish Branscombe would come back. I think if he did, I would ask him."

Railsford shifted his chair uneasily, and suddenly changed the conversation.

"How are the little girls?" asked he.

Poor monsieur! It was easy to turn him from any subject by a question like this. His eyes glistened at the mere mention of their names, and as he sat there and talked about them, with their portraits lying on the breakfast-table before him, Mr Bickers, Branscombe, even Railsford himself vanished out of sight, and his world held nothing but just those three little absent girls of his far away in his beloved France.

Railsford was tempted more than once during the day to absent himself boldly from the masters' meeting in the evening, and allow matters to take whatever course they chose in his absence.

"After all," he said to himself, "the fatal question will be put sooner or later, and then I must go down."

"Probably," said the bolder spirit within him; "but keep your feet, Railsford, my brave fellow, as long as you can."

So he braced himself up to the ordeal, and walked across at the appointed time, calm and collected, determined to "die game," if die he must.

It was a full meeting, but, to everybody's surprise, most of all Railsford's, Dr Ponsford was not present.

The head-master, as I have said, had the greatest belief in holding himself aloof from the settlement of any question which could possibly be settled without him. One might have supposed that the present question was one which would require his particular handling. Ultimately it would, no doubt; but meanwhile he would let his lieutenants sift the various issues raised, and send up to him only the last point for his adjudication.

Railsford was disappointed, on the whole; for his one wish was to have the matter settled once for all, and to know the worst before he went to bed that night.

Mr Roe, and Grover, and one or two more of his friends came forward to greet him as he entered, as if nothing was about to take place. But he did not feel actor enough to keep up the farce, and retired to his back seat at the first opportunity, and waited impatiently for the meeting to begin.

The usual routine business seemed interminable. The little questions of procedure and discipline which were brought up and talked over had very little interest to him, and once, when he found his opinion was being directly invited on some matter, he had with confusion to admit that he had not gathered what the question was.

At last Mr Roe said, turning over the agenda paper—

"That disposes of all the ordinary business. The only other matter is a personal question adjourned from our last meeting."

Whereupon everyone settled himself in his place expectantly. Mr Bickers rose briskly and made his speech.

"Mr Roe and gentlemen," said he, "I am sorry once again to trouble the meeting with the affairs of so very unimportant a person as myself, and I can only repeat what I have said before, and what I have a right to take credit for, that my only motive in doing so is my clear duty to Grandcourt, and the removal from a large number of innocent boys of a stigma under which they at present suffer."

Here someone said, "Hear, hear," and everybody agreed that Mr Bickers had begun well.

"In February last," continued he, "I was unfortunate enough to meet with some personal violence while passing the door of an adjoining house in the dark, I was seized from behind, enveloped in a sack, which was tied over my head and shoulders, in a manner which both gagged me and rendered me powerless to move my arms. My *feet* were also tied together, and in this condition I was dragged into a cupboard under the stairs and there left for the night. My impression is that two or three strong persons were engaged in the outrage, although the pinioning was performed by only one. I was released in the morning by my colleague in whose house I had been attacked, who, with his senior boys, untied my hands, and expressed himself as greatly astonished and indignant at what had befallen me. I fully believed at the time these protestations on my colleague's part were sincere."

Here Mr Bickers was beginning to get aggressive, and the backs of one or two of Railsford's friends, particularly monsieur's back, went up.

"That same morning, gentlemen, the doctor came and challenged the house to produce the offender or offenders. Every boy in the house was called over and questioned separately; said each one denied not only that he had done it himself, but that he had any knowledge of who had. Every member of the house, except the master of the house, was thus questioned. The master was not challenged.

"The house was disgraced by the doctor; and from that time to this the secret has been carefully kept. But capital has been made out of the supposed misfortune of the house to set on foot several ambitious schemes which depended for their success on the continued isolation of the house from the rest of the school.

"The master of the house was a prime mover in these schemes, and in consequence decidedly interested in preserving the new state of affairs.

"Now, gentlemen, you may ask why I make all this preamble—"

"Hear, hear!" from monsieur, and "Order, order!" from the chairman.

"I do so because I feel I have no right to take for granted that you all know what is nevertheless a notorious fact in Grandcourt.

"Now, gentlemen, it appears that my colleague's acquiescence in the disgrace of his house was not shared by some of his boys; certainly not by one—whose name I am not at liberty to mention—but whom I can speak of honourably, as being actuated by disinterested motives in securing justice to myself—which is a matter of small moment—and in removing a slur from the good name of Grandcourt.

"This boy took the trouble to make some inquiries shortly after the event, and succeeded in getting together some evidence, which, when I produce it, I think will convince you that little doubt remains as to the identity of the real culprit. I should have preferred if my informant might have been present here to state his own case, but he is naturally reluctant to come forward. He has, however, described to me what the nature of his evidence is; and I have his full authority for making use of that information now.

"In the first place, he claims to have found the sack in which I was enveloped, and which was left on the floor of the cupboard where I had been imprisoned, after my release. This sack, he tells me, bears the initials M.R., which correspond with the initials of the—"

"Midland Railway," dryly observed Grover amid some smiles, which roused Mr Bickers considerably.

"No, sir—the initials M.R. correspond with the name of the master of the house in which I was assaulted. They belong to Mark Railsford."

Railsford sat with his lips drawn contemptuously during this announcement, which failed to make the impression on the meeting generally which the speaker had expected. But he went on.

"In the second place, he found that the door, which closes by itself when not propped open, had been held open by a twisted piece of paper, which, on being unrolled, was found to be part of a newspaper, addressed to Mark Railsford, Esquire, Grandcourt."

This made rather more impression than the last; except on Railsford, who still faced his accuser scornfully.

"In the third place, a match-box was discovered on the ledge above the door, placed there, to judge by its freedom from dust, very recently. I ask you to notice three things in connection with this, gentlemen. A match was struck while I was being dragged into the cupboard; a match found on the floor that morning corresponds exactly with the matches in the box placed up on the ledge; and finally, the height of that ledge from the ground shows that it could only have been placed there by someone over six feet high; and the only person of that height in the house is the master, Mr Mark Railsford."

A dead silence followed this, and masters present wondered how Railsford could still sit so indifferent and unmoved.

"Now, gentlemen," continued Mr Bickers, after having allowed a due interval for this last shot to go home, "I should not be justified in repeating these assertions unless I were also prepared to lay before you the proofs on which those assertions are based. I therefore requested my informant to let me have these. He has done this, and this parcel,"—here he took up a brown-paper parcel from the seat beside him—"containing the articles I have mentioned, was placed in my hands just as I came to this meeting. I have not even examined them myself, so that I am sure you will do me the credit of believing that when I place them just as they are in your hands, Mr Chairman, I cannot be charged with having tampered with my evidence in any way."

Here he handed the parcel up to Mr Roe, amid dead silence.

"Had you not better open it yourself?" asked the chairman, who evidently did not like the business.

"No, sir; I request you will do so, and that Mr Railsford will confront the contents first in your hands, not mine."

"There is a letter here addressed to you," said Mr Roe.

"Please read that also," said Mr Bickers, declining to take it.

Mr Roe knitted his brow and tore open the envelope.

His brows went up with a start as his eyes fell on the opening words. He read the letter through, and then, turning to Mr Bickers, said, "This letter is not intended for reading aloud, Mr Bickers."

"Yes it is. I insist on your reading it, Mr Chairman."

"If you insist, I will do it; but I think you would be wiser to put it in your pocket."

"Read it, Mr Chairman," repeated Mr Bickers excitedly.

Mr Roe accordingly read, in a voice which betrayed some emotion:—

"'Sir,— I'm a cad, and a liar and a thief. Don't believe a word I say. You can tell anyone you like; most of them know already.

"'Yours truly,

"'Jerry Sneak.'"

The effect of the letter may be more easily imagined than expressed. The audience received it first with astonishment, then with consternation, and finally, as the light dawned in on their minds, with laughter. Railsford alone looked serious and bewildered.

As for Mr Bickers, his face turned white, and he looked for a moment as if he would spring at Mr Roe's throat. He snatched the letter from the chairman's hand and looked at it, and then stared round him, on the amused faces of his colleagues.

"You have been hoaxed, I fear," said Mr Roe.

Mr Bickers said nothing, but pointed to the parcel.

"Am I to open it?" asked the chairman.

"Yes, yes!" said the master hoarsely.

Mr Roe obeyed, and disclosed the turf amid another general laugh, in which all but Railsford and Mr Bickers joined.

The latter had by this time lost his self-control. He glared round him like a baited animal, and then, rounding suddenly on Railsford, exclaimed, "This is your doing! You are at the bottom of this!"

Railsford vouchsafed no reply but a contemptuous shrug. He was in no humour to see the joke. Disgust was his one sensation.

"Order, please," said the chairman. "These meetings, if they are to be of any value, must be conducted without any quarrelling. Mr Bickers, may we consider this unpleasant affair now at an end?"

"No!" shouted Mr Bickers. "I have been insulted! I don't care by whom! The matter is *not* at an end—not till I have received an answer from this Railsford here to my question! Let him get up like a man and say he did not attack me like a coward last term, and allow the blame and suspicion to fall on others; let him even get up and declare that he does not know anything about the affair. I defy him to do it! He dare not!"

A silence followed this violent tirade, and everyone turned to Railsford. He sat, motionless and pale, with his eyes on his accuser.

"Have you anything to say, Mr Railsford, or shall we consider the matter at an end?"

"I have nothing to say," said the Master of the Shell, sitting, "except that I refuse to answer these questions."

"Very good! Quite right!" said monsieur, springing to his feet. "When Meester Beekaire can speak like a gentleman, he—"

Here the chairman interrupted.

"I addressed my question to Mr Railsford," said he. "I can understand he declines, under present circumstances, to make any reply to these accusations. But may I suggest it would be most unfortunate if we had to adjourn this disagreeable question again? (Hear, hear.) I imagine it can be very easily terminated to-night. We are all ready, I am sure, to make allowance for a gentleman who is suffering from the irritation of a practical joke. His questions were undoubtedly offensively put, and Mr Railsford, as I say, was entitled to refuse to answer them. But I ask him, in order to close this painful controversy finally, to allow me as chairman of this meeting, to repeat those questions myself, so that he may have an opportunity, as no doubt he desires, of formally placing on record his denial of the charges which have been brought against him."

Railsford gasped inwardly. The long-expected blow was coming, and he felt it was no use to run from it any longer.

"The questions resolve themselves to two. First. Is there any foundation for the charge that you committed or in any way participated in the assault on Mr Bickers last term? And second, Is there any truth in the statement that you know who the culprit or culprits are? Mr Bickers, have I stated your questions correctly?"

"Yes," growled Mr Bickers. "Let him answer them if he can."

Every one now turned to Railsford, who rose slowly to his feet and fixed his eyes full on the chairman. His friends thought they had rarely seen a finer-looking man than he appeared at that moment, and looked forward with pleasure to applauding his denial, and greeting him as finally clear of the odious suspicions under which he had laboured for so long.

His reply was brief and clear:—

"Mr Roe and gentlemen,—The first question I answer with an emphatic negative. The second question I do not answer at all."

A bombshell exploding in the hall could not have caused greater consternation and astonishment than this avowal.

Grover, monsieur, and his other friends turned pale, and wondered if they were dreaming; others frowned; Mr Bickers smiled.

"I knew it!" said he. "I knew it!"

Mr Roe said,—

"You can hardly have heard the question properly, Mr Railsford; may I repeat it?"

"I heard it perfectly well," said Railsford.

"You are aware of the very serious nature of your reply? Do you give any reasons for your refusal?"

"None at all."

"I think," said Mr Grover, rising gallantly to protect his friend, "it would be well if this meeting adjourned. I submit there is no further business before us."

"I oppose that," said Mr Bickers, who had recovered his calmness rapidly. "I propose, Mr Chairman, that this meeting adjourn for five minutes, while the head-master is invited to come and assist our decisions."

This was seconded.

"If I may be allowed," said Railsford, "I should like to support that proposal."

After that, of course, it was agreed to; and for five minutes the meeting stood suspended.

Railsford's friends utilised the interval by begging him to reconsider his position, and if possible put himself right by stating all he knew. He thanked them, but said it was impossible, and finally withdrew again to his own seat, and waited anxiously for the doctor's arrival.

In due time the head-master arrived, with a tolerable notion of the object of this unusual summons.

Mr Roe briefly explained what had taken place, and reported the circumstances under which the head-master's authority was now invited.

For once the doctor looked genuinely distressed. Despite all his rebuffs, he had for some weeks looked upon the Master of the Shell as one of the most promising men on his staff; and he deplored the infatuation which now promised to bring his connection with Grandcourt to an abrupt end.

But there was no alternative.

"Mr Railsford," said he, "you have heard Mr Roe's statement; is it correct?"

"Quite correct, sir."

"And you persist in your refusal to say whether or no you have any knowledge as to who the persons were who assaulted Mr Bickers?"

"I cannot answer the question."

"You know that the inference from such a refusal is that you know the names and refuse to give them up—in other words, that you are shielding the evil-doers?"

"I cannot answer that or any question on the subject, Doctor Ponsford. I am aware of my position, and feel that I have no course open but to place my resignation in your hands."

Once more poor monsieur started up.

"Oh no. He has good reasons. He is not bad. He must not leave."

The doctor motioned him to be silent, and then, addressing Railsford said—

"Your resignation of course follows as a natural consequence of the position you adopt. It is better that you should offer it than that I should have to ask for it. I shall take a week to consider my duty in the matter. This meeting is now at an end."

Chapter Twenty Six.

Things go well with Mr Bickers.

It is not to be wondered at if the proceedings at the remarkable masters' session just reported leaked out somehow, and became the talk of Grandcourt. It was rarely that anything the masters did or said in their solemn conclaves made much impression on the complacency of their boys; but on the present occasion it was other wise.

Rumour had already been active as to the feud between Mr Bickers and the Master of the Shell, and not a few of the better-informed boys had heard that it was connected with the outrage last term, and that Mr Bickers's intention was to bring that crime home, in some manner best known to himself, to Mr Railsford.

The idea was generally pooh-poohed as a piece of vindictive folly. For all that, there was a good deal of speculation as to the proceedings at the masters' session, and, when it was over, curiosity to learn the result. The hurried summons to the doctor during the evening had not passed unnoted; the general opinion was that the "row" had come suddenly and acutely to a head.

When two superior officers fly at one another's throats the spectacle may be interesting, and even amusing, to the onlooker; but I never heard of it doing anything towards the promotion of discipline or the encouragement of good tone among the rank and file. The quarrel of the two masters at Grandcourt certainly failed to do any good to the school, and if it did less mischief than might have been expected, it was because up till now the parties principally concerned had had their own reasons for keeping it private.

Felgate was naturally anxious to hear the result of an entertainment to which he had, as he imagined, made so valuable a contribution. He therefore ventured to call on Mr Bickers the following morning for a little friendly chat.

His reception did not quite come up to his expectations.

"So, sir," exclaimed Mr Bickers, meeting him at the door, "you have thought me a fitting subject for one of your jokes, have you? What have you to say for yourself?"

Felgate looked at him in amazement.

"I really don't understand," said he. "What joke?"

"You wish to keep it up, do you? Very well, sir!" and Mr Bickers took down a cane. "You have thought fit to amuse yourself at my expense," said Mr Bickers. "I intend to repay myself at yours! Hold out your hand!"

"You are not going to punish me for—"

"Hold out your hand, sir!"

"Really, I acted for the best. If it was a mistake, I—"

"Do you hear me, sir? Hold out your hand at once!"

Felgate sullenly obeyed, and Mr Bickers there and then discharged his little debt, adding interest.

"Now go away, and don't dare to come near me again! Stay, take with you these tokens of your ill-timed humour; they may serve to amuse someone else. Begone!" and he thrust into his hands the unlucky parcel and closed the door in his face.

Felgate, smarting and bewildered, walked back to his house with the parcel under his arm, furious with Mr Bickers, and as eager now for revenge on him as yesterday he had been for revenge on Railsford.

What could have happened to make all his carefully laid scheme fall through, and set Mr Bickers, whom he had counted upon as an ally, thus suddenly against him? Had Railsford met him with some counter-charge, or turned the tables by some unexpected move in the face of his accusers?

That could not be, for already the rumour had spread through the house that Mr Railsford had resigned his post.

What did Mr Bickers mean by talking of a joke, and thrusting back upon him the very proofs which but yesterday had been objects of such anxious care and solicitude to them both?

Felgate flung the unlucky parcel down on the table, and called himself a fool for ever having meddled with it.

Was it possible he himself had been made a fool of, and that these precious proofs had after all been trumped up by that young scapegrace, Herapath, to hoodwink him?

At any rate, Arthur might have his property back now, and much good might it do him. He should—

Felgate started as he suddenly caught sight of what looked like a blade of grass protruding from a rent in the brown paper.

He looked again. It was not one blade only, but two or three. With an exclamation of consternation he tore off the covering and disclosed—the turf!

A joke? No wonder Mr Bickers's manner had been a trifle stiff that morning.

However had it got there? It was like a conjurer's trick. No one had seen or touched the parcel but himself. He had himself placed it in Mr Bickers's hands. Indeed, from the time he had taken the things from Herapath's cupboard till the moment of parting with them, he had scarcely had his eyes off it.

Stay! That evening he was at the Forum, he had left it for an hour unguardedly in his room. Yet, even then, he could almost have sworn the parcel had been untouched in his absence. Besides, the letter was there still, directed in his own hand.

He picked up the envelope, to satisfy himself it was the same. Of course it was; and he had explained in his letter what the articles were.

He took out the letter and glanced at it; and as he did so the blood rushed to his face, and he knew at last that he had been made a fool of.

It needed no great penetration to guess who it was to whom he owed his humiliation. So he armed himself with a ruler in one hand and the parcel in the other, and walked over to Herapath's study.

The proprietors were at home, and had apparently expected the visit, for an elaborate barricade had been drawn across the door by means of the table, bedstead, and other furniture, so that Felgate, when he looked in, could barely see more than the heads of his young friends.

"Let me in," he said, trying to push the door open.

"Awfully sorry; can't come in," said Dig cheerfully. "Herapath and I are having a scrub up. Come again presently."

"Do you hear me, you two? Let me in at once."

"Don't you hear, we're doing the place up?" said Arthur. "Go to some of the other chaps if you want a job done."

"I want you two; and if you don't let me in at once, I'll force my way in."

"Say what you want there; we can hear," said Arthur.

Felgate made a violent effort to effect an entrance, but without avail. The stout iron bedsteads held their own, and the wedge inserted under the door prevented it from opening farther than to allow the invader's head to peep in.

"I shall report you for this," said Felgate.

"Ha! ha! ha! you're not a monitor, my boy. Go and do it. We'll report you for invading our privacy. Say what you want there, can't you?"

"You know what I want well enough," said Felgate, forced at last to recognise that entrance was hopeless.

"What's the good of coming to tell us, then?" responded Dig.

"What business had you to go to my room the other evening?"

"Went to return your call," said Arthur. "Sorry we weren't at home when you called on us, and thought we'd do the polite and look you up. That makes us square, doesn't it?"

"Do you know I could get you expelled for coming and taking things out of my room?" said Felgate.

"Ha! ha! Do it! look sharp. We'll all go home together."

"I want the things you took away; do you hear? One of the masters has sent for them; they are to be given up immediately."

"Are they? Tell one of the masters, if he wants them he'd better go up the chimney after them."

105

"I shan't waste my time here any more. You'll be sorry for it, both of you, when I catch you."

"All right, wait till then. I say, you haven't seen a lump of turf about, have you? There's one missing."

"Ha! ha!" chimed in Dig. "How did you like the writing of the letter? Jolly hand our chaps write in the Shell, don't they?"

Felgate had not remained to hear these last two genial inquiries, but had returned, storming and raving, to his room.

The only game left him now was revenge. He would be very much surprised if that did not come off a little better than the last!

Arthur and Dig, meanwhile, were by no means in the elated spirits which their successful resistance to the siege might have warranted. Not that they were affected by the bully's retreating threat; they had heard that sort of thing from one or two fellows in their day, and their bones were still unbroken.

No; what afflicted them, and plunged them into a sea of wrath and misery, was the report circulated that morning and confirmed by reliable testimony, that Marky was going to leave Grandcourt.

At first they could not credit it. But when Ainger himself, with a long face, confirmed it, they were forced to believe their ears.

"Why?" they asked.

But Ainger had nothing to tell them on that score.

They therefore took the bold step of waiting upon the Master of the Shell himself.

"Marky," said Arthur, "it's not true you're leaving, is it?"

The misery of the boy's tone went to Railsford's heart.

"I am afraid it is true, Arthur. How did you hear?"

"Everybody knows. But, I say, why?"

"I have resigned."

"You resigned—of your own accord? Haven't you been kicked out, then? Aren't you obliged to go?"

"I am obliged to go, that's why I have resigned. You'll know all about it some day."

"But, I say, can't you withdraw your resignation and stay? Oh, I say, Marky, we shall be awfully up a tree without you here. Why ever are you going? Can't it all be squared?"

"No, old fellow, I fear not. But I am not going for a week yet. Let's make the most of the time, and get ahead with our work; for, remember, you've that Swift Exhibition coming near ahead."

"Work!" exclaimed Arthur, in disgust. "I'll not do a stroke of work more. I tell you what, if you leave, Marky, I shall leave too, and so will Dig, there!"

"My dear old fellow," said Railsford kindly, "you are talking like a little donkey. If you want to help me, you'll just determine to work all the harder now."

"I say," said Dig, shirking the question, "have you got into a row, Mr Railsford? Is it anything about—you know what?"

"You really mustn't ask me, boys; it's sufficient that I have to go, and I don't think you two will believe it is because I have done anything wrong."

"Rather not," said Arthur warmly. "But, I say, Marky, just tell us this—it wasn't us got you into the row, was it? It was awfully low of me to let it out to Felgate; but we bowled him out in time, just when he was going to send those things to Bickers. Did you see the nice trick we played him? He won't be able to do it again, for we burned the things. Such a flare-up! It isn't our fault you're going, is it?"

"No, not a bit," said Railsford. "Now you had better go."

They went and proclaimed their master's wrongs through the length and breadth of the house. The Shell took up the matter specially, and convened an informal meeting to consult as to what was to be done.

"Let's send him a round robin, and ask him not to go," suggested Maple.

"Let's get our governors to write to the doctor," said another.

"Let's all leave if he does; that's bound to make him stay," said a third.

Arthur, however, had a more practical proposal.

"What we'd better do is to get up a whacking petition to Pony," said he. "We've got a right to do it; and if all the fellows will sign it, he can't well let him go."

The question arose, Who was to write the petition? And after some discussion it was resolved to call the amiable Stafford into their councils. He at once suggested that if the petition was to be of any weight it should come from the entire house, with the captain's name at the head of the list; and a deputation was told off forthwith to wait upon Ainger.

He was not very encouraging, but said there would be no harm in trying, and undertook to draw up the petition and sign his name first underneath.

The petition was short and business-like:

"To Dr Ponsford. Sir,—We, the boys of Mr Railsford's house, have heard with great sorrow that he is to leave Grandcourt. We consider he has done more for our house than any other master, and feel it would be the greatest loss to all of us if he were to go. He does not know we are sending this. We hope it will have your favourable consideration, and make it possible for him to stay among us."

In two days this document received the signature of every boy in the house except Felgate and Munger, who contrived to evade it. Ainger took no trouble to press them for their signatures, and indeed stated, not in a whisper, that the petition would carry more weight without these two particular names than with them. Whereat Felgate and Munger felt rather sorry they had not signed.

A deputation was then appointed, consisting of the head boy in each form represented in the house, to convey the petition to the doctor. Arthur, not being the head Shell boy in the house, felt very sore to be left out, and prophesied all sorts of failure to the undertaking in consequence.

However, he was consoled vastly by a fight with Tilbury that same afternoon. Tilbury, though a signatory to the petition, was unlucky enough to brag, in the hearing of his comrade, that one reason he had signed it was because he believed Railsford had had something to do with the paying-out of Mr Bickers last term, and was a friend to the house in consequence. Whereupon Arthur, crimson in the face, requested him to step outside and receive the biggest hiding he had ever had in his life.

Tilbury obeyed, and although the combat was not quite so decided as Arthur had boasted, it disposed of the libel which had originated it, and made it clear to the house that those who knew best, at any rate, were now as firmly resolved to defend their master's innocence as last term they had been to glory in his guilt.

The doctor received the deputation politely, and allowed Ainger to read the petition and list of names without interruption.

When the ceremony was over, he said, quietly—

"The only fault I have to find with you is that you have presented your petition to me instead of to Mr Railsford. It is perfectly open for Mr Railsford to with draw his resignation. In that case it would fall to me to settle the question of his remaining here; and that would be the time for you to present your petition."

This was not very consoling; and the doctor's manner discouraged any further explanation.

Ainger therefore left the petition lying on the table, and withdrew his men to report the doubtful success of their mission to their comrades.

The week wore on, and in two days Railsford's short reprieve would be up.

He had already begun to get together some of his things preparatory to packing up, and had written out a careful paper of memoranda for the use of his successor. He had allowed the work of the house to be as little as possible disturbed by the coming event, and had even hurt monsieur's feelings by the peremptory manner in which he discouraged any representation being made by the masters with a view to avert his departure.

He had of course sent a plain, unvarnished account of his position to his "special correspondent," which happily reached her at the same time as a highly-coloured and decidedly alarming communication on the same subject from Miss Daisy's brother.

He received an answer full of courage, which helped him greatly. Yet as the day drew near he felt himself clinging desperately to his post, and hoping against hope, even at the eleventh hour, to see some daylight through his great difficulty.

Had he known that on that very last day but one Mr Bickers had received by the post a certain letter, he might have felt tempted to delay till to-morrow the final strapping-up of his portmanteau.

For Mr Bickers's letter was from Branscombe; and was as follows:—

"Sir,—I have been expecting to return to Grandcourt all this term, but I am sorry to say I have been ill again, and the doctor says I shall have to go abroad for some months. Before I go, I feel I must make a confession which will surprise you as much to read as it pains me to write it. I was the ringleader in the attack upon you last term at the door of Mr Railsford's house. I was very angry at the time at having been punished by you before all my house. But I am very sorry now for what happened, and hope you will in time forgive me. I know what trouble my conduct has caused, not only to you, but to Mr Railsford, whose house has been unjustly punished for what was my offence. There were three of us in it. One was another boy of your house, and the other was in Mr Railsford's house, only all he did was to show us the cupboard in which we put you. I should be glad to think, before I go away, that things are put right at Grandcourt by this confession. Please forgive me for my revengeful act, and, believe me, sir, yours truly,—

"S. Branscombe.

"P.S.—Please show this letter to Dr Ponsford and Mr Railsford."

This startling letter Mr Bickers read over several times, with great amazement and no less vexation. He was angry, not at the injury which had been done to himself, but because this letter had come just when it did.

To-morrow, in all probability, his enemy would have left Grandcourt, and then it would be less matter. For even if the truth were then made known, Railsford's offence in shielding the evil-doer would remain the same. But now this letter might spoil everything. It would, at any rate, postpone Railsford's departure, and might give him an opportunity of reinstating himself for good at Grandcourt.

Mr Bickers was in a quandary. He was by nature a vindictive, jealous, and fussy man, with a low opinion of everybody, and an extreme obstinacy in his own opinion. But he was not naturally a dishonest man. It was only when his other passions rushed out strongly in one direction, and his integrity stood on the other side, that his honour suffered shipwreck and went by the board.

It did so now, for Mr Bickers, having thought over the situation, deliberately put the letter into his pocket, and went about his usual avocations as if nothing had happened.

Any amount of excuses rushed in to his assistance. After all, there had been three culprits, and one of them belonged to the accused house. Railsford, no doubt, was shielding his own boy, and Branscombe's confession affected in no way his offence or the penalty attached to it.

On the whole, there was nothing to make Mr Bickers uncomfortable, and it was observed in the masters' hall that evening that he made himself quite agreeable, and even nodded in a half-friendly way to Railsford on the occasion of his last appearance at school-dinner.

After the Master of the Shell had retired to his house the doctor asked his other lieutenants to remain a few moments, as he had a statement to make to them.

Every one knew what that statement was to be.

"It is only right that I should inform you," said Dr Ponsford, "that I have considered it my duty to accept Mr Railsford's resignation, and that he leaves Grandcourt to-morrow. I confess that I do this with great pain and regret, for I have the highest opinion of Mr Railsford's abilities and character. But discipline must be maintained in a school like ours. I have no doubt that in acting as he has done Mr Railsford considers that he is acting honourably. I do not wish to impugn his motives, mistaken as I suppose them. But the fact remains that he virtually admits his knowledge of the offender last term, and at the same time refuses to give him up to justice. Under those circumstances I had no choice but to accept his resignation."

For a moment Branscombe's letter burned uncomfortably in Mr Bickers's pocket while the doctor was speaking. But it cooled again, and when Mr Grover said,—

"I am sure, sir, you will not misunderstand me when I say that your statement has caused some of us the deepest pain," he felt himself able to join in the universal "Hear, hear," with quiet fervour.

"We fully recognise," continued Mr Grover, "that under the circumstances you had only this one course left open to you. At the same time, we who know and esteem our colleague, feel that his removal will be a distinct loss to Grandcourt, and would like to add our own opinion to yours, that in the course he has considered it right to take, he has been actuated by conscientious and honourable motives."

Mr Bickers having said, "Hear, hear" once, did not feel called upon to repeat it at the end of this short speech, and was, indeed, rather glad to hurry back to his own house.

He had an idea that this time to-morrow he should feel considerably more comfortable.

Chapter Twenty Seven.

Clearing up, and clearing out.

Railsford's farewell evening in his house was not destined to be a peaceful one.

He had scarcely returned from the masters' dinner, meditating a few final touches to his packing, when Sir Digby Oakshott, Baronet, waited upon him.

The baronet was evidently agitated; and more than that, his face was one-sided, and one of his eyes glowed with all the colours of the rainbow.

"Why, Oakshott," said the master, "what is the matter? You have been fighting."

"That's not half of it," said Dig excitedly. "I say, Marky—I mean Mr Railsford; please Herapath wants to see you. He's in a bad way up-stairs. It's that cad Felgate. He's bashed us. He was in an awful wax about the dodge we played him over that sack, you know, and tried to pay us out the other day; but we kept him out. But he's been waiting his chance ever since; and when I was out of the study this evening, he came in, and gave it hot to Herapath. When I got back, Arthur was about done, and then Felgate turned on me. If I'd been bigger, I could have got a stroke or two in at his face; but I couldn't do it. I barked his shins though, and gave him one on the neck with my left. So he didn't get it all his own way. But, I say, can't you come up and see old Herapath? You haven't got any raw beef-steaks about, have you? He'll want a couple to set him right."

Railsford hurried up-stairs.

Arthur was lying on his sofa, blinking up at the ceiling with his one open eye—an eloquent testimony both to his friend's veracity and to the activity of his assailant.

"You see," he began, almost before Railsford reached the patient, so anxious was he to excuse his battered appearance, "he caught me on the hop, Marky, when I never expected him, and gave me no time to square up to him. I could have made a better fight of it if he'd given me time between the rounds; but he didn't."

Railsford made no remark on the unequal conflict, but did what he could to assist the sufferer, and reduce his countenance to its normal dimensions.

Arthur was far less concerned at his wounds than at the moral injury which he had suffered in being so completely punished in the encounter. He feared Railsford would entertain a lower opinion of him in consequence.

"If I'd have only known he was coming, I could have made it hotter for him," he said; "only he got my head in chancery early, and though I lashed out all I could, he took it out of me. Marky, do you mind feeling if my ribs are all right? I sort of fancied one of 'em had gone."

His ribs, however, were all there; and badly as he was bruised, Railsford was able to pronounce that no bones were broken, which greatly relieved both the boys.

The master helped the wounded warrior to undress, and then assisted him up to the dormitory, where, after carefully tucking him up, and advising Dig to turn in too, he left him and returned to his room.

His impulse was immediately to summon Felgate, and mete out to him exemplary chastisement for his dastardly act. But on second thoughts he remembered that he was, or rather he would be to-morrow, no longer master of the house. Besides, much as the chastisement might have relieved his own feelings, it would leave the house and everyone in it in much the same position as heretofore.

Putting everything together, he decided that his last official act should be to report the matter to the doctor next morning, and leave him to deal with it.

Having come to which conclusion, he strapped up his portmanteau, and sent an order to Jason for his cab to-morrow.

He was meditating an early retirement to bed, when a knock sounded at the door, and the three prefects entered.

It seemed a long while since their first embarrassed meeting in that same room at the beginning of last term. Much had happened since then. The house had gone down into the depths and risen to the heights. There had come disgrace and glory, defeat and victory. The ranks of the prefects themselves had been broken, and the master himself had ended his brief career amongst his boys. But as great a change as any had been the growing respect and sympathy between Railsford and his head boys.

It was long since he had learned the secret that sympathy is the golden key to a boy's heart. As long as he tried to do without it, sitting on his high horse, and regarding his pupils as mere things to be taught and ordered and punished, he had failed. But from the moment he had seized the golden opportunity presented by the misfortune of the house to throw in his lot with it, and make his interests and ambitions those of his boys, he had gained a hold which no other influence could have given him.

His prefects had led the way in the reaction which had set in in his favour, and perfect confidence bound them all together in no common bond.

"Do you mind our disturbing you, sir?" said Ainger. "We didn't want you to go without our telling you how awfully sorry we are. We don't know what will become of the house."

"I'm not sure that I much care," said Stafford.

"How good of you to come like this!" said the master. "For I wanted to talk to you. You *must* care, Stafford, and all of you. You surely aren't going to give up all the work of these two terms just because a little misfortune has befallen us?"

"It's not a little misfortune," said Ainger, "but a very great one."

"All the more reason you should not be knocked over by it. Didn't we all set ourselves to work last term in the face of a big misfortune, and didn't we get some good out of it for the house? It will be my one consolation in leaving to feel sure you will not let the work of the house flag an inch. Remember, Railsford's is committed to the task of becoming cock house of the school. Our eleven is quite safe. I'm certain no team in all the rest of the houses put together can beat us. But you must see we give a good account of ourselves on prize-day too. Some of the boys have nagged a little lately in work. We must keep them up to it—not by bullying—nobody will work for that—but by working on their ambition, and making the cause of each boy the cause of the whole house."

Railsford, as he uttered these words, seemed to forget how soon he would have to say "you" instead of "we." He had hardly realised yet what that meant.

"We'll try hard," said Ainger. "But what we wanted to say, besides letting you know how sorry we are, was to ask if it's really necessary for you to go. Is there no way of getting out of it?"

"None at all, that I can see," said Railsford.

"Fellows say you know who it was assaulted Mr Bickers last term and won't tell. Perhaps it's to save some fellow in the house from being expelled. But—"

"My dear fellows," said Railsford, "don't let's spoil our last evening by talking about this miserable affair. I can't tell you anything at all: I can only ask you to believe I have good reasons for what I'm doing. They ought to be good reasons, if the price I have to pay is to leave Grandcourt, and all of you."

It was evidently no use trying to "draw" him further; and as the first bed bell sounded shortly afterwards, they withdrew after a cordial but dismal farewell.

"I shall see you again in the morning before I go," said he.

The prefects walked away abstracted and downcast. It was all very well for him to say, "Keep the work up when I am gone." But how were they to do it? He was the pivot on which all their work had been turning; and without him what chance was there of keeping the house together for a day?

"Come in here a minute, you fellows," said Ainger, as they reached the captain's door. "We *must* do something to stop it."

"That's a very feeble observation to make," said Barnworth. "Is that what you want us to come in here for?"

"No, hang it, Barnworth! there's no time for chaff at present. What I want to say is, have we tried every possible means of finding out who scragged Bickers last term?"

"I think so," said Stafford. "Every one in the house has denied it. If it's one of our fellows, it's probably the biggest liar among us."

"Which means Felgate?" said Ainger.

"Or Munger," said Barnworth.

"It's not Felgate," said Ainger, "for he has burnt his fingers in trying to fix it on Railsford himself; and it he was the real culprit, you may depend on it he'd have kept very quiet."

"Munger *has* kept quiet," said Barnworth.

"Munger! Why, he's a fool and a coward both. He could never have done such a thing."

"Let's ask him. I'll tell you why I mentioned him. I never thought of it till now. The other day I happened to be saying at dinner to somebody that that affair was going to be cleared up at last, and that the doctor had been in consultation with Bickers and Railsford about it the evening before—you know, that's what we were told—and would probably come across— this was an embellishment of my own—with a policeman, and point the fellow out. Munger was sitting opposite me, and when I began to speak he had just filled his tumbler with water, and was going to drink it. But half-way through he suddenly stopped, and put the tumbler down with such a crack on the table that he spilt half the water on to the cloth. I didn't think anything of it at the time, but it occurs to me now."

"Well," said Ainger, "it's an off-chance. Staff, do you mind bringing him?"

"The one thing to do," said Barnworth, while the messenger was gone, "is to frighten it out of him. Nothing else will do."

"Well," said Ainger, "if you think so. You must back me up, though."

After a long interval, Stafford returned to say that Munger was in bed and refused to get up.

"Good," said Barnworth; "I like that. Now, Staff, you amiable old boy, will you kindly go to him again and say that the prefects are waiting for him in the captain's study, and that if he is not here in five minutes they will have to do without him. I fancy that's true, isn't it?" he added, appealing to his colleagues. "Let's see if that doesn't draw him. If it does, depend upon it there was something in that tumbler."

Barnworth was right. In less than five minutes Munger appeared, half-dressed, and decidedly uneasy in his manner.

"What do you want me for?" he demanded, with an attempt at bluster.

"What do you mean by not coming when we sent for you, when you know perfectly well what you are wanted for?"

"What am I wanted for?" asked Munger, glancing nervously round.

"You know well enough, Munger."

"How do I know, till you tell me?" snarled the boy.

"If he doesn't know," said Barnworth to Ainger, significantly, "we must do as we proposed. I'll go and get my papers and be ready for you in a minute."

This meaningless speech had a remarkable effect on Munger. He stared first at one prefect, then at the other; and when Barnworth rose as if to leave the room, he said,—

"Wait—don't do that. What is it you want to ask?"

"You know that as well as we do. Are you going to say what you know, or not?"

"I don't know how you got to know anything about it," began Munger; "it's a plot against me, and—"

"We don't want all that," said Ainger sternly. "What we want to know is, did you do it yourself, and if not who else was in it?"

"Of course I couldn't do it myself. *You* couldn't, strong as you are."

"You helped, then?"

"I had nothing to do with the—the scragging," said Munger. "I—Oh, I say, Ainger, you aren't going to get me expelled, surely? Do let us off this time!"

"I'm not the head-master; you'll have to ask him that. Your only chance is to make a clean breast of it at once. What was it you did?"

"I only opened the door of the boot-box, and helped drag him in. I had nothing to do with the scragging. Branscombe did all that himself, and Clipstone hung to his legs."

It needed all the self-control of the three prefects to refrain from an exclamation of astonishment at this wonderful disclosure.

"Are you telling the truth?" demanded Ainger.

"I am—I swear it—I never even knew what they meant to do till an hour before. It was Clipstone's idea, and I—owed him money for betting, and he had a pull on me, and made me do it. But I swear I never touched Bickers except to help pull him in."

"Now, one question more. Was there anyone else in it, but just you three?"

"Nobody, as sure as I stand here."

"Very well, you can go now. We shall have to tell the doctor, of course, and there's no knowing what he will do. But it's been your best chance to make a clean breast of it while you had the opportunity."

The wretched Munger departed to his bed, but not to sleep. He could not conceive how Railsford first, and then these three prefects, should have discovered his deeply hidden secret. Not a word about it had escaped his own lips. Branscombe was away, and Clipstone scarcely anyone in Railsford's house ever saw. But the secret was out, and what kept Munger awake that night was neither shame nor remorse, but fear lest he should be expelled, or, perhaps worse, arrested!

The three prefects sat late, talking over their wonderful discovery. "It's good as far as it goes," said Barnworth. "But it doesn't clear up the question how Railsford got to hear of it, and what his motive has been in shielding the criminals. It can't have been on Munger's account, for the two have been at war all the term; and I don't suppose since the affair he has exchanged two words with either Branscombe or Clipstone."

"Don't you think," said the captain, "that now we do know all about it, we might go and ask him?"

It was a brilliant suggestion, and they went.

But Railsford was in bed and asleep; and his visitors, important as was their business, had not the hardihood to arouse him, and were reluctantly obliged to postpone their explanation till the morning.

Even then they seemed destined to be thwarted; for Railsford had gone for a bathe in the river, and only returned in time for call-over; when of course there was no opportunity for a private conference.

But as soon as breakfast was over they determined to catch him in his room, and put an end to their suspense there and then.

Alas! not five minutes before they arrived, Railsford had gone out, this time, as Cooke informed them, to the doctor's.

It seemed a fatality, and who was to say whether his next move might not be to quit Grandcourt without even giving them a chance?

"The only thing to do is to go and catch him at the doctor's," said Ainger; "we've a right to go—at least I have—to report Munger."

"All serene," said Barnworth, "better for you to go alone. It would only put Pony's back up if we all went."

For once in his life Ainger felt that there were some dignities connected with the captaincy of a house; and for once in his life he would have liked to transfer those dignities to any shoulders but his own.

But he put a bold face on it, and marched across to the doctor's.

"Perhaps I shall only make it worse for Railsford," said he to himself. "Pony will think it precious rum of us to have let two terms go by without finding the secret out, and then, when it suits us to find it, getting hold of it in half an hour. So it is, precious rum! And if Railsford has known the names all along and kept them quiet, it's not likely to make things better for him that we have discovered them on our own account. Anyhow, I'm bound to report a thing like this at once, and it's barely possible it may turn something up for Railsford."

As he crossed the quadrangle a cab drove in, and set down a tall, elderly gentleman, who, after looking about him, advanced towards the prefect, and said,—

"Can you direct me to the head-master's house?"

"Yes, sir," said Ainger, "I'm going there myself. It's this way."

It wasn't often strangers made so early a call at Grandcourt.

"A fine old building, this," said the gentleman; "how many houses are there?"

"Eight," said Ainger.

"And whose do you belong to?"

"Railsford's. That's his, behind us."

"And which is Mr Bickers?"

"This must be the father of one of Bickers' fellows," thought Ainger. "That one next to ours," he replied.

The gentleman looked up at the house in an interested way, and then relapsed into silence and walked gravely with his guide to the doctor's.

The doctor's waiting-room was not infrequently tenanted by more than one caller on business at that hour of the morning. For between nine and ten he was at home to masters and prefects and ill-conducted boys; and not a few of the latter knew by painful experience that a good deal of serious business was often crowded into that short space of time.

This morning, however, there was only one occupant when Ainger and the gentleman were ushered in. That occupant was Railsford.

"Why, Ainger," said the master, scarcely noticing the stranger, "I did not expect you here. What are you come for?"

"To report a boy."

"Which one, and for what? Is it a bad case?"

"It's Munger, sir, for being one of the party who assaulted Bickers last term."

Railsford started. And it was an odd thing that the gentleman, although his back was turned, did so too.

"How did you discover that?" said the master.

Ainger briefly explained, and the gentleman, evidently disturbed in his mind, walked to the window.

When the conference between the other two had ended the latter turned abruptly and said,—

"Excuse me, but I accidentally overheard you just now mention a matter in which I am very much interested. In fact, it is about it that I am here to see Dr Ponsford at present."

At that moment the doctor entered the room. The other two naturally gave way to the visitor, who accordingly advanced and greeted the head-master.

"Allow me to introduce myself, Dr Ponsford; I dare say you do not remember me. My name is Branscombe. You know, of course, the painful business on which I have come."

"I hope, Mr Branscombe, your son is no worse. We should be sorry to lose him. We looked upon him as a promising boy."

The gentleman looked hard at the doctor.

"You surely say this to spare my feelings. Dr Ponsford. Of course I understand my son can never return here."

"Is that so? I am truly sorry."

"You would be the last to wish him to return to a school in which his name has been so disgraced."

It was the doctor's turn to look astonished.

"Disgraced? Branscombe was always one of our model boys."

"Until last term," said the father.

"I don't understand you," said the doctor.

"Surely, Dr Ponsford, you know by this time my son's offence. I do not attempt to excuse it. He voluntarily took the only right step to take in his position by confessing."

"Pardon me," said the doctor, "but I still do not understand. What confession do you refer to?"

"Has not Mr Bickers communicated the contents of my son's letter to him, written two days ago? He must have received it yesterday morning. In it my boy confessed that he, assisted by two others, had been the author of the outrage on Mr Bickers last term. He is deeply repentant, and wishes by this confession to put right all the mischief which has resulted from his act. But surely Mr Bickers has shown you the letter?"

"He has neither shown me it nor mentioned it."

"Is it possible? My boy was so anxious and restless about the affair that I promised him to come down and see you; fully expecting that long before now you would have been made acquainted with everything. Would it trouble you to send for Mr Bickers?"

"Certainly," said the doctor. Then, turning to Ainger and Railsford, he said, "Would you two come again later on? and on your way, Ainger, will you ask Mr Bickers to come here?"

"Excuse me, doctor," said Mr Branscombe, "but I should much prefer if these two gentlemen remained. I believe, in fact, that—although I do not know them—they have come to see you on this same business that I have."

"Perhaps, Railsford—" began the doctor, when his visitor broke in, "Railsford! Is this Railsford? Why, to be sure, now I look at you. How ungrateful you must have thought me! but you slipped away so suddenly that day when Mrs Branscombe and I arrived, that in our excitement and anxiety we scarcely had time to look at you; much less to thank you. Indeed, it was only lately my son told me how devotedly you had tended him; and it breaks his heart now to think that you, of all persons, have suffered almost more than anybody by what he did. Surely, sir, Mr Bickers showed *you* his letter?"

"No, I have not seen or heard of it," said Railsford. "But I know what you say your son has now confessed; and have known it since the time of his illness. Dr Ponsford, I am at liberty now to explain myself; may I do so?"

"Certainly," said the doctor sternly.

Railsford thereupon gave an account of the boy's sudden illness, and of the accidental manner in which he had learned, from the boy's delirious talk, of his own guilt and the guilt of his confederates.

"I could not but regard a secret so acquired as sacred," said he; "and even though by keeping it I was actually shielding criminals, I should have been a greater traitor to betray them than to shield them."

"May I say, sir," put in Ainger at this point, "that the prefects in our house last night received a confession from Munger, which corresponds exactly with what Mr Branscombe says?"

"Except that I did not mention the names of the other two culprits," said Mr Branscombe. "My son did not even name them to me."

"Munger was not so particular. He says Clipstone suggested the affair, and assisted Branscombe to carry it out; while he himself held the light and helped drag Mr Bickers into the boot-box. That was what I had come to report to you now, sir," added he to the head-master.

Dr Ponsford looked half stunned with this cascade of revelations and explanations. Then he went up to Railsford and took his hand.

"I am thankful indeed that all this has happened now—in time. A few hours more, and it would have come too late to prevent a great injustice to you, Railsford. Ainger, go for Mr Bickers, and come back with him."

Mr Bickers had a tolerable inkling of what awaited him, and when he found himself confronted with all the overwhelming evidence which was crowded that morning into the doctor's waiting-room, he hauled down his colours without even coming to close quarters.

"Yes," said he sullenly, "I did keep back the letter. I considered it better for Grandcourt and everyone that Mr Railsford should go than that this old affair should be settled. After all, I was the person chiefly interested in it, and if I didn't choose to do what would vindicate myself, I had a right to do so. My opinion is that there will be no peace at Grandcourt while Mr Railsford is here. If he is now to remain, I shall consider it my duty to resign."

"I hope not, Mr Bickers," said Railsford. "Now that this unhappy secret is cleared up, why shouldn't we forget the past, and work together for the future? I promise for myself and my house to do our best."

"Thank you," said Mr Bickers dryly. "The offer is a tempting one, but it is not good enough. Good-morning."

Late that afternoon Mr Bickers drove away in the cab which had come to take Mr Railsford.

It was an occasion for rejoicing to nobody—for everybody agreed with Railsford that it would have been possible even yet to make a fresh start and work together for the good of the school. But, as Mr Bickers thought otherwise, no one complained of him for leaving.

Another cab came on the following day for Clipstone, whose departure was witnessed with rather more regret, because he was a good cricketer, and not quite as bad a fellow as he often tried to make out. His expulsion was a salutary warning to one or two who had looked up to him as a model—amongst them to Munger, who, transferred, with a heavy bad mark against his name, to Mr Roe's house, thought over his former ways, and tried, as well as a cad of his temper can do, to improve them in the future.

Jason surely was making his fortune fast. For the very next day yet one more cab drove into the square, and, after a brief halt, drove away with Felgate. He left Grandcourt regretted by none, least of all by Arthur Herapath, who, with a beef-steak on his cheek and linseed poultice over his temple, whooped defiantly at the retreating cab from his dormitory window, and began to feel better and better as the rumble of the wheels gradually receded and finally lost itself in the distance.

Chapter Twenty Eight.

"Dulce Domum."

The great 20th day of July had come round at last, and Arthur Herapath was in an unwonted flutter of excitement. For was not this speech-day, and were not Mr and Mrs Herapath and Daisy due by the 9.40 train?

Ever since, a week ago, Arthur had heard that he had run a dead heat for the Swift Exhibition with Smythe of the School-House, he had not known which end of him was uppermost. He envied neither Smedley his gold medal nor Barnworth his Cavendish scholarship. He condoled patronisingly with Ainger on not having quite beaten the captain of the school, and virtually hinted to Wake, who had won the first remove into the Sixth, that, if he cared to come and sit at his feet, he might be able to put him up to a thing or two for Plumtre medal next Christmas.

Sir Digby was scarcely less elevated; for he had won the Shell History prize by a deal of tremendous hard work. And as he had never done such a thing in his life before, he scarcely knew what to make of it.

Fellows told him there must have been an awful shady lot in against him; but that didn't satisfactorily explain the great mystery. Railsford told him it was the reward of downright work; and he inclined to think such was the case himself.

Arthur of course gibed at the idea.

"All gammon," said he. "It's a lucky fluke for you, and I'm glad for your *mater's* sake. But I wouldn't say too much about it if I were you. It'll make the fellows grin."

"Why should they grin at me any more than you?"

"Well, you see, I was in the running for the Swift. They put it down to me last term, so I was bound to pull it off."

"You only pulled off half of it, you know," said Dig.

Arthur looked not quite pleased at this reference, but laughed it off.

"Oh, of course, I can't object to go halves with young Smythe. If I'd known he was quite so hot on it, I might have spurted a bit more. But I'm glad I didn't, poor young beggar. He'd have been precious cut up to miss it."

"What about that boat on the river?" asked Dig, who did not swallow the whole of this. "Are you going to buy the front or back half of it?"

"Young Oakshott," said Arthur, with all the dignity of a Swift exhibitioner, "don't you make a bigger ass of yourself than you can help."

The term had ended well for Railsford's house. Although restored to their equal rights with the rest of Grandcourt, the spirit of enterprise and achievements which had been born during the troubles of last term survived, and begot an equal spirit in the other houses, who felt their *prestige* in danger from the bold challenge of these latest aspirants.

The match of Railsford's against the School did not come off; for the Athletic Union, of which Railsford had been chosen president by acclamation, decided to limit the contests to house matches only. But though deprived of an opportunity of asserting themselves against all Grandcourt—which might have been of doubtful benefit—the house beat successively the School-house, Roe's and Grover's houses, and, as everyone had foreseen, ended the term as the crack cricket house of the school.

How they would fulfil their other and more ambitious scheme of becoming the "cock house" for studies, remained much longer a doubtful question. No one of course supposed for a moment they would carry off all the prizes they entered for; and, after the removal of the ban upon the house, it was pretty generally calculated they they would do a great deal less than they would have done under the old order of things.

But Railsford was not the man to allow the house to rest on their oars because of a single success. Surely, he represented, it was not to go out to all the school that Railsford's fellows could only work when they were in a bad temper? Glorious as it would have been to clear the prize list when they were isolated and sulky, it would be still more glorious to show that not less could they do it when they were in good cheer and shoulder to shoulder with the rest of the school. Besides, if they won all the athletic events and none of the scholastic, people would be sure to say any fools can excel in sports if they let all their books go by the board.

Thus Railsford whipped up his house to their great effort, and the result was that to-day's prize list showed that nearly half the honours of the examinations had fallen to Railsford's boys. Not a few there were who looked gloomy that the result was no better. They grudged the school the other half. But there was no gloom on the master's face as he read the list down and saw the reward of his labours.

He was proud, but his pride was not on account of Mark Railsford, as six months ago it might have been, but of every boy, senior and junior, who had put his back gallantly into the work and made a name for the good old house.

But this is a tedious digression to make, while Arthur and the baronet are putting on their Sunday "togs" and brushing up their Sunday "tiles" preparatory to going down to meet the 9.40 train from London.

They were up to the business; they had done it before; they knew how essential it was to engage half a dozen cabs off different parts of the rank, so as to be sure of getting one; and, not for the first time in their lives they "bagged" three or four porters in advance with a similar object.

The platform, as usual, was full of Courtiers waiting for their "people," and many was the passage of arms our Shell-fish engaged in to beguile the time.

"Hullo! here's a lark," said Arthur, presently, when the arrival bell had just sounded, "here's Marky—do you see him? I say! won't he blush when Daisy goes and kisses him before all the fellows!"

"Look out," said the baronet, "here comes the scrimmage."

The train was steaming into the station, and as usual the boys all along the platform began to run; and woe betide those who either did not run too, or were not lucky enough to get a perch on the footboard.

Our young gentlemen were far too knowing to suffer disadvantage through neglect of one or another of these simple expedients.

"Here they are!" yelled Arthur, waving to his chum; "spotted them first shot! Go on, Simson, cut your sticks off this step; these are all my people in here. How are you? Dig's here; we've got a cab. Fetch up some of our porters, Dig, I say."

Amid such effusive greetings Mr and Mrs Herapath and Miss Daisy Herapath alighted and fell into the arms—or rather, civilly shook hands with their son.

"Hullo, Daisy! Marky's here. There he comes. Here she is, Mr Railsford; here's Daisy! I say, Daisy," added he, in a confidential whisper, "you'd better not kiss him before all the fellows. Wait till you get up to our study."

Railsford arrived before this piece of fraternal counsel was ended, and solved the difficulty by quietly shaking hands all round, and asking Mrs Herapath if she had had a comfortable journey.

Arthur had the mortification of seeing five out of his six cabs drive gaily off under his very nose with other fellows' people inside; and his temper was also further ruffled when all his porters waited on him at the door of the sixth for their fee; however, he had the presence of mind to tell them to wait till he came back in the evening, and then, slamming the cab door, hopped up on the box beside the driver—no Grandcourt boy had ever been known to ride inside a four-wheeler with his people—and drove off.

It was a gay scene in the great quadrangle that summer morning—fathers, mothers, sisters, cousins, and aunts were all mixed up in one glorious crowd, with their boys mounting guard over them and introducing them right and left to all the other boys within call.

Mr and Mrs Herapath, like their son, were up to the business, and quietly led the way through the throng towards the hall where the speeches were to be delivered and where, as they knew by experience, it was better to look for a seat too early than too late.

Arthur and Dig, however, were by no means disposed to waste Daisy in so unprofitable an occupation, and therefore haled her off to their study. Some of us, who know the young lady, are able to excuse the pride with which these two gallant tenders towed their prize into port—for as Dig shared Arthur's study, of course he shared his sister on this occasion. It wanted a very few dropping and facetious introductions on the way, such as, "Daisy, you know, my sister," or "What cheer, Sherry?—ever hear of Chuckey?" or, "No good, Maple, my boy, bespoke!" to set the rumour going that Daisy Herapath, Marky's "spoon," was come, and was "on show" in Herapath's study.

To her credit be it said, the young lady bore her ordeal with exemplary patience and good-humour. She liked everything she saw. She admired the study so much. What a pretty look-out on the old square—what a luxurious lunch—ah! Arthur had not forgotten her weakness for marmalade—and so on.

The boys voted her a brick; and Arthur went so far as to say he hoped she and Marky would fix it up in time for her to come and be dame of the house before he left.

All this time—would you believe it?—the poor Master of the Shell was sitting in his study, very bashful, and wondering whether he would get a chance of speaking to Daisy during the day at all. She had been spirited away from under his very eyes, in the most truculent manner, by her graceless brother; and it seemed very doubtful whether he would be allowed—

Mrs Hastings at this moment knocked at the door and handed in a dainty little note addressed to "Mark Railsford, Esquire," from the doctor's niece.

"Dear Mr Railsford," wrote Miss Violet, "will you and Miss Herapath join us at lunch before the speeches? I should so like to make her acquaintance.

"Yours truly,—

"Violet Ponsford."

So Railsford, armed with this authority, sallied forth boldly to recapture his Daisy. He thought he knew where to find her, and was not mistaken. The little impromptu lunch was in full swing when he entered the festive study. He had rarely felt so embarrassed, and the manifest excitement of his two pupils at his arrival did not tend to restore him to ease.

And now occurred a wonderful case of presence of mind on the part of two small and tender boys. No sooner had Railsford entered, and somewhat hesitatingly advanced to the table, preparatory to stating his business, than Sir Digby Oakshott,

Baronet, winked at Arthur Herapath, Esquire, and Arthur Herapath, Esquire, kicked Sir Digby Oakshott, Baronet, under the table; after which both rose abruptly to their feet and bolted from the room, making the corridor echo with their laughter!

They explained afterwards that they wanted to bag front seats for the speeches; and that, no doubt, was a highly satisfactory reason.

At twelve o'clock, when the Earl of Somebody, and Sir Brown Robinson, and the other local celebrities and governors of the school entered the hall, that usually dingy room was packed from end to end by a brilliant and expectant crowd.

The radiant faces of the boys peeped out from among the phalanges of their no less radiant people. The prize boys on the front benches kept up a running fire of talk and cheering; the masters in their gowns beamed right and left, as if all of them put together could not give a fellow a hundred lines if he asked for it; and the college servants, grouped at the doors, smiled as if no cloud had ever ruffled their temper since last speech-day: while the doctor, as he rose, resplendent in his academical robes, and called for silence, looked as if no more solemn question had engaged his attention all the term than the arrangement of his strings and the droop of the scarlet hood on his back.

Then speech-day began. My readers hardly want me to describe so familiar a scene. They will be able to picture to themselves, better than I can picture it for them, how Smedley was cheered when he got up to deliver the English Oration in honour of the old school; and how he blushed and ran short of breath when he came to the quotation from Milton at the end, which had something about a Violet in it!—how, when Ainger rose to give the Greek Speech, his own fellows rose at him amid cries of "Well run, sir!" "Well hit!" "Well fielded!" and cheered every sentence of the Greek, though they had not an idea what it was about—how Barnworth was similarly encouraged through his Latin Oration with cries of "Jump it out!" "One inch more!" mingled sometimes with "False quantity!" "Speak up, prompter!"—how, after the speechifying was done, the examiners rose and made their reports, which nobody listened to and everyone voted a bore.

How, next, Dr Ponsford rose with a rustle of his silk gown, which was heard all over the hall in the dead silence, and proceeded to tell the Earl of Somebody and the other distinguished guests what everybody knew, namely, that the school had now come to the end of another year's work, and etcetera, etcetera. But how, when he took up his list, and the tables containing the prizes were wheeled forward and uncovered, attention once more awoke, the boys on the prize benches settled their cravats, and felt if their hair-partings were all right, and then sat back in their places with a delightful simulation of indifference—

The reader knows all about it; he has been through it. He knows the cheers which hailed the announcement that Smedley was going up to Oxford with a Balliol scholarship in his pocket, and that Ainger had won one of the minor scholarships at George's. He does not need to be told of the shouts which greeted the appearance of boy after boy from Railsford's house on the platform steps to receive his prize; or of the grim smile on the doctor's face as a youthful voice from the prize benches, forgetting the solemnity of the occasion, shouted, "Marky again, bravo us!" Nor when presently Arthur Herapath was called up to receive a piece of paper informing him that he was the winner of half the Swift Exhibition, or when, close behind, Digby Oakshott—the doctor scurrilously omitted his full title—trotted up to accept the Shell History prize—can anyone who has been in such a scene before fail to imagine the cheers and laughter and chaff which the public appearance of these two notorious characters evoked?

So the ceremony went on—and the reader, I think, can bear me out when I say that, after an hour of it, I distinctly saw—for I was there, near the front—several ladies yawn behind their fans, and otherwise show signs of fatigue, so that when the poor little Babies, who had done as honest work as anybody, toddled up to get their little prizes, scarcely anybody looked at them, and were glad when they were polished off. Which I thought a shame; and resolved, whenever I am head-master of a public school, I shall turn my prize list upside down and call the Babies up first.

It was all over at last; and then followed that wonderful event, the speech-day dinner, when boys and visitors all sat down promiscuously to the festive board and celebrated the glories of the day with a still more glorious spread.

Arthur and Dig were in high feather. They had, I am sorry to say, "shunted" their progenitors up to the doctor's table, and, in the congenial society of some of their own "lot," were jammed in at one of the side tables, with just elbow-room enough to do execution. Arthur was comfortably packed between Sherriff's sister and Maple's second cousin, and cheered by game pie and mellowed by ginger ale, made himself vastly agreeable.

"See that chap with the sandy wig!" said he to Miss Sherriff, "he's a baronet—Sir Digby Oakshott, Baronet, A.S.S., P.I.G., and nobody knows what else—he's my chum; aren't you, Dig? Sherriff's sister, you know, make yourself civil, can't you? Dig can make you laugh sometimes," added he, aside, to his fair neighbour.

Then his genial eye roamed up and down the room and lit up suddenly as he perceived, with their backs to him, Railsford and Daisy dining happily at the next table.

He gave a whistle to Dig, and pointed with his thumb over his shoulder. Dig, who was in the middle of a pull at the ginger ale, put down his tankard suddenly and crammed his handkerchief into his mouth.

"Such a game!" said Arthur to Maple's second cousin on his right. "Look round, behind you. Do you see them?"

"See whom?" asked the young lady.

"Those two. Regular pair of spoons; look at him helping her to raspberry pie. Oh, my word!"

"Who are they?" asked his neighbour, laughing.

But Arthur was at that moment busy attracting the attention of all his friends within call, and indicating to them in pantomimic gesture what was going on.

"Oh," said he, hearing the question at last, "that's Marky, our house-master, you know; and he's spoons on my sister Daisy—just see how they're going it. Do you want to be introduced to my sister? I say, I'll—"

"Oh, no indeed, not yet," said the young lady in alarm, "presently, please."

"All right. Dig, I say, pass the word down to those fellows to fill up their mugs, do you hear? And fill up Sherriff's sister's mug too, and all those girls' down there. Look out now, and keep your eye on me."

Whereupon he rose and made a little speech, partially audible to those immediately round him, but supremely inaudible to the two parties specially concerned behind.

"We're going to drink a toast," said Arthur. "I vote we drink the health of jolly old Marky and my sister Daisy; there they are behind, going the pace like a house on fire. Gentlemen and ladies, I vote we drink their very good health, and the sooner Daisy's the dame of Railsford's the better larks for us."

The toast was honoured with much enthusiasm; and there were loud cries for a speech in return. But the Master of the Shell was making speeches of quite another kind, and utterly unconscious of the flattering little demonstration which was taking place behind him; he was telling Daisy in whispers the story of the term, and feeling himself rewarded for all he had gone through by her sympathetic smile.

The dinner ended at last, and but one more ceremony remained. This was the time-honoured cheering with which speech-day at Grandcourt always came to an end.

Smedley and the prefects walked in procession to the head table and ranged themselves behind the head governor's chair, while everyone stood up.

"Three cheers for Grandcourt!" called the captain.

And you may fancy the earthquake that ensued.

Then in regular order followed—

"Three cheers for the doctor!"

"Three cheers for Miss Violet!"

"Three cheers for the governors!"

Then again, in regular order, the captain of each house stepped forward and called for three cheers for his own house, all of which were vigorously given—each house being on its mettle to drown all the others.

Last in the list Ainger stepped forward and called for "Three cheers for Railsford's!"

Then Arthur and Dig and the rest of the house got upon their chairs and put their backs into the shout; and everyone allowed that, whatever else Railsford's wasn't first in, it could carry off the palm for noise. At the end of the third cheer a voice called out,—

"One more for the cock house!"

Whereat Arthur and Dig and the rest of them got on their chairs again and yelled till the roof rang.

Then amid a multitude of promiscuous cheers for "the captain," "the prefects," "the cook," "Jason," "the school cat," "Thucydides!" and finally for "Dulce Domum!" Grandcourt broke up for the holidays.

Let you and me, friendly reader, say good-bye here amid all the cheery bustle and excitement of the crowded quadrangle. It is better to part so than to linger about talking morality till the great square is empty—till the last of the cabs has rumbled away out of hearing—till the echoes of our own voices come back and startle us from behind the chapel buttresses. If we wait till then, we part sadly and miss the promise of a meeting again. But if we part now, while Arthur, on the box of his cab, with his "people" safely stowed inside, is whooping his noisy farewells right and left—while Smedley, with his Balliol scholarship in his pocket, is leaving Grandcourt for good, and casting his last shy look up at the doctor's window—while Messrs Roe, Grover, and Railsford are talking cheerfully of their Highland trip in August—while monsieur, humming *Partant pour la Syrie*, is hurrying away to his own dear France and his still dearer little girls—while Ainger and Barnworth, the old and the new captains of Railsford's, are grasping hands at the door—if we part now, we part not as those who bid a long farewell, but as those who think and talk of meeting again.

117

Printed in Great Britain
by Amazon

41454624R00066